VIOLET SMOKE

"For my sake?" she jerked away from him, a white-hot rage exploding in her chest. "You used me, Whip! You took my body—my virginity—everything I had to g—give . . ." Her voice broke and she could not continue. "What we did was wrong, so very wrong . . . I thought it was right and wonderful, but now I see how cheap and dirty it really was . . ."

Angry now, he moved closer and seized her face in his hands. "Listen to me, you little fool . . . I am an honorable man. Despite everything else, I am honorable . . ."

She tore his hands away from her face and inched away from the heat of his body. Even now, at this terrible moment, her treacherous flesh was capable of succumbing to overwhelming passion.

LOVE'S BRIGHTEST STARS SHINE
WITH ZEBRA BOOKS!

Violet Smoke

KATHARINE KINCAID

PINNACLE BOOKS
WINDSOR PUBLISHING CORP.

PINNACLE BOOKS

are published by

Windsor Publishing Corp.
475 Park Avenue South
New York, NY 10016

First printing: June, 1988

Printed in the United States of America

For Richard, again, who keeps me believing in miracles. Especially the miracle of love.

Prologue

Dear God, would she get there in time?

She had never paddled a canoe before—and certainly not on a swollen mist-shrouded river long after midnight. In the bow, Shadow whined and whimpered, his massive gray body trembling with eagerness to get to his master. He, too, had never been out on the river in a canoe, and she feared that at any moment the wolf's fearful frantic movements would dump them both overboard.

Struggling to keep the canoe headed straight downstream, she realized that there was really no need to paddle; the current was strong and swift. The greatest danger lay in the churning, tumbling debris being swept downstream on the flood. The pale, wavering light of a crescent moon silvered the floating, bobbing objects—logs and tree branches mostly—which threatened to smash into the delicately balanced craft and upset it.

The fog obscured all else. Tendrils of mist clawed at the canoe from either side, and the banks of the river were swallowed in the hungry, seething vapor. Her stomach cramped with fear; what awaited her at the end of this journey was sure to be far worse than what faced her now.

A damp breeze smelling of wet earth and wood smoke stirred her long braided hair. She fancied she could hear agonized groans and screams in the far distance—unearthly sounds carried by an unseasonably warm keening wind. What if she was too late? What if he had already been sacrificed to the blood lust of the savages and their evil British allies?

Dear God, no—it couldn't be! If he should die before she even had a chance to plead for him, to beg for mercy from General Proctor, the British commandant at Fort Miami, she did not know what she would do. Probably she would die. She would have no choice in the matter. If what everyone was saying turned out to be true—if indeed, Proctor was allowing the savages to torture and murder the Americans they had taken captive this morning— then she would stand little chance of leaving the fort alive.

But her own death would not matter, if *he* was dead.

Oh, God, how she wished she were somewhere else, where the wickedness of men could not harm her, where her dreams could not be stamped into the dust by moccasined feet dancing a death dance. How she wished she were enfolded once more in the heated embrace of her beloved. Was it only a few nights ago that she had lain in his arms, writhing in ecstasy as his mouth tortured and inflamed her body?

What agony to remember! How impossible to

forget. He had done things to her that she had never imagined any man doing. He had exceeded the bounds of her imagination.

"Woman," he had said, "I am going to make love to you as you have never even dreamed of being loved. I am going to love you everywhere... *here*... and then I will love you *here*..."

His lips had tenderly, scorchingly, traced a tingling trail across her breasts and down her belly. "Open yourself to me," he had commanded. "I want you, *need* you..."

And she had opened herself to him, allowed him total access to every quivering inch of her flesh. Finally, in a fever of wanton abandonment, she had rolled on top of him and claimed the same rights of intimacy and ownership. She had loved and beguiled every inch of his lean muscled hardness, driving him to a peak of throbbing desire that had exploded like a flaming British fireball between them...

What would the savages do to his splendid male body, already scarred and violence-branded, which she had tried so hard to soothe and gentle?

It wasn't difficult to imagine. This very night, the settlers were hunched before their campfires behind the strong walls of Fort Meigs. There, in hushed, fearful voices, they were whispering of past atrocities and speculating about present ones. They were straining to hear the voices of the damned begging for mercy on the restless spring wind. They were weeping and praying, and the faces of the soldiers were dark with anguish over the fate of their captured comrades.

Startled, she looked up from her paddling. She

had heard something; she *did* hear something. Oh, merciful God . . . what she heard raised the hairs on the back of her neck. And in the bow of the canoe, the hackles of the great gray beast stood on end. A growl rumbled in his throat; he shook so hard that the canoe rocked in protest.

The canoe caught on something in the water, and suddenly she realized how very close to shore they had drifted. The outlines of the still-naked trees became starkly apparent, and through the trees shone a reddish haze. She used the paddle to free the canoe, then maneuvered it closer to shore.

She noticed the bunching of Shadow's muscles, and before she could stop him, the animal sprang from the canoe into the shallows. Cold wet droplets sprayed her, and at the same moment, the riverbed scraped the bottom of the canoe.

"Shadow! Wait for me—wait!" Scrambling to her feet, she stepped from the rocking craft and did not even care that it seemed to leap away from her, as if reluctant to touch the accursed shore.

The animal bounded away through the trees. Sighing, knowing that she no longer needed him to show her the way to Fort Miami, she let him go. Once inside the fort, he would go straight to his master. He would cause a commotion—for he hated and feared Indians almost as much as she did. It would be easy to follow his trail.

And it would be easy to gain entrance to the fort. As she mounted the riverbank and passed through the fringe of surrounding woodland, she saw that the gates were flung wide in careless abandon, drawing her onward toward the yawning maw.

The smoke from countless campfires curled toward the black sky, and tongues of crimson vapor entwined with the purple mist. The cries of the damned assaulted her ears. They were no longer recognizable as human voices—the voices of men who had once whispered love words to their wives and sweethearts, who had teased their children and complained about the rigors of war on a lonely frontier.

These were the cries of men delivered up to unimaginable tortures and suffering, and for a moment, she could not go forward. It seemed as if every step she had ever taken had been leading toward this moment.

No longer subject to conscious direction, her feet began to carry her down the path toward the gate. Images rose from her past; she saw her life unraveling before her like the unraveling of a hem of a skirt. Her thoughts went spiraling away from her, away from a present that was too stunningly terrible to contemplate. They went winging back to the past . . . to the abandoned child she had been and the fulfilled woman she had finally become . . .

She reached the gate and paused there, only dimly realizing that she was smiling. Yes, she would greet death with a smile. Her beloved awaited her; that was reason enough to smile. Soon—oh, yes, quite soon—they would be forever united. What was a little fear or pain when the reward would be so great?

Holding herself as erect as an Indian princess, she entered Fort Miami. Calm and fearless, she walked straight into hell.

Chapter One

Philadelphia
January 1799

An icy wind howled down the chimney and rattled the parlor windowpanes. Reverend Abel Cormorand hurried to lay another log on the grate in the blackened fireplace. "Heaven spare us, Tabby! I cannot remember a worse winter than this. Pray God no one needs me tonight."

The striped orange cat on the sofa narrowed her eyes to two green slits. She waved her white-tipped tail, her expression conveying her thoughts: Silly fellow—if I were you, I would not venture out for any reason.

Abel shook his finger at her. "Don't be telling me what a fool I am to bother with poor folks when I could be the vicar of Christ Church here in Philadelphia if I chose. Just think where *you* would be if I hadn't taken you in off the streets. 'Inasmuch as ye have done it unto one of the least of these my

13

brethren, ye have done it unto me,' you know."

Bored with a scriptural quotation she had heard many times before, Tabby yawned and closed her eyes. Abel drew a shabby horsehair chair as close to the crackling fire as possible and eased his large, stooped body into it. He adjusted his wire-rimmed spectacles, ran a hand through his thinning hair—shoulder-length and pewter-colored—and reached for the black leather Bible on the table beside him.

"Now, Tabby, what message will the Lord be sending us tonight?" he wondered aloud, paging through the well-worn volume.

Feeling a thrill of nervous anticipation, Abel shut his eyes and randomly opened the book. This was how he had first discovered his destiny; it had been written plainly beneath his fingertips: "Come follow me, for I shall make you fishers of men."

The Lord had been speaking to Peter and his brother, Andrew, but the call had echoed in the very marrow of Abel's bones. And later, when he had been offered the prestigious vicarship of Christ Church, a different course of action had been revealed to him: "Blessed are the poor in spirit; for theirs is the kingdom of heaven."

He had known immediately. The vineyard in which he labored must include the worst fruits of society. No Christ Church for him, with its impressive membership roster: George Washington and Benjamin Franklin, to whom people always said that he—portly, homely, silver-haired Abel Cormorand—bore a startling resemblance.

His questing fingers roved down the page and stopped. Abel opened his eyes and read, "Chapter thirteen, Verse thirteen, of Saint Paul's letters to the Corinthians: 'And now abideth faith, hope, charity, these three; but the greatest of these is charity.'"

With a shiver, he leaned back in his chair. "Ah, Tabby! That is one of my favorite passages. The Lord must be telling me something important—if I could only guess his meaning."

Tabby ignored him, and Abel, clutching the leather volume to his chest, jumped to his feet. He began to pace the small parlor, ponderously avoiding the worn red sofa, two padded chairs, and three small tables set on a threadbare Turkish carpet with a faded pattern of red and yellow roses. A single candle in a wall sconce flickered at his passing.

What was the Lord's message? he wondered. What was being asked of him now—and, equally important, would he prove worthy of the task?

In answer, the fire leaped and popped, sending a shower of sparks out onto the rug. Wrinkling his nose against the smell of burnt wool, Abel hurriedly stamped out the cinders. Tabby opened her eyes and meowed a complaint at the noise. His paste-buckled shoes thumping on the floor, Abel almost did not hear another sort of thumping. But then the sound came again, and he stood perfectly still, his heart leaping into his throat.

The summons was so thin and weak it could scarcely qualify as a knock, but Abel was filled with certainty that someone in desperate straits had come out on this blustery cold night to seek his aid. Someone—the Lord himself—had seen fit to test his courage and commitment.

"Pray God I have enough strength and perseverance!" he muttered to Tabby.

Four long strides took him out of the parlor and into the shadowy hallway. He hurried to the door, grasped the doorknob, and was overcome by a sense of impending fate. Trembling, he paused long enough to peer through the fan-shaped windowpane into the darkness. Snowflakes whirled in a great black void. Nothing or no one was visible.

Could he have been mistaken? Could he have imagined the divinely dictated summons? He yanked open the door and saw three tiny snow-covered figures shivering on his doorstep. Snow mixed with sleet buffeted them. The wind roared past them into the house. Shaking with cold, the children leaned together against the blast.

God in heaven. He had never expected *this*. "Come in quickly. Come, come . . . hurry now," he urged through chattering teeth.

The tallest of the trio pushed the smaller figures forward into the hallway. Abel wondered why he had not thought to light a candle in a glass and bring it with him. He wrestled with the door, shutting it against the wind, and then turned and spoke into the inky darkness. "Into the parlor with you, where it's nice and warm. Don't worry about tracking snow . . ."

The rosy glow of the fire drew them unerringly down the hallway. "Here now," Abel clucked. "Take off your shoes and put them on the hearth to dry."

He looked at the feet of his three small visitors. The children wore no shoes. Seeking warmth, their tiny bluish toes burrowed into the carpet as if trying to elude his gaze. Abel was shocked. His eyes

16

traveled up the stick-thin legs of the nearest visitor to the ragged edge of her too-high hem, over the hem and up the patched dress to the edge of her thin little shawl. That useless wisp of covering framed a pinched white face, trembling lips, and eyes the color of blue violets.

"Why, you—you're just little girls!" he blurted in a voice gone squeaky with amazement.

The child nodded. She moved closer to the others and gave them a little nudge toward the fire.

"B-but surely you were not sent here alone! Why, you—the biggest one—can hardly be more than five or six!"

Still shivering, the violet-eyed child held up five fingers. She opened her mouth but could not yet manage to speak. Her other hand snaked from beneath the shawl and held out what appeared to be a wadded handkerchief.

A folded piece of parchment paper dropped from the handkerchief, and Abel caught it before it struck the floor. Noting that the parchment was the cheapest kind, he opened the note and read: "I kan't tek care uf em no more. Please find good homes fer em."

Written in black ink with several words crossed out and rewritten, the missive bore no address or signature.

Fingering the chilled parchment, Abel exploded, *"Well!"*

Tabby jumped a foot into the air and poured herself off the sofa in a single fluid motion. All three of the children's heads swiveled to watch the animal disappear beneath a chair. Only her long tail protruded, switching with annoyance.

"Well," Abel said more quietly.

Three pairs of eyes darted back to him: one violet, one green, and one—the eyes of the smallest child, a mere toddler—a tear-filled blue. The toddler sniffed, furrowed her brow, and began to cry huge silent tears.

"Three's hungry," the eldest child announced.

A sound somewhere between a cough and a sob issued from the green-eyed child, and the eldest volunteered, "Two's feelin' poorly. An' I ain't—I'm *not* feelin' so good neither."

Abel was jolted into action. "Tea. Hot tea. That's what you need—no, milk! I always keep milk on hand for Tabby, and that's what children should drink. I'll heat milk for you and make tea for myself."

Two cups of tea, six mugs of scalded milk, and a tin of biscuits later, Abel still felt inadequate to cope with the challenge of three abandoned little girls. The children sat quietly on the sofa, stroking an ecstatic Tabby sprawled across the knees of all three.

Abel leaned forward on his chair and studied them. Thus far he had learned nothing about them other than that they were called One, Two, and Three, and apparently knew no other names for themselves. Watching them, he was appalled by the callousness of a parent who would number children rather than name them.

Was it only the play of firelight on their faces that gave them such a fragile, innocent beauty? Now that they were fed and warm, their color had returned, and he was stunned by their dissimilar appearances.

18

Beneath her tattered shawl, the eldest had been hiding long, shiny ribbons of straight black hair. The middle child had cascading waves of auburn, and the youngest, a wealth of blond curls.

Perhaps their mother had been one and the same, but their fathers must have been different.

Abel frowned and fingered the handkerchief in which the note had been wrapped. The square of white silk—the finest he had ever seen—was trimmed with lace and embroidered with a gold flowerlike emblem. A fleur-de-lis, he believed it was called. And beneath the fleur-de-lis were the initials M de H. He wondered how three urchins had come to possess something so grand. Surely, it did not belong to them or to anyone they knew.

"Did you steal this?" he held up the handkerchief and gave the oldest child a stern glance. Children of five or six were often trained to pick pockets; the depraved custom had been imported from England, along with several other nasty habits that wounded the sensibilities of honest men.

The violet eyes flashed. "That's Maman's."

Ah, now they were getting somewhere. "And who is Maman?"

"Maman," the child repeated. "She went to sleep, and they put her in a long box and tuk her away."

Abel's heart constricted with pity. Here, no doubt, was another poor woman who had fled the tyranny and upheaval of the Old World only to fall prey to the unexpected perils of the New—yellow fever, most likely, and grinding poverty.

"And your—um—papa?"

The child shook her head. "Got no Papa."

19

Abel sighed. Just as he had thought, the mother had been unmarried. In order to buy bread, she must have sold herself to the sailors on the waterfront—or to the fine gentlemen on Society Hill. Not even the Quaker influence in Philadelphia had eliminated one of man's oldest, most wretched sins.

"Did you—um—where did you—?" Dreading the child's answer, Abel hesitated to ask his next question: Where had the children been living and who had been caring for them? His imagination conjured a dark, cheerless row house where men came and went silently, ashamed of their evil purposes.

He held out his arms, inviting the eldest child to confide in him, to unburden herself. Perhaps she was too young to know the awful things that had been going on right under her nose; he hoped so. If she did know, it might haunt her all her days. "Is—is there anything you wish to tell me, my child?"

Misinterpreting his gesture, the child dug her fingers possessively into Tabby's fur. She could not have been pried apart from the animal. "Are you gonna tek keer of us?" she demanded. Her large violet eyes darted to her sisters, then came back to him.

The steady glances of the three children impaled him, and Abel knew that the moment of decision had come—and was there even a shred of doubt regarding what his decision must be?

He could not send them away, barefoot and shivering, into the snow and the cold. No, not even in summer could he have returned them to the pit of evil from which they had somehow miraculously escaped. Nor was there a suitable home for orphans or *any* place where speculation about their past would not damage and harm their future. In the cruel world of 1799, the daughters of prostitutes could not normally expect to live better lives than their mothers had endured—unless someone obliterated their past altogether.

Abel's knees creaked as he left his chair and knelt down in front of the sofa. His hands had begun to shake, and his throat felt dry—but his bones were full of certainty.

"From now on," he said softly, "you must call me Uncle Abel. I will be your mother, your father, and all the family you will ever need. I will feed and clothe you and teach you to speak properly. I will comfort you when you awake frightened in the night . . . I will . . ."

Overcome with emotion, he stopped and swallowed. How he was going to manage all that, he had no idea; sometimes the Lord was distinctly silent concerning details. Only His general mandate was unmistakably clear: "Suffer the little children to come unto me . . ."

Abel pressed the silk handkerchief into the hand of the eldest child. "You may keep this to remember your *maman*—and we will pray for her every morning and every evening. Pray God she has repented her sins."

The eldest child and the middle one returned his gaze solemnly, their eyes large and shining, brilliant as jewels. The toes of the smallest child wriggled against his waistcoat. She giggled and withdrew her feet.

"Uncle Abel Cormorand," he repeated. "That is my name, and we will tell everyone I am your uncle and your guardian. No one but you and I need know the truth, and in time, even you will forget. Sometimes, you see, the past is best forgotten."

The children nodded, seeming to drink in every word, and a disturbing thought occurred to Abel. He could not call his new nieces One, Two, and Three. The names they ought to be called came to him like a thunderbolt.

"And your name," he said to the violet-eyed child, "will be Faith Cormorand, because you did not doubt the Lord's goodness when you led your sisters through the cold dark night."

Faith did not smile, but the color of her violet eyes deepened to a hue that Abel had only seen in the sky long after sunset. God in heaven, he thought. This child will grow to be more beautiful than Ruth, more tempting than Salome . . .

Embarrassed by the surge of fierce protectiveness he now felt, he turned his attention to the middle child.

She cocked her head, and her green eyes, the color of beech leaves in the spring, were filled with expectation. "You are Hope Cormorand," he said, and his heart lurched a second time. With her auburn hair, green eyes, and vivid coloring, this child would arouse the hopes of many a young man in years to come.

She dimpled with pleasure, and he knew, without knowing how he knew, that Hope Cormorand would cherish her own sweet hopes and seek love with a joyous optimism. Oh, pray God she is not hurt or disappointed, he thought.

Last, he turned to the baby who sat tugging at his sleeve. He would never have characterized himself as sentimental, but now his heart melted like butter. She will be the golden one, he realized—the blessed one.

Her hair was already the color of ripe wheat glowing in the sunlight. Her eyes were the exact shade of a summer sky, and her skin was as rosy as a peach.

"You may be the smallest, but do you not know that the greatest of the three virtues is Charity?" he whispered. "You are Charity Cormorand."

"Unca' Abul," she chortled, throwing her tiny arms around his neck.

He opened his arms to embrace Faith, Hope, and Charity, but Tabby suddenly scrambled from the children's lap, clawed her way up his waistcoat, and leaped from his shoulder to the mantelpiece. There, she arched her back and hissed at him.

"My poor Tabby." Sighing, Abel rose stiffly to his feet, lifted down the cat, and cradled her in his arms. Smiling apologetically, he turned to the three little girls. Obviously, his new family was going to require some getting used to—on the part of all of them, including Tabby.

"Tabby isn't accustomed to sharing, you know. We must all help her to get over feeling jealous."

Faith slid off the sofa and came to stand beside him. Lacking a pocket on her shabby dress, she tucked her mother's silk handkerchief in her sleeve, then reached up to stroke Tabby's head and scratch behind her ears.

"It's all right, Tabby," she piped in her sweet young voice.

Now that everything had been decided, the child sounded calm and confident. Abel was stunned by the change in her; her belligerence had disappeared. "Uncle Abel b'longs to all of us," she continued brightly. "And we b'long to him. You'll see—it'll be all right."

And to Abel's utter amazement, Tabby began to purr. The cat, it appeared, had no further doubt— and suddenly, neither did he.

Chapter Two

Northwestern Ohio
April 1813

"Faith, are you ready? Hurry, my child, we've a long way to travel before nightfall."

Faith took one last look around the little cabin that had been home to her and Uncle Abel during five of the longest months she had ever known. Finally, they were leaving, and she could scarcely contain her joy and relief. "I'm coming, Uncle Abel!"

Her feet seemed to sprout wings as she hurried to the rough-hewn puncheon table, took up several large bundles, and departed the one-room shelter without a single backward glance. She and Uncle Abel were setting out for a destination they had never seen and knew precious little about, but anything had to be better than the cold lonely winter they had just endured.

All they did know, in fact, was that the River

25

Raisin settlement on Lake Erie, called Frenchtown, had no resident missionary. It did boast a sizable Catholic population, but such religious differences were immaterial; Uncle Abel was not going there to serve the whites, but to "minister to the poor savages," and she was going there to help him—at least at first.

Faith came out of the cabin and stole a critical look at her uncle. A winter in the Ohio wilderness had not improved his health or appearance. Perhaps if they had made it to the settlement before winter set in, he might not have lost so much weight or fallen prey to the many minor ailments that had sapped his energy and strength. At least, she thought happily, his mental alertness had remained intact.

As he stood surveying the limitless forest around them, his eyes twinkled with a wry good humor. Unaware of his stooped, cadaverous appearance, Uncle Abel greeted her with a toss of his scraggly silver mane, nearly unseating his tricorne. "The weather is lovely for our journey, don't you think so, my dear?"

Faith smiled. No one in his right mind would consider a chill, damp, mist-shrouded morning perfect weather for traveling, but in some ways it was a blessing that Uncle Abel often refused to acknowledge just how bad things were. All winter long he had extolled the wonderful goodness of the Lord, who had so miraculously provided them with an empty cabin just when they needed it—while she had dismally wondered what had sent the inhabitants fleeing from their well-stocked larder and wood pile, and what had prevented them from ever returning.

"Yes, Uncle Abel," she agreed. "The weather is superb."

Uncle Abel hitched his bundles a trifle higher beneath one arm. In his free hand he carried a walking stick, and over one shoulder he wore a musket. Being a man of strong conviction when it came to violence, he had staunchly resisted learning to load or fire the weapon, but she had managed to persuade him to bring it along for appearance's sake, if not for actual protection.

Uncle Abel looked up at the small patch of sky directly overhead and grinned encouragingly. "Yes, fine weather for traveling. But how else could it be, eh? The Lord has brought us to this fair land, and he will guide us to our destiny. Did you leave a note for the owner of the cabin, my child?"

Though she knew that few in the wilderness could read, Faith nodded. "On the table . . . I apologized for having eaten all their dried meat, squash, and corn, and used their firewood."

"Well, I expect the Lord will provide for them, too, my dear, just as he did for us."

Faith forbore to mention her doubts and fears about the fate of the cabin's previous occupants. Uncle Abel would never have admitted that Indians were capable of attacking and killing people for no good reason. Yet she knew this to be true from the tales of fellow travelers on the Philadelphia-to-Erie leg of their long journey the previous autumn.

"Shall we go?" She put more confidence into the

question than she felt.

Apparently not realizing that she was still watching him, Uncle Abel took a deep steadying breath and squared his frail shoulders. He did not look capable of hiking through miles of trackless forest in search of a river called the Maumee. But at least this time there was no snow to deter them, and she had to assume the zeal that had carried her uncle this far would keep him going until they reached their destination.

Thinking seriously now of what lay ahead, Faith shivered. Once they found the Maumee, they must somehow cross it, follow it to Lake Erie, and then follow the shoreline of the lake to the River Raisin. Uncle Abel insisted that the journey could take no more than a day or two at most, and Faith hoped that he was right. As she had already learned from painful experience, distances in the wilderness were often deceiving.

Reciting a Psalm to give them courage, Uncle Abel set out leading the way. "To you, O Lord, I call; O my rock, be not deaf to me, lest, if you heed me not, I become one of those going down into the pit . . ."

Twenty Psalms later, Uncle Abel suddenly stopped walking. Faith hurried to his side. Having been so long shut up in a cabin, he was panting from the unaccustomed exertion, and his face was damp and pale. But true to his nature, he smiled and tried to forestall her anxious questions. "Ah, Faith, how I wish that your sisters, Hope and Charity, could be with us on this adventure . . ." Breathing deeply, he

28

leaned back against a tree.

They had been trudging due north—a convenient direction since tree moss always grew on the north sides of trees, and in this endless forest, trees and tree moss abounded. Ahead of and behind them, there was nothing to see but trees.

Knowing that it was useless to discuss the frailty of his health, Faith sat down on a decaying log and sighed loudly. She might as well pretend that she was the one who needed a short rest. "Don't worry about Hope and Charity, Uncle Abel. Hannah Turner will take good care of them. Hannah is the best housekeeper in the entire country—and when we get settled, we can send for them."

Her sisters and Hannah Turner had accompanied them from Philadelphia as far as Erie, Pennsylvania, where they were to remain with Hannah's relatives until spring. If last year's hostilities between England and America had by now abated, American ships would soon begin plying Lake Erie, and Hope and Charity could board a ship at Erie and be in Frenchtown by early summer, if not before. Faith only hoped that the girls would not set forth until hearing from her that she and Uncle Abel were safely settled and organized to receive them.

Thinking of her sisters, she grinned. She really need not worry about them arriving any sooner than absolutely necessary. Neither of her sisters had much interest in saving the souls of savages, though they had been careful to hide that fact from Uncle Abel. Indeed, Faith could not imagine her pretty, vivacious sisters willingly burying themselves in the

29

wilderness and settling for ignorant backwoodsmen who could neither read nor write. Hope, at seventeen, pretended to scorn men, yet drew them as clover drew bees. Charity, at sixteen, was more beautiful and marriage-minded than either of her older sisters.

More than likely both girls would find reasons aplenty to remain in Erie where Hannah had already assured them that they would always be welcome. Hannah's relatives, two maiden cousins, had been delighted to have youth and laughter invade their dull household—and had even begged Faith and Uncle Abel to remain in Erie. But her dedicated uncle had, of course, refused.

Faith could never have allowed him to set off for the wilderness by himself, and besides, she rather fancied the idea of taking part in a stirring adventure. Something was waiting for her out here in the wilderness—something grand and exciting. She was sure of it—and it was *not* just saving souls, or getting scalped. She could not have explained it to anyone. But just sitting on a log suddenly filled her with such impatience that she unthinkingly leaped to her feet.

"Rested now?" Uncle Abel peered over his spectacles at her. "Ready to go on?"

"Oh, yes!" Her own eagerness embarrassed her. Fortunately, Uncle Abel seemed to have recovered from his shortness of breath, and she did not have to add guilt to her discomfort. "Thanks for stopping, Uncle Abel. You always seem to know when I'm growing tired."

They trudged deeper into thick primeval stands of oak, beech, chestnut, and walnut, whose tightly closed green buds were just beginning to open. Faith lost count of the many varieties of trees, and as she trudged along, her thoughts kept straying to her future. What would she do in Frenchtown once the mission was open and on its feet?

At nineteen, she was already considered too old to attract the most eligible men, and here in the wilderness, there did not seem to be any men, eligible or not, to attract. Even if Frenchtown was swarming with prospective husbands, she could not simply go up to one of them and propose marriage; after all, she had her pride.

And she did not really know how to banter with men, to signal her interest in them in that sly way so many other girls, including her own sisters, obviously were born knowing.

That very ignorance might mean she was doomed to be a missionary, an occupation she could only halfheartedly embrace. What other possibilities were there—teaching school? Becoming a seamstress? None of these appealed to her.

Indeed, she could think of only one thing that fueled her excitement, that spoke to her sense of adventure. And of course, it wasn't possible. A woman couldn't clear her own land, put up her own cabin, plant her own crops, and proclaim herself mistress of all she surveyed. She wouldn't even know how to go about it . . . so why did the idea persist?

Was it because she alone remembered the terrifying rootlessness of their past? Hope and Charity had forgotten the sheer horror of wandering about in the dark and cold, knowing that no one wanted them, that they belonged to no one, and that no one cared if they lived or died—but Faith had not forgotten it. All those glowing windows she had longingly looked into—and none of them were hers . . .

Not even Uncle Abel's love could obliterate those earliest, most frightening memories; she wanted something—someplace—all her own. *That* was what she yearned for, and why she had come so great a distance and was willing to go even farther. Here, things might be different. This was a *whole* new world, with a new set of opportunities. Maybe, here, a woman *could* have her own place if she really wanted it. Maybe, if she worked hard, planned and schemed . . .

"Faith dear, did you remember to pack Hope and Charity's miniatures?" Uncle Abel had stopped and turned on the nonexistent path.

In her preoccupation, she almost ran into him. "Their miniatures?" She had to force herself to concentrate on the question. "Why, I thought you packed them. You said you were afraid I would forget them."

Uncle Abel's spectacles bobbed up and down apologetically. "Did I say that? Dear me, child, I don't remember . . ."

Faith eased her bundles onto the ground. Over the winter, her uncle had grown occasionally forgetful. She was sure that the condition was only temporary, a consequence of enforced idleness combined with

32

bouts of illness, but now she could see him agonizing over it—and with reason.

The precious miniatures in their tiny, delicate gold frames had cost a small fortune to have painted, but cost had been no object when it had come to obtaining likenesses of Hope and Charity to take into the wilderness.

"Now, let me think . . ." Frowning, Uncle Abel fingered his chin. "I put them under the mattress—or maybe it was inside my hat . . ."

Hopefully, he set down his bundles and removed his tricorne. His gnarled fingers groped across his pewter-colored hair, but no miniatures appeared. "God forgive me . . . You see, I wanted to keep them safe until I rolled my blanket, but when I rolled it, I never thought of the miniatures . . . didn't think of them until just this moment. And of course, now it is too late."

He looked so upset with himself that Faith jumped to put the blame where it belonged—on her own shoulders. She ought to have checked for the miniatures herself. "Look, Uncle, there is another fallen log over there. Why don't you sit down and say a prayer while I go back to look for them?"

"Oh, my dear, do you think you should? We really ought to forge ahead. Or else you should stay here and I'll go back . . ."

"*I'll* go," Faith insisted. "It's *my* fault that we forgot them. You shouldn't have to think of everything. I'll leave my bundles here, and it won't take nearly as long to go back as it took to get here. It really isn't too far. Just promise me you will stay

33

here and . . . and . . ."

She wanted to say "rest" but thought better of it. A moment's irritation came over her; sometimes it was difficult to maintain the pretense that all was as it should be. Sometimes her uncle's relentless optimism was downright exasperating.

"Just stay here," she pleaded. "Don't worry. I won't get lost."

Uncle Abel patted her hand reassuringly. "You, my dear Faith, will never be lost. The Lord will always show you the way."

"I am certain he will," Faith responded, feeling less reassured by the minute. She hated to think of the time they would lose—and of having to spend the night or nights in the forest if they didn't make it to Frenchtown before dark.

"Lovely child." Uncle Abel communicated his gratitude with the gentle pressure of his palm pressing downward. "As beautiful and stalwart as her name."

Embarrassed, Faith withdrew her hand and hurried away through the trees. Compliments always made her feel uneasy. She did not have the striking coloring of her sisters, but her curves were more ample than theirs and her nature less selfish. She knew these things about herself, but took no pride in them. They were accidents of nature, not something she had earned.

Being the eldest, she had been schooled to think of her uncle's and her sisters' needs before her own. And having silky black hair and strangely colored eyes was something that had merely happened.

Whoever her mother and father had been, they had bequeathed to her a physical legacy and a position of rank among her siblings that had shaped and molded her entire life. She could not remember when she had not been responsible for others, when she had been free to think of no one but herself.

Snagging her skirt on a protruding root, she stopped and freed it, reflecting that she would never have chosen to be the eldest, to be burdened with so much responsibility. There was a wildness, a rebellion inside her, that was quite at odds with her outwardly calm, staid, dependable personality. Sometimes she felt as if she were not the woman whom others thought she was. It was not just her desire to do something different with her life or even to own her own square of earth; it was something more . . .

Had she known her parents—especially her mother—she might have known herself better. But as it was . . . sometimes she dreamed the strangest, most disturbing dreams . . .

An image from a dream of the night before returned with stunning clarity: Wearing a silk chemise, she was sitting on the side of a bed, and a man was sitting beside her. She could feel the warm pressure of his arm around her waist, could smell his faintly musky masculine odor. A shivery feeling came over her as he began to stroke her ribs through the delicate fabric. He pulled her closer and whispered into her ear, "Touch me . . . You know you want to. Go ahead and touch me . . ."

And she had wanted to touch him, had wanted, in

fact, to do more than just touch him. Shyly, wary of her own feelings, she had run her fingertips over the muscles of his massive chest. He had whispered something and seized her hand, pressing it downward between his well-muscled thighs . . .

Her own thighs had begun to quiver. Heat had enveloped her in a burning wave. And now, at the mere memory of how she had felt during the night, erotic images flooded her mind: a man's naked, well-muscled body moving to cover hers, his hands exploring her own naked flesh, her hands exploring his flesh . . .

Fleeing these vivid specters, she ran faster through the mist-shrouded forest. Would a man desire such intimate caresses as much as she desired them? Would he, too, be filled with tumultuous, scarcely controllable emotions?

She could scarcely discuss such things with an uncle who was a minister or even with her younger sisters. Yet she wondered; was she normal or had she perhaps inherited some strange, unmentionable disposition? Uncle Abel always seemed reluctant to talk about her past, and other than her mother's white silk handkerchief in which, she abruptly remembered, her sister's miniatures had been wrapped, she had no clue—no clue whatsoever—as to who she was or where she had come from.

Determined not to let these unanswerable questions continue to haunt her thoughts, Faith fairly flew through the trees toward the cabin. And when a man suddenly stepped out in front of her, she could not stop herself from colliding with the wall of his

36

chest. Her breath was knocked from her own chest, and she would have fallen if he had not grabbed her and held her upright, less than a hand's span away from his body—a body that was even more muscular than the body of the man in her dreams . . .

A chill morning mist obscured the line of Indians and red-coated soldiers stealthily winding its way along the banks of the Maumee River. But behind a screen of underbrush, the lone man stretched out on the damp ground had no difficulty counting his quarry. Six hundred British regulars, eight hundred Canadian militiamen, and over fifteen hundred Indians were on the march, headed toward the new American Fort Meigs, an encampment farther downriver on the high southern bank of the Maumee.

The scout swore silently as the British army's commanding general, Henry Proctor, rode past: "Damn bloody bastard. I'll see you in hell before we're through. You can have the high seas and the whole of Canada, but *not* the Northwest Territory."

A tall, ghostly figure wearing little more than a breechclout, a musket, and slashes of black and white war paint followed closely behind the general. The scout gripped his long gun and fought the urge to shoot. He should have known Tecumseh would be with Proctor. Still, the shock of seeing the Indian who had once been his friend, but was now his sworn enemy, brought back a storm of memories.

Long ago, Tecumseh's gentle, powerful voice had

37

entreated him. "Take care of our Shawnee sister. She is special, different . . . and she will never willingly bring you sorrow or unhappiness."

And special she had been—Moon Daughter, of the soft doe eyes and shining black hair. Tecumseh, renowned leader of the united tribes, had not spoken falsely, but neither had he lifted a finger to prevent the tragic death of the lovely Shawnee girl.

The scout gritted his teeth and wrenched his thoughts back from the past. He had a job to do and must do it unseen. General William Henry Harrison was depending on him. The pitiful group of settlers and soldiers at Fort Meigs would lose their lives if he was discovered and could not return to warn them.

He flexed his fingers; they had grown stiff while he lay motionless, and now they tingled. He frowned, resenting any reminder that his body was not always the servant of his mind, but had a will—and needs—of its own. He had neither eaten nor slept in the past twenty-four hours. His control was in danger of slipping, and darkness threatened, a darkness in which he knew he would succumb to violent urgings to gain release from his pain.

Despite his best effort to banish them, the memories of Moon Daughter—innocent Moon Daughter lying motionless and bloodied on the trampled grass in front of their lodge—twisted knifelike in his heart. He could still hear her voice whispering his name, still see the light fading from her eyes. Hurt and surprise had crumpled her mouth; it had trembled like a bruised wildflower. Even at the end, she had not understood that white men and red could not live peaceably side by side, hunting the same forest and prairie. She had never realized that the two races would always be enemies, murdering one another, murdering their own if they voiced a protest . . .

The scout shifted his weight and peered through the underbrush. The line had thinned and only a few straggling Indians brought up the rear. He wondered if Proctor thought savages were more expendable than soldiers, or if he had discovered the truth: The wily, fierce warriors were better able to defend themselves from surprise attack. The last man in line—tall, naked, and wearing a necklace of bear claws—was more fierce-looking than most. His muscles rippled like an animal's as he moved soundlessly through the swirling fog.

The scout waited until the Indian was past him, then leaped to his feet. A roaring began in his ears. He felt light-headed, almost disembodied. The acrid scent of the Indian's body, smeared that morning with bear grease and paint, assaulted his nostrils. Another smell—that curious odor of pride worn almost exclusively by the arrogant Shawnee— enraged him beyond all turning back. Now he welcomed the darkness that blotted out reason and conscience.

The scout's moccasined feet carried him forward down the path beside the river. More silently than an Indian, he trod the carpet of leaf mold and decayed vegetation. The Indian never once looked behind him—and the scout easily caught him in a bone-crushing grip about the neck.

"This one is for you, Moon Daughter," he hissed into the startled man's ear. "Indeed, they are *all* for you."

Unable to make a sound, the Indian struggled for his life. The scout pitted his hatred against his enemy's strength. His powerful right arm, corded with muscle, closed inexorably around the man's windpipe. The satisfying crunch of breaking bones sounded in his ears. The Indian's body sagged against him, but the scout made one last upward jerking motion before he allowed the man to fall.

"I'll make you pay for what you did to her—you and the others. One by one I will hunt you down. Your whole nation will pay . . ."

The scout released the Indian's body and stood a moment looking down at it. Already, his sense of satisfaction was fading, his pain beginning to throb anew. Moon Daughter would never have understood the savagery of which he was now capable. He did not understand it himself. Worse yet, he had done this for her, but she seemed farther away from him than ever.

Did not the Bible teach "An eye for an eye, a tooth for a tooth?" Why, then, he wondered, was the taste of vengeance so bitter?

The scout stepped back from the body and retreated a safe distance into the forest. He breathed deeply, filling his lungs with untainted air. The scent of the damp earth was soothing. The innocent flutter of a nearby pheasant calmed his racing heart. He stood quietly, allowing the vast peacefulness to penetrate to his inner core. Then, as if in those few moments he had become a new person, he gave a high whistle. The cheerful call of the bobwhite bounced from tree to tree.

A moment later, a large gray shape came hurtling forward out of the underbrush. "Easy, boy . . ." The scout braced himself and held out his hand, palm downward in a friendly nonthreatening gesture. "Easy now, take it easy."

The enormous animal struck him squarely in the chest, its two front paws almost knocking him over. The scout laughed and ruffled the fur around the creature's neck. Its long pink tongue lolled from its mouth, making it appear to be grinning.

The scout accepted an affectionate swipe on his cheek, then pushed the animal back down on all fours. "Come on, Shadow. Our work here is done. It's time we headed for the fort."

Shadow wagged his tail and frolicked like a puppy. The man patted the beast's huge gray head, snapped his fingers in front of its nose, and strode off into the trees. But he did not get far before Shadow suddenly stopped, growled low in his throat, and bared his teeth.

Stepping behind a shagbark hickory, the scout hurriedly set down his rifle and seized the hunting knife strapped to his waist. He strained to see through the palisade of trees, but before the reason for Shadow's warning came into view, there sounded a loud rustling of underbrush and snapping of twigs.

No Indian, soldier, or experienced woodsman would move so carelessly; it had to be some wayward settler—and a foolish one at that.

Heaving a sigh of annoyance, the scout sheathed his knife and waited until the figure was almost upon him. Then, grunting his disgust, he stepped from behind the tree . . . and even before he caught a glimpse of enormous violet-colored eyes, he knew that the soft body rushing into his arms was that of a young full-breasted woman . . .

Quickly recovering her footing and jumping back, Faith looked up into blazing green eyes, more feral than a cat's, and was overwhelmed by the sheer force and strength of the man who stood before her. Surprise etched his harshly cut features, and for a long breathless moment, he stood silently staring down at her.

Struggling to swallow her own surprise, Faith stared back at him, and details of his appearance struck her with the force of blows.

Above his disturbing green eyes, locks of dark wavy hair swept his forehead. His skin was the color of tanned leather, and the tiny web of lines about his mouth told of much hard living in the open air.

He had to be years older than she—and yet, he seemed strangely ageless, as powerful and strong as an oak tree, as harsh and unforgiving as a mountaintop in winter. A sudden uneasiness caused her knees to buckle. She swayed, and the man stepped closer, his fingers digging into her upper arms.

"Who are you?" he demanded.

She could not defy the authority in his voice. "Faith Cormorand," she gasped.

Her eyes sought something less hostile than his face, and came to rest on several startling slashes of white cutting through the dark matted hair on his chest. Neither the boldness of his half-open shirt nor the wicked-looking scars did anything to reassure her.

Swept with anxiety, she glanced away and discovered something even more frightening: Scarcely a leap from where she stood, an enormous timber wolf crouched. Its lips were drawn back from its teeth, its amber eyes gleamed, and a growl issued menacingly from its throat.

"Look!" She raised a trembling finger and pointed. "A—a wolf!"

The animal gathered itself to spring.

"No, Shadow!" At the man's reprimand, the beast cringed. Its tail swept the ground abjectly. Amber eyes grew mournful and sought forgiveness.

"See what you have done—or made me do." The stranger muttered something low in his throat and slapped his leather-encased thigh. Tail wagging joyfully, the wolf bounded forward, his eagerness to be forgiven apparent in every movement of his huge trembling body.

Faith maneuvered herself so that the tall figure in buckskins stood between her and the creature. "I didn't make you do anything." Indignation sharpened her tone. Was she supposed to apologize for hurting the feelings of an animal who could have torn her apart? "That—beast was going to

43

attack me."

The man's fingers gently stroked the wolf's furry ears, but his chilling glance denied any such gentleness toward humans. "No, he wasn't. He was only warning you to keep your distance. Shadow is basically a docile fellow—far more so than his master."

Taken back by the man's hostility, Faith saw no reason to disagree. A shiver crept along her spine. She did not want to be alone with this man or to make him angry—and apparently she *was* alone with him and had already stirred his ire. "I—I'll be on my way, then. If you will excuse me . . ."

In a blur of sudden movement, the stranger caught her wrist. Looking down, she saw that his fingers were surprisingly long and graceful, not short and blunt as she had somehow expected. But the strength in those fingers could not be ignored. Her wrist was firmly imprisoned.

"No, you won't. I don't know what you are doing here in the middle of nowhere, but it's my duty to order you to Fort Meigs with the rest of the settlers."

Astounded by his peremptory manner, Faith blurted, "I am not headed toward Fort Meigs. I don't even know where it is."

"I'm going there myself. You can follow me."

"But—I don't want to follow you!"

"You will do as I say." The stranger's hand tightened. "There's no time to waste."

Truly frightened now, Faith stepped backward. Futilely, she tried to disengage herself from his powerful grip. "I don't think you understand—"

"No, it is you who do not understand! You are in danger here and must leave immediately."

"Danger? Why, I hardly think—"

The haunting cry of some forest creature interrupted her. It came from far off in the distance, but the wolf's ears pricked, and Faith sensed danger. The mist seethed and pulsated with it. For a full silent moment, she seriously considered the stranger's demand. She would have to go back and get Uncle Abel, of course, and then explain . . . No, the whole idea was absurd.

No one had the right to order them about or to cause further delays in their plans. Besides, she knew her uncle; nothing on earth could dissuade him from going to the River Raisin settlement.

"I'm sorry, but I cannot," she said quietly.

His green eyes glinted. "Cannot or will not?"

Resisting the impulse to tremble, Faith stood her ground. "Both, I'm afraid."

The stranger moved closer and seized her shoulders with savage urgency. "You silly little fool! What is the matter with you? Must I carry you out of the woods slung over my back? Fort Meigs is the safest place for you now!"

The man was mad, Faith thought—or else she was mad, standing there allowing him to threaten her. Could she escape down the path and run back to Uncle Abel? Another furtive glance at the man's lithe, muscular body convinced her to abandon that idea. He would easily catch her.

"I am warning you," the stranger growled. "There is little time, and I am losing patience."

Faith lifted her chin and fought to remain calm. Another woman, one of her own sisters perhaps, might resort to tears and entreaties in this situation, but she would not. Nothing in this wilderness—no, not in the entire world—could cause her to grovel and beg; by the sheer force of her determination, she would convince him to leave her alone.

"Sir, you had better go without me. I am not your responsibility. And if there's any trouble, I can handle it."

"Damnation!" the stranger swore. His anger, barely held in check before, now seemed to explode. In less time than it took to blink, his hands found her waist and lifted her high off the ground. The hard edge of a protruding collarbone grazed her midsection, and Faith jerked backward to keep from falling head downward over his shoulder.

Rigid with shock, she pounded on his back, neck, shoulders—whatever was handy. When that brought no result, she entwined her fingers in his thick wavy hair and tugged with all her might. "Put me down at once! You have no right to do this! Put me *down!*"

As if she bothered him less than a fly and weighed no more than a haunch of deer meat, the stranger began walking. For a single moment, panic got the better of her. "Uncle Abel!" she screamed. "Come quickly and bring the musket."

The stranger put her down with a bone-jarring thud. "Then you aren't out here all alone. I suspected as much—and you could have spared us both time and trouble by admitting it at once."

"I don't have to admit anything, you—you arrogant jackanapes!" Flushing, Faith bit her lip. She had never stooped to calling people names, but never had she been so provoked.

The stranger's eyes narrowed. A muscle twitched threateningly in his jaw. "If a jackanapes is related to a jackass, someone should teach you better manners—or better cuss words. If I had the time, I would take you over my knee and give you a lesson with a hickory stick here and now."

Faith half expected him to make good on his threat. She backed away. The wolf's cold, wet nose brushed her hand. Startled, she jumped and jerked her fingers out of reach of his powerful jaws.

A derisive look accompanied the stranger's short laugh. "I told you Shadow would not hurt you—but there is scarcely a brave alive who would not greatly enjoy relieving you of that long black mane of hair. It would make a fine trophy to hang from a lodge pole."

Her hands flew to her hair. In her struggles, the neat knot at the back of her neck had come undone, and the solid blue-black mass had tumbled down about her shoulders. No man but Uncle Abel had ever seen her with disheveled hair; she felt doubly vulnerable and exposed. With all the dignity she could muster, she began plaiting her waist-length tresses into a braid.

The stranger eyed her with a mixture of contempt and exasperation. "Well, are you going to tell me where to find your uncle—or must I go looking for him myself?"

"My—my uncle is waiting for me nearby. We are on our way to the settlement on the River Raisin where we plan to open a mission for the savages . . . Not that it's any business of yours," she added defiantly.

"Bible toters," the stranger scoffed. "I might have guessed it."

How dare this man mock and revile them! Faith fixed him with her haughtiest stare. "We make no apologies for our beliefs, sir!"

Angrily, she finished braiding her hair, then wondered what to do with the heavy coil. She had no ribbon or twine with which to tie the end. A brown piece of vine clinging to a tree caught her eye, and she started toward it.

But the stranger's hand reached out and grasped hers. He drew her close—so close that she became aware of the heat and odor of his body—and of his increasing anger.

"Can you and your uncle really be such fools? These woods are full of British soldiers and renegade savages who would as soon shoot or scalp an American as look at one. This entire territory is enemy held."

Enemy held? What in heaven's name was he talking about? "We can take care of ourselves!" she flared. "We have a musket!"

Even as the words left her mouth, she remembered that neither she nor Uncle Abel had any idea how to use the aged and rusty gun. Furthermore, it had been months since she had spoken with a human being other than her uncle. In that time, *any*thing might

48

have happened in the world at large—even all-out war with the British.

Quelling her mounting panic with a supreme effort of will, she resolved never to reveal to this arrogant stranger her ignorance or her fear. "We *do* have a musket," she repeated. "And we're not afraid to use it."

The stranger scowled. "I see no musket."

Suddenly, he grasped her chin and tilted it upward, forcing her to look at him. She had never seen eyes so coldly searching. They were the color of green glass—or green ice.

His tone of voice was equally cold. "Little idiot . . . In these woods there are no churches, no schools, no fine congregations of kindly, righteous people. I doubt there is even a God. There is only violence and savagery—and where you are concerned, most probably there will also be lust."

"L-lust?" she stammered, no longer doubting a single word he said.

His menacing nearness and her unaccustomed loss of confidence combined to send tremors through her body. The tremors reminded her of . . . the lust or passion or whatever it was that had so often invaded her dreams at night.

Amazed that, under the circumstances, such associations would even occur to her, she tried to pull away from him, but his hands once again encircled her waist. He pressed her to him, crushing her full breasts against his chest. The hard contours of his male body burned through the fabric of her dress. She writhed and struggled, but with threatening calm, he held her still, compelling her to endure his embrace and to look into the dazzling green depths of his eyes.

This can't be happening to me, she thought, shocked by the rush of liquid heat to her loins and the furious thudding of her heart. Her cheeks flamed, but she was powerless to move or to glance away from him.

"Have you no idea what a band of men would do to you if they came upon you alone? Do you think your Bible would save you then? Believe me, I know what men are capable of, especially those men who have reason to hate. Don't think, because you are a woman, that you will be spared. On the contrary, a woman can bring out the worst in a man; she can turn him into a vicious rutting animal."

"I—I . . ." Faith's voice refused to function. Was he talking about himself—or about savages and British soldiers?

She dropped her gaze to his lips and was stunned to discover them only inches from her own. Unthinkingly, she moistened her lips with her tongue . . . If he did not let go of her, if he forced himself on her, she did not know what she would do. Incredibly, it wasn't just *him* she feared; it was her *own* reaction to him, her own totally unmanageable responses; they terrified her more than anything.

The stranger's arms tightened, squeezing the breath from her lungs. "You've got to get out of here, little idiot," he hissed in her ear. "Don't you understand? You have nothing to fear from me; I never ravish foolish little virgins—but unfortunately, the same cannot be said for *others.*"

The warning growl of the timber wolf alerted both of them to someone's approach. Like a hammer striking an anvil, fear slammed down on her consciousness.

Dear God, it's the others!

She twisted in the stranger's arms, and a split second later, Uncle Abel's best preaching voice boomed into the clearing: "Unhand my niece, sir—or I shall blow off your head!"

Chapter Three

Giddy with relief, Faith started to laugh hysterically—something she had done only once or twice in her life. Then she saw the barrel of the musket pointed straight at them. Abruptly, she fell silent and stiffened. In his inexperience, Uncle Abel might blow off both their heads.

The stranger displayed not the least alarm. His grip relaxed, and he stepped away from her. With one hand, he signaled to the wolf, and the animal dropped to the ground, its watchful eyes and twitching nose betraying its unceasing vigilance.

"Sir, I doubt that you will blow off anybody's head," the stranger said. "That musket is neither primed nor cocked—as any woodsman can plainly see."

"It isn't?" Uncle Abel sounded both relieved and disappointed. He turned the weapon around and peered down its muzzle. "Dear me, I knew it was useless to carry a musket, but Faith positively insisted. Didn't you, my dear?"

Faith flushed with embarrassment. It galled her that this cocksure stranger had discovered how weak and vulnerable they really were. "Never mind, Uncle Abel. The musket isn't necessary. Now that you are here, you can explain to this *gentleman*"—she gave the word unwarranted emphasis—"that we have no need for his protection."

"His protection?" Uncle Abel frowned and adjusted his spectacles. "But I thought . . . My eyesight is none too good, 'tis true, but it looked as if he was trying to force his attentions on you."

Flushing even more deeply, Faith acknowledged the error she, too, had been guilty of making. "We—we had a misunderstanding, an argument—that's all. And the gentleman was trying to prevent me from walking away in the middle of it. He—he was not actually forcing his attentions . . ."

The stranger folded his arms complacently across the broad expanse of his chest and shot her an inscrutable glance—a look, almost, of amusement. Anger rose hotly in her breast. Never in her life had she met anyone so boldly arrogant. The man was insufferable. Were it not for the shock to her uncle, she most definitely would slap his face.

Attempting to regain her pride and her dignity, shredded and tattered now, she crossed the small clearing. "Really, Uncle Abel. I am quite all right. But I cannot seem to convince Mr.—Mr. . . ." Blushing furiously as she remembered her body's response to the stranger, she turned back to him. "I don't believe you told me your name."

The green eyes rudely assessed her. "No, ma'am, I

don't believe I did. It's Whip Martin, in case you are interested."

His tone suggested that her interest must surely be personal. Incensed, Faith whirled back to her uncle. "I cannot convince Mr. Martin that we are in no danger and do not need to be ordered about like children!"

"Danger? Ordered about like children? I demand that you explain this matter, sir. You have rendered my niece quite distraught."

"That's not the worst of it!" Faith's indignation almost choked her. "He insists that we follow him to some f-fort!"

"Meigs," the stranger said. "Camp Meigs, some call it. The place is named after Return Jonathan Meigs, of whom you may or may not have heard."

"Of *course* we have heard of the governor of Ohio," Faith snapped. She stepped into place beside her uncle and gave the stranger what she hoped was her most withering glance.

Unexpectedly, he grinned. At least, Faith interpreted the sardonic quirk of his lip as a grin. "And have you also heard why he is called *Return* Jonathan Meigs?" His patronizing drawl left no doubt that he enjoyed confusing and humiliating her.

"No, I have not, nor do I wish to hear it. We have been delayed on our journey long enough." Faith tucked her hand under her uncle's arm and pointedly tugged on it. "Uncle Abel, I am afraid we will have to leave the miniatures behind. We have wasted too much time now for me to go all the way back to the cabin."

"But there's no need, child!" Uncle Abel's face lit up. "I found the miniatures. I don't know why I did not remember . . . I wrapped them in your mother's silk handkerchief, exactly as we carried them here from Erie, and put them in my shot bag."

Whip Martin snorted, and from the corner of her eye, Faith saw that he was scowling again. "You would be better off to carry shot in your shot bag—and powder in your horn. As I have been trying to tell your niece, these woods are swarming with Indians and British soldiers. It's a wonder we aren't all dead and scalped by now—as indeed we would be if Proctor were not so intent on attacking the fort instead."

"Proctor? Henry Proctor? Do you mean the British colonel at Fort Malden?" Uncle Abel asked. "Why, I have heard that he is an honorable man, sir!"

"Henry Proctor is now a general," Whip said curtly. "We are at war, and he has formed a strong alliance with the savages to seize control of the entire Northwest Territory."

Uncle Abel looked stunned, exactly the way Faith felt. Before their departure from Philadelphia, they had known about the threat of impending war with the British. But because of a treaty that had supposedly been in force since 1795, they had not expected to be in any way affected. How naive and foolish they had been to place their trust in a mere piece of paper! Faith saw at once that everything had changed, and by the slump of her uncle's shoulders, she knew that he, too, recognized that awful fact.

"But," she blurted, "if soldiers and Indians, an entire army, are going to attack this fort, why do you want us to go there?"

"The fort is well designed and well situated. It may be undermanned, but General Harrison has taken every precaution to make it a place of safety . . . Of course, he can do nothing to protect those who insist on wandering around in the woods."

"We are *not* wandering around in the woods. We know exactly where we are going, and our destination, too, should be a safe place." Growing more certain of this as she thought about it, Faith again tugged at her uncle's sleeve. "We must leave, Uncle."

Uncle Abel was silent for a moment, his expression thoughtful. Then he sighed and nodded. "Yes, yes, we most definitely must. Now it is even more urgent that we begin our work among the savages . . . 'Tis a pity, though, this stirring up of hostilities, this warmongering among honorable men. When we get to Frenchtown, I shall cross over to Malden and speak with the British authorities. They cannot help but listen to the counsel of a man of God."

Whip Martin's deepening scowl would have stopped a charging buffalo. "Sir . . ." He glared at Uncle Abel. "Man of God or not, any remaining Americans have been ordered to go immediately to the fort. Most have already left the area. General Harrison will take no responsibility for those who refuse to obey his orders."

Uncle Abel drew himself upright. "I am the

57

servant of the Lord, sir, not of the general. My place is in Frenchtown. God will provide all the protection we need."

Disbelief and barely controlled fury contorted Whip Martin's dark face. Despite her increasing concern, Faith felt a spurt of satisfaction. This opinionated stranger might think he could order a mere woman about, but against the rock-hard moral strength of Uncle Abel, he would have little effect.

But the capitulation she expected did not come. Instead, Whip Martin snapped his fingers, and the timber wolf rose from the ground. "You must have been heading north, were you not?" His tone was deadly calm, almost disinterested.

"North! Of course, it was north. Do you think we do not know in which direction we ought to be traveling?" Uncle Abel cocked his head and peered over his spectacles at Whip Martin. "My good man, we are not fools, you know."

"That, sir, remains to be seen." Whip gave the wolf another signal, a simple nod of his head.

Uneasily, Faith eyed the animal as it glided into the center of the path down which she and Uncle Abel would need to proceed.

"Since you refuse to take my advice, perhaps you will accept Shadow's. He seems to think that north is a bad direction in which to travel."

As if on cue, Shadow growled and bared his teeth. His menacing presence filled the narrow path, and Faith knew a moment of stunned defeat. For the second time that day, she protested, "Why, you— you have no right!"

Whip Martin's lifted eyebrow stopped her cold. "I have every right," he said smoothly. "Someday you may even thank me for saving you from the consequences of your own stubbornness."

Whip watched Faith Cormorand kneel beside the river and dip water into her cupped hands. Gingerly, she drank, and he could not help noticing how delicate and graceful her movements were, even when she was angry. She had not spoken the entire afternoon. Now, at twilight, she was still not speaking, but her silence no longer irritated him. Instead, he had grown thankful. It was safer to travel with a silent woman than a noisy one.

He did not know why her silence should bother him anyway. In an hour or two at most, they would be at Fort Meigs, and she would be General Harrison's responsibility, not his. General Harrison would send her south to Fort Greenville as soon as possible, and likely he would never see her again. Which suited him fine. The last thing he needed in his life was another woman—especially an ignorant easterner.

Nevertheless, the slender grace of the girl's rounded figure pleased his critical eye. Even her simple brown homespun dress could not conceal the fact that she was a lady—gently reared and as out of place in the wilderness as he would be in a parlor. Her hands were slender and white, her hair a glossy blue-black, and her eyes the most unusual color he had ever seen: a changeable blue-tinged violet.

When she looked at her uncle, her eyes seemed as blue as Lake Erie, sparkling on a summer's day, but when she looked at him, they turned a smoky violet. He had never seen eyes so expressive. And if her face and figure were not enough to attract a man's attention, her air of innocence alone would have done it.

He wondered if she had ever been kissed, then chided himself for even wondering. Obviously, she was untouched, and he would enjoy being the first to touch her. But involvement with a young innocent like Faith Cormorand could only mean trouble. He could never give her anything but sorrow—and could never expect anything but sorrow in return. This he knew from experience.

He knelt down on one knee and dipped a handful of river water. He was thirsty but had long ago learned to keep his appetites under strict control. Self-denial made him more vigilant—and now, so close to the fort, he could not afford to let down his guard for a single moment.

The closer they got to the fort, the more dangerous the wilderness became. Until this moment, steering clear of Proctor's and Tecumseh's scouts had been relatively easy. Shadow had seen to that. But the wolf was unusually wary and skittish now, constantly scenting the still air and making brief forays into the underbrush.

Only one thing could make him so uneasy: the presence of many men, especially of savages. Though Shadow had been a mere abandoned pup with an injured paw at the time, he well remembered what a band of savages had done to Moon

Daughter, the gentle Shawnee maiden who had rescued him from a flock of buzzards. Now, Shadow trusted no one but Whip—and only because Moon Daughter had loved and trusted him.

Whip watched as his pet slunk down the riverbank and nosed the water beside Faith Cormorand. The girl gasped and stepped sideways, wetting the hem of her dress in the eddying current. She stood looking down at the wolf as he lapped water in a hurried, furtive manner, and Whip suspected that she was struggling to overcome her fear. Tentatively, she held out one hand as if she meant to stroke Shadow's head.

Growling softly, Shadow cringed away from her. Whip said nothing. It pleased him to be the only human being to enjoy the wolf's friendliness and affection. He doubted that Shadow would harm the girl, but neither would the wary animal make friends with her. Little Jeffrey Foster, the son of a settler at the fort, had tried again and again to win Shadow's approval—thus far, to no avail. Shadow growled whenever the boy became too bold, but otherwise ignored him.

In brief moments of retrospection, Whip had to concede that his pet was much like himself; he neither wanted nor needed human closeness.

The hairs on the back of his neck prickled warningly, and Whip looked up from Shadow to discover Faith's smoky eyes upon him.

"I thought you said Shadow was docile and friendly." Her soft cultured voice held a note of accusation.

Whip frowned at the familiar use of his pet's

name. "I said he was basically docile; I did not say he was friendly."

"Then you mean that he is docile only when he is left alone."

Was she being sarcastic? No—sarcasm would not come naturally to her. And at the moment, there was more of a question than a challenge in her eyes.

"That's right," he agreed. "Shadow appreciates his privacy and independence."

The girl glanced away from him. "So do I," she said proudly.

Both her tone and her comment surprised him. He would have thought her to be like most other white women he knew—always clinging, always meddling, especially in the affairs of men. His own mother had been like that, until she died of cholera when he was only eleven.

Gruffly, he changed the subject. "Where is your uncle? I told him to stay close by."

"He is close by. But sometimes one must attend to needs of a personal nature."

A warm color crept up the girl's cheeks, and Whip bit back a grin. Faith Cormorand blushed more easily than any child or woman he had ever met. Perhaps that was why he enjoyed goading her—being even ruder than was normally his nature. Her physical responses intrigued him.

"Your uncle's modesty could get him killed—if his ignorance doesn't do it first."

"My uncle is not ignorant!" came the quick defense.

Whip held up his hand to quiet her. Nervously,

she glanced toward the surrounding screen of black-limbed trees, then moved nearer to him. "He is not nearly so stupid as you seem to think," she continued indignantly. "He may not be a woodsman, as you are, but—"

"But he can read and write and recite every verse in the Bible," he finished for her.

"Yes!" she hissed. "Can you?"

Whip had a renewed urge to shake some sense into her. "If I could, would it help to protect me from the savages? Would it put food in my belly or skins on my back?"

She drew up her slim form in a haughty manner that struck him as ridiculous—since she barely came to his shoulder. "You forget, Mr. Martin, that until this morning, we managed very well without you."

He had forgotten. Indeed, he could not begin to imagine how they had done so. A man who could not even properly load and fire a musket was certain to live a very short, hungry life in the wilderness.

"What did the Lord do?" he drawled cuttingly. "Send manna from heaven to sustain you? I had been wondering what kept you alive this long."

The violet eyes sparkled with anger. "I see that you are no stranger to the Bible yourself, Mr. Martin. Perhaps if you tried living according to the Lord's word, instead of mocking it—"

"I am not mocking it—or you. I am asking questions. How did you manage to come so far without suffering harm? How long have you been here? Who has looked after you? Has no one told you what danger you have been in?"

The girl's lower lip trembled, but she quickly bit down on it and glared at him. "You ask questions that are none of your business, while my uncle and I ask nothing from anyone except to be left alone to do the work for which we came here."

Whip had to admire her spirit, if not her lack of logic. How could she allow her loyalty to a misguided old man to so becloud her reason? He sighed. She sorely tried his patience. Not only that, but the memory of her quivering lower lip—and her efforts to conceal it—made him feel absurdly ashamed, as if he had been trying to hurt her instead of help her.

"Go find your uncle," he snarled, "before the savages get to him."

It had grown so dark that Faith could scarcely see a hand's length in front of her. And the shreds of mist that had lingered all day had thickened into fog as dense as wood smoke.

She leaned against a damp tree trunk and groped for Uncle Abel's hand. His cool, clammy palm and shaking fingers reminded her that fog was said to bring on attacks of ague. Certainly it brought on chills and disorientation. She could not keep her teeth from chattering.

"Do you see anything, child?"

"Hush," Faith reminded him. "Mr. Martin said not to make a sound—just to wait until he comes back for us."

Uncle Abel removed his hand, and Faith guessed that he was fidgeting with the musket again.

Before Whip Martin left to scout the fort, he had shown them both how to prime, load, and cock the heavy old flintlock. Then he had given Uncle Abel strict orders: if they were attacked, he was to fire on their attackers, and Whip would somehow get back to them.

Uncle Abel had argued briefly that those who fought by the sword would perish by the sword, but finally, he had agreed. Whip had then turned to Faith and demanded, "If he loses his nerve and is incapable of firing, will you at least try?"

She had promised that she would. She had watched and listened carefully. And now that she knew how to measure and pour the powder, slip a patched ball into place, and ram it home with the ramrod, she felt certain that firing the thing would be the easiest part of the process.

"I hope no one comes along, dear Faith," Uncle Abel rasped in her ear. "I should hate for either one of us to have to shoot one of God's creatures. Truth to tell, I don't think I could live with myself if I killed someone."

I could, Faith thought—if he was trying to kill me.

She patted her uncle's arm and whispered, "You wouldn't be able to hit anyone, Uncle, even if you tried. You've had no practice. But don't worry. Mr. Martin will come for us soon, and when we get to the fort, we will probably find a nice hot meal awaiting us."

"I hope so, child," Uncle Abel said wearily. "I know we would have found one at Frenchtown tonight."

Faith wished she could be as certain as her uncle.

Despite the darkness, the dampness, and the chill— or perhaps because of them—she was almost glad they were within firing distance of Fort Meigs. A fort meant hot food, shelter, and human companionship, all of which she desperately desired. In all probability, had they gone to Frenchtown instead, such things might still be another day or two away.

Yes, she would have been quite content to be where she was—if it were not for Whip Martin.

Standing there in the dark, listening to every sound and trying not to be frightened, she thought about the man who had forced them to accompany him through the forest. What a strange name he had—Whip. Yet it suited him. He gave the impression of coiled violence, of waiting to lash out and wound others.

She did not like anything about him, least of all his ability to slice through her defenses and leave her feeling overwhelmed and ineffectual. She was accustomed to being in charge, being in control. For all his stubbornness and actual bullheadedness at times, Uncle Abel deferred to her in almost everything. She had made the household decisions, disciplined her younger sisters, and, when necessary, persuaded her uncle's parishioners to supply necessary funds to support them all.

Not even Hannah Turner saw a need to question her decisions. Instead, the old housekeeper was her staunchest ally.

And I have always managed our affairs with an even temper, being kind to all and impolite to none, Faith thought with great satisfaction.

66

But she had never before run into a challenge like Whip Martin. In the space of a single day, he had managed to make her lose her temper repeatedly—and to say things no proper lady with a strict upbringing would ever say. Worse yet, he had made her *feel* things . . . things she wasn't certain that she wanted to feel.

Just thinking about him caused a wild fluttering in her lower abdomen and a creeping sensation of warmth.

She was exasperated and angry with herself. Why had she allowed Whip Martin to bully them, to take complete control of their lives? And why was she helplessly permitting the mere thought of him to have such a ridiculous effect on her?

The smallest of sounds, no heavier than a footfall, jerked her attention back to the present. She peered into the threatening darkness and tried to identify the shapes she saw. There, on the left, was the small twisted hackberry tree garlanded with antler velvet.

Whip had pointed it out to her: "You see these shreds of rotted velvet? Some big buck cleaned his antlers here late last summer. The tree will serve as a landmark. Don't stray more than a few steps away; it's going to be damn hard to find you in the dark as it is."

"We won't," she had promised in an irritated voice. How long ago had that been?

To her right and all around her, other trees pressed close upon them. Their weird shapes reminded her of giants silently standing guard. One of the trees, shorter than the rest, moved toward her, and for a moment, Faith could not breathe.

"U-Uncle Abel!" she whispered. "Fire the musket!"

"What? What—Who?"

"Uncle Abel, the musket!"

"Oh, my dear, I . . . I can't see to aim it!"

Without hesitation, without even thinking, Faith tore the weapon from her uncle's hands, pointed it at the walking tree, and squeezed the trigger. Nothing happened. And then, as if the musket belatedly remembered its duty, a thundering roar split the night.

Faith was knocked backward. Her head and shoulders slammed into a tree trunk, and the darkness shattered into brilliant orange flowers. They hung in the air like wavering stars, then disappeared into nothingness. Faith blinked to clear her vision and still the pounding in her temples.

She was amazed to discover herself sitting on the ground, the hot barrel of the musket still in her hands.

"God's mercy, child! . . . Faith, dear, are you all right?"

Before she could answer, another voice said wearily, "Well, you've done it now. Every savage in the forest will be headed in this direction. If we value our scalps, we had better get moving."

Faith still could not see clearly, but she needed no clue other than the man's voice to guess the identity of her walking tree. "Mr. Martin . . ." Her voice cracked. She could not bear facing him and asking the all-important question: "I'm sorry . . . Are you all right?"

There came a pause before he answered. "No, Miss Cormorand, you creased my shoulder and damn near blew me to kingdom come."

He paused again, giving her a chance to wonder: Was that a note of grudging admiration underlying his mockery?

". . . But you're not a bad shot—for a woman."

It *was* admiration, she realized in astonishment. He admired her for shooting him!

Chapter Four

Faith tried to rise from the damp ground, but her legs stubbornly refused to obey her orders. They wobbled, and she fell down again. Her weakness drove home the enormity of what she had done—shot and almost killed another human being.

In the brief moment of afterglow following the musketfire, she had been able to make out the form and shape of her victim—and he had been clutching his shoulder. Blood was probably streaming down his side at this very moment, and though she could see nothing now, the mere thought of having caused such damage made her stomach heave alarmingly.

"Faith, dear, get up. Hurry."

Uncle Abel seized her arm and attempted to drag her to her feet. Then another hand reached down and hauled her upright to stand beside the lean, battered body of the man she had just shot.

Almost as if he could read her thoughts, Whip Martin hissed in her ear. "There's no time for you to

71

be sick now, Miss Cormorand. We've got to get out of here."

Sick indeed. She was *never* sick, and recalling that made her immediately feel better, or at least more like her normal self. "How badly hurt are you, Mr. Martin?"

She reached out and touched the sleeve of his shirt. His muscles tensed at her exploratory touch, and beneath her fingertips, the buckskin was wet and sticky.

"It doesn't matter how badly hurt I am; we don't have time to deal with it."

"We'll *make* time," she insisted. "You are bleeding like a stuck pig, and the savages will be able to follow us by blood scent alone if nothing else."

"Now, how would you know that, Miss Cormorand?" His scornful tone held the least bit of surprise and respect. It had only been a random guess on her part, but his reaction gave her the confidence she needed to seize the hem of her skirt and begin ripping off a thin strip of cloth.

"Here . . . Hold still. I'll bind your wound." The darkness made her fumble, but she managed to tie the cloth tightly around his upper arm.

He winced and then snapped, "If you're going to do it, at least do it right. Tighter—make it tighter . . ." He groaned, and she winced to think of the pain she was causing.

But no sooner did she have his wound bound than he pulled away from her and turned to Uncle Abel. "Old man, can you see enough to stay close on my heels?"

"I—I cannot see much at all, but I will try," Uncle

Abel answered.

A push from behind propelled Faith forward into the darkness. She stumbled over a tree root and was spared a nasty fall only by Whip Martin's good arm catching her about the waist. Her weak-kneed clumsiness annoyed her almost as much as his surefooted strength, as he murmured against her hair, "Get behind me and hook your fingers through my belt. Can't you hear them coming?"

Faith strained to hear or see anything. The night was darker than the inside of a copper kettle, and Uncle Abel's heavy breathing, along with the pounding of her own heart, blocked out every other sound. Quickly, she stepped behind Whip and did as he ordered, hooking the fingers of one hand through the length of rawhide around his waist. With her free hand, she reached back and grasped her uncle's gnarled fingers.

Uncle Abel grunted as she was jerked forward, dragging him along with her, and she could only guess at the strain the headlong flight would cause his large, unsteady body. She could scarcely keep one foot moving surely in front of the other. Low-hanging branches snagged her hair and whipped her face, and obstacles beneath her feet rose up monsterlike to trip her.

A furry body brushed past, and a scream bubbled up in her throat, until she realized that it had to be the wolf—and then she felt strangely comforted. The fearsome beast would no doubt warn them if any Indians were close in front or behind.

They ran for some distance, dodging unseen objects and twisting and turning so often that Faith wondered if they were going in circles. Then Uncle Abel's fingers slipped from her grasp. "Wait—stop!" she cried as Whip, unaware that he had lost a follower, continued his forward rush.

He stopped suddenly and bolted back to her, colliding with her yet again. The warmth and solidness of his broad chest offered a brief moment of reassurance. Then his whispered snarl cut into her like a horsewhip. "What is it? We are almost there, but they are gaining on us."

"Uncle Abel . . . He's fallen behind."

"Shadow!" Whip said urgently. And the big animal again brushed past her, this time headed in her uncle's direction.

They groped their way back along the trail and discovered the old man collapsed on the ground, his arms clasping a sturdy tree trunk. Brazenly kneeing the wolf aside, Faith dropped down beside her uncle and pried his hands away from the rough bark. "Uncle Abel? It's only a little farther. Mr. Martin says we're almost there."

Uncle Abel's breathing sounded loud and labored. "It's n-no use. Go on without me . . . I c-can't run anymore."

"Nonsense." Whip knelt down beside Faith. "Do you fancy being roasted alive or having your skin peeled off strip by strip? Get up, old man. You endanger all of us."

With her on one side and Whip on the other, Uncle Abel succeeded in struggling to his feet. But they had not gone more than a step or two when Faith heard a high-pitched undulating sound that made the hairs stand up on the back of her neck.

Whip paused in midstep. A growling and snarling came from behind them, and Faith could imagine the wolf facing the unseen danger, raising its hackles, and crouching to attack their attackers. From somewhere to their left, another undulating sound began, swelled in volume, then died out on a lingering note that seemed to mock and taunt them.

All at once, the forest began to vibrate as other voices took up the eerie cry and passed it from one to the other. Faith had never known such fear as that which pierced her heart and lungs; the simple act of breathing became suddenly difficult.

"What shall we do?" she panted. "They're so close—"

Whip's free hand clamped over her mouth, effectively silencing her.

"Be still!" he growled in her ear.

Then, to her utter amazement, Whip threw back his head and took up the cry himself—with every nuance of mockery and menace the other cries had contained. Frozen to the spot, Faith gripped Uncle Abel's arm as Whip's taunting yell echoed and reechoed in the mist. Then he was dragging Uncle Abel forward. "Hurry. Their confusion will not last long. And when they realize I am a white man who dares to use their war cry . . ."

The consequences he left unspoken frightened Faith far more than anything he could have said. Onward they ran through the tunneled darkness. Faith's chest muscles began to hurt. She felt as if she were running through a dream—a nightmare. The weight of Uncle Abel's body dragged on her like an anchor; if Whip had not been on her uncle's other side—half dragging, half carrying—she could not have kept moving forward.

At last they stopped, and Faith looked ahead to see a dull orange glow visible above the trees. Her heart lifted, and she knew without asking that the light must be coming from the fort.

Whip's voice sounded low and hoarse. "There's a cleared area—twice the distance of a stone's throw—all around the fort. You will use the entrance nearest us, and I will go around and use one on the farther side."

"But why?" Fear clamped down on her throat. She could not, she suddenly realized, bear the idea of Whip leaving them alone again.

"I will provide a diversion," he growled impatiently, "while you and your uncle sneak in safely—or would you rather we all walk out together and die under a hail of arrows and musketballs?"

"But won't *you* be killed?"

Whip didn't answer the question. Instead, he pointed through the trees. "Do you see the stockade? The entrance is along the wall a short distance to the left. Wait here until you hear my cries, and then run as fast as you can to the gate. Beat on it and shout something so that the soldiers will know to open for you—but don't shout too loudly. With any luck, the savages will be heading for the other side by then."

"No!" Faith surprised herself by her own vehemence. "They will kill you! You can't—"

Whip's hand clamped over her mouth again. "Do as I say. I know what I'm doing . . . Old man, can you walk by yourself now?"

Huffing and puffing, his chest rising and falling as

he gasped for air, Uncle Abel merely grunted. But before Whip Martin turned to leave, the old man managed a rasping farewell: "God go with you, my son."

Then the tall scout was gone, almost as if he had melted away into the darkness. The brush rustled as Shadow followed him, and Faith and Uncle Abel were alone once more.

Faith clung tightly to her uncle's arm. No longer daring to speak nor even to make a sound, she edged toward the rim of the clearing. The dull orange light she had seen glowed a trifle brighter, outlining the barricade of sharp-pointed stakes that formed the stockade around the fort. But the light from the campfires within did little to illuminate the dark shadows at the base of the palisade.

Faith was relieved. They would not be as visible as she had feared. Moreover, a pall of wood smoke hung over the fort and mingled with the swirling shreds of mist to limit visibility even further. The smoke smelled deliciously sweet and inviting, reminding her of the nearness of food and shelter and the comfort of friendly human beings.

As she stood waiting anxiously for Whip's signal, Uncle Abel squeezed her hand. "It will be all right, my dear," he whispered. "We have only to trust in the Lord."

Despite herself, Faith smiled. Perhaps the Lord *was* looking after them. Or at least He had sent Whip Martin in His stead.

She peered toward the fort but could not discern its size or shape. The palisade of stakes stood at the top of a steep slope where earth had been piled high to form an additional protective barrier. A dark depression in the forbidding wall far to her left gave the only indication of the entranceway Whip had mentioned. To her right, an angular black shape indicated a blockhouse.

No light lit the outer wall; the distance between forest and fort yawned like a stretch of desolate wasteland.

If Whip Martin did not succeed in drawing the attention of the savages, she and Uncle Abel would be easy targets. Yet, if he did succeed, how would he ever get to safety himself?

The night seemed to grow blacker while she pondered the terrible risk he had taken for their sake. There must be something she could do to help *him* get to safety, too—but what?

The eerie silence was abruptly shattered by a bloodcurdling yell from the other side of the fort. Faith started so violently that Uncle Abel grasped her arm and cautioned, "Not yet. We had best wait a moment more."

The yell ricocheted from tree to tree and ended in a scornful ringing challenge. "Come on, you bastards! Come and get me. Don't you know a white man's voice when you hear one?"

"Oh, dear," Uncle Abel said. "I didn't know he was going to incite the poor heathens."

The phrase "incite the poor heathens" prompted a wild improbable idea. Faith linked her arm in her uncle's and stepped away from the shelter of the trees. "I think we had best go *now*, Uncle Abel. Before the 'poor heathens' discover that he is not alone."

Breaking into a half-run, she pulled Uncle Abel across the cleared space leading to the entrance of the fort. Gouged by spade and pickaxe, the ground was raw and uneven. Tree roots protruded everywhere, and they had to make several detours around tree stumps.

Faith fought down rising panic. Maybe her idea was stupid; maybe it couldn't possibly work. Their own danger was too great for her to worry about saving Whip Martin . . . yet, wasn't he risking all to save them?

Her flesh prickled in anticipation of being struck by arrow, tomahawk, or musketball. She fancied she could hear running footsteps converging on them from the woods. Supporting her uncle as best she could, she ran faster—with Uncle Abel panting and grunting to maintain the pace.

From far away came the sounds of scuffling and men shouting in a language Faith did not recognize. A single shot rang out. Then the night erupted into a frenzy of loud explosions and war whoops. Assailed by full-scale terror yet still hoping her plan might work, Faith shoved Uncle Abel toward the heavy picket gate. "Go on," she gasped. "Tell them to let us in—to open up or we'll both be killed."

"Yes . . . oh, yes," he muttered. Her shove had propelled him forward, and she heard the satisfying thump of his body colliding with the gate. "Hello! Is someone there? Please let us in!" he begged. "The savages are right behind us. Open the gate!"

She heard him pounding and knew it would only be minutes, perhaps even seconds, before the huge gate swung inward. She began shouting as loud as she could. "Come on, y-you savages! We're over here now! We've fooled you, haven't we? Come and get us if you can."

"Faith, what are you doing? Come over here quickly!" Uncle Abel pounded even harder on the gate. "Open this gate! My niece has taken leave of her senses. We're going to be killed!"

Throwing back her head, Faith screamed as loud and as long as any savage. If the Indians didn't hear her, it wouldn't be for lack of trying on her part. She screamed and screamed, then fell abruptly silent as her throat closed in protest at the unaccustomed strain on her vocal cords.

Had it worked? She strained her eardrums to listen. *Yes.* The shouts and war whoops were changing direction—coming nearer. Growing louder.

"Please open the gate!" Uncle Abel pleaded.

It seemed an eternity before the huge gate swung inward, and someone—several blue-coated figures carrying torches—grabbed Uncle Abel and dragged him inside. She wasted no time in joining him. Another soldier grabbed her, and she stumbled to one knee, clawed his jacket to pull herself upright, then whirled around to see what was happening outside the fort. The big gate swung closed in her face, and she heard thudding sounds against the walls of the stockade. Pish! Pish! Pish!

"Ma'am—get out of the way!" The soldier shouted at her, dragging her back.

She did not at first realize what the thudding sounds were, until muskets thundered close by, and she saw soldiers standing on an earthen platform, returning the fire through the pickets.

"Faith, dear . . . Oh, thank God you are safe!" Someone's arms came around her; Uncle Abel's voice penetrated her consciousness. "Dear child, speak to me . . . Are you quite all right?"

Faith turned and saw her uncle's fear-filled eyes. His spectacles sat askew on his nose, and his hat had been knocked to one side. His dignity had suffered badly, but otherwise he looked intact. "Tell me, dear," he inquired with a catch in his voice. "Are you hurt? Do you need assistance?"

Flinging her arms around her uncle, she hugged him. She could not believe they both had arrived unharmed. "No, I'm fine, Uncle Abel—and you?"

".J-just out of breath, my dear." He leaned back to look into her face, the light from nearby torches and campfires illuminating his bewilderment. "When you started screaming . . . oh, dear child . . . I didn't know what to think."

He looked her up and down as if doubting that she had told him the truth.

"I'm perfectly fine, Uncle Abel . . . no wounds, no blood." She stretched out her arms to show him.

"But the screaming—why did you scream, child?"

"I—I was creating a diversion, the way Mr. Martin did for us. I was trying to give him a chance to reach safety."

"A *diversion!* But you could have been killed . . . We both could have been killed. It might not even have worked . . . Oh, dearest Faith, sweet child . . ."

"We were *not* killed," she insisted. "We are safe." She hugged and kissed Uncle Abel again. But even in the midst of her joy and relief, she felt a sharp pang of dread. Had it really worked? She and Uncle Abel were safe, but what of Whip Martin? What of the man who had saved their lives?

Whip lay perfectly still and breathed deeply of the acrid scent of gunsmoke. To his amazement, he was still alive, but his shoulder hurt abominably, and the distant sporadic sounds of musketfire told him that the fight continued. He knew he should get up. But the pallet on which he lay felt uncommonly soft and comfortable, and he sensed, without even needing to open his eyes, that he was in a safe enclosed place— the nearest blockhouse probably.

He lay still and listened, sensing, too, that he was not alone; women were in the room with him. He could smell them; they had a sweeter odor than a man's, mixed as it was with the fragrance of herbs, cooking, and wood smoke.

Their voices buzzed and blurred together, and he had difficulty distinguishing one from the other. He realized that the blow he had taken on the head—the one that ought to have killed him—had no doubt scrambled his brains a bit. Remembering how the war club, or whatever it was, had come crashing down on him out of nowhere, he became aware of a dull thudding in his temples and a tenderness at the back of his scalp where his head touched a rolled-up blanket or pillow.

His whole head began to throb, and he dismissed the thought of immediately going back to the fight. No, he would simply lie here for a moment and celebrate the fact that he was still alive, when he ought to be lying scalped and dead or dying in the clearing outside the fort.

The question plagued him: Why wasn't he dead?

He could not understand it. Perhaps General Harrison's Kentucky recruits were not such useless greenhorns after all. Realizing what he was trying to do, they must have diverted the savages away from him. When he felt better, he would get up and thank them—and also find out whether little Faith Cormorand and her uncle had made it to safety inside the fort.

The image of the girl's enormous frightened eyes—as violet-hued as spring flowers—sprang to mind. Though she had made every effort to conceal it, he had known that she was afraid. Her eyes gave her away. Even in the dark, they had glittered, or perhaps he had merely imagined them the way they had been earlier that afternoon when he had imprisoned her in his arms.

Ah, but she was a stubborn, brave little thing, in addition to being quite the softest bit of humanity he had held in months. And if he had died in an effort to save her, it would not have been any great loss, he reflected.

Life was cheap—his life especially. He did not expect to live a long time. When living was such a burden, what did it matter how many chances he took? Taking risks was a challenge—a game to ward off boredom. And he had nothing whatever to lose by playing it. Yet . . . it amazed him how much he was enjoying the sensation of having escaped once again.

A clear feminine voice cut through his self-absorption. He turned his head slightly, the better to hear what the woman was saying.

"Will he be all right, do you think?" The tiniest tremor underscored her words.

"I b'lieve so, but he's taken a bad blow t' the head. He'll need rest and hot grub for a few days."

The second voice sounded older and more mature than the first, and it had a distinctive backwoods twang. Whip recognized it as belonging to Nancy Foster, Jeffrey's mother. He thought he knew the first voice, too. He could hardly mistake those soft well-educated tones, so out of place in the wilderness. Slowly, squinting against the light from a tallow candle, he opened his eyes.

Faith Cormorand stood beside his pallet, her pale, earnest face turned toward the heavily pregnant Nancy whose jutting belly filled the entire space between the two women.

"I would be happy to see to his care," Faith murmured. One of her delicate white hands fluttered in his direction. "It's the least I can do. Mr. Martin could have been killed trying to save us from those savages."

Looking worn and tired, Nancy Foster sighed and rubbed the hollow of her back. "Whip Martin has made a habit out of almost gettin' kilt . . . Do you have any experience in nursin' full-growed stubborn men?"

"I have cared for my uncle since I was just a little girl—and he, too, can be very stubborn."

"All right, then, if you know what you are gittin' into, I guess the job is yours."

The two women smiled at each other, and

something passed between them—a look of silent understanding, as if the foolishness of men gave them an instant bond of shared experience that transcended their disparate backgrounds.

Whip felt oddly left out and discomfitted. "If you two wish to discuss my stubbornness, I wish you would do so out of my hearing," he growled. "I would like to enjoy this rest you are so determined I shall have."

At the sound of his voice, Faith looked startled and stepped back, but Nancy bent over him, holding the candle so that its arc of light shone full into his eyes. "So you been lying there spyin' on us, while I was worryin' myself to the point of an early labor wonderin' if you had gone and gotten yourself kilt this time."

"And if I had, would you have mourned me? Or would you have told Jeffie, 'See? That's what comes of being a rootless no-good spy'?" Whip managed a small grin despite the pain the movement caused him.

Nancy Foster was the only woman he knew with whom he could feel marginally at ease. Not only was she eight months gone with child, but she was also happily devoted to her husband, Tom. And she treated all men in a scolding, good-natured manner that neither threatened nor invited familiarities.

Nancy's plain round face and soft hazel eyes lighted up with the challenge of teasing. She handed the candle to Faith and tucked a wispy strand of brown hair back under the white ruffled kerchief covering her head. Then she leaned over Whip to smooth a blanket that he hadn't even noticed. "Even rootless no-good spies deserve to have someone worryin' over them. Jeffie is out in the tent frettin' himself half to death over you and that mangy ole wolf of yours."

Whip frowned. "Where is Shadow? The last I knew he was right beside me."

"Well, he wasn't there when the soldiers dragged you through the gate—and you're *not* gittin' up to go look for him."

Whip started to rise anyway, but was stopped by the pain in his head and shoulder and by the look on Nancy's face. "So help me, Whip Martin, if you don't stay on that pallet, I'll sit right down on your chest!"

Grudgingly, Whip settled back on the pillow. He knew when he was licked. Nancy was as big as a mule right now and twice as stubborn. If she sat on him, he would go nowhere, wounded and hurting as he was. Instead, he switched his growing annoyance to Faith; the girl's mouth was twitching strangely, as if she might burst out laughing.

"So, Miss Cormorand, you said you would nurse me. Well, I'm waiting . . . You could start by cleaning out that flesh wound in my shoulder. I only hope you can do as well fixing the damage as you did when you inflicted it."

The violet eyes widened. All traces of humor fled from them. "Yes, of course, Mr. Martin," she responded in her proud, stiff way. "I'll see to your shoulder immediately."

He studied her a moment, enjoying the effect of his rudeness. A blush crept up her neck and suffused her face, mottling her cheeks a delicate rose color.

He wondered if the blush had begun in her bosom and was tinging her sweetly upthrust breasts a rose color, too. Pointedly, he looked at them until her cheeks flushed a flaming scarlet.

A clucking Nancy moved across his line of vision. She gave him a scolding look, which he ignored, and reached down on either side of him to plump his pillow. "If you'll just b'have yourself, Whip, I'll leave you in Miss Cormorand's hands. Jeffie'll be waitin' t' hear how you are, and Tom should soon be comin' t' the tent now, too."

"Don't worry about me, Nancy," Whip drawled with his heaviest sarcasm. "I'm too damn tired to be of much trouble to anyone . . . Give my best to Jeffie and Tom."

He waited until Nancy had left the room, then shot the blushing dark-haired girl a long, scathing glance. "Well, Miss Cormorand. Do you mind if we get started . . . before I bleed to death?"

Wordlessly, the violet-eyed beauty reached for his shoulder. At her mere touch, pain lanced through him like a hot poker, cleansing his thoughts of all mischief. Nor did he any longer have the will to wonder about the origins of Faith Cormorand's blushes.

Chapter Five

"You're sure you really want t' do this?" Nancy heaved the heavy bundle of soiled clothing into Faith's waiting arms. "They're awfully muddy. They was filthy before, an' two days of solid rain hasn't improved 'em any."

"I'm positive," Faith insisted, maneuvering the large bundle under one arm so that she would have room under her other arm for her own smaller bundle of clothing and Uncle Abel's musket.

"It's the least I can do for you, Nancy, after all you and your family have done for us—giving us clothes, food, blankets, and household utensils to take the place of those we left behind somewhere in the woods."

"Well, don't you worry none about all that. We settlers gotta share an' share alike. We gotta stick t'gether an' help each other out, like I done tol' you the day before yesterday. Praise God Whip found you. Why, it gives me the shivers just t' think what might've happened if you an' your uncle *had* made it

89

to Frenchtown. Right this very moment, you'd be prisoners of the British, an' who knows what would've happened then? Them bloodthirsty redcoats would probably have turned you over to the savages to be tortured an' killed."

"Yes, from what everyone has said, I'm afraid they would have . . . Can you hitch my musket a little higher on my shoulder? . . . Oh, no, there goes a bundle. They aren't tied up tightly enough."

Nancy helped Faith to retie both bundles of clothing and get everything situated for her climb down the steep riverbank to wash laundry with the other women. The rain had driven off the savages, but it had also turned the ground around the settlers' tents into a muddy quagmire, so General Harrison had given permission for the women to take advantage of the bright, warm sunshine to wage war on mildew and mud.

Punching Nancy's bundle into a more compact shape, Faith tried not to think about the terrible story Nancy had told her—a story she and Uncle Abel had since heard several times from others at the fort.

Eight hundred soldiers under the command of General James Winchester had gone to Frenchtown in January and been surprised by an enemy force of two thousand. Frenchtown had fallen to the British and their savage allies, and few Americans had survived capture, imprisonment, and torture.

They had died most horribly, and the "Frenchtown Massacre," as the affair had come to be called, was still causing a wave of fierce hatred and resentment to roll through the nearby states of

Kentucky and Pennsylvania. Indeed, so great was the reaction that a flood of Kentucky volunteers was expected to arrive at the fort any day now.

Faith found it incredible that human beings could so cruelly butcher and slaughter others, and she could not understand why General Proctor, the British commandant, had allowed such atrocities to happen. How absurdly foolish she must have sounded, protesting to Whip Martin that she and Uncle Abel could take care of themselves! He must have thought she was addlepated—for indeed, he had warned her that Frenchtown was in enemy-held territory, though he had never mentioned the massacre.

Momentarily closing her eyes against the sun's glare, she wondered when she would find the right moment to properly thank the tall, surly scout; she had not seen him since the night of their arrival. On the rainy morning after, she had dashed through the pelting rain, lost her way twice, and arrived at the blockhouse soaked to the skin, only to discover that her patient had left his pallet before first light.

Now she had to thank him not only for risking his life for her and Uncle Abel but also for forcing them to accompany him to the fort in the first place. It would not be easy to apologize to that darkly handsome arrogant man, yet apologize she must. Because of Whip Martin, their lives had been spared not once but twice.

"There, now . . ." Nancy eased the last bundle into place beneath Faith's right arm. "Is that any better?" She stepped back and eyed Faith critically. "It's too much for you t' tote, lass. Maybe I should come with you after all. I could at least carry the musket."

Forcing thoughts of Whip Martin into a dim corner of her mind, Faith hugged her bundles and replied with a hearty firmness. "No, you had better stay here. If the Indians *do* come back while the women are outside the fort, how will you ever run up the hill to the stockade? Besides, you promised to keep an eye on Uncle Abel for me."

The last thing Faith wanted was for Nancy to accompany her; in addition to washing laundry, she had important business to attend to outside the fort—business of which her new friend would never have approved.

"So I did . . . Is your uncle still sleeping? How's his rheumatism t'day? This sunshine should be good for him." Nancy glanced toward Faith and Uncle Abel's tent, a small triangular affair of canvas and stout wooden poles.

Captain Eleazar D. Wood had forced five soldiers out into the rain to provide the simple accommodations near the Foster family, and at first, Faith had felt guilty about it. But her uncle's severe bout with rheumatism, brought on by the heavy rains, had quickly dissipated her feelings. She was deeply concerned about his health and hoped that he would sleep long this morning—and not worry about her leaving the stockade. He, too, would have tried to stop her from doing what she intended.

"Yes, he's still asleep, and I hope he stays that way. He needs a great deal of rest if he is to regain his strength."

"I'll look in on him after a bit," Nancy promised. "Come along, then, at least I can walk with you as far as the gate."

They began to wind their way through an obstacle course of barrels, tents, dray wagons, and people hurrying to and fro. Faith looked about with interest. Despite the many precautionary measures being taken, an air of tense expectancy hung over the huge enclosure—as if mayhem and madness might overtake it at any moment.

The faces of settlers and soldiers alike were lined with the strain of living so close to danger and under such uncomfortable circumstances. From day to day, one never knew what might happen; indeed, one could only be infinitely glad that General Harrison seemed to know what he was doing, carving out this refuge in the middle of the fierce wilderness.

The fort itself was enormous—encompassing more than eight acres of ground on the high east bank of the Miami of the Lake, or the Maumee River, as the waterway was sometimes called.

With the exception of eight blockhouses and four elevated gun batteries, the whole was entirely enclosed by thick timbers—the high picket fence Faith had seen on the night of their arrival. As yet, she did not know the location of everything, but from where she and Nancy now walked, she could just see the top of the largest magazine—a protected earth-covered mound where powder and other combustible materials were stored.

The magazine was always guarded, and Nancy's husband Tom had told her that anyone entering the place had to remove his boots and put on felt slippers so as not to strike any sparks and blow up the entire fort.

To their right, a huge breastwork called the Grand Traverse was under feverish construction, and to their left, a smaller breastwork was already half complete. When both were finished, the sea of tents surrounding them on all sides would be protected from musket and cannon fire coming from the river or the woods.

Faith recalled her surprise on learning that the blockhouses, sturdy as they were, were not used as living quarters but were employed instead as defensive positions. From each one, cannons poked through wall openings on the first floor, and fifteen to twenty soldiers stood guard around the clock on the second floor.

The only other log structures in the fort were storehouses for the precious supplies hauled up from Fort Washington at Cincinnati. Even the officers slept in tents, and crowded in among them were two hundred or more horses, oxen, and mules.

Carefully negotiating her way around a dismantled wagon and four milling mules, Faith pointedly ignored the admiring glances of two blue-coated soldiers. Her gaze fell on the triangular roof of the distant blockhouse where she had last seen Whip, and upon being reminded of him for the second time that morning, she felt a sharp twinge of annoyance.

Actually, she told herself, she ought not to feel too disappointed if she never saw Whip Martin again. The whole business of cleaning and dressing his wound had been most unpleasant. His mocking green eyes had watched her every move and embarrassed her into total silence.

The opportunity to thank him for saving her life and Uncle Abel's had slipped past, and learning that they were doubly indebted to him had not made her feel any better. If only she could arrange to meet him—accidentally, of course—and express her gratitude, she could then put behind her the sense of unfinished business between them. She could concentrate on forgetting that she had ever met him or had felt such a stirring attraction for a man who was stubborn, arrogant, and entirely too dictatorial.

"Nancy," she said, slowing down to accommodate her longer strides to those of her pregnant friend. "Have you seen Mr. Martin lately?"

"Saw him just last night, Faith, an' gave him a piece of my mind for jumpin' out of bed so fast followin' that bump on the head." Nancy shot her a knowing look, her hazel eyes dancing with sudden mischief. "You been worryin' about him?"

"No, of course not," Faith denied, fighting the fluttery feeling provoked by the mere mention of his name. "It's just that Uncle Abel and I never got a chance to thank him for—you know—all he's done for us."

"He's done plenty for a whole lot of folks, includin' me an' my family. But he don't go lookin' for no pats on the back. No sirree, that's not his way . . . Of course, if you really feel beholdin', you an' your uncle can come t' dinner t'night and thank him. Whip promised me that he would come, an' I was workin' up t' askin' you anyway 'cause there's someone I want you t' meet."

"Someone you want us to meet?" Faith suppressed her excitement at the possibility of seeing Whip again by directing her attention to the dinner invitation.

"Yep, someone who escaped that tragedy at Frenchtown. Her name is Adrienne Langlois, an' seein' as how you an' your uncle were headin' t' the place where she lived, I thought you'd have lots t' talk about."

"Oh, we'd love to meet someone from Frenchtown!" Faith cried with genuine pleasure. She knew Uncle Abel would be even more eager than she was; despite his dismay at hearing about the Frenchtown Massacre, he had not abandoned his dream of ministering to the savages. If anything, he had grown more determined, believing that the savages acted as they did because they had never been taught to act any differently.

"Well, then, it's settled . . . You an' your uncle an' Adrienne an' Whip can eat supper with us, an' afterwards, we'll all go over t' the settlers' campfire. It's been too wet for a campfire these last couple of nights, an' everyone'll be anxious to set an' visit and talk about how we're gonna git on an' help one another when all is safe again."

"That sounds like fun!" Faith exclaimed. "We'll be there for certain."

"I thought you would." Nancy grinned, and Faith detected a sly gleam in her eye—a matchmaker's gleam. "I jus' thought you would," she repeated. "And now here we are at the gate. I'll let you go on alone from here."

* * *

96

Faith finished her washing long before the other women and carefully hung blankets and clothing to dry on the low bramble bushes and brush lining the shore of the placid swollen river. She had done her work quickly, not lingering to gossip or to enjoy the freedom of being out of the stockade, and then, casually ignoring the warning of watchful soldiers, had managed to separate herself from the others and make her way slightly upstream.

She waited until the guarding soldiers were looking in the opposite direction. Then, snatching the musket, she ducked behind the trees that leaned out over the water. Hurriedly, she climbed the steep bank and set off through the forest.

The Foster family had been wonderful about sharing their meager possessions, but Faith simply could not bear the idea of having lost her own belongings in the woods on the night when Whip had brought her and Uncle Abel through the darkness to the fort. She had thought long and hard on the matter and come to the conclusion that their packs could not be far away. Inside those packs were things they needed and could ill afford to lose, and if the Indians had truly departed the area, as everyone believed, now was the time to retrieve them.

Remembering which gate they had entered that night, she had a good idea of the direction in which to retrace their path. The problem was in remembering exactly where they had dropped the packs. Most likely, they were near the small, twisted hackberry tree where Whip had left her and Uncle Abel when he went to scout the fort. If she could locate that tree, finding the packs would be easy . . .

Holding the musket at the ready in case an Indian suddenly jumped out from behind a tree, she hurried through the woods and prayed that her search would not prove fruitless. This morning the forest was dappled with sunlight and smelled wonderfully fresh and green. What had been tightly closed buds several days before were now delicate, unfurling green leaves.

Here and there, tiny purple and white flowers were poking up from the damp leaf mold, and Faith fancied that she even heard bird calls echoing and reechoing through the trees. At her approach, a chipmunk leaped across a log and scurried into the brush, and she smiled and inhaled deeply of the promise of spring.

She walked a long way without seeing anything that looked like her twisted hackberry tree. The tree had been so distinctive that it seemed impossible she could have missed it. Coming to a standstill, she looked about in puzzlement. Could it have been so far from the fort? Or had she walked right past it without seeing it?

"My dear Miss Cormorand," drawled a familiar mocking voice. "Why is it that I always find you where you have no business to be, in the middle of the woods all by yourself? Though I see that this time you have at least taken the precaution of arming yourself."

Almost dropping the musket in her surprise, Faith whirled around to confront glowing green eyes that swept her from head to toe with a single penetrating glance. Under such avid scrutiny, she wished she were wearing something other than Nancy Foster's faded too-snug dress.

"Mr. Martin—you startled me."

"Did I?" Whip Martin leaned casually against a
tree trunk . . . "The truth is that Shadow and I could
hear you coming long before we ever saw you—and
if *we* could hear you coming, so also could any
savages in the area."

"There *aren't* any savages today," Faith responded defensively. Her glance fell on the wolf,
crouching doglike but wary at Whip Martin's side—
and then she noticed the bundles that Whip held
bunched together under one muscular arm. "Why,
you found our things—the packs I came here to look
for."

With studied politeness, Whip held them out to
her. "It was really no trouble to find them. Shadow
did the searching; he took your scent from the
bandage on my arm."

Marveling that Whip had found the wolf and that
Shadow could locate anything of hers or Uncle
Abel's, Faith slung the musket over one shoulder in
order to free her hands to receive the bundles. As
Whip gave her the packs, their fingertips touched,
and a primitive, elemental awareness—something
amazingly close to lightning—sparked from his
fingertips to hers.

Not knowing whether he, too, had felt it or
whether she had only imagined it, she desperately
sought to hide her sudden confusion and embarrassment in some safe topic of conversation.
"How—how *is* your arm?"

She lowered her eyes to escape his searching gaze,
yet was unable to resist watching him through the

99

fringe of her eyelashes. He was wearing a clean buckskin jacket, the long sleeve of which hid his injury from view. To her immense relief, he did not hold himself as if his shoulder still pained him.

"Better," he grunted. "The wound was minor, nothing to be concerned about."

"But your head!" she exclaimed, recalling her worry on that rainy morning when she had rushed to the blockhouse only to find him gone. "Nancy said you were to rest, but when I went to the infirmary the next day, you had already left. I was going back to look after you!"

His left eyebrow quirked sardonically. "I am sorry to have disappointed you. But I had better things to do than to lie in a blockhouse—though I am certain that your tender ministrations would have proved most enjoyable."

His scornful amusement made Faith wonder why she had been feeling ashamed for never having properly thanked him for his help. Now that the opportunity to do so had once again arisen, all she wanted to do was to set him back on his heels—not thank him.

"I—we—that is, my uncle and I . . ." she began.

"Wish to express your gratitude that I have found and delivered your belongings into your safe-keeping?" He nodded toward the packs in her arms. "There's no need. I only came after them because I didn't want the savages to have them. And as I said, Shadow found them in no time. It was merely a pleasant morning's work."

"Then perhaps I should thank Shadow!"

"Perhaps you should," he said evenly, ignoring

the bite in her tone. "It would be a good idea for you and Shadow to learn to tolerate each other. There might be times when I would do best to leave him at the fort with you."

"Leave him with *me?*" Astounded, Faith eyed the enormous amber-eyed creature with ill-concealed distaste. "Why would you want to do that?"

"I would never *want* to do so, Miss Cormorand, but I can conceive of possible moments when it would be to his benefit and mine for him to stay at the fort instead of following me everywhere I go. The other night, he became separated from me, and I did not know if he had been killed or not. In fact, he had been struck down, though not seriously hurt, and it took me a full day of searching in the rain to find him. Now, if I had someone with whom I could leave him when I know there will be danger . . ."

"Of course," she murmured meekly, unable to think of a good reason for refusing when she was so indebted to him. "I'd be happy to look after him whenever you—whenever it becomes necessary."

"Thank you." He grinned a dazzling white-toothed smile and stepped closer, causing her heart to begin racing madly. "Tell me, Miss Cormorand, was it you who diverted the savages' attention by screaming your pretty head off two nights ago? And did you do it on purpose, or were you just giving in to panic?"

So he *had* somehow found out about that. She herself had almost forgotten it. "I—I was just trying to help you. I thought if it worked when you tried it, it ought to work when I did it."

He stood looking down at her, a strange expression softening his harshly carved features. "It worked. The Indians were distracted just long enough for the soldiers to open the gate and haul me through it."

"I'm glad. I was so afraid for you . . ."

"Were you, now?"

"Yes, I . . . I . . ." With his burning green eyes probing hers, she hardly knew what she was saying, much less doing, and when he gently took the packs and her musket and set them down beneath a tree, she did not protest, but chose to interpret the gesture as a gentlemanly offer to carry the things back to the fort for her.

He then moved to stand so close in front of her that she could feel his breath caressing her face. The scent of him filled her nostrils—a pleasant aroma of clean buckskin and crushed herbs underlaced with pine. She wondered briefly what he washed himself with and was assaulted by a sudden image of him— naked, glistening wet, magnificent—stepping from some stream or river after bathing.

As she thought of him like that, her cheeks burned fiery hot, and he grinned and tilted her chin, forcing her to look him directly in the eye. "What is it about you, Miss Cormorand, that makes me so angry and yet so . . . pleased?"

She was sure she didn't know. Indeed, she felt exactly the same way about him. Without waiting for an answer, he rubbed his thumb along the curve of her cheek, then reached behind her back and fumbled with the mass of plaited hair at the nape of her neck.

Her hair tumbled down around her shoulders,

and his fingers raked through it while she stood rooted to the spot, unable to say a single word of protest against such liberties. All her presence of mind, her tedious self-control, seemed to have vanished like a wisp of smoke into the sunlit air.

"Ah . . . this is the way you should always wear your hair, flowing freely down your back." He drew out a single strand of the blue-black mass and wound it around his fingertip, as if the look and feel of it enchanted and excited him. His other hand caressed her neck, moved to her cheek, and one finger slid down to her lips and lightly traced them.

His touch was infinitely gentle, infinitely warm, like the touch of the April sun, yet she shivered from head to foot.

"Mr. Martin . . ." Her breath came out in a low moan. She did not recognize the sound of her own voice. "Please don't . . . don't do anything more. I have to go now . . ."

He stared at her a moment, the very air between them throbbing with taut expectancy. She felt as if she were standing on the very edge of a precipice she hadn't even known was there, as if she were trembling at the brink of it and almost falling . . . falling . . .

"Not yet," he whispered. "I can't let you go just yet."

Watching her intently, he leaned closer and experimentally brushed his lips across hers. The effect was startling, like a brushfire igniting between them. He slid his arms around her waist and pulled her against his lean, hard body.

"Mr. Martin . . ." The breath was crushed from

103

her lungs; she felt giddy and light-headed and feared she might faint. "Mr. Martin, please . . ."

"Have you never been held like this, little Miss Cormorand? Have you never felt passion stirring within you like a sweet hot flame?"

"No, I . . ." She was feeling it *now*, and the lie would not come out. "Mr. Martin, I don't even know you," she protested instead.

"Do you think if you knew me better, you would want this?" He pressed his lips to the hollow where her shoulder joined her neck. "I assure you, if you knew me—the kind of man I am, the things I've done . . ."

His words dissolved into a half-dozen burning kisses that moved up her neck to her ear, tracing a sensuous, smoldering trail. He paused, took her face between his hands, and lowered his lips ever so gently to hers. Even though she had been longing for it, expecting it, the kiss took her by surprise. Never had she dreamed that a kiss could be like this . . . gentle, so gentle, yet causing the earth to shudder and the sun to burst into flame.

She closed her eyes against the radiant brightness and felt his lips begin to press harder, to make demands upon her. His tongue probed, seeking hers. His arms tightened around her quivering body, pressing her ever closer to him. She gasped and tried to draw breath, but he seemed to be taking all of her air, to be swallowing all of her into him.

For a long blissful moment, the kiss continued, summoning feelings, desires, half-forgotten dream images . . . in which she freely surrendered all that he was demanding . . .

Then his mouth broke away from hers, and his hands found her arms—reaching now to steal around him—and he thrust her away from him.

Rudely startled, she opened her eyes to discover him glaring at her. The burning green had gone wintry blue, chilling her to her innermost depths.

"We shouldn't be doing this," he growled.

"Why?" The question was out of her mouth before she even knew she had asked it.

His eyes raked her. No man had ever looked at her quite that way—as if he might rend, tear, and devour her on the spot. But also as if he hated her. "I don't think you would want to know, Miss Cormorand . . . I don't think I would want to tell you . . ."

She searched his face for some clue—even looked at his pet wolf for an answer. But Shadow was lying on the ground with his nose between his paws, his attention all for his master.

"Is it—are you married?" she blurted in an agony of wondering.

"Not anymore," he answered curtly, mysteriously.

Not anymore. Each word seemed like a blow aimed directly at her heart. If he wasn't married, then what awful secret was he hiding?

"M-Mr. Martin . . ." She swept her long unbound hair back from her burning face.

But without a breath of explanation, he turned and snatched up her packs. "I'll leave these at Nancy's for you," he said, and then he left her— disappeared into the forest with Shadow loping after him.

Chapter Six

Whip Martin had not yet arrived when Faith and Uncle Abel took their places on a puncheon chair and a sawed-off log in front of the cookfire outside Nancy's tent. Jeffrey Foster had gone to the well to get fresh water for the herb tea that Nancy wanted to brew, and Jeffrey's father, Tom, was nowhere to be seen.

The early evening light was still long and golden, which made Faith glad that Whip was not there. She feared what her face might reveal when she saw him again. By now she had convinced herself that she was a total fool for having allowed a man about whom she knew nothing to kiss and caress her. What little she did know about him should have been enough to deter her: Whip Martin exuded violence and a barely controlled savagery.

His best friend was a wolf. He obviously took orders and advice from no one and thought himself better than anyone else. His taciturn heroism notwithstanding, he was harsh, moody, difficult, and scornful of everything that mattered to her. In short, she should not have permitted him to arouse anything in her but polite disdain.

This morning had been a mistake—one that would never be repeated. She simply needed to learn to keep her emotions under better control.

With a smile that even she knew was overly bright and false, Faith inquired after the other missing dinner guest. "Where is Adrienne Langlois this evening? I do hope she is going to come."

"Yes," Uncle Abel added, "I hope I have not gone to the trouble of shaving my beard and cleaning my boots for nothing."

Roguishly, he grinned at Faith, both of them knowing that *she* had been the one to clean his boots, and had she not insisted, he probably would not have bothered to shave or to make himself presentable. Cleanliness was not one of her uncle's strong points, and wifelike, she often had to remind him to tidy himself, especially when his joints were stiff and any extra movements were painful.

Nancy chuckled, her bulging midriff shaking. She was busy stirring something in a black caldron suspended over the fire on sturdy branches. "Adrienne'll be along any minute now—don't you worry. She's anxious t' meet you both . . . Hope you don't mind the same old supper you probably been eatin' since you got here. This here stew is all I could manage."

"Oh, we don't mind!" Faith insisted before Uncle Abel could express his disappointment over the lack of fresh vegetables, meat, fish, and fruit. Unfortunately, at the moment, no one in the fort had anything but moldy flour, salt pork, and dried beef. The rain, the time of year, and the savages had seen to that. "Now, what can I do to help?"

Nancy directed her to keep watch over the bread. The dough was baking Indian-style, meaning that it had been wrapped around a stick and inserted into the ashes.

Faith had just determined that the bread was indeed done and was removing the sooty mass when she became aware of someone watching her. She looked up to discover a small, slim woman standing nearby and staring at her with a stunned, disbelieving expression, as if she knew her—or as if she were seeing a ghost.

"Adrienne!" Nancy hooked her ladle over the edge of the caldron and wiped her hands on her white apron. "You're just in time. I was gonna start dishin' up the stew now. It's done and so's the bread."

She took the woman's slender hand and drew her forward. "Adrienne, this is Faith Cormorand and her uncle, the Reverend Mr. Abel Cormorand . . . Faith, Mr. Cormorand, this is Adrienne Langlois, the woman from Frenchtown I told ya' about."

Still staring at Faith, the woman moved closer. "Faith Cormorand?" she asked softly, in lightly accented English. "You and your *oncle*—your uncle—you are related by blood?"

"Why, I . . . that is, we . . ." Faith evaded, wondering why the woman asked such an odd question.

Uncle Abel came to her rescue. Having risen to his feet a moment before, he now lumbered to Faith's side and smiled down at the petite woman. "Of course, we are blood-related, madam, and from a very fine old family, too."

Faith barely had time to comprehend her uncle's lie before Adrienne Langlois nodded politely. "Oh, I see. *Bonjour, mademoiselle et monsieur,* I am very pleased to meet you."

The woman's soft French accent died out on a doubtful note, and Faith shifted awkwardly from one foot to another as Nancy began to bustle about. "Here, now, Reverend, can you move that stump closer so's Adrienne don't have t' sit so far away? . . . Yep, that's th' way. Now ever'body can jus' sit down an' I'll serve supper."

For a moment, Adrienne continued to stand perfectly still, regarding Faith with shadowed brown eyes—eyes that revealed nothing but guarded interest and even, perhaps, hostility.

I can't have offended her, Faith thought. I have never met her before, or anyone else named Langlois.

Yet there was something vaguely familiar about the proud way the Frenchwoman held herself: slim shoulders thrown back almost defiantly, chin lifted in a manner reminiscent of royalty. Adrienne Langlois had once been beautiful. Though her face bore the scars of the dreaded smallpox and though, beneath her white ruffled kerchief, her neatly coiled brown hair was streaked with gray, she still maintained a certain beauty, an air of being someone important.

Faith could not look away from her thickly lashed brown eyes. They were large and sad, as if they had seen much suffering.

110

"Faith, you wanna pass out that bread now?" Nancy asked, and Faith moved quickly to do so while Adrienne sat down on the tree stump and arranged her skirts as delicately as a queen.

Uncle Abel was quite charmed. "Are you comfortable, dear madam? That stump is not too low or too high for you?" he inquired solicitously.

"No, *monsieur*. It is perfect."

Nancy passed to each of them a wooden trencher of hot stew and then, without ceremony, sat down to eat the simple meal herself. They ate in awkward silence, until finally, balancing her trencher expertly on her knees, Nancy sighed and said, "I'm so sorry Whip is not here—nor Tom. An' I fear t' know the reason why. They been summoned t' meet with General Harrison, and that, put t'gether with the way the soldiers've been workin' so hard t' build th' Gran' Traverse, worries me much this evenin'."

Faith paused in the act of lifting a gravy-soaked piece of bread to her mouth. Nancy had not furnished them with cutlery, and she was trying, in a less than refined manner, to eat without being overly sloppy. "What do you think it means, Nancy?"

"I think it means a siege is imm'nent—don't you think so, too, Adrienne?"

"Of course. I think you are right." Adrienne dabbed at her mouth with a small square of linen, and Faith noticed that she seemed not at all distressed by having to eat with her fingers. Indeed, she looked as though nothing in the world could distress her—except perhaps dining with Faith herself.

"Did you not notice, when the women went down

111

to the river this morning, that the guards were very nervous?" Adrienne directed her question to no one in particular, but since neither Nancy nor Uncle Abel had gone down the steep riverbank with the women, Faith assumed that the woman was speaking to her.

Ashamed to admit what she had really been thinking of and where she had gone during that time, Faith shook her head. "I thought they were just worried that the savages might still be lurking about."

Adrienne Langlois folded her handkerchief into a perfect square. "*Certainly* the savages *are* still about—they are always everywhere. But now they are waiting."

"Waiting for what, Madame Langlois?" Having finished eating, Uncle Abel turned to give the woman his full attention, and Faith noticed a streak of gravy on his chin.

She wished that she, too, had thought to bring along a handkerchief—not the lovely silk one that had belonged to her mother, of course, but one of plain linen or homespun, like Adrienne Langlois's. Thinking of her mother's handkerchief made her remember Uncle Abel's lie. Why, she wondered, had he not told the truth?

It struck her as very odd, but then it was very odd that Madame Langlois had asked if they were blood-related. People usually just assumed that they were. Indeed, Faith could not even remember the last time she had explained their true relationship to a stranger. It was something private that none of them—especially Uncle Abel—considered necessary to explain or discuss.

"The savages are waiting for the British batteries across the river to begin bombarding us with cannonballs," Adrienne said calmly, jerking Faith's attention back to the conversation.

"British batteries—where?" In her eagerness to search for their belongings, Faith had seen no fortifications across the river, and the thought that they had been there, unbeknownst to her, was not a pleasant one.

"*Excusez-moi,* but you do not seem very attentive —or observant. The British have broken ground in four places and have been most industriously occupied these past several days—so much so that I expect they will soon be ready to commence."

The rebuke was so gently spoken that Faith could not take umbrage, and anyway, Uncle Abel jumped in quickly with another question, his attention positively riveted on Adrienne Langlois. He leaned forward incredulously. "Commence? Do you mean commence firing on us?"

"That is exactly what I mean, *monsieur.* The ultimate purpose of the English is to annihilate every last one of us."

The Frenchwoman's words—so genteelly spoken —struck terror into Faith's heart. Promptly, she lost her appetite. What had been the experiences of this gently bred woman to enable her to speak so matter-of-factly of impending death and destruction? Just how much of the Frenchtown massacre had she witnessed?

"Are you judging the British and guessing at their intentions, Madame Langlois?" With a disap-

113

proving thump, Uncle Abel set down his trencher on a nearby log. "Only the Almighty has the right to judge the actions of human beings. Perhaps the intentions of the British are honorable after all, and we need only expend the time and effort to try to understand them."

A spark of anger lit Adrienne Langlois's large brown eyes. "Or perhaps you see things the way that you would prefer to have them, Reverend Cormorand, instead of the way they are."

Taken aback, Uncle Abel adjusted his spectacles and peered more closely at the Frenchwoman. "You may be right, Madame Langlois, but I had rather err on the side of expecting too much from my fellow man than be guilty of expecting too little."

The woman smiled, her pockmarked face becoming almost pretty. "I am sorry, but my past experiences have not taught me to see things as you do. Perhaps, if we were to speak more about this, either this evening or in the future . . ."

Now she will tell us about Frenchtown, Faith thought, but before the fascinating conversation could go any further, Nancy grunted and said, "I ain't so certain we have a future."

Faith was saddened to see her normally cheerful new friend looking so glum. Obviously, the idea of a siege had upset her, for it would almost certainly have a grave impact on her own immediate future and that of her soon-to-be-born child.

"I don't mind admittin' that I'm a mite skeered," Nancy admitted with a rueful grin. "Though I try not t' show it in front of Tom or Jeffie."

"I guess one can't help being afraid," Faith offered

114

consolingly. "But General Harrison is surely a fine general. He *did* defeat the savages at Tippecanoe, remember?"

Nancy nodded. "That he did—but we're awful far from any other settlements or American forts. A hundred miles or more, with the Black Swamp between us and any sort o' civilization." She gazed off toward the western sky, where the sun was now setting in a blood-red haze, then sheepishly glanced back at them. "Oh, don't mind me; if I wasn't so near my time, I would look at this all as some gran' adventure."

"That is the way to look at it—as only a grand adventure. Do not take life so seriously, eh?" Adrienne rose to her feet and reached for Nancy's trencher. "A little more of this good stew, perhaps? You need to build up your strength for *le petit, n' est-ce pas?*"

"*Le petit?*" Nancy questioned.

"The little one," Adrienne translated.

"Yes, the little one." Nancy's round face softened and grew less worried and pinched. "At least, there's a minister here now. I'm so glad that you an' Faith got here safely, Reverend Cormorand. You'll be able to christen—"

"Ma! Ma!" A child's voice piped. "I brung the water you wanted."

Faith turned to see the young boy toting the heavy wooden bucket, as he weaved his way between the closely strung tents and came toward them. Brown-haired and hazel-eyed like Nancy, he was thinner and his body leaner—like his pa, Faith thought. Freckles dusted his nose.

115

"There's a good boy, Jeffie," Nancy said. "But I was beginnin' t' think I would need to send someone after you—or have t' go lookin' for you myself."

Jeffrey Foster set the bucket down at his mother's feet. Water sloshed on his hand, and self-consciously he wiped it on his brown homespun pants. "I had to wait in line," he explained, "with some soldiers from the Pennsylvania Blues."

His shining eyes and excited tone betrayed his admiration for that distinguished regiment. "They promised t' take me t' the Gran' Battery, so's I can see how an eighteen-pounder is loaded an' fired."

"Jeffie, no," Nancy scolded. "You know what I already told you: You're *not* t' go near the batteries or cannons."

"But I'm eight years old, Ma," the child returned with a wounded air. "And Pa said I could have my own rifle when I git to be ten. B'sides, I want to see the . . . the artiller—artiller . . ."

"Artillerists?" Adrienne supplied graciously, her brown eyes twinkling in obvious liking of the eager young boy.

"That's right, the artillerists! I want t' see the artillerists blast the gawddamned old redcoats right off the face o' the earth!"

Grunting with the effort, Nancy stood up. "Jeffrey Foster! There'll be no more talk of blastin' the redcoats, damned or otherwise. And if you go anywhere near the batteries, I'll take a hickory switch to your behind. You understan' me?"

Jeffrey's disappointment showed in the downward pull of his soft young mouth. He hung his head and looked at his bare dirty feet. "Yes, Ma . . ."

"And you'll put your shoes on now and greet our guests—and then eat your supper if you hope t' go with us t' the settlers' campfire."

"Yes, Ma . . ." Jeffrey slid a sideways look at Faith, and she gave him an encouraging smile. It seemed a shame to have to dampen his bright enthusiasm—but of course, his mother was right; the batteries were no place for a child.

"I ain't too certain it's good for Jeffie to fall under the influence of all these young hotheads," Nancy lamented as the boy ducked into the tent. "Do forgive him for swearin', Reverend Cormorand."

"Oh, don't worry, my dear lady . . ." Uncle Abel dismissed the apology with a courtly wave of his gnarled hand. "I shall give him my very best sermon on the subject. What concerns me more is the thirst for blood of these young soldiers. It appears I have been neglecting my duty since arriving here; there are those who obviously need my counsel."

Adrienne Langlois raised a skeptical eyebrow. "But are not soldiers supposed to feel anger toward the enemy?"

"Anger, Madame Langlois? But surely, you have heard the entreaty, 'Love your enemies and do good to them that hate you'?"

"Yes, but with a siege about to begin, I question whether—"

The beginnings of this second polite argument were cut off in midsentence as Tom Foster strode into the clearing around the cookfire, pulled up a sawed-off tree stump, and sat down on it with little regard for social amenities.

"Nance," he demanded. "You got somethin' t' fill

the bellies of a coupla hungry fellers?"

As yet, Faith did not know Tom well, but she sensed that he was excited and trying hard not to show it. A tall, lean, rangy man whose Adam's apple bobbed when he talked, he was dressed in fringed buckskins with a powder horn dangling at his side.

Another man in buckskins came into the clearing behind Tom, and Faith's heart began to hammer as she recognized him. Tom gestured to Whip with a large callused hand. "Git yourself a stump, Whip, and light down on it. We're gonna need some hot grub."

Nancy motioned Whip to her own puncheon chair and hurried to ladle out two more trenchers of stew. Jeffrey sidled out of the tent in his heavy leather shoes. At the sight of Whip, expectancy lit his narrow freckled face, and within moments, he began to fidget impatiently.

Everyone else, including Faith, sat waiting politely for the customary greetings and then some explanation of what had happened at the meeting with General Harrison. As her eyes met Whip's, Faith felt a thrumming tightness in her chest. Almost imperceptibly, he nodded, setting off a tiny explosion of excitement and pleasure. She wanted desperately to ignore him, but his very presence, it seemed, had the power to unleash wildly erratic waves of hidden emotion.

Finally, Jeffrey could stand it no longer. "Where's Shadow?" He piped. "Didn't you bring him?" Disappointment laced the boy's tone.

Casually resting his hand on the boy's thin shoulder, Whip Martin sat down on the puncheon chair. "Well, now, I might have, but I was afraid he might not take kindly to all these people. He doesn't like to be bothered, you know."

"Oh, I wouldn't bother him, I swear it! I didn't mean t' make him growl the las' time. I only wanted him t' play with me." Jeffrey's lower lip trembled, and his eyes pleaded. "I swear I'll never tease him again."

Whip's expression grew stern. "You know he's a wild creature; you can't treat him as you would a dog."

"But *you* do," the boy pouted.

"That's because I've known him since he was a pup. He'll take it from me, but from anyone else, he's likely to forget himself and bite."

"I'll mind not to pet him or poke a stick at him," Jeffrey promised. "Please, Mr. Martin, if you call him, I know he'll come."

For a moment, Whip studied the boy with such a searching expression that if he had been looking at her, Faith knew she would have blushed. Her cheeks would have turned that horribly revealing crimson that she had no way to control, especially when Whip Martin looked at her in that penetrating way of his.

"All right, I'll call him, but only because I know I can trust the son of Tom Foster to keep his word."

"Yes, sir!" Jeffrey said.

Whip turned and snapped his fingers. A moment later, the big gray wolf loped around the corner of the tent. But at sight of the people gathered so close to his master, he stopped beside Whip and flattened his ears.

"Shadow, down," Whip commanded softly.

Growling low in his throat, the wolf dropped to a crouch. But as his master's hand came down on his head, he put his nose between his two front paws and lay looking mournfully at everyone, who in turn, stared silently back at him.

"Jiminy!" Jeffrey breathed. And Faith could see that the boy was aching to go up to Shadow and touch him. She understood now why Whip had asked her and not the Fosters to keep him. Jeffrey would have too hard a time keeping away from the animal.

"Here, Whip—some hot stew." Nancy handed him a trencher and also gave one to her husband.

Tom dug in right away, but Whip nodded to each of the others, and said, "Evenin', Adrienne, Reverend Cormorand . . ." He shot a particularly long, meaningful look at Faith. "And a good evening to you, too, Miss Cormorand. Have you all eaten already?"

It did not escape Faith's notice that he called everyone else by a first name but formally addressed her and Uncle Abel. It was as if he took pleasure in singling them out for subtle ridicule.

"Yes, we've eaten," she answered brazenly, determined to show him that she was not at all bothered by what had happened between them earlier in the day. "And we have just been wondering what was keeping you so long."

"There is trouble?" Adrienne inquired in her soft French accent.

"There is always trouble," Whip grunted noncommittally. But a long, slow glance, a kind of unspoken message, passed between the two, and Faith's curiosity, as well as her jealousy was aroused. Her feelings must have shown on her face, for Adrienne suddenly turned to her and Uncle Abel.

"Monsieur Martin saved my life. He was the one who led me and several other settlers out of Frenchtown only moments before the British attack . . . Poor foolish General Winchester would not believe there was any danger, even when Monsieur Martin warned him."

"Where are the others, then?" Faith asked. "The settlers who came with you."

Adrienne's nostrils delicately flared, indicating that the question did not please her.

"They didn't make it," Whip said curtly. He tore off a piece of bread and thrust it into his stew. "They came with us a short way, then decided to go back. Some people can be very stubborn when it comes to taking orders from a stranger. They think they know better . . . and sometimes prefer to die rather than admit they are wrong."

So he was still angry at her—even after this morning. His hostile attitude stung like a lash. Yet Faith could understand better now why he had been so enraged by their initial refusal to accompany him to the fort.

"Whip saved our lives, too!" Nancy said fondly. She sat down near Faith on the sawed-off log. "The savages were headin' for our cabin and no doubt would've killed us all and burnt down our place. Whip got there first and made us take what we could carry an' hide in the woods. Them savages looked and looked, but they didn't find us. An' o' course, after that, it was too dangerous t' do anythin' but come here t' the fort."

She plucked at her skirt and frowned. "'Twas a shame—leavin' our place so sudden. We had 'er all made up for winter—all the provisions we needed and a big load o' firewood put by, too. I wonder if our cabin's still standin' or if the savages was so mad about us escapin' that they went an' burnt 'er after all."

"You—you left your cabin filled with supplies and firewood?" The image of the tiny neat cabin sprang to Faith's mind—and with it, the knowledge that there could not be two such cabins so coincidentally stocked and vacated. "Did it have a fine featherbed and a puncheon table and a well that was newly dug?"

"It did right enough," Nancy said in surprise. "But how would you know that, Faith?"

Everyone looked at her, and for a moment, the men's mysterious meeting with General Harrison faded into unimportance. Even Tom stopped shoveling stew into his mouth and eyed her curiously.

But before she could explain, Uncle Abel harrumphed with sudden understanding: "Why, it seems we were the recipients of the Fosters' good planning and foresight. That must be the self-same cabin where Faith and I took refuge when winter closed in upon us."

"We were very fortunate to find it," Faith admitted. "I—I left a note to thank you for the use of your provisions and firewood."

From the corner of her eye, she saw Whip Martin shake his head, probably in disbelief at their stroke of dumb luck. She had a good idea what he was thinking and wanted to kick herself for letting everyone know how they had survived their own foolishness. No one with the least bit of sense would have risked getting caught by a snowstorm so far from any settlement.

As if aware of her embarrassment, Nancy patted Faith's knee kindly. "Well, I sure am glad somebody got the use of our place through the winter. At least, that means it's still standin'."

"It was when we left it," Faith affirmed in a small voice.

Taking his cue from his wife, Tom mopped up the last of his gravy and stuffed the bread into his mouth. "That well give you any trouble?" he asked in a polite muffled tone.

"Not a whit, sir!" Uncle Abel assured him, and Faith wondered how her uncle would know, since she had usually been the one to draw water.

"Glad t' hear it . . ." Tom glanced over at Nancy. "You see, girl, the place wintered well. All that backbreakin' labor was worth it, I guess."

"Oh, it was, Tom! It was . . ." Nancy's voice suddenly thickened with suppressed emotion. "An' I wish we were t' home right now."

Furtively, she dashed a hand across her eyes, then stood abruptly. "Does anyone care for more stew? . . . Whip? You ain't hardly et a bite, an' that's not like you."

"I'll have some more, Nancy, as soon as I finish this." Whip lifted his trencher and began eating.

"You best eat it up right good, Whip, ole boy," Tom Foster said. "Are you goin' t' tell 'em or am I? I think they're imaginin' worse than it is."

Whip paused between mouthfuls. "You go ahead and tell them, Tom. It isn't anything, really."

But Faith knew it must be something, because Tom put his trencher down on the ground and leaned forward. Between the locks of his straggly long brown hair, his eyes shone with excitement. "There's a ship comin' into the bay—an American ship. Not one o' them big uns like the redcoats got patrollin' all along the lakefront—but a little un. Only it's big enough t' be loaded down with supplies and some canisters o' grapeshot—stuff that sure will come in handy when the redcoats start blastin' us from across the river."

"That is wonderful news!" Adrienne exclaimed. "All I am hearing from the soldiers is how little ammunition we have. They say that when the siege begins, there will not be enough shot to fire back at them."

But Faith did not think the news was so wonderful. She looked at Whip and knew without asking how this wonderful bounty would be transported from the ship to the fort: He and Tom Foster were going to go after it.

Nancy must have had the same idea, for she rose and took a quick step toward her husband. "Is that what you're so het up about—the general asked you and Whip t' go git it?"

Tom could not quite conceal his pride. "We're the only ones who know the land an' waterways hereabouts, Nance. Besides, even if they knew the way, General Harrison's recruits don't amount to a hill o' beans. They haven't any experience. First sign o' trouble, they'd panic an' run, leavin' everythin' t' the savages an' the redcoats."

Nancy's back grew rigid; she stood still and regarded her husband with wide frightened eyes. "But you ain't a soldier, Tom! You're a backwoods farmer. Why should you take all the risk?"

Whip put down his plate. "That's exactly what I said, Nancy, but your husband was able to convince the general otherwise."

Tom looked from his wife to Whip and back to his wife again. A scowl settled over his lean features. "I can't sit back an' do nothin', Nance. Not when I know that half the men in this fort are sick with swamp fever an' the other half can't hardly find the firin' end of a musket!"

Faith bit her lip. She disliked witnessing a family squabble, but despite her feelings, she *was* interested. She hadn't known that conditions were so bad.

"But you ain't a soldier," Nancy wailed again, as if that simple statement made all of her objections clear.

Tom snorted and stood up. His big hands sought his wife's shoulders, and he looked deep into her eyes. "Hell, I know I ain't, Nance, but Whip here'll look after me. You trust him t' bring me back safe, don't you?"

Nancy turned to Whip. In the deepening twilight, Faith saw that her hazel eyes were pleading for reassurance. "Whip? Is it gonna be real dangerous?"

Whip stood also. His eyes were darkly shadowed, and Faith knew his answer even before he spoke. "You know it will be, Nancy, but there *is* something more you should know. And it's the only reason why I finally agreed to let Tom come with me."

He paused, and Faith grew conscious of the crackle of a log in the cookfire, the throaty murmur of men coming from the tents beyond, and the soft sigh of the evening breeze as it hurried a huge bank of clouds across the sky. She squinted to see better, because the clouds were bringing down a curtain of darkness on the small drama being played out in front of Nancy's tent.

"What is it?" Nancy pleaded.

"There are two young women aboard that ship," Whip said. "General Harrison does not know who they are or why they're so anxious to get here, but they stowed away at Erie, Pennsylvania, after the captain refused them passage."

Fear—like an icy hand—reached out and clutched Faith's heart. She jumped to her feet, her trencher clattering to the ground just as Adrienne exclaimed, *"Mon Dieu!* Why would two young women wish to come to a place where war is raging?"

Across the cookfire, Whip's narrowed green eyes caught and held Faith's. He could not possibly know what she was thinking, and yet it seemed, despite the gathering darkness, that he could read her face, her eyes, her very thoughts.

"I—no, it couldn't be," she whispered, even as the thought solidified and filled her with an awful certainty.

"Couldn't be what, dear Faith?" Uncle Abel rose and grasped her arm. "My dear, you look positively faint."

Her thought was almost too terrible to put into

126

words. She turned to him and groped for his hand. "It couldn't be Hope and Charity, could it, Uncle Abel?"

Her uncle's head jerked up. His spectacles almost fell off his nose. "Hope and Charity—*here? . . . Now?*"

Whip Martin's voice sounded close behind her. "And who, may I ask, are Hope and Charity?"

She whirled to tell him but was stopped by the anger flashing from his eyes. Exasperation was stamped on every feature, and he heaved an exaggeratedly long, weary sigh. "No, don't tell me . . . Knowing you, Miss Cormorand, I think I can guess."

Chapter Seven

If Whip Martin could guess the identities of Hope and Charity, well, then, let him guess.

Subduing her annoyance as best she could, Faith said quietly, "Mr. Martin, I would like to go with you to meet this ship."

Shocked silence greeted this announcement. Then everyone began talking at once.

"But Faith dear, I can't believe that Hope and Charity would stow away aboard a ship!" Uncle Abel cried.

"Hope and Charity—they are Faith's sisters, *n'est-ce pas?*"

"Your sisters! Why, Faith, you didn't tell me you had two sisters!"

Then, over all the voices, came the one that Faith most dreaded. "You would like to do *what,* Miss Cormorand?"

She met Whip's mocking green eyes with a glance as steady as his own. "I want to go with you to meet this ship. I think—I believe that the two young

129

women on it could be my sisters. If they are, I would like to tell them to return to Erie until this conflict with the British passes."

"Oh? . . . And do your sisters have better sense than you do? Would they accept your suggestion if they have gotten it into their stubborn little heads to come into enemy-held territory?" Whip snorted. "Somehow, I doubt it."

Faith could feel the heat of anger rising to stain her cheeks. "My sisters are accustomed to accepting my authority. I have been looking after them since I was five."

"But my dear, how can you be so certain that those two young women are Hope and Charity?" Uncle Abel gestured apologetically to the others. "My other two nieces were to have met us in Frenchtown this spring. But of course, when we arrived here at the fort and heard about the massacre, we realized that everyone in Erie must have heard about it, too. However, my housekeeper would never have allowed the girls to sneak aboard a ship and come all this way during such dangerous times."

"Uncle Abel." Faith could scarcely control her exasperation at her uncle's naiveté. She was even more exasperated by her own denseness. Why had she not realized before this how upset her sisters must be? "Uncle Abel, if indeed they *are* the young women on the ship, they have come only because they are worried sick about us. Hope and Charity don't know that we spent the winter at the Fosters' cabin. They probably think we made it to French-town, and they may have come to find out if we are still alive."

The play of soft orange light from the fire emphasized her uncle's sudden loss of color and the dark hollows beneath his cheekbones. Slowly, he got to his feet. "Then I, too, must meet this ship. I am the girls' uncle; it is my duty."

"Now, just a minute." Tom Foster held up his hand.

But before he could finish, Whip Martin raised both hands. "No one is going anywhere," he growled authoritatively. "Except Tom and myself and the other two men whom General Harrison assigned to the mission."

"You are not going alone, then?" Adrienne Langlois asked.

Whip shook his head. "It will take at least four of us to get everything ashore and safely hidden or buried—two to do the work and two to stand guard. We can't risk traveling with any more than that, and we aren't even going to try to bring the supplies back here all at once. When everything is hidden, we can go back and retrieve it a little at a time."

Upon hearing this, Faith blurted, "But what about my sisters? Won't they be in great danger? What will you do with them?"

"They are the reason I am taking Tom."

Whip glared at her accusingly, as if the entire affair were her fault. "He and I will go aboard ship, and while I am supervising the transfer of supplies to our boat, he will find out who these women are and what they want—and he will also tell them we cannot bring them back to the fort with us . . . Unfortunately." He bit out each word. "The *Sea*

131

Sprite's captain will also need to be told—and convinced. He sent word with his messenger that he intends to dump the women into the lake if we don't take them."

"Dump them into the lake!" Uncle Abel sputtered. "How dare he make such a threat? Are chivalry and honor dead? Why, I never heard of such a thing!"

"And I never heard of women making such damn nuisances of themselves," Whip retorted. "Frankly, I can't say I blame him. Alex Cummings is a good man—and a brave one. But he'll have hell's own time trying to bring the *Sprite* into the mouth of the Maumee without the *Queen Charlotte* catching him."

"The *Queen Charlotte* . . ." Searching her memory for the last time she had heard that ominous name, Faith tried a quavering guess. "Isn't that the big British warship from Malden?"

Whip nodded, his expression grim. "She goes three hundred ton or more and has enough firepower to blow a little sloop like the *Sea Sprite* out of the water a hundred times over. But Alex knows what he's doing. Not only have I met the man, but I've heard good things about him as well. I trust his ability, or else I would never even attempt this venture. He's coming in tomorrow night under cover of darkness, and if we're lucky, the British will never even know he was here."

As full knowledge of the danger of this mission sank into everyone's consciousness, Nancy threw her arms around her husband and clung to him. "When're you goin', Tom? An' when can we hope t' see you back agin?"

Tom Foster hugged his wife, then smoothed a wisp of hair away from her tear-filled eyes. "T'night, Nance. An' if all goes well, we'll be back—not t'morrow night but th' night after."

"Pa!" Jeffrey Foster tried to throw his arms around both his parents, but their combined girth—made even greater by Nancy's pregnancy—was too wide for him. "Can't I go with you an' Whip? I ain't no lady like Faith, an' I ain't no ole man like the reverend."

"Jeffie!" Nancy gasped.

Jeffrey stepped back defiantly. "Well, I ain't, Ma! An' I wouldn't be no trouble. I could be a help. Me an' Shadow could both be a help."

Tom Foster moved away from his wife. Silhouetted against the fire's glow, he stood looking down at his son with more than a hint of pride at his audacity. "I know you could be, Jeffie. But I need you more here t' look after your Ma. I can't leave her alone right now with her time so near. She needs a man t' tote water an' firewood, an' t' pertec' her if need be."

"Aw, Pa . . ." The battle between his desire to take part in a grand adventure and his sense of responsibility toward his mother was evident on Jeffrey's earnest young face. "Aw, Pa," he said again and, obviously hoping for support, looked pleadingly at Whip.

But support was not forthcoming. "Listen to your Pa, Jeffrey," Whip admonished. "Besides, Shadow isn't going either. I'm leaving him here to look after Miss Cormorand."

133

Now it was Faith's turn to gasp. Whip shot her a warning look, and she managed not to blurt out what she was thinking—that she didn't *need* looking after, especially by a wolf.

"Shadow's not goin' either?" Jeffrey asked doubtfully.

"Nope. He has more important things to do here. And I couldn't take him out on a boat anyway. He doesn't like water. But even if he did, he would still have to stay here and attend to his duties."

As if he knew that his responsibilities were being discussed, Shadow lifted his nose from his paws and turned pleading amber eyes on his master.

Whip leveled a finger at him scoldingly. "No complaints, Shadow. A true soldier never complains."

Jeffrey appeared to swallow whatever he was going to say next. And Whip then turned to Tom and said, "It's almost time to go, Tom. Finish saying good-bye, and then meet me at the west gate. I'll just see Miss Cormorand back to her tent and get Shadow settled there."

Tom nodded, and Faith found Whip at her elbow, ready to escort her someplace she wasn't yet ready to go.

"I'll bring you back here afterwards, if you like," Whip said low, for her ears alone. "It's only Jeffrey I'm thinking of—and Shadow."

Seething inwardly, but not wanting to show it in front of so many interested onlookers, Faith nodded to her uncle. "I'll be right back, Uncle Abel."

"But the wolf!" Uncle Abel motioned to Shadow. Sensing his master's imminent departure, the big

134

gray animal had already risen to his feet. "Will he be all right with us, do you think? He might not want to stay when he sees Mr. Martin leaving."

"No need to worry, Reverend. Shadow will do as I tell him." Abruptly, Whip seized Faith's arm and steered her into the darkness between the tents and out of earshot of the others.

She twisted away from his grip as soon as she could do so without being seen. "And does everyone do what you tell them to do, Mr. Martin?"

Standing in the deeply shadowed narrow space between two tents, she confronted him with all her pent-up ire—which was mixed with another emotion she did not yet want to acknowledge; fear for Whip's safety as well as that of everyone else involved in this venture, including, perhaps, her own two sisters.

His tall form blocked out the light from the scattered lanterns and cookfires in front of the tents. Breathlessly aware of the startling width of his shoulders and of how well his fringed buckskin shirt fit across the muscled expanse of his chest, Faith fought the urge to extend her hand and touch him. Strong and stalwart, she would have to call him, and always—infuriatingly—in control.

"If it's looking after Shadow that's bothering you, you needn't even worry about feeding him. Just let him out of the fort for a while tomorrow morning, and he'll get a meal for himself."

Whip's nearness was so disturbing that she carefully looked away from him. "He won't follow you?"

"He might, but by then I will have crossed the

135

river, and he'll lose my scent. When he finally discovers that I've gotten into a boat and gone farther downriver, more than likely he'll just come back here and wait until I return. That's what he usually does—waits somewhere near the point where I left him."

"You have everything all figured out, I see."

"Not quite . . . I don't have *you* figured out, Miss Cormorand."

The unexpected personal remark, spoken in a throaty growl, caught Faith by surprise. Uncertain where the conversation was now leading, she peered up at him in the semidarkness. Under his steady scrutiny, her heart began to pound and her knees to shake. He was so close to her now that, had she leaned forward, she could have brushed the tips of her breasts against him.

Struggling to conceal her nervousness, she ventured a timid question: "What do you mean?"

The glint of his even white teeth suggested a smile—or one of his mocking grins. "You are full of surprises, Miss Cormorand. A band of angels would have a difficult time keeping up with you and your frequent requests: to provide empty cabins when you need them most, to rescue you from savages and enemy soldiers. And did you also petition for your sisters to keep you company while the fort is under siege?"

"I will thank you to leave my sisters out of this!"

Whip's tone grew even more mocking. "No doubt you get what you want without even asking—merely because you are so virtuous."

"My virtue—or lack of it—is hardly any business

136

of yours, Mr. Martin!" Too angry to remain in his presence even a moment longer, Faith would have stalked away, but Whip caught her by the arm.

"You are wrong, my little Miss Cormorand, it is very much my business. It's a distraction and a challenge . . . those enormous innocent eyes . . . Why is it that whenever you're near me, I can hardly keep my hands off you?"

He reached for her and pulled her close to him, so close that his body's response to her nearness was stunningly evident. His clean pine scent invaded her nostrils, and the memory of the morning's kiss brought a rush of heat and giddiness. He bent his head and nuzzled her cheek, then ran the tip of his tongue around her earlobe . . . Such tiny caresses, yet they made her feel amazingly weak, as if her legs had turned to liquid and were flowing out from under her.

"Lovely, innocent Miss Cormorand . . . Someone will always want to look after you, but I suppose a mere man would never satisfy you. Your prayers and your Bible will be comfort enough when you awaken in the long lonely night."

What was he talking about? What did he mean? She was not that way at all. He spoke as if she were a dried-up piece of leather, a woman of no feeling. If he only knew what he was doing to her . . . She drifted for several moments, aware of nothing but the tender elusiveness of his lips and tongue on her earlobe, inflaming her, exquisitely torturing her . . .

Someone inside one of the tents coughed and grunted. She froze, but there was no other sound.

"Mr. Martin, please . . . someone will see or hear

137

us." Ineffectually, she tried to push him away, but her heart was not really in it. Sensing that, he took advantage. His lips moved down to the hollow of her throat, nudged her head back. She reached up to steady herself, and her hands somehow found the back of his neck and then his hair.

The dark curls had a life of their own, and even as she reveled in the thick, silken texture of them, she could feel him once again undoing her hair. His kisses burned her throat, her cheeks, her forehead, her closed eyes, and he raked his fingers through her tangled tresses. She slid her arms around his waist and gave herself over to the sensual pleasure caused by his eager exploring lips.

His hand strayed to her breast and gently cupped it.

"Mr. Martin, you've got to stop," she pleaded breathlessly, unnerved by the ferocity of her desire.

He did not remove his hand, but instead made the barest trace of a circle with his thumb. "Do you really want me to stop, Miss Cormorand?" he rumbled in her ear. "Has no one ever touched you like this before?"

No one ever had, of course, but it was not just the touch that jolted her nerve endings and thrilled her soul; it was that it was Whip Martin who was touching her. The unseen precipice she had first sensed that morning yawned before her once more, inviting her to leap, to swoon, to fall . . . to spiral downward in flaming rapture and glory.

From somewhere beyond the concealed hollow between the tents, came the low murmur of men's voices. The small interruption was enough to drag her back to cold reality.

She was doing it *again,* allowing this man she didn't even know—this man she actually disliked—to take unseemly liberties with her.

"M-Mr. Martin, you have to go. Tom Foster is waiting." The excuse sounded lame, but she could think of nothing else to say. Reluctantly, she pushed away from him. "I—I want you to go now ... please."

Something flickered in his eyes. Slowly and deliberately, as if he didn't know how they had gotten there, he removed one hand from her hair and the other from her breast.

"Then of course, I'll go. Your concern for my safety overwhelms me, Miss Cormorand, I had not realized that you cared."

The return of his mocking tone finally succeeded in breaking the spell, and she almost hated him for it. "I *don't* care, Mr. Martin," she retorted. "My concern is only for my sisters—if indeed they are on the *Sea Sprite.*"

Drat. Why did her voice have to quiver? Why couldn't she speak to him as coolly as he had just spoken to her?

"If they are on the *Sprite,* Miss Cormorand, they deserve to be keelhauled."

"No, they deserve to be sent back home again."

Keelhauled indeed. Was violence his response to everything? Her sense that Whip Martin was capable of anything grew stronger, filling her with shivering uneasiness. Never, she realized in a spurt of mingled amazement and honesty, had she been so intrigued by a man—or so drawn to one, despite

139

herself. That fact alone was reason enough for anxiety; but what about his dark secrets? What about his past, which was somehow affecting his present and future?

"Come along, then, my gentle innocent," he mocked, taking her arm. "Shadow, heel."

And the animal whom Faith had all but forgotten followed them to her tent.

Whip cursed softly to himself as the prow of his bateau scraped against the side of the sloop looming high above him in the darkness; the noise was unnaturally loud and would carry far across the placid waters of the bay.

Behind him, Tom Foster exclaimed, "God Almighty, that'll draw the attention o' the *Queen Charlotte* for sure."

Whip cast a worried glance at the horizon. The jutting edge of an island partially concealed the gently bobbing lantern lights of the British warship. He waited a moment, but there was no further sound. Evidently, the watch on the *Charlotte* saw little need for alarm. The night was calm, and in the sheltered anchorage off Turtle Island, secure in the knowledge of their superior size and weaponry, the enemy did not expect trouble.

Nor were they going to get it. If all went well, he and Tom could transfer the supplies in two or three trips from the sloop to the shore, and the *Sea Sprite* would be gone before sunrise.

Whip grabbed hold of the sloop's line, and after making certain that Tom also had hold of it, slung himself over the side of the bateau and began climbing. In a moment, he was on deck, and Alex Cummings, the big blond captain of the *Sprite*, was leading him into a lanternlit cabin, from which no light escaped through the masked portholes.

"So far, so good, eh?" Alex grinned and handed him a mug of rum. "We've time for a quick one, I should think. Good to see you again, Whip."

Whip raised the pewter cup in salute, before draining it in one long swallow. The rum burned his throat and warmed his insides; he licked his lips in appreciation, then turned his attention to the man who stood before him in the sparsely furnished narrow cabin.

Alex Cummings was dressed like a buccaneer or a pirate, all in black, which made a startling contrast against the bright golden hair on his thickly muscled arms and chest. He gave the impression of great physical strength, though he stood not quite as tall as Whip and had a more compact body. His eyes were a sparkling blue and as friendly as a frisky pup's. Whip suspected that Alex found great favor with the ladies—unlike himself, who was usually regarded as too taciturn and unfriendly.

Thinking of ladies, he wondered where the two troublesome young women might be. "I hear you have two stowaways. Would their name happen to be Cormorand?"

"How did you know?" An angry flush spread across the captain's face, surprising Whip, who knew him to be amiable. At least, Alex Cummings had been amiable when Whip first met him at Fort Detroit, long before the war with the British had cut

141

off American shipping.

"There is a young woman at Camp Meigs who suspects that her two sisters might have followed her and her uncle out here to find out what happened to them," he explained.

"*Faith* Cormorand!" Alex snapped. "So she's still alive. Hope and Charity told me about her. Well, for the sake of you and General Harrison I only hope she isn't half as bothersome as her two little sisters. I have never met a more difficult pair. My sympathies are with you."

"They needn't be." Whip fingered his mug. "I'm not taking those girls back with me."

"What?" Alex bellowed.

Whip tried hard not to wince as the captain's voice reverberated through the cabin. "I said I'm not taking the young ladies back with me."

Alex slammed down his mug on a round wooden table, and rum sloshed over the cup's side onto the polished wood. "You damn well better take them! They can't remain on board my ship. The older one is as willful and stubborn as a mule, and the younger has my crew at swordpoint over what she means when she smiles at one of them."

Whip raised one eyebrow. He did not doubt that one of Faith's sisters would be as stubborn as she was, but he wondered about the other one being flirtatious. Faith herself never flirted—at least not intentionally. It was one of the things that made her so desirable; she seemed genuinely unaware of her striking beauty.

Guiltily, he pulled his thoughts from her. "I'm sorry, Alex, but General Harrison doesn't want to be

142

responsible for any more civilians. We will soon be under siege. The redcoats are going to start bombarding us any day now—and not only that, but God knows how I would manage to get two young females past the Indians and back to the fort."

From the set of Alex's jaw, Whip wondered if the man was even listening to him. "You're just going to have to try, Whip, because I'm not going to keep them aboard. One more day with them, and I will do as I promised—dump them into the lake."

Whip suppressed the urge to grin. Here was a man after his own inclination: If a woman caused trouble, he would do something drastic. White women especially needed to be put in their place—except Nancy Foster, of course, who already seemed to know her place: pregnant and generally uncomplaining.

"I understand how you feel, Alex, but until you get back to Erie, why not simply lock them in a cabin?"

Alex Cummings frowned. "You don't know, then? I'm not going back to Erie. I'm sailing toward Malden to keep track of British naval operations. Our warships being built at Erie are almost complete. You'll see the tide turn when the *Niagara* and the *Lawrence* begin plying these waters."

A look of pride banished the scowl on Alex's face. "Damn! But they are beauties. The haughty *Queen Charlotte* won't stand a chance. I only hope I'm there when the day of reckoning finally comes."

Whip shifted uncomfortably. Alex Cummings, the seaman, had little understanding of what was happening on land. Perhaps, the war with the British *would* be won on the lake, but in the meantime, what were the Americans at Fort Meigs to do—hold out forever?

Never had Whip felt so isolated, so cut off rom civilization, as he did in that moment, listening to Alex Cummings talk about what *might* be—God knew when. He was twenty miles or more from the comparative safety of the fort, and each step back could be his last. He didn't want to think about distant naval battles; if he could just survive tonight, he would be more than satisfied.

"Look, Alex . . ." Impatience edged his tone. "The women will surely be safer on the *Sea Sprite* than in a besieged fort. Don't you think—"

"No, I don't think." Alex cut him off, his eyes no longer sparkling, but darkened to a stormy blue. "They took their chances; now they can live with them—or die with them, as the case may be. I won't endanger my ship or my crew any further by having a couple of fluttering females aboard when we are playing hide and seek with the British . . . Besides," he added, unsympathetically, "as you will soon discover for yourself, they haven't the slightest idea of how to conduct themselves during times of danger. And I haven't time to train them or play nursemaid any longer. That, my friend, I leave to you."

Whip set his own cup down on the table. Giving himself time to compose his expression into congenial lines that belied the state of his emotions, he examined his long gun as if he had forgotten he had brought it and wanted to make certain it was primed

144

and loaded.

"All right, then. They go with me," he conceded graciously. But his mind began spinning like a child's wooden top as he considered various ways of "accidentally" leaving the ladies behind. He would insist on transporting the ammunition and supplies to the mainland first. Then, on the last trip, after the bulk of the weaponry was safely ashore, he would simply "forget" to return to the ship. What could Alex Cummings do then, with the *Queen Charlotte* right on the opposite side of the island?

He resisted the impulse to smile. Alex would be as mad as a hornet, but no matter. It was better to have to face the wrath of the big blond sea captain one day than to be saddled with two females who promised to be every bit as difficult as Faith herself.

For an instant, as he thought of Faith, Whip could almost feel the violet-eyed girl's voluptuous curves pressed against his body. He remembered the tantalizing fullness of her breast cupped in his palm, and the blood boiled in his loins, warming him far more than the rum.

Grudgingly, he dragged back his errant attention and concentrated on the matter at hand. "Let's get on with it, shall we, Captain? I haven't got all night, and I suspect that you haven't either."

Chapter Eight

Faith awoke to the sound of twittering birds. Shortly thereafter, the drum and fife sounded reveille. She lay still for a moment, trying to remember what it had been like to live without drumrolls directing her day. Did the soldiers and the militia never tire of all that toodling and tooting? She knew now that the army of the United States obeyed the drums even when it was under fire from the enemy. When muskets thundered and cannons boomed, drum signals were the only reliable means of communication among officers and their men.

And muskets had been thundering continuously for the past two days.

The early morning air was not chill, but Faith pulled her faded red woolen blanket more closely around her shoulders. Yesterday had frazzled her nerves. For most of the morning and all afternoon, the savages had kept up a steady tattoo of musketfire. They were not content merely to fire at the walls of the stockade, but instead climbed the trees, which had not yet been completely cleared on the west side of the fort, and then fired down into it.

She could not believe how wiry and monkeylike they were. She had never seen a monkey, except in books, but she imagined that the brown, wrinkled-faced creatures must closely resemble the grinning savages who swung themselves easily into and out of treetops.

Would today bring more of the same? The Grand Traverse was growing larger and higher each day as the soldiers worked day and night with spade, mattock, and pickaxe to finish it, and everyone was saying that its completion would come none too soon. Across the river and slightly to the right, the British batteries were almost finished, too. Weapons and ammunition continued to pour into them from British supply routes by way of Lake Erie, while all of the American supplies had to come through the wilderness from Cincinnati, by river and land transportation.

It would not be many more days, she realized, until the isolated fort came under full siege, and then the design of Camp Meigs, with its massive breastwork, sturdy blockhouses, and river-facing abatis—a barrier of brush and outward-pointing sharpened stakes—would be severely tested.

Faith shivered and wished she could remain huddled in her tent, curled up on her pallet, until it was all over. She closed her eyes and tried to imagine that she was safe in her bed at home in Philadelphia, but something nagged at her. On top of everything else that was happening, some special event was due to occur. Suddenly remembering what it was, she sat bolt upright: Whip Martin was due back today.

He and Tom Foster should have made it back to the fort sometime during the night—and if they had, she would soon know if the girls on that sloop, the *Sea Sprite,* were Hope and Charity. She would find out if they were safely embarked on a return voyage to Erie.

Best of all, she hated to admit, she would see Whip again, and the mere thought of that set off a wild fluttering of butterfly wings in her stomach.

Scrambling off her pallet, Faith dipped into a bucket of well water she had fetched on the previous evening. She washed carefully and quietly, so as not to awaken Uncle Abel. Next, she combed out her hair and arranged it in thick plaits at the nape of her neck. Finally, she changed from her white linen nightdress into a dress the color of cornflowers.

Of the four dresses she owned and had brought to the wilderness, this one was her second best, and she wore it only on festive occasions. Briefly, she considered donning her Sunday lace collar, then discarded the idea and instead tied a sturdy white apron around her waist.

Whip Martin did not deserve her Sunday lace. He did not even deserve her cornflower-blue dress. Lace and bright colors were hardly the appropriate garb for a siege, and she wondered why she wanted to impress such an arrogant infuriating male animal anyway. In a last moment of doubt over her choice of apparel, she seized a white ruffled cap, such as other women about the fort often wore, and jammed it down over her glossy hair.

She herself despised the silly little head coverings,

149

but maybe this one would give Whip Martin the message: His opinion that her hair should flow freely mattered not one whit to her. Nor did anything else he thought of her.

Still, as she surveyed herself in the tiny round mirror she had carried all the way from Philadelphia to Erie and then to Ohio, she knew that she looked exceptionally pretty. The dress brought out the color of her eyes and emphasized the round fullness of her breasts. The rosy, expectant glow of her cheeks embarrassed her, but she told herself that she was blushing only because she was anxious for news of her sisters.

Uncle Abel stirred on his pallet, then resumed his loud snores. Silently, she undid the flap of their little tent and went out.

Jeffrey Foster sat outside, so close to the entrance that she almost tripped over him.

"Jeffie! What are you doing here?"

The boy jumped to his feet, his freckled face contorted into a worried frown. "You didn't forgit, did you?"

Having indeed forgotten, she heaved a sigh. Yesterday, she had promised to take him over to the Grand Battery to watch the artillery drill this morning. Nancy still would not allow him to go with strangers, nor would she dare to venture so close to the cannons herself. Their thundering booms always startled the baby in her womb, she said.

Fearing that Jeffrey might sneak there by himself, Nancy had given grudging permission for Faith to accompany the boy—and to keep him at safe distance.

"No, I didn't forget," Faith fibbed. "Did your father come home last night?"

Jeffrey shook his head. "No, ma'am. An' Ma sat up half the night waitin' for him."

Faith felt a stab of guilt. How could she have slept so soundly, knowing the danger the men had been facing? Perhaps she had come to depend too much upon Whip Martin's ability to get himself and others out of tight corners.

Hiding her own disappointment, she offered her hand to the boy. "Well, come on, then. I'm sure he'll come tonight, Jeffie, after it gets dark. He probably just couldn't make it back as soon as he and Mr. Martin expected."

"Aw, I ain't worried about Pa. Whip'll take care o' him. Whip can do anything." Jeffrey's thin young face radiated confidence. "Did Shadow come back t' the fort yet?"

Faith sighed again. The problem of Shadow was another thing she had forgotten. On the morning after Whip's departure, she had let the unhappy animal out of one of the rear gates, and he had not returned, though she had checked the gate repeatedly during the day and before retiring to her tent at night.

Now she did not expect him to return until Whip did. The wolf had neither drunk the water nor eaten the meat she had tried to give him. Instead, haughty and silent, he had lain for the entire night on the exact spot where Whip had ordered him to stay. He had growled once when Uncle Abel ventured to speak to him and again when Faith accidentally nudged his paw, and the next morning, she had decided to let him out to hunt, as Whip had suggested.

Shadow had perked his ears when she walked toward the gate and called to him, and then, seeing his chance to escape, had slipped out of the fort and raced into the woods.

"Well, I suppose we could check the gate once more," she said to Jeffrey. "Though I doubt that we'll find him waiting there."

They threaded their way through a complicated maze. Tents, remnants of the previous night's cookfires, stacks of kindling and firewood, and tepees of rifles, which had been stood on their butt ends and leaned against each other to form triangular arrangements, littered their path.

Even at this early hour, with dawn but a short time behind them, the entire camp was astir. Men were busy cleaning weapons, polishing boots, brushing down their uniforms, and setting their tents to rights. The watch had recently changed, and other men were crawling into the tents to take the place of those who had just crawled out.

Faith knew that four hundred soldiers were usually on duty at any one moment. And those who were not on duty wasted little time socializing with the civilians who were crowded into the fort alongside them. Winter, followed by the cold, wet spring, had taken a harsh toll. As Tom Foster had pointed out, half the men were sick with recurring fever or other ailments, and they cherished the meager rest time allotted to them.

Nevertheless, as she passed the tents and lean-tos,

152

several young men caught her eye and nodded to her.

"Hey, pretty lady, where are you off to so early in the morning?" One brash young soldier called out. Having been earnestly engaged in conversation with a blowsy-looking young woman carrying a bundle under her arm, he stepped back and gave Faith an admiring glance that swept her from head to toe.

"Oh, she ain't in'erested in *you!*" The girl with the bundle placed her free hand possessively on the young soldier's arm. "She's one o' them nose-in-the-air settler women who think they're better'n us."

Faith ignored them both. Her usual discomfort at addressing strange men asserted itself, and the girl's comment did not deserve a friendly response. Frankly, she did not know what to make of the women camp followers, who, like this girl, served as laundresses—and God knew what else—to the men of the United States Army.

Camp followers were supposedly married to noncommissioned officers, and their behavior was strictly governed by orders from General Harrison. In the interests of preserving her virtue, if a woman's husband died, she was quickly wed to another. But to Faith, the women seemed a crude, unkempt, loudmouthed lot whose morals were highly questionable. She much preferred the company of the settlers, with whom at least she had something in common: exile in a dangerous place not of her own choosing.

She and Jeffrey arrived at the gate, and without a word to the soldiers standing guard there, Faith

153

marched straight to it and peered between the pickets. Unlike the wall, the gate had a space of several inches between each pair of timbers so that the soldiers could look out or poke rifle barrels through it.

"Ma'am," one of the soldiers said, "I wouldn't do that if I was you. Some savage is likely t' see your pretty blue dress an' use it for target practice."

Faith turned to see who had spoken. A young man in a black and white-trimmed jacket and white linen gaiters gazed steadily back at her. She knew by his tall black felt shako, with its white cockade feather, that he was a member of the infantry, but he looked so young and apple-cheeked that she wondered if he could be that much older than Jeffrey. He also had the same backwoods twang as the Foster family.

"I'm just trying to see something," she explained.

The young man grinned. "Ain't nothin' out there t' see but them redskinned devils an' a powerful lot of trees."

He stopped grinning and grew serious, as if suddenly mindful of his duties. "Iffen you're thinkin' of goin' down t' the river or out t' the sinks t' dump refuse, you best change your mind. The way them Injuns been firin' at us lately, th' general won't give his permission t' open the gates today."

"I wasn't thinking of that at all," Faith hastened to assure him. "You haven't seen anything like—like a dog, at the gate, have you?"

"A dog, ma'am?" The soldier rolled his eyes at his comrade, who was avidly listening in on the exchange. "You mean a reg'lar ole coonhound or

154

some other kind of huntin' dog—that what you mean?"

"No, I mean a creature like a wolf, a big gray animal with amber-colored eyes."

"Why, no, ma'am, I ain't seen any such critter. You lose a wolf, now, did you?"

"What kind o' wolf was it?" the second soldier asked. "A big nasty one with sharp teeth that eats up pretty ladies in blue dresses?"

Faith didn't know whether to laugh or be angry. The two young soldiers had friendly, mischievous faces and were obviously enjoying baiting her. They were just boys, she realized, and not nearly as intimidating as their uniforms and bayoneted rifles would suggest. She was about to hazard a smile and explain that indeed she *was* actually looking for a real wolf, when Jeffrey's excited cry demanded her attention.

"I see somethin' out there, Miss Faith!" He was pressing his face to the gate and peering between the pickets. The back of his head and his shoulders twitched excitedly. "Somethin' jus' moved—I saw it!"

The two soldiers sprang to the gate, and the apple-cheeked boy grabbed Jeffrey by the shoulder. "Come away from there, boy, b'fore you git—"

A sharp report and a puff of smoke issued from the trees across the clearing. Jeffrey spun around and slammed into Faith, and she had a terrifying glimpse of someone—more than one person— running along the rim of the woods toward the entrance. Then the two young soldiers blocked her

155

view, and one of them banged her with his elbow as he swung his rifle around and jammed its muzzle through the pickets.

"Cover 'em!" the apple-cheeked soldier shouted. "Sound the alarm."

The quiet morning seemed to explode with the sound of their rifle fire as they shot over the heads of whoever was running toward the fort. Soldiers began converging on Faith from every direction. From somewhere behind her, a drum began to beat out the signal for attack. Beruuuuuum! Beruuuuum! Berum-pi-ty bruuuuum.

The sound sliced through her. Holding Jeffrey firmly with two hands, she sought to drag him out of the way, behind the breastwork that offered shelter to anyone near the gate. Only then did she realize that he was clinging to her, dragging on her, seemingly unable to coordinate his feet.

"Jeffie, stand up—move!" she cried.

"I—I can't, Miss Faith."

Looking down, she saw that his thin little face was so white that every freckle stood out clearly. His hazel eyes looked dazed, frightened. And then she saw something else: an ugly spreading red stain on the front of his shirt.

With a puzzled expression, he glanced down at it, then up at her, as if he could not understand what had happened.

She removed one hand from his shoulder. Her palm was glistening wet with his blood. He sagged against her.

"Dear God, Jeffie," she gasped, hugging him,

supporting him as he fell. "You've been shot."

An hour later, Faith sat on a puncheon chair outside Nancy Foster's tent. She tried to pray but could not even think of the words to the Our Father. Uncle Abel sat across from her in the hot sunshine, and his lips moved soundlessly as he fingered his worn leather psalmbook. His tricorne was pulled down low over his eyes to shield them from the sun, and Faith could not see his expression. But she guessed that he must be feeling the same way she did—wretchedly miserable and in a state of shock.

Jeffie. Jeffrey Foster. How could that lively little boy be lying so pale and still inside his mother's tent?

Leaning forward slightly, she tried to hear what was happening inside the tiny canvas shelter. But the sounds of sporadic musketfire as the soldiers exchanged volleys with the savages in the trees made eavesdropping impossible—and the tent itself was too small for her to squeeze in beside Nancy, Jeffrey, Adrienne Langlois, and the chief medical officer of the fort.

Surgeon Smythe, a very young man with a curling mustache, had advised her and Uncle Abel to wait outside and pray—and that was what she in turn was advising the other settlers. On hearing the awful news, everyone had gathered nearby; and a little way off, under a sturdy young oak tree that had somehow escaped being cut down for firewood, a knot of women camp followers had come together to offer silent sympathy.

157

Many off-duty soldiers and militiamen were also standing or lounging about, and Faith reflected on how sad it was that a tragedy had been necessary to bring together the disparate groups in the fort. Why couldn't simple friendliness have done it sooner?

"Oh, and he is only eight years old!" One settler woman sighed against her husband's shoulder. "We are doomed here at this fort. I tell you we are doomed."

"Hush that kind of talk," growled a militiaman in a fringed green hunting jacket and red woolen cap. Angrily, he straightened his knapsack. "The boy ain't dead yet, an' we ain't neither."

"But we might be soon," another woman wailed. "How long can we hold out after the redcoats start to bombard us? And if we stick our noses outside this fort, the savages will git us."

The pop-pop-pop of gunfire underscored her words. A musketball zinged against a branch of the nearby oak, and except for Faith and Uncle Abel, everyone moved closer to the looming protective mound of the Grand Traverse. Behind it, Faith noticed dispassionately, sweating infantrymen in heavy woolen jackets were digging trenches as if their lives depended on them—which they probably would.

"Well, if we ever git outa here alive, it'll be too late t' put in crops. We might jus' as well forget about plantin' anythin' this spring."

Faith glanced at the man who had spoken. He, like most of the men, looked more like a trapper or a trader than a farmer. As she watched, the man spat out a stream of tobacco juice, then wiped his mouth with the back of his hand. "Yes, sir," the man grunted. "Tomorrow's the first o' May, an' it'll be too late t' plant this year if we don't git outa here soon. I still gotta clear some stumps from my corn field."

"Huh," snorted a man in a coonskin cap. "I gotta rebuild me a cabin. The Injuns took and burnt everythin' but my oxen—an' the army took them."

A plump older woman with a dirty apron and straggly black hair put her hands on her hips and glared at everyone. "The army owes *me* forty-eight dollars for twenty bushels of corn, ten bushels of potatoes, my breakfast table, and two big copper kettles they took from me."

She had a French accent, much coarser than Adrienne Langlois's, and Faith remembered hearing her name at the settlers' campfire: Archange Jacques. She had come from a place farther downriver, called Presque Isle. A widow, she and several of her grown children had managed to escape the enemy and come to the fort the previous February. They had remained there ever since, complaining of the army's injustice.

Someone else recounted his troubles, and still another told his sad tale, and Faith wondered at the insensitivity of her fellow refugees. A child lay wounded and possibly dying inside the tent, and yet the bystanders could think of nothing but their own trials and tribulations. As terribly as these people had suffered, she wished they would just be still.

Her eyes sought the clear blue sky overhead, and for a moment, that brilliant arc seemed a mockery and an obscenity. The sky should not be so blue

159

when a child lay dying, nor should the oak tree be sprouting tender green leaves, nor should a Johnny-jump-up be raising its purple head beside the tent.

Would Jeffrey Foster live to see summer steal softly over the land, even as spring was now doing? A gentle breeze rustled Faith's skirt; she could smell the sweet scent of growing things mixed with the bitter burnt odor of gunsmoke.

Then Uncle Abel's most eloquent tones suddenly cut through the murmur of voices around her. "The Lord is my shepherd; I shall not want. He maketh me to lie down in green pastures; he leadeth me beside the still waters. He restoreth my soul . . ."

Faith closed her eyes and allowed the soothing words to flow over her. At times like these, Uncle Abel more than made up for his small eccentricities. Tears sprang to her eyes. Right now, courage was exactly what she had need of—and the words of the Twenty-Third Psalm seemed to give it to her.

Then she heard the sound of a woman weeping—a hopeless, broken sound that could only be coming from Nancy's tent. The voice itself sounded like Nancy's, as over and over, the woman moaned softly, with despair, "Jeffie . . . Jeffie . . . dear God, no—not my darlin' Jeffie . . ."

Uncle Abel stopped reciting, and even the muskets and long guns chose that moment to fall silent.

The young surgeon with the curling mustache opened the flap and stepped out of the tent. The sleeves of his gold-trimmed dark blue uniform were rolled up above his elbows, and he was wiping his hands on a bloody rag. He looked around at the tense faces, and his shoulders sagged; he shook his head in a gesture of defeat.

Several women burst into tears. Faith felt her own tears rising and beginning to flow down her cheeks, hot and salty. She fumbled in her apron pocket for a linen handkerchief, but before she could wipe away the wetness, someone touched her arm.

"Ma'am? Are you Miss Cormorand?"

It was the apple-cheeked young soldier who had been guarding the gate that morning.

"Y-yes," Faith answered. "I am Miss Cormorand."

"Ma'am, General Harrison wishes you t' come t' his headquarters." The young soldier glanced at the weeping women and somber-faced men. He swallowed hard, as if keeping his composure right now was the most difficult thing he had ever done. "I'm sorry about the boy, ma'am—but could you please come right now? The general said to tell you it was important."

Faith did not think anything could be more important than mourning a dead child. But she also saw no need to keep this pleasant young soldier—who was trying so hard to be militarily efficient—waiting any longer than was necessary.

"Yes, I'll come," she said. And it was only as she stumbled after him, angrily swiping at her tears, that she thought to wonder how General Harrison could possibly know her name. She had never met him, never spoken to him, and if he suddenly crossed her path, she would not recognize him—except for his officer's gold epaulets. Why would he want to

161

see her?

She resented the intrusion, being torn away from the others at this moment of fragile camaraderie brought on by grief and sorrow. But she soon realized that she need not have felt so alone; the sound of weeping followed her all the way to General Harrison's tent.

Chapter Nine

General William Henry Harrison's tent, the Grand Marquee, was round and spacious, about three times as large as those that housed five men to a single shelter. But the man himself was not in the least imposing. When Faith's arrival was announced, he came out of the tent to greet her, and she was startled to see him dressed in a soiled old rifle shirt and a slouch hat instead of the gold-braided uniform and epaulets she had expected.

His hair was combed forward over his forehead, his eyes were large, intelligent, and close-set, and his lips were thin and tense-looking. His nose was his most dominant feature.

He did not stand as tall as Whip, she noticed, yet there was something about him—some intensity or nervous energy—that set the man apart from others. Or perhaps, she decided, she was merely in awe of him because of his reputation. Impressed by his defeat of Tecumseh at Tippecanoe, some of the settlers had mentioned that someday the general might go far in politics, especially if he could once again hold firm against the Indians.

Suddenly nervous about displaying her emotions so publicly, Faith dabbed at her tear-stained cheeks. The general took her arm and walked a short distance away from the tent and out of earshot of the guards. He paused and smiled kindly, giving her a moment to compose herself, then spoke in a dignified low voice: "The young boy who was shot. Was Surgeon Smythe able to do anything for him?"

Faith struggled to keep from breaking down completely. "No, he died a few moments ago."

"I am so sorry to hear that, Miss Cormorand . . . a needless tragedy. I have become so used to seeing men die that I think almost nothing of it anymore— but a child . . . well, that is different. I must go over and see his mother."

Faith nodded. "She would appreciate that."

Nothing else came to mind to say, so Faith simply stood and waited for the general to tell her why he had sent for her. They had come to a stop in front of the forge where weapons and iron tools were mended. The fort smithy was dunking a red-hot piece of metal into a bucket of water, and the metal hissed and steamed. Faith was grateful for the distraction.

"Miss Cormorand," the general said, "your sisters are here."

Not certain she had heard correctly, Faith stared at him. "Here? But—but I thought they would be going back to Erie—if indeed they were on that sloop."

"They were on it." A frown creased the general's

brow. "And indeed they *were* supposed to be transported back to Erie. But something happened . . ."

An enormous lump came into Faith's throat. *Whip.* Had Whip been hurt? Or Tom Foster! No, not Tom, she thought. God wouldn't take the father and the son on the very same day—would He?

The general suddenly looked tired and impatient —even haggard, as if he were exasperated beyond the limits of his endurance. But when he spoke, his voice was calm and controlled, very much a gentleman's voice: "Your two sisters boarded Mr. Martin's bateau while he was in the cabin speaking with Alex Cummings, the ship's captain. The other gentleman, Tom Foster, had gone below, into the ship's hold, to ascertain the amount of goods that were to be transported. When Mr. Martin came out and saw the women in the bateau, he ordered them to disembark until such time as all of the goods and ammunition were safely carried to shore. Your youngest sister—the blond one—refused . . ."

At this point in his explanation, the general sighed. "Apparently, she did not wish to hazard being left behind on the ship, which is exactly what Mr. Martin intended to do. He threatened to carry her off bodily. She still refused—and began screaming when he attempted to make good on his threat."

"She began screaming?" Immediately, Faith knew that something terrible had happened. A woman's screams would not go unheard in the dead of night, especially out on the water where sound would carry so far. Someone—the enemy—must have heard her.

"The *Queen Charlotte* was anchored nearby,"

General Harrison continued. "And it became necessary for Mr. Martin to depart precipitously for the mainland. Your two sisters, of course, had to come with him since they were already in the bateau. He had to leave the supplies and ammunition behind on the *Sea Sprite*—and he also left Tom Foster behind."

"T-Tom didn't make it back?"

"No, Miss Cormorand, he did not. He is still aboard the *Sprite*. And I have no idea whether or not the sloop was able to escape the *Queen Charlotte*. The last Mr. Martin saw of either of them, the *Charlotte* was pursuing the *Sprite* out into the bay. She may have escaped. I do not know—and it will be some time, I expect, before word of what happened reaches us here."

Tears welled once more in Faith's eyes. "Poor Nancy . . . I—I don't know how I can tell her all this."

The general gave her a small, tight smile. "Fortunately for you, Miss Cormorand, I am not in the habit of assigning such distasteful duties to others. I intend to go now to her living quarters to tell her myself—and also to express my condolences on the death of her son."

He waved a slim aristocratic hand in the direction of the tent. "Your sisters and Mr. Martin are within. You can thank him for bringing them here to safety. I doubt that any other man in camp could have done it. But he and that wolf of his seem to lead a charmed life . . . Good day to you, then, Miss Cormorand. And do try to keep those obstreperous young ladies under control. Mr. Martin said that you were more likely to succeed at doing so than your uncle."

"You may be certain that I will control them. Good day to you, General—and thank you."

General Harrison bowed. It was a courtly gesture more appropriate to a parlor than to a fortified encampment, but Faith was oddly touched. She dropped a quick curtsy, then stepped back out of his way. He proceeded to walk toward Nancy's tent in the company of two soldiers who had been standing at attention nearby.

Left alone, except for the ever present soldiers passing to and fro, Faith took a deep breath. She wished that she had more time to collect herself before being reunited with her sisters. Neither was she any more anxious to come face to face with Whip.

It must have been Whip and her sisters whom Jeffrey had seen when he peered through the gate— was it only several hours ago? The span of time seemed much longer—a lifetime, at least.

Slowly, she walked toward the general's tent and drew back the flap. The first thing she noticed was Shadow, stretched out on the wooden floor. His amber gaze followed her as she stepped inside. In addition to the wood floor, other luxuries caught her eye—a small round table and two chairs; an actual bed with a mattress, sheets, and two pillows; a washstand and pewter basin; crockery and crystal stemware instead of wooden trenchers.

General Harrison's uniform hung carefully suspended between two tent poles, and his high black boots, polished to a gleaming black, stood off to one side, as if awaiting his speedy return.

Faith's sisters, Hope and Charity, were sitting on the two chairs by the table; their heads were bowed. Whip was standing behind them, his back to her and to them, as if he were too angry even to look at them. Probably he was, she thought, and no one could blame him, least of all Faith.

Charity looked up and saw her. "Faith!"

In a flurry of rose silk skirts, the pretty blond girl was on her feet and crossing the wooden floor to throw her arms around her sister. Hope stood also, and Faith noted that she, at least, was dressed in sensible brown homespun rather than silks and lace. But her bright auburn hair fell in a curling wave from beneath a straw bonnet that could only be described as frivolous. It was tied with an orange silk bow and decorated with tiny silk flowers.

Faith had a moment to wonder why the girls had chosen to wear such fripperies; both their dresses were stained and torn, and Hope had an angry red scratch along one cheek.

Then Charity engulfed her in a hug so enthusiastic it took her breath away. Hope smiled tremulously and came forward to embrace her also. But the moment of joyous reunion quickly fled. Both girls drew back, and Charity's blue eyes clouded and filled with tears.

"Please, Faith, don't be angry. This whole thing was my fault, I admit it. But we were so worried about you and Uncle Abel. There was no way to get here but to stow away aboard the *Sea Sprite*."

"I tried to talk her out of it," Hope said in her surprisingly low, melodic voice, which at the moment was aquiver with strain. "But when she threatened to come on her own, I thought it best to come with her . . . Really, Faith, we had no idea it would be so dangerous or cause so much trouble."

"And I wouldn't have screamed and alerted the British if Mr. Martin hadn't grabbed me!" Charity shot a glance of embarrassment at Whip's broad, stiff back. Having the same propensity to blush as Faith, her cheeks burned a pretty pink. "When I felt his hands on me, I—well, I just screamed."

"He—put his hands on you?" The moment it left her mouth, Faith regretted having asked such a stupid question. It sounded as if she were accusing him of wrongdoing.

Slowly, Whip turned around. Smoldering with scorn, his eyes raked her, and she saw that his mouth was rigid with anger. "I assure you that I intended to do her no harm, Miss Cormorand. I was only going to put her off the bateau, but she, apparently having inherited the same stubbornness from which you suffer, behaved like a little hoyden. I had to slap her smartly to get her quiet, and by then the entire British navy had been apprised of our exact location."

"I'm so sorry, Faith!" Tears spilled down Charity's rosy cheeks. Her golden curls bobbed up and down as she put her hands to her face and wept. "I am really, truly sorry."

The corner of Whip's upper lip curled in obvious disgust. "All the tears in the world won't undo what's done." He shot Faith a glance so filled with loathing that a shiver ran down her back.

"Well, here they are, Miss Cormorand—your sisters. I hope you are happy to see them, because it cost a great deal to get them here . . . and now, if you will excuse me, I must explain to my best friend's wife why her husband is not here to share her burden of sorrow."

"Whip . . ." She could not let him continue his bitter tirade.

He stopped her with an explosive, "No! I don't want to hear it, Faith. A soldier told me Jeffrey had been shot, and I knew when I first saw your face that he was dead. Well, people die every day. We could all be dead tomorrow. Who was he anyhow but a bothersome kid? So now he's gone—so what?"

He shoved a chair to one side. It made an ugly scraping sound. Hope and Charity stared at him, aghast at his callousness. Faith herself could find no words to respond to Whip's cynical tirade. But she knew, without knowing how, that he did not mean what he was saying.

Whip stalked to the entrance, then stopped and looked down at her. "It's probably just as well he died young, before he could discover how stupid and futile life can be . . . but you wouldn't know about that, would you?"

His glance raked over the three of them, then came back to Faith. "None of you would know, Miss Cormorand, and if you are luckier than the rest of us poor sons of bitches, none of you ever will."

Then, before Faith could say another word, he was gone, striding out of the tent with Shadow close on his heels.

Shaken to the core, she turned to her sisters. Hope's face was ashen; her lips trembled. Charity

170

was sobbing in short, choking, little gasps, like a child.

"Welcome," she whispered. "Welcome to Fort Meigs."

Jeffrey Foster was buried just before sunset.

It fell to Uncle Abel to conduct the short memorial service, but he discovered, to his chagrin, that he could scarcely keep his hands steady long enough to open his psalmbook and begin the proceedings.

Abel hated funerals, especially those of children. The death of young Jeffrey Foster had wounded him deeply. But he promised himself that no one would ever know how he felt. After all ministers were supposed to take these things in stride. They were supposed to tender comfort to others, not be in need of it themselves.

So he stood at the foot of the small yawning grave and resolved to make his big voice boom with emotion. Regardless of his own feelings, he would shore up the wavering spirit of the boy's mother and of his own three nieces.

The soldiers began heaping earth over the small oak coffin, which had taken four men all afternoon to build from the last standing tree in the fort. Abel stole a glance at Faith, Hope, and Charity. His nieces stood together beside Nancy Foster and Adrienne Langlois, and even though the girls were unnaturally subdued and red-eyed, the mere sight of them gladdened his heart.

He knew he should be angry with the two younger ones—ought even to scold them for having endangered themselves and caused so much trouble—but he was so happy to see them again that he couldn't do it. A man needed to have his chicks about him in his old age, needed to see them, to hear their laughter, and yes, even to soothe their tears. He needed to be near them. Despite the sorrows of the day and his shaking hands, he felt younger than he had in years.

Besides, he knew he could depend on Faith to properly chastise them. Faith was his rock and his fortress, the one he could always count on, whether in small things like finding his misplaced spectacles, or in large ones like disciplining her sisters and comforting Nancy Foster. He was so very proud of her—his dear, dependable Faith.

Still dressed in her cornflower-blue dress, the one he liked so well, she was bending down to take up a handful of soil. When she had done so, she linked her arm in Nancy Foster's and gave the woman a wavering sympathetic smile. Nancy nodded through her tears. With Faith and Adrienne Langlois—one on each side—Nancy walked to the small mounded grave and sprinkled soil on the earth that covered her firstborn.

Faith said something to her, and Nancy gave her a bleak look and stepped back; then Faith walked to the grave and threw down her own handful of soil.

On the other side of the grave stood a scowling Whip Martin. With disturbing intensity, the man watched Abel Cormorand's eldest niece.

Now, there is a troubled soul, Abel thought. A

172

man who has turned his face from God and even refuses human companionship.

Abel wished that he knew what to say to such a man. He knew from experience that most men might ignore the Almighty throughout most of their lives, but in moments of stress and danger, they came hurrying back to religion like frightened children. And if they feared that death was imminent, their newfound piety could be truly amazing.

Abel had been kept busy all that day. As soldiers and militiamen visited Nancy's tent to pay their respects, many lingered afterward for a word or a prayer with him. With each passing day, as everyone prepared for the siege, the prospect of death loomed nearer.

But Abel did not think Whip Martin would reconcile himself with his Maker even on his deathbed.

The man was cold and stubborn. Here, where there was scarcely a dry eye to be seen, Whip Martin stood unblinking beside the grave. His mouth and his eyes were awful to behold, so stern and unyielding were they, as if he contemplated revenge, not sorrow. What could the man be thinking—and why did his blatant hostility so obviously radiate toward Faith?

Then Abel had a flash of insight: Perhaps the scout's hostility was really not hostility at all, but something far more volatile. Yes, Abel realized, there was hunger in the man's eyes—naked, desperate hunger. Whip Martin looked like a man whose need for love and comfort was so great as to be almost inconceivable.

173

Abel's glance strayed back to Faith, and to his surprise, he discovered his eldest niece surreptitiously returning Whip's hungry glances. Unless one knew her very well, as he did, one would never notice how uncharacteristically furtive and full of longing she looked. Her eyes would sweep across Whip, steal a glance, dart away, and then return again, as if she were irresistibly drawn to him but dared not admit it even to herself.

A match between these two would be most unlikely, but the more he thought about it, the more likely it became. Whip Martin was not the man he would have chosen for Faith, but there could be no doubt of the attraction between them.

Well, Abel thought. A strong woman needed a strong man, and Faith was stronger than most women. She was even stronger than most men. He himself often found it difficult to hold his own against her. In her own quiet way, she was formidably stubborn and uncompromising—and it would take an equally formidable and uncompromising man to win and hold her respect.

Were it not for Whip Martin's apparent godlessness, the surly scout would be a good choice for Faith. She would meet her match in him.

Wishing that life would pose easier problems, Abel sighed inwardly. Of course, godlessness was not necessarily an irremediable condition—but with Whip, one could not be certain. Abel resolved to pray over the matter and to be on the lookout for some way he might yet manage to reach the man.

Someone coughed. Startled by the sound, Abel fumbled with his Bible and lost his place. Then he noticed that Adrienne Langlois was looking at him. The Frenchwoman's large brown eyes were luminous with tears, but her pockmarked face was serene. She, too, it appeared, had stood at many a graveside.

Adrienne nodded toward his book, and he realized that everyone was waiting for him to begin. He cleared his throat, opened the book at random and, trusting that the Lord would choose the right selection, began to read.

"Have mercy on me, O Lord, for I am in trouble; mine eye is consumed with grief, yea, my soul and my belly . . . For my life is spent with grief, and my years with sighing . . ."

From the corner of his eye, he saw Faith frown. Her wide violet eyes connected with his and flashed disapproval; she did not find this Psalm very comforting.

He wondered if he ought to switch to another, then decided against it. He knew, if she did not, that the choices of the Lord may not always be man's choices, nor did one always want to hear what the Lord wished to say. He persisted, pushing his voice to its God-given utmost . . .

"I am forgotten as a dead man out of mind; I am like a broken vessel . . . But my trust is in you, O Lord; I say, 'You are my God.'"

Onward, he plowed through the lengthy Psalm, and when he came to the part that began, "How great is thy goodness, which thou hast wrought for them that fear thee," he knew that the selection was indeed inspired. The Psalm now concentrated on exhorting the faithful to trust in the Lord.

The dead have no more need of exhortations, he thought. It is the living who have need of them. And he raised his voice even louder, so that his listeners, especially Whip Martin, could not fail to hear.

"For I said in my haste, I am cut off from before thine eyes; nevertheless thou heardest the voice of my supplication when I cried unto thee . . .

"So I say unto you . . ." He looked up, closed his psalmbook with a dull thud, and fixed a baleful glance on Whip. "Love the Lord, all ye his saints; for The Lord preserveth the faithful, and plentifully rewardeth the proud doer . . . Be of good courage, and he shall strengthen your heart all ye that hope in the Lord."

Faith held the rushlight, in its little iron holder, over the exhausted form on the pallet. She breathed a sigh of relief. Nancy Foster was asleep at last.

She lay on her side, her knees drawn up, with the enormous bulge of her unborn child resting against a rolled-up blanket. She had gone to sleep hugging the blanket, which had belonged to Jeffrey.

Nancy's plain round face was tear-streaked and dirty, and her brown hair was knotted and disheveled. Faith did not think that her own could look much better, but there would be time enough on the morrow to worry about appearances. Or perhaps, on the morrow, there would no longer be any need for concern with such trivialities.

Following the military salute fired over Jeffrey's grave, General Harrison, resplendent in his gold-braided jacket and buff gaiters, had warned the settlers that the siege on the fort would probably begin in the morning. Everyone was to take down the tents at first light and establish quarters in the trenches behind the Grand Traverse.

The soldiers had been laboring all day and well into the night digging bombproof sanctuaries into the side of the traverse—and there, like moles or groundhogs, everyone would live until the siege was over.

Faith was at least grateful that Nancy would have one more night in the tent—a night to rest and prepare for tomorrow's challenges. She did not know how much more her friend could take. She did not know how much more she herself could take. She felt mentally and emotionally drained; yet, she knew that if she lay down, she would never be able to sleep. Her body was as tense as a fiddle string.

Adrienne Langlois came into the tent. Faith turned to place a finger to her lips in warning, but the Frenchwoman merely smiled. "Do not worry, *chérie*. She will not waken. When the body can take no more, the mind cannot keep it awake, no matter how much it clamors . . . Here, give me the rushlight, and you go on back to your own tent. I will sit with her."

Handing Adrienne the light, Faith marveled at how calm the Frenchwoman was. Her slim shoulders were still resolutely erect, and her face betrayed no inner turmoil. Indeed, she seemed almost untouched—removed from all emotion. Faith recalled that only at that first meeting, when Adrienne's scarred face had registered shock, had she seen any indication of the woman's feelings.

177

Adrienne Langlois had magnificent self-control.

"How do you do it, Adrienne?" she blurted.

Adrienne peered questioningly over the light. "Do what, *chérie?*"

"Remain so calm—so uninvolved." Faith hoped she hadn't offended the woman by being so blunt, but Adrienne merely smiled, revealing a dimple in her cheek that Faith had not noticed before.

"Ah, *ma petite,* when you have lived as long as I have and seen the things that I have seen, you will not need to ask that question."

"What sort of things have you seen?" Faith bent to pick up an article of Jeffrey's clothing, which she did not want Nancy to find lying on the earthen floor in the morning.

She straightened, and Adrienne's glance dropped to the homespun shirt, then came back to her. "I do not think you would really wish to know, *chérie,* but if you do . . . Well, it is a tale that does no good by repetition, except to stir memories I would prefer to forget."

"I would like to hear it," Faith insisted, "if you can bear the pain of remembering . . ."

Adrienne shrugged. "I am used to a little pain . . . Someday soon, then." She held out her hand for Jeffrey's shirt. "Why don't you give that to me? I will dispose of it. And then do go and get some sleep . . . Your sisters are staying in your tent?"

Faith placed the garment in Adrienne's free hand and nodded. "Yes, and I don't know how I will fit in beside them. Uncle Abel has moved out and is sharing a lean-to with a trapper who offered to take him in—but even so, you know how little space there is in these things . . ."

She gestured around Nancy's tent, which was crammed with one other blanket-heaped sleeping pallet besides the one on which Nancy was sleeping, the puncheon chair on which Faith herself had been sitting, and various household items. The Fosters kept most of their belongings outside, wrapped in canvas against the weather; even so, the tent was crowded.

"You will manage, as we all must," Adrienne responded, not unkindly.

Before she departed, Faith thought of something else. "What—what are you going to do with Jeffrey's shirt?"

Adrienne held up the garment and regarded it with the same thoughtful expression she had worn earlier upon looking at it. "I will give it to someone who is suffering very much right now because of the boy's death. Perhaps it will bring a measure of comfort."

"Who is that?" Faith wondered aloud. Having picked up the shirt to avoid Nancy's finding it, after all of Jeffrey's things except a few mementos—such as his blanket—had been removed, she was curious.

"Monsieur Martin," Adrienne said. "I believe he blames himself for Jeffrey's death."

"Blames himself! But why would he do that? Jeffrey was shot by some savage who just happened to see him peering through the gate. His death had nothing whatever to do with Whip. If anyone should be blamed, it is I—I took him to the gate!"

"No one is to blame," Adrienne said firmly. "But men think they can control everything in life, and

179

when they discover that they cannot, they often blame themselves. You know how they are, *chérie*."

Faith did not know—but she intended to find out. If Whip thought such a ridiculous thing, she would set him straight immediately, this very night. Jeffrey's death was a tragic accident. She could accept that. Why couldn't he?

"Give me the shirt," she demanded, and before Adrienne could protest, she snatched it from the Frenchwoman's hand and stalked from the tent.

Chapter Ten

Faith had no idea where she might find Whip
Martin at this hour of the night, but find him she
would. His display of bitterness in General Harrison's tent was now perfectly clear to her—oh, why
had she not guessed the reason for it herself?

Whip must have been aware that Jeffrey had seen
him—or her sisters—running toward the fort. And it
was also possible that the young soldier at the gate
had told him that she and Jeffrey were there looking
for Shadow. In his typically arrogant, twisted way,
he could possibly have concluded that if it were not
for his own presence outside the fort—or the
presence of his pet—Jeffrey would not have stood
there so long and drawn the attention of the savages.

But such painful speculation could go on forever;
it could trap everyone in a web of guilt and self-
recrimination. If only *she* had not decided to go
looking for Shadow . . . if only the young soldier
had been quicker to warn them . . . if only Jeffrey
himself had not been so curious.

What was the point of it all?

Jeffrey was dead, and nothing could bring him back—certainly not blaming oneself for what an enemy had done. And if she had to awaken Whip from a sound sleep to tell him so, she would. But first, she had to find him.

Cookfires still smoldered in front of tents and lean-tos, and their fragile light prevented her from stumbling in the darkness. Large angular shapes gradually separated themselves into the quartermaster's storehouse, the meat house, and various storage sheds. Here and there a lantern gleamed, as some lone soldier, settler, or militiaman refused to give any quarter to the shadows of the night.

Faith headed for that section of the encampment where the scouts were billeted. She had never ventured there before, but Nancy had once mentioned that Whip had his own tent there. Disdaining to share his living space with anyone but Shadow, he had provided his own shelter—just as he had provided his own weapons and clothing.

Most of the scouts were independent creatures who came and went as they pleased, submitting to army discipline only in times of war and danger—and even then, they did everything possible to maintain their autonomy from the soldiers and the militia. Reportedly, General Harrison put up with them only because he had no choice; no one in the army knew the area half so well as the scouts, and few could shoot, track, or interpret the actions of the Indians as well as they—many of whom were said to be half Indian themselves.

Faith thought about this as she hurried toward the

area, and fear prickled up her spine. If she didn't see Whip or anyone who could tell her his whereabouts, she didn't know what she would do when she got there. She had to count on finding someone still awake—a likely possibility considering the number of men who were lounging quietly in front of their tents.

Evidently, the expectation of being besieged tomorrow had made many of the soldiers edgy. They were no more able to sleep than she would be if she returned to her tent.

Rounding the corner of a shadowy log-walled structure, she came to the section belonging to the scouts. A gasp of surprise escaped her: Several of the tents were tall triangular affairs of the type she had thought that only some tribes of Indians used— tepees, they were called, or lodges.

Instead of canvas, they were made of animal hides, and instead of the typical settlers' and soldiers' campfires, which were contained in square excavations in the grassy sod, the campfires of the scouts who slept in the tepees were contained in stone-ringed circles.

Then she noticed another strange thing: All of the entrances to the tepees faced east. And some of them had strange symbols painted on them; their bright colors were clearly distinguishable even in the darkness.

Faith hesitated to walk into the midst of these exotic structures. Hoping to see someone who was still awake—or even better, Whip himself—she paused and looked about. The smoke curling up from the dwindling cookfires cast an eerie pall on the tepees; for a moment, she wished she hadn't come.

But determination forced her onward; she had never backed down from responsibility or an irksome task in her entire life. Only Whip Martin had been able to make her feel timid and inept—and it was high time she finally faced up to him.

Taking a deep breath, she began walking through the clutch of tepees. Something—an animal lying in front of the entrance to one of them—growled at her, and looking down, she saw the amber glint of Shadow's eyes, watching her every move.

It struck her as almost funny that she could be so glad to see the unfriendly creature. Then a wave of sorrow washed over her; if Shadow were only less temperamental, less inclined to hostility, perhaps he would have remained with her in Whip's absence— and perhaps she would never have gone to the gate with Jeffrey to look for him this morning . . .

No, she reminded herself. No more useless speculation.

She looked the animal square in his amber-glinting eyes and thought: I am going to win you over yet, Shadow. For Jeffrey's sake, I am going to prove to you that *some* humans other than Whip can be trusted . . .

"What are *you* doing here?" a familiar voice demanded. "Do you care nothing for your reputation? Get inside at once—before someone sees you and draws the worst conclusions. A minister's niece has no business wandering about a camp of anxious men in the dead of night."

Faith almost bolted inside the tepee where Whip Martin's tall form stood framed in the entranceway.

The interior was pitch black, and she wondered after all if she was crazy to have come. Never once had she given a moment's thought to her reputation or to the chances she was taking by seeking out Whip Martin alone in a tepee. Belatedly she recalled what had happened the last two times they were alone together.

She spun around just in time to see the flicker of a yellow flame, as he held a taper to a tallow candle in a lantern. The candle wick caught the fire and glowed more brightly, illuminating his hostile, questioning face and the entire inside of the tepee.

Unnerved, Faith looked away from him and saw that the interior was almost painfully neat and lavishly comfortable. A platform made of pine boughs and rushes ran along the inside wall of the structure. Instead of blankets, it was heaped high with soft pelts in rich, dark colors and provided ample space for sitting or sleeping.

Containers made of hides, bark, or rushes stood like a row of soldiers beneath the platform, and weapons, including a long bow and a quiver of arrows, hung from the poles supporting the tepee. A small stone-ringed circle in the center gave evidence that a cookfire could be lit within the lodge as well as without, and Faith guessed that such a fire would also make the shelter warm and cozy.

"I had no idea . . ." she began in amazement.

"That I lived like a savage?" he finished for her. "Really, Miss Cormorand, just because I despise them and would kill every last one if I could doesn't mean that I am averse to enjoying the benefits of their style of living . . . As you can see, their lodges offer a measure of comfort rarely found in the wilderness."

"Oh, but you can't mean that—about killing them. I mean . . ." She met his eyes over the glow of the lantern. "They are human beings, after all. They cannot be all bad, surely."

"Love thine enemies, eh, Miss Cormorand?" His green eyes narrowed in scorn. "I wonder that you can still believe such pious claptrap after what happened to Jeffrey this morning."

Faith glanced down at Jeffrey's shirt. "I still believe it," she said softly, and raising her eyes to his, insisted, "I will always believe it. The only thing that sets us apart from the animals in the forest is our capacity to forgive."

"More claptrap," Whip growled.

He hung the lantern from the center lodgepole so that its arc of light bathed the luxurious furs on the sleeping platform in a soft orange glow. Then he strode to the platform, sat down on it, and leaned back, arrogantly folding his arms across his chest. From the waist up, she noted with a slight shiver, his muscular torso was naked.

Barefoot and tousle-haired, he wore only his snug-fitting fringed buckskin pants. Above them, the bandage on his shoulder gleamed whitely against his dark skin. "Now, Miss Cormorand, suppose you tell me why you have come here? If you were any other woman, I would suppose you were in need of . . . comfort, but since you are who you are—the niece of a minister—I must assume some other reason has brought you here to my lodgings."

Faith blushed under the implication of what he

meant by "comfort." All at once, she felt ridiculous. She had come to offer solace, but apparently he had little need of it.

"I—I—came to give you this." She held out the shirt. "It belonged to Jeffrey, and I thought—I wanted to tell you . . ."

All the things she had meant to say refused to come out of her mouth. In silence, Whip stared at the shirt. She thought she saw a wetness spring to his eyes, but then his dark brows slanted downward in his all too familiar scowl. He leaped to his feet and towered over her.

"What do you think you are doing?" he ground out between clenched teeth. "Sneaking here to my tepee in the darkness, bearing silly little remembrances of someone who is dead."

He snatched the shirt from her trembling hands and held it up. "Well, this is what I think of you and your soft heart, Miss Cormorand!"

There was a terrible rending sound as he ripped the shirt in two. He dangled the two halves in front of her eyes and snarled, "There! Let the dead be dead . . . I have had enough of mourning in my life. And I don't need you or anyone else trying to get close to me."

Faith was so shocked by his actions that she could scarcely comprehend his words. She only knew that she had made a terrible mistake by coming here; she must get out and away at once. Whirling to take her leave, she almost fell over an iron kettle and a large basket with a lid. They had been standing beside the ring of stones, and she had not noticed them so near her feet.

187

Kicking them to one side, she had reached the entranceway when he suddenly called her name: "Faith!"

His tone held such savage urgency that it brought her to a standstill—and only then did she realize that he had not used his usual sarcasm-tinged "Miss Cormorand."

"Faith . . ." he repeated raggedly.

Slowly, fighting back tears, she turned to face him.

He was looking at her strangely. A muscle twitched in the strong, stubborn jaw, and the green eyes held naked, wordless suffering. Instinctively, she knew what was happening: He was crumbling inside.

Something—some dark, awful thing that was even worse than Jeffrey's death—was tearing him apart.

"Mr. Martin—Whip . . ." Her feet took her a single step in his direction. Swept with uncertainty, she stopped.

He vaulted across the narrow space, and any protest she might have made was lost in a riot of sensory impressions: the feel of his arms locking around her body, dragging her to him; the warmth and roughness of his skin as his head descended and rubbed against her cheek; his pungent, piney odor, as his presence enveloped her in a tight cocoon from which there was no escape.

Noises rumbled from his throat, but they sounded more like growls of torment than human endearments. His lips found the hollow where her neck joined her shoulder; then he was tilting back her

188

head and assaulting her mouth with hot, swollen kisses.

"Whip!" she managed to gasp, but he was like a strong driving wind; she could not speak or think or resist his strength. Passion seethed between them—a palpable living presence whose demands would not be satisfied by a mere touch or word or glance.

She began to respond.

Her arms stole around his neck, hesitantly at first—then she abandoned all pretense of refusal. She leaned into his embrace and welcomed the assaulting sensations. Her breasts began to feel heavy and swollen. A liquid feeling bubbled in her loins. Dimly, she knew that his lips were ravaging and bruising her mouth, and her breasts would probably be bruised from having been crushed so hard against his chest.

But the discomfort was delicious . . .

He broke away from her lips, and his hot breath singed her earlobe. "Faith . . . Faith," he groaned.

Then his hands found her hair and tugged and pulled until the heavy black mass came tumbling down. He buried his face in it. "Lovely Faith . . . lovely innocent child . . ."

A tiny voice whispered that she should stop; this passionate interlude had gone far enough. But another voice, stronger than the first, responded: You want this. You have wanted this from the first moment when you saw this man in the woods. And this man—this arrogant, stubborn, suffering man—needs you. You will destroy him if you turn away. Besides, you want him too much, he is too magnificent, you have gone too far to stop now . . .

189

This was meant to be, Faith told her bedazzled self. And there did seem to be an essential rightness in the way her body responded to his. His mouth claiming her mouth, his hands invading her back, her hips, her shoulders, her hair, set her flesh aquiver—and made her desire an invasion that was even bolder and more intimate.

She did not protest when suddenly he lifted her like a child in his arms and carried her to the skin-heaped platform. He laid her down and stood for a moment raking her with his smoldering green eyes.

"If you are going to say no, say it now, Miss Cormorand, while there is still a slight chance that I can keep myself from raping you."

"You will not rape me . . ." And then, with the perfect honesty she was just beginning to practice, she added, "I want you—to do this . . ."

He emitted a throaty growl and flung himself down beside her, taking her in his arms and maneuvering himself so that she felt the pressure of his full arousal against her thigh.

"Don't be afraid, little Faith . . . I promise to be gentle—as gentle as ever a man can be with a maiden . . . Here, touch me. It will not be so frightening as you think."

She had often dreamed of touching that which sprang so boldly between a man's strong thighs, but now that the opportunity had come, she was overcome with shyness. He must have guessed her thoughts, for he took her hand and, watching her eyes to judge her reaction, pressed it downward to the forbidden place.

The protrusive shaft was throbbing even through

his buckskins, and after a moment, he pulled her fingers away.

"Little one," he rasped. "If you continue to do that, I will surely rape you; there will be no other word for it."

Then he was on top of her, tugging at her clothing, sending the buttons flying as he jerked the cornflower-blue dress down from her shoulders.

Her full aching breasts thrust up between them, her nipples contracting at the sudden rush of his breath upon them. She was embarrassed by the hot rosy flush that began in the valley between the curved white mounds and quickly spread to the mottled peaks. She had always thought herself too large—too extravagantly fashioned.

But Whip Martin did not seem to think so. His green eyes consumed her. "My God, you are beautiful," he breathed. "More beautiful than I had thought . . ."

His head dipped, and with mingled shock and delight, she experienced the exquisite sensation of having her nipples licked, nuzzled, pulled, and suckled. Her breath was coming in short little gasps when he had done with kissing and fondling them; then he leaned back to study her face.

"Shall I give you more, Miss Cormorand?" He chuckled low in his throat. "Did you ever, in your virginal dreams, imagine that it could be like this?"

Even in his lovemaking, he needed to mock her. Instinctively, she reached for *his* nipples.

They were small and flat, buried in crisp, crinkly dark hair that tantalized her fingertips. At her touch, his nipples grew erect, and he moaned and jerked away when she squeezed them. The reaction emboldened her, and she grew more confident with her caresses, exploring his bare chest, his shoulders, his muscular back with eager roving hands.

Curiosity fueled her desire. She wanted to know every inch of him, to be better acquainted with the mysteries of his body than she was with her own. The scar ridges beneath her fingertips briefly reminded her of his constant hostility.

I must soothe away his hurts, she thought. I must give him peace and comfort. Tomorrow, we all may die, but tonight . . . tonight . . . Oh, God, she prayed, let me heal him!

Abandoning all restraint, she used her hands and mouth to perform benedictions, psalms, and beatitudes on the long lean length of Whip Martin's body and soul.

At last, with a muttered oath, he stripped away the remnants of the blue dress, and she lay totally naked and exposed before him. Glazed with passion, his eyes roved over her, scorching her flesh and making her ache to possess him—to own this proud, distant man who belonged to no one but a wolf. Holding her glance with his own, he gently inserted a finger where no man before him had ever before entered.

"It will hurt," he whispered. "But only this one time."

The gentle exploration of his finger belied the warning. She relaxed and opened her thighs. The sweet ache in her loins was building . . . building. In one lithe motion, he poised himself above her. His breath blew moist and hot on her forehead. She reached for him, and he came plunging down, down into her body.

A tearing pain seared through her, to be quickly replaced by a throbbing. She arched upward, knowing that she now possessed his body but still wanting something more—there had to be something more.

"Oh, my sweet little Faith . . ." he growled against her ear.

And then he began to move within her. She locked her arms and legs around him. He rose, plunged again, rose and plunged—again, and again, and again. A wildness overtook him. All the violence and savagery that she had ever sensed in him surged to the surface.

A wetness sleeked his entire body as he drove into her, pumping his seed into the deepest inner core of her, filling her, consuming her, causing her to throb with an ecstasy that she had never imagined to exist.

The sheer surprise and intensity of the wondrous sensation caused her to gasp. And still, he did not cease his driving. With one mighty thrust, he plunged into her quivering flesh and let out a single agonized cry.

It sounded like a name, but it was not her name.

Her eyes flew open. Her body stiffened. He must have sensed the change immediately; he levered himself off her damp body and glanced down at her with a dazed expression—as if it were an effort for him to remember where he was and who she was.

She had never known such awful hurt, such terrible unwarranted rejection. "Who," she managed to choke, "who is Moon Daughter?"

Chapter Eleven

"Moon Daughter!" Whip exploded. "How do you know about her?"

The old hostility was back in his tone, and the glance he gave her as he rolled off the platform and stood up was hostile, too. He reached for his buckskins and began tugging them on—while Faith covered herself as best she could with what was immediately available: her hair and her hands.

Only a moment before, she had known not the least embarrassment at her nakedness, but now she was utterly shamed. The rosiness of her skin—still glowing from Whip Martin's lovemaking—shamed her even more. Desperate to retrieve her dress, she, too, scrambled off the platform and, turning her back to him, gasped a defiant explanation: "You—you spoke her name."

Having secured his pants with a leather thong, Whip grabbed her by the shoulders, turned her around, and hauled her to him. It seemed that he was always hauling her to him—and with the same exasperation.

"What are you talking about? When did I ever mention Moon Daughter to you?"

His voice held the slightest tremor, and she knew without any doubt that Moon Daughter was someone he had loved—and still loved. Tears gathered in her eyes and threatened to spill over. "You called out her name when you lay with me . . . when you . . . when you . . ."

Comprehension dawned on his face; then the scowl she had learned to dread once again contorted his handsome features. "I could not have," he denied flatly. "I do not make love to one woman while thinking of another."

"I could not have known her name otherwise," Faith retorted in despair. A sense of outrage welled up in her. "Who is she? And why do you live in an Indian tepee and sleep on furs and know so much about how to—how to pleasure a woman?"

The boldness of this last inquiry appeared to surprise even him. He stared down at her, his green eyes sweeping across the disarray of her tangled hair and naked body as if he were somehow shocked by it—or by himself.

When he did not answer, she bit her lower lip. She had not meant to ask so many prying, embarrassing questions. They had somehow just popped out. And with a sense of inevitability, she knew the answer to every one of them. "Moon Daughter is—was your wife?"

And then it occurred to her that perhaps Moon Daughter had not truly been his wife. Perhaps she had just been a loose woman—a wanton heathen who lay with him and sought his love without ever having considered marriage to him at all. She had heard of such unholy alliances; among the scouts, before this conflict forced the taking of sides, it was not uncommon for half-breeds to seek the companionship of Indian women without benefit of marriage. But Whip! Nancy had said that he was a full-blooded white man.

Faith shivered, and Whip's large, warm hands began to knead her bare shoulders with slow deliberation. "Yes. She was my wife," he admitted finally. "Though we were never married in a manner that your uncle would approve of. Perhaps even you would not approve."

Faith winced. So they had lived together and shared the intimacies of married life without actually ever being married. Somehow that made it even worse. "And this lodge. It was *her* lodge?"

Whip nodded, and the naked agony in his eyes was more than she could bear to see. She averted her own eyes, but everywhere she looked she saw things that must have belonged to the beloved Moon Daughter. Things that she had no doubt used or cherished—furs on which she must have slept and lain with Whip. The woman had possessed not only Whip's body but his soul as well.

Faith had to know the rest of the story; no matter how terrible, she had to know it. "What—what happened to her?"

Whip paused, and when he finally answered, his voice was curiously flat and unemotional, as if he had willed himself to bury his true feelings, to hide them forever from sight.

"She died at the hands of Tecumseh's followers—a vicious lot who disapproved of her marriage to a white man and hated her gentle peace-loving ways. They raped and tortured her in the most savage manner possible, then left her broken body where I would be certain to find it."

"Where—was that?"

"In front of our tepee—this tepee. She died in my arms. I buried her, then gathered together all I had left of our life together and went to Frenchtown. Shadow and I have been seeking her murderers ever since."

"Shadow? Shadow knew her?"

"Shadow worshiped her. She rescued him from a flock of vultures when he was just a pup with an injured paw. He tried to defend her, I am certain of it, but someone clouted him over the head with a war club—and for a long time afterward, he would not even allow me to touch him."

"Oh . . ." Faith let out a long, painfully held breath.

She had many more questions. How had Whip come to meet the Indian girl? After they became lovers, had they remained among the Indians or had they gone off somewhere to live by themselves? But, for now, she had heard enough, more than enough, more than she had ever wanted to hear.

She stepped away from Whip and leaned down to pick up her dress, which was draped across the platform.

Whip towered over her. "'Oh'? That's all you have to say—'oh'?"

She straightened. What more did he expect from

198

her? What more did he want? His love for his dead "wife" was chillingly obvious. Now she could understand everything—why he was so cold and hostile. Why Jeffrey's death had caused such a bitter outburst. And why he risked his life so often for others with such little apparent self-concern.

Whip Martin was sick with grief. He was consumed by it. It ate at his very soul. He could not even lose himself in another woman's body. The memory of Moon Daughter pursued him even there.

"I—I am so sorry for you . . . and for me." She stifled a sob and began pulling her dress over her head.

He tugged the garment down and settled it over her shoulders so that he could see her face. "I don't want your pity, damn you! Don't you understand why I have told you all this?"

She did not want to look at him, or she would begin to cry like a baby. Turning her attention to adjusting and fastening her torn and bedraggled dress, she whispered, "I know why you've told me. I understand. And you needn't worry: No one will ever know about what happened here tonight. I don't hold you responsible. I should have said no; I shuld have stopped you . . ."

"Stopped me, hell." He seized her shoulders again and forced her to look at him. "I may have said her name, Faith. I don't know. But she was not the one I was thinking of when I spilled my seed in you . . ."

He pulled her closer, his hands dropping to her buttocks and molding her body to his. "She was not here in this tepee when we were joined together, when I was doing this to you . . ."

He rubbed against her, letting her feel the strength of his new arousal. "Not because of her did I desire and take you. It was for your own sake. Do you understand? For your own sake, Faith."

"*For my sake?*" She jerked away from him, a white-hot rage exploding in her chest. "You *used* me, Whip! You took my body—my virginity—everything I had to give . . ." Her voice broke, and she could not continue for a moment. "What we did was wrong, so very wrong . . . I thought it was right and wonderful, but now I see how cheap and dirty it really was . . ."

"Don't, Faith . . . don't. It *was* right and wonderful."

An expression of hurt came into his eyes. But she didn't care anymore; she *wanted* to hurt him. "No! It was deceitful and ugly!"

Angry now, he moved closer and seized her face in his hands. "Listen to me, you little fool . . . I am an honorable man. Despite everything else, I am honorable . . . In the morning, I will go to your uncle. I will tell him everything. He can marry us tomorrow, if you like."

"Marry us!"

"We'll marry as soon as possible . . . Oh, Faith, I *want* to marry you. Despite what you may think, I care for you a great deal."

"Stop it!" she cried. "Will you please stop it!" She tore his hands from her face and inched away from the heat of his body. Even now, at this terrible moment, her treacherous flesh was capable of succumbing to overwhelming passion, a passion she ought not to have felt—and must refuse to feel

200

again. "I can't marry you, Whip . . . I can't."

For a single second, looking up into his brilliant, pain-ravaged green eyes, she allowed herself to wonder what she might have said if he had asked her before she learned about Moon Daughter.

Instead of resorting to mere words, she would have thrown herself in his arms. She would have offered him her body again and again, as often as he wanted it. Then she would have flown from the tepee, run joyously to her uncle, to her sisters, to anyone who would listen. She would have wept happy tears as she spread the wondrous news: Whip Martin loves me . . . He wants to marry me. He loves me . . . as I love him.

The image of what might have been made the present moment even more bitter.

"I—I'm sorry," she apologized in a shaky voice. "But you see, I have responsibilities—my uncle and my sisters. They need me. I have to look after them. Why, Uncle Abel can't even find his spectacles without my help—and Charity, she's so young and featherheaded, she never thinks of the consequences of her actions. You saw that! You know how she is—and Hope. She's so sad and quiet now. That's not like her at all. Something's bothering her, and I must find out what it is."

"Faith . . ." he began, coming toward her.

Her babbling ceased. She stared at him, suddenly hating what he had done to her, the way he had reduced her to a sniveling, brokenhearted weakling. Oh, she would never forgive him for that—for stripping away her pride, for shredding her dignity, for making her love him while he still belonged body

201

and soul to the ghost of another woman.

"Faith . . ." He reached for her.

But she slapped ineffectually at his hands, snatched up her shoes from the floor, spun around, and ran out of the tepee. And she did not stop running until she was certain that he was no longer following her, no longer calling her name, and indeed could no longer see her as the night swallowed her in darkness.

Whip watched Faith run away through the looming tents and tepees, her black hair streaming behind her, her shoes clutched to her full breasts. He pursued her only a step or two, called her name only twice more, before he realized the futility of his actions. The girl wanted nothing more to do with him, not now, not tonight—and perhaps not ever. He had wounded her too deeply, although he had not intended to do so.

He did not remember saying Moon Daughter's name. He did not remember saying anything in that moment of exquisite rapture, that fleeting, perfect moment when he had totally possessed Faith Cormorand. How could it have happened—how?

Unlike some men, for whom coupling was a casual act, he had held himself in reserve from women. He had eased his passions by killing Indians and driving himself, day after day, into a state of near total exhaustion, so that when he lay down at night, the need for a woman's soft body was the furthest thing from his mind.

If he had called out Moon Daughter's name, he

202

had done so only because—after all this time—his tortured mind still remembered, still resisted his efforts to forget. He had always cried out her name in the act of possessing her, but never—not once when he was sheathed in Faith's lush body—had he confused the two women.

They were nothing alike, except for the spontaneity, the innocent wonder, the unconditional surrender with which they had both responded to his lovemaking. He had not expected to discover this childlike generosity in any woman other than his dead wife. Now to have found it, only to have it slip once more from his grasp, filled him with a familiar numbness.

Whip remembered that numbness often followed a serious injury. He had experienced it once before, after taking an arrow in his chest, and he had often heard dying men speak of it. Numbness preceded death, and he wished, instead, for the wrenching pain he had known when Moon Daughter died. At least in pain he knew he still had a chance at life; he knew he might one day heal. But this time . . .

"Appears to me you have lost her, my friend," a male voice suddenly spoke to him from the entranceway of a nearby lean-to.

Startled, Whip whirled about and then, seeing who it was, relaxed.

The voice had come from Peter Navarre, a man well known to him and to almost everyone else at Fort Meigs. The six Navarre brothers had lately lived at Frenchtown and had tried, with as little success as Whip, to convince General Winchester to beware of the trap set by the savages and the British.

Peter now served as a runner and messenger for General Harrison. He, like Whip, was one of those precious few who understood the Indian mentality. He, too, had grown up among them and lived among them, and members of his family had married Indians.

Peter knew Whip's background: how his father had been a fur trader, how his mother had died of cholera when he was only eleven, and how his father had then settled among the Shawnee, taking a Shawnee wife, trading and trapping with them until his death in a canoeing accident two and a half years later.

The boisterous Navarres had even adopted Whip for a time and seen to it that he received a rudimentary education. Whip had applied himself to books with a burning zeal, devouring everything he could find, including the Bible, to such an extent that the Navarre brothers, especially Peter, had often poked fun at him.

But then, one fresh spring morning, the lure of the green forest and the freedom he had known there as a boy, among the savages, had proven too great for Whip. He had shunned Peter's big-brotherly advice and sought his destiny among the Shawnee. There, not much later, he had met and married Moon Daughter.

All of this history flashed through his mind, as Whip stood looking at Peter Navarre and saying nothing. Peter, seated on a stump, unconcernedly lit a pipe with a taper he had thrust into the embers of his cookfire.

"Yes siree, Whip my boy, I think you have lost that pretty little lass . . . Name is Faith Cormorand, isn't it?" Peter drew on his pipe, held the smoke in his lungs, then expelled it in a long, silvery wisp. His face and hands were in darkness, but the smoke from his pipe was clearly visible.

Whip confirmed Faith's name with a slight jerk of his head. It did not surprise him that Peter knew; Pete knew everything and always had. Of all his brothers—Jacques, Robert, Antoine, Francis, and Alexis Navarre—Peter had the greatest ability to instantly size up a situation.

He did this by first observing details, people, places, mannerisms that most folks never noticed. He made it his business to know who came and who went, who stayed, who had a quick temper or a slow one. Whip knew these things about Peter Navarre and was not pleased to have his recent nocturnal activities fall under the man's penetrating scrutiny.

"Why aren't you sleeping instead of spying?" Whip finally growled.

Peter chuckled, his amiability an effective shield against Whip's prickliness. "Can't sleep. Got too much on my mind. I thought I would just sit a spell and study the night—and then things got so interesting in your tepee that I had to stay up and see how it all came out."

"It came out badly," Whip said in a manner meant to cut off any further comments or questions.

"I could see—and hear—that. You lost a fine upright little lady who gave in to her feelings for you tonight. I've been watching her about the fort— unbeknownst to her, of course. I've seen how the

205

soldiers ogle her, and she never pays them the slightest heed. Yes, a fine, upstanding lady she is—and as pretty as I've ever seen, with that hair the color of a crow's wing and those eyes the color of violets."

"You prattle on like an old woman. Do things never change?" Whip drew up a log and sat down across from his old acquaintance. He did not analyze why he was willing to undergo such abuse as Peter would no doubt hand him; at the moment, anything seemed better than returning to his empty silent tepee.

Peter chuckled again. "No, Whip, some things never do change. I see you are still stubborn and willful, intent on doing things your own way—and be damned to anyone who interferes."

"Be damned to you then," responded Whip.

They sat in silence for a while, Peter puffing on his pipe and Whip marveling at himself. He could not remember how long it had been since he had sat in relaxed proximity with another human being.

Occasionally, when the need for human companionship had become overwhelming, he had sought out Nancy and Tom Foster or Adrienne Langlois, his only real friends at the fort. But even with them, he was always slightly on edge, unable to completely let down his guard. Only with Jeffrey, on one or two occasions, had he been able to forget his uneasy vigilance. Of course, Jeffrey was a child—and therefore harmless.

He wondered if his ability to sit quietly with Peter Navarre stemmed from numbness or from the fact that his long suppressed physical cravings had finally been satisfied. If so, if he had known that all he needed was to plunder a woman's body, he would have done so much sooner. He would have responded to the invitations often flashed at him in the eyes of the women camp followers. And perhaps, had he done that, he would not be in his present predicament.

"Where is that wolf of yours tonight?" Peter tamped out the bowl of his pipe against the end of Whip's log.

"Shadow?" Whip hadn't noticed the creature's absence until just this moment. He shrugged his lack of concern. "He probably got disgusted and left when he heard what was going on inside the tepee. Shadow doesn't hold with folks getting too friendly —with me or with him."

"He reflects his master's sentiments," Peter sagely observed.

Whip snorted. "We have both learned that friendliness doesn't pay."

Another silence followed, in which Whip had time to remember what he had known from the beginning —that he should have left Faith Cormorand alone. He had suspected how much he could hurt her; what he had not fully perceived was how much he would hurt himself. Or had he guessed that, too, and simply ignored his own instincts?

"You think the reinforcements from Kentucky will make it here before the redcoats start blastin' us?" Peter asked.

Whip started. "What?" With effort, he focused on the question as Peter patiently repeated it. "No," he responded wearily. "Clay won't be able to get through in time."

"Oh, I don't know. Green Clay is a good man. 'Course, someone might have to go out and bring him in."

The comment hung in the air like a persistent noxious odor, and Whip realized that Peter meant that one or both of them would probably be drafted for that purpose. "Makes no difference to me, I'll go," he muttered.

"You have nothing to lose," Peter said, and Whip knew from his tone of voice that he was grinning—enjoying the opportunity to needle him some more.

He almost yawned with indifference. "Willie Oliver get back yet?"

Captain William Oliver had been sent out to reconnoiter with General Clay on the same night that Whip and Tom had gone to meet the *Sea Sprite*.

"Nope . . . and that's probably as good an indication as any that Clay isn't within marching distance of us yet. Anyhow, I just hate t' think of him and his men coming down the river under the guns of the British."

"So do I," Whip agreed, but he could no longer maintain even the slightest interest in a conversation that normally would have absorbed him.

He stood so abruptly as to be markedly rude. "Be seeing you, Pete . . . and I'd appreciate it if you didn't mention that you saw Miss Cormorand leaving my tepee tonight."

Peter stirred in the dark entranceway of his lean-to. "I don't carry tales, Whip; you know that. We go back a long way together, and I have never told a living soul about you and your little Moon

Daughter. General Harrison thinks you hate Injuns on account of the color of their skin, and whenever he brings up the subject, I just let him go on thinkin' that."

The mere mention of Moon Daughter's name was like having salt poured on an open wound. Standing there, in close company to the only man in the fort who knew the story of his life—who he was and where he had come from and how his life had been shattered—Whip experienced a resurgence of his old desire for revenge.

Suddenly, he felt strong again. What did it matter if Faith Cormorand had run away, hurt by something he had said? Nothing had changed for him; he should be glad she had refused his offer of marriage. Marrying her would only have complicated and confused things.

He had a duty—a quest that she would never be able to understand. Sooner or later, she would try to stop him. She would fix those big violet eyes on him and beg him to leave off hunting and killing, to let his vengeance rest. No! He would never forgive and forget. He had no patience with such a weak approach to one's enemies.

Renewed in purpose, he turned and strode toward his tepee, scarcely hearing Peter's parting shot: "G'night, Whip. Hope you can sleep."

But as he entered the place where he and Faith had so recently been joined in flesh and spirit, he saw the torn pieces of Jeffrey's shirt lying on the matted floor. He picked them up, folded them, and stroked the rough homespun fabric for a moment.

How had Faith guessed how much it would mean

to him to have something of Jeffrey's?

He reached under the sleeping platform and withdrew a basket with an intricately woven design. Setting down the shirt, he removed the lid from the basket and debated whether to place the shirt on top of the other contents or beneath them.

Succumbing to impulse, and because he had not opened the basket in months, he took out the garment that lay neatly folded inside. It was a fringed dress of the softest, finest white doeskin with a bodice embroidered with red beads and blue and white quills.

The dress had been Moon Daughter's—the one she had worn for their wedding ceremony and their first night alone in the lodge together. He did not unfold it, but instead, closed his eyes and crushed it to his face. He tried to remember how she had looked in the dress. He had come into the tepee and seen her kneeling beside the cookfire, her head shyly bowed, her long, glossy black braids hanging straight down the front of her flat bodice, almost to her waist.

Her graceful figure was as slim as a boy's, but Whip had only to look at her to set his heart to pounding, his blood to racing. Slowly, she had raised her head to return his devouring gaze.

He struggled to remember her face—but the face he saw in his mind was not Moon Daughter's. Nor were the eyes. Instead of warm brown eyes, Indian eyes, he saw eyes the color of spring violets. Enormous purple-shadowed eyes that misted with tears as they gazed at him. He saw the rosy blushing cheeks, the tender curved lips, the lovely blue-black

210

hair of Faith Cormorand.

He tried and tried—but he could not summon the image of Moon Daughter. And he knew that somehow, against every measure of probability and against his own fierce resistance, Faith Cormorand had stolen his heart.

Could she also have done the impossible—healed his soul?

Chapter Twelve

"Faith . . . Faith, wake up! The fort is under siege!"

Still locked in the throes of anxious slumber, Faith did little more than stir at the sound of Charity's voice. She had been aware of the booming and vibrating as shells whistled and exploded nearby, but she had thought she was merely dreaming. And now, even though she knew the booming was real, she could not throw off her lethargy.

Exhaustion had settled into every bone and muscle. Her thighs ached, and so did her loins. She felt stiff and sore all over. It could not have been more than an hour or two at most since she had finally fallen asleep, with her feet and half her body outside the tent. Why, she wondered, should she rush to get up merely because the British had finally mounted their attack?

She could just as well die lying down as standing. Indeed, it would be far more convenient and comfortable. And after what had happened last night between her and Whip, after what she had learned about him, she didn't much care if she did die. Her enthusiasm for living had certainly died a little.

Charity shook her shoulder. "Faith, get up! Oh, it's so exciting! The soldiers look so brave and dashing in their uniforms. And the dearest young captain just came by to tell us to take down our tent and go immediately to one of the bombproof areas. I hope he will return to see if we have obeyed his order."

Faith released an audible groan and opened her eyes.

Charity was leaning over her, blond curls falling forward across her pink cheeks, blue eyes sparkling. "His name is Daniel Cushing, and when he smiles he dimples."

"Who dimples?" Trying to ease the throbbing in her temples, Faith ran one hand across her forehead. Her voice came out more sharply than she intended. "Whomever are you talking about?"

"The young captain!" Charity bubbled. Leaning closer, she grinned, revealing her own dimples, then continued in a lower voice. "What shall I do, Faith? I can't decide whom I like best—Captain Cushing or a young woodsman named Jacob Brent whom I met at the well this morning."

Faith groaned again. How could she ever have thought that Charity would be bored in the wilderness? The girl obviously regarded the fort as some sort of banquet table, loaded with treats for her choosing. After only one day, Charity already knew the names of two young men. Faith herself had been there five days—no, six—and had yet to meet anyone but the Fosters, Adrienne Langlois, and a few other married or otherwise unavailable men.

Whip Martin, of course, did not count. Nor could she bear just yet to think about him.

She yawned exaggeratedly and sat up. "Where are Hope and Uncle Abel? Do they know we are to take shelter in the bombproofs?"

Something whined overhead, and Faith instinctively ducked. There came a loud thud as the missile buried itself in a wall of earth—one of the traverses probably—and she waited with bated breath for an explosion.

None came, and she relaxed. It was still something of a mystery to her how cannons, field guns, and howitzers worked and what sort of ammunition they used. She knew only that some threw balls of six-, twelve-, or eighteen-pound weight and others threw canisters of grapeshot, explosive shells, or large, heavy pieces of metal.

Rumors had lately flown about the fort that the British had siege guns capable of throwing twenty-four-pound cannonballs, while the largest that the Americans could throw were eighteen pounds. Jeffrey could probably have explained more about the various pieces of artillery, but when Faith remembered this, she carefully turned her thoughts from the subject and realized that Charity had still not responded to her question.

"Where are your sister and Uncle Abel?" she repeated.

Charity ceased snatching up their belongings and

215

shrugged. "Someone has already been wounded, and Uncle Abel went to comfort him. Hope must have gone with him."

Uncle Abel might be kept quite busy this day, Faith thought. Wide awake now and much less resigned to dying than she had been only moments before, she scrambled off her pallet and joined Charity in assembling their things for the move to the bombproof hollows the soldiers had dug in the side of the Grand Taverse.

Hope came into the tent a few moments later just as Faith was hiding her torn cornflower-blue dress in the folds of a blanket. Until she had time to mend it, she didn't want either of the girls to see it and be prompted to ask embarrassing questions. "Well . . ." she said to Hope. "Where have you been? I trust you haven't been ogling young men like your sister."

Hope tossed her mane of abundant, glistening, auburn hair. Her green eyes flashed. "I have only been to the quartermaster's. I have no interest whatever in men, young or otherwise. Indeed, I shouldn't complain if every last one of them were suddenly swept from the face of the earth."

Stunned by the disturbing bitterness of Hope's tone, which echoed her own bitterness, Faith stared at her sister. Hope straightened her wiry shoulders and stared back, her small, boyish figure bristling with defiance, as if she were daring Faith to defend the entire male sex.

Faith had no wish to do so, but her curiosity was piqued. Hope had been so subdued—and with good reason, considering the circumstances surrounding

216

her arrival at Fort Meigs. But even given recent events, this barely suppressed hostility was totally unnatural in a girl who was normally cheerful, optimistic, and outgoing.

Something besides Jeffrey's death and the strain of the sudden departure from the *Sea Sprite* was bothering her sister.

Hope thrust a small canvas sack into Faith's hands. "Here—coffee. I bought it from the quartermaster . . . If we are going to be so uncomfortable, living like groundhogs, at least we can enjoy some of life's amenities. I wanted to buy sugar or molasses to sweeten the coffee, but they cost too much. However, if you want some . . ."

"No, no . . . this will be fine," Faith murmured, accepting the treasure. Her own thrifty nature had prevented her from indulging in such luxuries, especially since most of the other settlers could not afford to purchase them from the quartermaster. "I didn't know you'd brought money, Hope."

"Of course I brought money!" Hope flared. "You don't think I would have come unprepared. Luckily, I hid it in my bodice; Mr. Martin made us leave everything else behind in the bateau."

"Perhaps we can recover your things later," Faith offered consolingly, suddenly remembering her meeting with Whip in the woods. Then she also recalled their first wonderfully sensuous kiss—even then a kiss of betrayal—and she quickly set the coffee inside a black kettle at her feet. "Or perhaps not . . ."

"What?" Hope asked.

The rat-tat-tat of musketfire and another distant

boom spared Faith from having to explain. Instead, she straightened and briskly warned: "Girls, we had better get busy. If we stay here much longer, we may be blown up."

"Not that it would matter much." Hope bent to pick up the kettle and then turned away, but not before Faith saw the tears glistening in her sister's bright green eyes.

Momentarily forgetting her own misery, Faith stepped closer to Hope's rigid back. "Hope, what is it? What has happened to make you so—"

Another explosion—this one much closer—caused the tent to shake, and Faith realized that this was neither the time nor the place to question her sister. "Oh, my goodness!" Charity shrieked, and all three girls flew into a wordless frenzy of activity. Within minutes, nothing remained but to dismantle the tent and carry it away.

"Do you think you can manage the rest?" Faith panted. She had not really exerted herself, but as the musket and cannon fire had increased, so also had the painful throbbing in her head. "I want to check on Nancy Foster. She may need help with her tent."

"Why do you need to check on her? Weren't you with her most of the night?" Hope's green eyes were oddly penetrating, almost suspicious, Faith thought. "It was certainly very late when you came in—I heard you."

"Y—Yes, it was late. But I felt I should stay with Nancy as long as possible," Faith lied, hating herself for the falsehood. "And I don't want to leave her alone too long today . . . I suppose—if anything good can come out of this siege—it will be to take

Nancy's mind off Jeffrey and off her husband's absence."

Hope seized the canvas flap of the tent and made ready to tug it down. "Hah! If she's really suffering, nothing can help her."

Again, Faith was stunned by the echoing bitterness and truth of Hope's observation. She vowed to find out what was wrong in the first private moment that presented itself.

"Hurry to the bombproofs. I will join you there. And if Uncle Abel appears, make him go there with you."

"Oh, we will!" Charity trilled. "Don't worry about us. If we have any problems, I'll just find Captain Cushing."

"I hardly think that will be necessary," Faith commented dryly.

She hurried out of the tent, straightening her slightly tousled hair as she did so. On her arrival during the wee hours of the morning, before lying down to sleep, she had brushed and plaited her hair, changed her dress, and tried to obliterate every sign of her union with Whip. Outwardly, she knew that she was reasonably presentable; inwardly, she had changed forever.

She had gone from girl to woman in a single night—and she felt as if that, combined with her misery, must surely be stamped on her every feature. But perhaps it was not so strange that her sisters noticed nothing different about her. Charity, after all, was busy conquering new beaux, and Hope was obviously wrestling with some great problem of her own.

Faith sighed. Her responsibilities weighed heavily on her this morning. She realized that what she had told Whip last night was true: She wasn't free to marry. Perhaps one day, when Hope and Charity were safely married and Uncle Abel was settled into his work among the Indians . . .

She sighed again. It would be some time before Uncle Abel sufficiently recovered from last winter's illnesses to be able to manage without her. Even then, he would need someone to cook and clean for him, to mend his breeches, to shine his boots . . . Taking care of him was a full-time occupation, and it was wrong of her to resent performing these tasks. Hadn't Uncle Abel gone far beyond his Christian duty by joyously assuming the burden of raising all three of them?

She, more than anyone, knew how often he had gone without necessities so that they might have hair ribbons, lace collars, and flowered bonnets.

Faith arrived at Nancy's with a heart as heavy as an anvil. But she put a determinedly cheerful expression on her face for Nancy's sake—and was surprised to find Nancy already up and about, calmly packing her things.

"Good mornin'. They're poundin' the hell out of us, ain't they?" Nancy finished tying a bundle of blankets and gave a sharp twist to the length of rawhide.

"Good morning . . ." Faith concealed her amazement. She hadn't expected Nancy to be so completely in control of her feelings. The woman's plain round face was pale and blotched, but her eyes were clear and her glance unwavering. Her quiet strength

220

of character made Faith feel a rush of shame.

"Here, let me help you," she offered, as Nancy picked up the bundle and began to carry it out of the tent.

"I can do it," Nancy insisted, brushing past Faith. She set the bundle down outside the tent and returned for another. "I don't want anyone fussin' over me. I got to be strong. Tom'll expect that of me. Till he gets back, I got to just keep goin'."

She paused long enough to lay a protective hand on her distended belly. "This little one needs his mama. I can't give up. He's gonna get born in a coupla weeks, an' I gotta be ready for him."

She picked up another bundle and hurried out of the tent with it, leaving Faith to blink back a sudden rush of tears. Nancy Foster was one of the strongest human beings she had ever met. How could she—self-centered Faith Cormorand—have wasted a single moment feeling sorry for herself?

As the sounds of the siege increased in intensity, Faith and Nancy dismantled the Fosters' tent and carried their belongings to the Grand Traverse.

The scene there was a milling mass of confusion and excitement. Faith had expected short tempers and constant disagreements over who would be bunked where in the narrow cavelike trenches behind the Grand Traverse. Instead, an almost festive mood prevailed. Exhausted soldiers, who had risen before dawn to finish work on the project, slapped one another on the shoulders and called congratulations.

Their elation infected the settlers, who took due note of the accomplishment and were awestruck.

221

Faith could not believe that the men had built the Grand Traverse in only three days. It was a wall of earth ten to fifteen feet high that ran the entire length of the camp. In back of it ran a smaller traverse, and at each end of the long snakelike walls stood additional traverses. Other embankments shielded the well, the quartermaster's house, the powder magazines, and the gates.

The construction of the Grand Traverse had been concealed from the enemy's view by the sea of tents surrounding it on all sides. But now, with all the tents coming down, the wall of earth would be clearly visible from across the river—much to the surprise and chagrin of the British, who had no doubt expected the Americans to be easier targets.

"Haw! Wonder what them bastards're thinkin' now," a scar-faced militiaman boasted. He grinned at Faith, revealing a mouthful of broken yellow teeth. "They thought they could jus' git their cannon in place an' pick us off like nestin' turkeys, but we showed them what we're made of, didn't we? Give the Newnited States Army a coupla spades and mattocks, an' there ain't nothin' we cain't do!"

Faith nodded and passed by him without speaking. She was watching for the girls and Uncle Abel—and also, helplessly and uneasily, for Whip.

Nancy stopped walking when she saw Adrienne Langlois coming toward them. She eased her bundles to one side and rested them on her hip. Adrienne smiled, her brown eyes lit by the excitement that surged around them like an invisible foaming wave.

"Look no farther, *mes amies.* I came early and

222

found a place for all of us. It is close to the well, so we won't have to walk far for water . . . Come, I will show you."

Adrienne's ramrod-straight back proceeded ahead of them down the length of the traverse. They passed the quartermaster's house on the left and were soon at the other end of the fort from where they had been previously camped. Faith's uneasiness increased. The area was near the spot where Whip's tepee had stood, but the poles of the structures no longer pierced the sky. The tepees, tents, and lean-tos had all been taken down.

Faith, however, could not help looking for Whip's tall, lean form. Every time she caught a glimpse of a man in fringed buckskins, her heart leaped into her throat. This senseless reaction disgusted her, but she could no more stop it than she could have stopped breathing or blinking against the sting of the thick wisps of gunsmoke floating over the Grand Traverse.

Adrienne led them to a large hole in the ground near the base of the traverse. She pointed down, and Faith saw that the hole was actually a deep, cavelike hollow. One had to climb downward to enter it. Inside the hollow, Adrienne had laid out sleeping pallets, household utensils, and other accoutrements and had staked out a piece of canvas overall.

"To keep off the rain," she explained, gesturing to the makeshift roof. "We shall be wading in mud if it rains, but at least our heads will be dry."

Faith's dismay must have shown on her face, because Adrienne wagged a finger at her. "Do not look so sad, *chérie*. It is not forever. I lived in a gully

223

without any roof for three days when I was escaping the guillotine in France. And it was in the cold season, too."

Having already guessed that Adrienne had had a turbulent past, Faith was nevertheless taken aback. More and more, she felt like a weakling beside these strong, capable women. She turned to take Nancy's arm and help her into the shelter, but Nancy was already climbing down the embankment.

"It looks right good, Adrienne. I've got some salt pork for supper. Let's put the kettle on."

Adrienne had saved the space on the right for Faith, her sisters, and her uncle, and Faith went back through the busy throngs to look for them. She found Charity half in tears beside their belongings, while Hope struggled to unfold the unwieldy lump of canvas that had been their tent.

"We can't live in *there!*" Charity wailed, pointing to the trench. "Look!" she gestured to her dress and shoes. "I cleaned these last night, and already they are covered with mud. What are we going to do? I'm a mess!"

Hope shot her sister an angry look. She thumped the canvas to knock off a fat beetle. "If you weren't so vain, you wouldn't care how you look. Really, Charity, you are such a baby . . . I had to take down the tent by myself, Faith. Our little sister didn't want to disarrange her curls."

Faith's anger boiled to the surface. Why couldn't her sisters display some of the poise and calmness of Nancy Foster, who had so much more to complain about? She willed herself not to shout at them. "Adrienne has saved us a place farther on down. It is

224

less muddy there and closer to the well. We shall be next door to Nancy and Adrienne. Please help me carry our belongings down there."

"But Faith, we just carried them here!" Charity protested.

"Oh, she's just afraid that Captain Cushing will not know where to look for her when he comes back," Hope complained. "Besides, he and I did most of the carrying. *She* just followed along looking pretty."

"I did not! I—"

"Stop it!" Faith finally exploded. "Pick up these things immediately. Everyone else is making do, and so shall we—without complaints. I won't tolerate another word from either of you."

The sharpness of her tone startled the girls into instant embarrassed compliance. Hurriedly, Hope refolded the canvas, and Charity grudgingly helped her. Faith gathered up more than she could comfortably carry, and the two girls struggled to help her hoist the canvas and carry it. The heavy, unwieldy thing made their best efforts look ludicrous. Much as she hated to admit it, Faith realized that they needed a man to help them. Ordinarily she would not have subjected her uncle to strenuous activity, but if he could just help a little with one end of the canvas . . .

She was about to suggest that they cease struggling while she went to look for him, when they were suddenly joined by three young soldiers with the red cockade feathers of the artillery in their caps.

"Might we be of some assistance, ladies?" The tallest of the three smiled and bowed. "We must

225

shortly repair to the Grand Battery, but I believe we have time to lend you a hand."

A denial leaped to Faith's lips, but before she could voice it, Charity's silvery little laugh erupted. "Of course you can help us! Why, we would be ever so grateful, wouldn't we, Faith? Three strong, handsome gentlemen would make this move ever so much easier and more pleasant."

The three soldiers grinned, and Faith could feel her cheeks go hot with embarrassment. The glances of the young men betrayed their pleasure in discovering three young women obviously unprotected and ripe for masculine attention.

One of them, the shortest and least handsome of the trio who had a large, red wart on the end of his nose, shot Faith an appraising look, as if he might be considering purchasing her for a brood mare. "I say there, little violet-eyed lady, you just give those bundles to me. Why, I'd be right proud to carry them for you."

And probably to bed me, too, Faith thought with a burst of anger. The young man's expression could almost be called a leer.

"Thank you, gentlemen, but I really don't think we need your—"

"Why, whatever are you saying, Faith?" Charity's pink lips turned down in a pout. "You know we can't manage all this by ourselves. If I have to carry this nasty old tent much farther, why . . . why, I might faint!"

The tall soldier stepped nearer and took Charity's end of the canvas. "Now, we can't have *that,* can we, little lady?"

Practically swaggering, he gazed down into Charity's sparkling blue eyes, and she blushed and giggled until Faith wanted to throttle her. Hope, at least, had the good sense to hang on to her end of the folded tent as the third soldier tried to take it from her. She glared at the young man and snapped, "Sir, I'm neither so weak nor so desperate as my sister. I can carry this end myself."

"Red hair and a temper to match!" the soldier crowed. "This must be my lucky day."

Faith noticed that they were beginning to attract attention. Everywhere she looked, she saw men—and most of them were grinning and watching the spectacle with unconcealed interest. She was relieved when a cannon ball slammed into the other side of the traverse, causing all of them to jump and sending the spectators scurrying back to their tasks.

"Now, don't you be afraid," the wart-nosed soldier cautioned her. "Them redcoats can't aim worth a damn. And they sure as hell can't shoot anything over the top of the traverse. We're safe as long as we stay behind it."

"But won't you be exposed when you are on duty in the Grand Battery?" Hope asked curtly.

The soldier turned to her with a little click of his booted heels. "Yes, ma'am, I will, but that's my job, you see. We can't spare any horses or oxen to drag the cannon back into place after it recoils, and I'm one of the eight men who do that every time we fire off one of our own eighteen-pounders."

The three girls stared at him. Surely, Faith thought, they hadn't heard him correctly. Was he saying that men were more expendable than horses,

227

mules, or oxen?

"Yes, ma'am," the soldier chuckled on seeing her expression. "That's me—cannon fodder. And now, iffen you give us your bundles, we'll help you to get wherever you're goin'."

On that sober note, Faith could not say no. She nodded to Hope, who grudgingly gave up her end of the canvas, and the six of them proceeded down the length of the traverse to the sound of artillery fire punctuated by Charity's giggles. "My goodness, you boys are so courageous—and so strong. Why, I don't know how you can stand it, right out there in front of the fort, with the redcoats shooting right at you."

"And the Indians, too, ma'am. Don't forget the Indians."

"Oh, my goodness yes, the Indians!"

With every step, Faith grew more determined to curb her youngest sister's flirtatious nature before it got her into serious trouble. As they approached their camp, she breathed a sigh of relief. Now the soldiers would leave, and before Charity could begin another flirtation, she would take her aside and forbid her to engage in conversation with any more overly eager young men.

A tall buckskinned figure strode hurriedly toward them, and as Faith recognized him, her breathing stopped. A scowling Whip Martin came to a standstill in front of her, his scathing glance sweeping across the soldiers, her sisters, and herself.

"Well, Miss Cormorand . . . I'm glad you have finally gotten here."

Behind his sarcastic drawl, she sensed a frightening urgency; drawing closer, she searched his face for some hidden clue as to what was the matter now, on top of everything else that had gone wrong between them.

"Do you know where your uncle is?" Whip demanded.

It took a moment before she realized that he was asking a question to which he already knew the answer. "Where is he?" she gasped. "He—he didn't take a musketball, did he?"

Yesterday's tragedy rose freshly painful in her memory, followed by a surge of sharp anxiety. "Where is he, Whip? Tell me."

Whip bowed stiffly to the soldiers. "If you will excuse Miss Cormorand, I believe she has important business elsewhere—and it would seem that you gentlemen also have important business awaiting you."

This last he emphasized with a nod in the direction of the booming cannons before pushing his way through the middle of the group, thereby blazing a path for her to follow. Faith did not wait to see how the soldiers would react to such rudeness. Trusting to Nancy and Adrienne to look after her sisters, she hurried after him.

"Stay there!" she called back to her sisters. "Set up camp. I'll return as soon as possible."

Then, her heart pounding with fear, she began to run to keep up with Whip's long, angry strides.

Chapter Thirteen

"Can't you at least tell me what has happened or where we're going?" Faith pleaded. She caught up to Whip and grabbed his arm. "Please . . . my uncle isn't hurt, is he?"

"Not yet, but he will be soon enough." Whip stopped walking and glared down at her. "Is there to be no end to the trouble you have brought? Your sisters are spoiled, stubborn, and addlebrained. They haven't a lick of sense, and your uncle . . . well, he is worse than the two of them put together. You should never have allowed him to set foot in the wilderness."

Faith bristled at a truth she had sometimes suspected but did not like to hear from Whip. "That may be. But we are all here now, whether you like it or not. And I will do everything I can to keep them from causing any more trouble."

At her defiant half-agreement, Whip flashed her a look of surprise. Then he scowled again, his green eyes taking on the hue of gray-green thunder-

231

clouds. "And you, Miss Cormorand—who will keep *you* from causing trouble?"

His husky tone suggested that the trouble she had caused was far more intimate, personal, and devastating than anything caused by her sisters or her uncle. A lightning bolt of tension crackled between them.

"I am sorry," she said stiffly, not trusting her voice to remain steady. "I intend to keep out of your way from now on. You need not even see me."

"That will be difficult. Since I am camping right beside Nancy and Adrienne, and you chose to set up camp on the other side of them."

"Adrienne invited me to camp there! We have to look after Nancy."

"No, you don't. With Tom gone through the fault of your featherbrained sisters, I feel responsible, and I will see that she is taken care of. There is nothing you can do that Adrienne and I cannot do better."

He folded his arms confidently across his chest, as if to dare her to dispute what he had said, as if he could not imagine anyone defying him.

"Who do you think you are?" Faith hissed. "You can forget about all of us—Nancy, Adrienne, my sisters, my uncle, and me. We don't need you. We can look after ourselves. Why don't you just—go off somewhere and kill Indians? You aren't capable of doing anything else, least of all comforting a pregnant grieving woman!"

The green eyes burned with a dangerous light. "That is exactly what I am going to do, Miss Cormorand. And I thank you for reminding me of my responsibilities. I had gotten a bit soft—

232

bothering about *any* woman. Now that I see the error of my ways, I will set about immediately to change things, to take up my old habits and activities. I might even bring back a few bloody scalps—just to let you know I'm working hard."

"You—you are despicable. Twisted. Sick."

"Am I, Miss Cormorand? Then perhaps in a rare moment of compassion, you might condescend to say a prayer for me."

"You are beyond prayers!"

Whip gave her a stiff little bow. "Whatever you say, Miss Cormorand. But I would have thought that none of us are beyond prayers—not even you."

He turned on his heel and would have left her standing alone in the shadow of the Grand Traverse, except that she remembered what they had both forgotten in the heat of anger: Uncle Abel. Whip had still not told her where her uncle was or what was wrong.

"Whip . . . wait."

He turned back to her, and a flicker of hope or expectancy crossed his face, only to disappear as quickly as it had come. His scowl deepened, and she thought it must be permanently imprinted there by now, never to be erased. "Your uncle is over there." He pointed. "Waiting to get his fool head blown off."

Faith looked in the direction of Whip's accusing finger. Her rage drained out of her, to be replaced with a hard-edged panic. Not a hundred yards away, Uncle Abel stood atop the large mound of earth that covered the fort's main powder magazine. In one hand, he held a large wooden cross fashioned from

233

two saplings lashed together, and in the other, he held his psalmbook. His eyes were closed, and his lips were moving, but through the din of whining missiles, and the boom of the fort's cannon as it returned the British fire, she could not hear what he was saying.

Whip's stinging tones momentarily reclaimed her attention. "Since you don't need my help, I will leave you to get him down yourself—before General Harrison has him thrown in the guardhouse. The British have been trying to discover the location of the magazine all morning. If they do, and if they ever learn to aim properly, they will blow this whole fort to hell and back."

"Oh, my God! Hasn't anyone told Uncle Abel that?"

"Zealots and fools are indisposed to listen to mere reason. They have their own way of seeing things, as doubtless you already know."

She did know and was smitten with horror. "Uncle Abel!" she cried, gathering up her skirts and beginning to run toward her uncle.

The magazine stood behind the Grand Traverse and was covered with several layers of logs and a shield of earth. Several smaller breastworks had been erected around it. But even as she ran, Faith could see that the protection was not enough. If a cannonball or shell landed square on the roof of the magazine, it would either collapse or explode.

A detachment of soldiers was frantically digging and hauling more soil to the base of the magazine. Faith guessed that they intended to reinforce the barrier as soon as it was safe to crawl on top of the exposed roof. The roof was only a little lower than the top of the Grand Traverse—and Uncle Abel, who was not much taller than she, towered above that high protective ridge.

A young officer, looking worried, stood at the base of the magazine. He motioned to her uncle and entreated, "Come down, sir. You really must come down. Don't force me to come up after you."

Uncle Abel either did not hear him or was pointedly ignoring him. The young officer glanced skyward, as if expecting a shell to come screaming down at any moment. Another man, his fringed hunting jacket identifying him as a member of the militia, perched atop the Grand Traverse, and Faith wondered why *he* was allowed to expose himself to possible death or mutilation when it was so obviously wrong and dangerous for her uncle to do so.

"Look out near the meat house!" the militiaman cried.

Faith heard a whine and saw a missile come flying through the air. It veered off toward her right and smacked into the breastwork protecting the meat house, which stood nearby. A puff of smoke went up, accompanied by a frightful hiss.

"You guessed that 'un, right!" A sweating soldier called out to the militiaman.

A short, cocky fellow, the militiaman grinned from ear to ear. "I always guess 'em right! Why do you think I'm sittin' up here if it ain't t' warn you when t' duck? But that ole buzzard"—he pointed to Uncle Abel—"he's crazier than a black bear with a musketball stuck in his arse."

And now Faith could hear her uncle, his big voice rising and falling in a long-winded prayer. Caught up as he was in his prayer, Faith knew she stood little chance of gaining his attention, but she rushed to the side of the young officer and called, "Uncle Abel! Uncle Abel, look down here—it's me, Faith."

The young officer shot her a surprised glance. "Is that man really your uncle?"

She wondered what he expected her to reply: No, he was her aunt? She nodded her answer, then added in a sort of apology for her unspoken sarcasm. "He—he is probably not feeling well. The—the heat and noise, you know."

She herself felt suddenly faint. Her dress clung wetly to her perspiring body, and the musket and cannon fire, which she had almost ignored until this moment, began to vibrate in her very bones.

Uncle Abel did not open his eyes, and Faith knew she would have to climb on top of the magazine in order to make any impression on him. When her uncle prayed, he would often block out other sounds—anything that might intrude on his concentration. Uncle Abel prayed wholeheartedly, and Faith hoped that the Lord was listening and diverting cannonballs from him.

"Look out near blockhouse number four!" Atop the traverse, the little militiaman began hopping up and down excitedly.

The young officer grabbed Faith's arm as she hitched her skirts even higher and made ready to mount the steep incline of the mound. "Miss, you can't go up there, even if he is your uncle."

"But how else can I get him down? He doesn't hear

236

me—or you. Or if he does, he is determined to ignore us. I know my uncle; once he decides that something is right and proper, he can't be swayed . . . and he must think it's right and proper to protest this siege from the rooftop of the magazine."

"Begging your pardon, miss, but your uncle is plumb crazy . . . I was hopin' to avoid this, but if you can't talk him down from there, I'm gonna go up with two other soldiers and carry him down bodily."

Nervously, the young officer wet his lips. Faith noticed that he had straight brown hair peeking out from beneath his black shako, brown eyes, and a cleft in his chin. Charity would have found him handsome, but Faith found him weak. His lips were as soft and pink as a girl's. Occasionally, they twitched.

He looked too young, too frightened, to have such an important job as guarding the magazine, she thought. For a fleeting moment, she wished with all her heart that she had not driven Whip away with her sharp tongue. How much easier this task would be if she had his surly, taciturn strength behind her!

"I—I'll try again." She cupped her hands around her mouth and shouted as loud as she could. "Uncle Abel—please! They will put you in the guardhouse if you don't come down. You are endangering all of us. If the British guess where you are standing . . . Oh, please listen to me! You've got to come down at once. You don't realize what could happen!"

Uncle Abel opened his eyes and looked down at her. To her immense relief, he was bright-eyed and lucid; at least he did not appear to have gone mad.

"Faith, dear, stay back, please," he said calmly. "I know exactly what could happen, but I must take my chances, as we all must if this insanity continues."

A stooped but dignified figure in his black frock coat and tricorne, Uncle Abel hugged his psalmbook more tightly to his paunchy belly and clutched the wooden cross with whitened gnarled fingers. "When the British see this"—he raised the cross higher—"they will think twice about firing upon it. They are God-fearing men, after all, as are we Americans. And if both sides would only remember that, this siege could quickly be brought to an end."

"But it's so dangerous," Faith started to protest, only to be stopped short by her uncle's suddenly fierce expression as cannons boomed and thundered in the distance.

"Should we be slaughtering one another like base savages? Should we be endangering our immortal souls as well as our bodies?" He thumped the base of the cross on the earthen rooftop. "No, by God, we should not! And while I have breath in my lungs to protest this madness, I shall do so—in the most visible manner possible."

"Oh, Uncle Abel, you are right, of course, it *is* madness, but—"

"Bomb—to the quartermaster's! Look out, Quartermaster!" the little militiaman shouted behind her.

Uncle Abel flinched but otherwise ignored the missile whistling through the air toward the quartermaster's house. "O Lord, forgive us our iniquities. Spare us thy divine and righteous wrath. In your eyes, we are not British, Indian, or American. We are all thy sons and daughters, united before thee. When we die, we shall all be gathered together in thy kingdom, except for those who refuse to do thy will—those who sally forth bearing arms and armaments . . ."

This last coincided with the departure of several soldiers who suddenly came out of the magazine carrying canisters of grapeshot and barrels of gunpowder to be rushed to the batteries and blockhouses.

Uncle Abel frowned and cried out reprovingly, "Forgive them, Lord, for they know not what they do! And I say unto them, lay down your armaments. And we shall raise the flag of truce to our enemies. We shall invite them to sit down with us and discuss our differences in a peaceable manner."

"Look out by the magazine!" the militiaman bellowed.

On hearing that, Faith began to claw her way up the incline. "Uncle Abel, get down! The magazine is going to be hit. Get down!"

She did not know how she arrived at the top so quickly, but as she scrambled to her feet, a missile whined overhead, falling wide of the magazine and slamming harmlessly, with a hiss and a sputter, into one of the breastworks.

"Good-bye, if you will pass . . ." With a cocky grin, the militiaman saluted the aborted bomb, and Faith realized that he had known all along that it was not going to hit them.

"Why, you . . . you . . ." she sputtered, at the same time brushing off her dusty skirt.

"Sorry, miss, but I just wanted to see if your uncle was on as friendly terms with the Creator as he pretends to be or whether he might be scared into climbing down."

Faith turned to see what had become of Uncle Abel. He was still standing in the center of the mound, face pale as milk and raised to the sky, eyes tightly closed behind his spectacles, looking for all the world like a man about to become a martyr— reluctantly, but very, very bravely.

A lump came into her throat; never had she been so proud of him, but never had she been so afraid for him either.

"Brute! *Chien!* Dog!" A familiar French voice rang out. "You up there on the traverse—you should be ashamed. And you, Lieutenant, an officer, cowering on the ground while two civilians are exposed to danger."

Faith looked down and saw the petite, enraged figure of Adrienne Langlois. Hands on her hips, the little Frenchwoman was standing over the young officer who had instinctively followed his training and dived to cover. Frowning sheepishly, the officer got to his feet. Adrienne gave him a look of pure disgust, then turned her ire back to the cocky militiaman.

"You think you are so wise and brave, *monsieur,* with your ability to predict where the shells will hit. But how much braver is he who stands his ground, praying for our deliverance, while all around him the world explodes with evil and madness. The Reverend Cormorand is not mad, he is the only one among us who truly sees. *Mon Dieu!* The rest of us are all blind—as I was myself until a few moments ago."

Faith had never expected to see Adrienne so

animated. Her brown eyes glowed with an inner fire. Her ordinarily calm voice sounded almost strident. She shouldered the young officer out of the way and directed her attention to Uncle Abel.

"Monsieur Cormorand, come down at once so I can tell you how proud I am of you. Never have I seen such courage. You are the very flower of American manhood. No mere Frenchman could match you."

What her uncle thought of these outrageous compliments, Faith could not ascertain. He suddenly shook his head as if to clear it, and the hand that held the cross began to tremble. Groaning softly, he almost dropped the crude wooden symbol, and to Faith's intense concern, he did let go of his psalmbook, which plopped heavily to the ground without his even noticing it.

"Ah, Faith dear," he murmured sadly, "I'm not so strong as when I was younger . . . All at once, I do not feel so well . . . Everything is spinning."

Was it merely the tension of the moment, or was her uncle succumbing to another outbreak of illness? Faith rushed to his side. "Please, Uncle Abel, come down now. You aren't completely well yet. And you've made your point—really, you have. Here, you go first . . ."

Ignoring the fallen psalmbook in her anxiety to remove him from danger, she led him to the edge of the roof, but he was protesting even as he went. "First, the little Foster boy and then, this morning, a fine young infantryman . . . and as I was reading a Psalm over him, they brought in another and yet another—so tragic! We must do something to stop this carnage . . . It is our Christian duty to protest in whatever peaceable means is available to us."

Understanding better now what had driven her uncle to this desperate act, Faith was tempted to take his place on the roof. But when another missile whined overhead, she frantically urged him onward. "Hurry, Uncle Abel. There must be some other way . . . Adrienne? Can you take my uncle's hand as he comes down?"

"Oui, chérie. I am here, and I will help."

The young officer quickly positioned a makeshift ladder of sawed-off logs against the side of the magazine, but as Uncle Abel came to it, he stopped. "Faith, perhaps we should at least leave the cross up here so everyone can see it. It could serve as a reminder, a moral reproach to the hard-hearted . . . or perhaps, in a few moments, I will feel better and can remain here myself . . ."

Faith ducked as a barrage of missiles whined past them and exploded nearby.

"Look out by the meat house and quartermaster!" For the first time, the little militiaman looked as if he were in danger of losing his bravado. "Damn! They're gettin' close enough t' singe our beards, Reverend!"

"Uncle Abel, *please* . . ." Faith begged. In her own heart, she believed in what he was trying to do, but she could not allow him to delay a single moment longer. In truth, she did not think that anyone besides herself—and perhaps Adrienne—even understood his motives. If he were killed, his death would serve no purpose; he would simply be

242

mourned as a crazy old man who had taken one too many chances.

"Please," she repeated.

In answer to her plea, Adrienne's pale face and worried eyes suddenly appeared at the top step of the ladder. *"Monsieur,* you must come down at once. I—I am in desperate need of your wise counsel. You must tell me how best to comfort Jeffrey's mother. That is why I came in search of you. Poor Nancy is bereft. She is weeping and calling her son's name even now."

Faith knew that this was not true, but she was grateful to Adrienne for trying whatever ploy was necessary. And the ploy appeared to be working.

His brows wrinkled in concern, Uncle Abel threw one unsteady leg over the edge of the mound and handed down his cross. "Nancy? Nancy is weeping? Why, then I must go to her directly . . . Faith, get my psalmbook. I dropped it, I think."

Faith glanced back toward the fallen book. She did not want to take time to retrieve it, for it seemed that the barrage of missiles had suddenly increased. Thuds and muffled explosions sounded on every side, drowning out the voice of the little militiaman and the shouts of the soldiers who were hastily throwing dirt up onto the roof in a last panic-driven effort to provide more covering. Apparently having given up on Uncle Abel, even the young officer had joined the effort.

Faith glanced back and saw her uncle's body and then his head disappear as he unsteadily climbed down.

"Oui, mon cher," she heard Adrienne encourag-

ing. "One more step . . . Now here you are at the last one. Just so, steady now . . ."

Good, he was almost down, and knowing that her uncle was safe gave Faith the courage to go back for his treasured old psalmbook. Without it, he would be lost—and might even try to come back for it.

"Faith! Faith Cormorand, where are you going? Come down from there—you little idiot!"

The voice and the epithet sounded achingly familiar, but it couldn't be, she thought. Whip had not wanted to help her. He had been too angry.

Without bothering to see who it was, she sprinted to the center of the magazine roof and snatched up the fallen book.

"Oh, m' gawd, look out by the magazine!"

Something in the militiaman's tone made Faith realize that this time he wasn't joking. With book in hand, she straightened. Round, dark objects were hurtling around her, but her feet would not respond to the urgings of her brain: Run. *Run.* Jump off the roof. It might be your only chance.

"Faith—Faith, run!" A man shouted, and she knew with certainty that it *was* Whip. The top of the ladder shook as if someone were scrambling up it. Still, she could not run—or do anything but stand and stare.

A round dark object slammed into the ground at her feet. It was a large leaden ball with a long, sizzling stick protruding from it—and it lay within scant inches of her toes. Even as she watched in dumbstruck horror, the wick grew brighter. A small spark raced along it toward the casing.

This was it, then. This was how it felt to die. She

struggled to remember the words to a prayer—any prayer—but just then a man came hurtling over the edge of the magazine's roof. He landed atop the instrument of doom and rolled away from her onto his back. His strong, lean hands tore at the fuse and ripped it from its casing. Cursing, he threw it away from him.

The still smoldering wick hissed as it hit the dirt and sputtered out, and the man was left cradling the unexploded shell in his reddened palms.

"Whip . . . oh, dear Lord in heaven," she whispered, dropping to her knees in front of him.

For a brief, stunning moment, his eyes bored into hers. He had come back to help her after all. He did . . . he *must* care for her . . . love her . . . return her passion . . .

"Miss Cormorand, will you get the hell off this roof?" Whip leaped to his feet, hauled her up, and shoved her toward the ladder. "Go—get moving!"

"Whip . . . I . . . I . . ." She turned to him, tried to thank him, to throw her arms around him.

Anger leaped from his eyes. *"Now!"* he roared.

At that, she broke away from him, ran to the ladder, and descended as fast as she could.

No, it wasn't love or caring that he felt for her; it couldn't be. It was something else—a desire to prove to her how incompetent she was, how superior *he* was. It was the bitter, dark side of him that drove him to take risks no one else would ever take, to save lives when no one else could or would save them. It was everything that she despised and feared about him.

Yet—why *had* he come back? And what, for a

245

single moment, had she seen in his eyes? Dare she hope—or ought she only to despair?

Faith, Adrienne, and Uncle Abel walked back toward the bombproof in utter silence. Uncle Abel knew what had almost happened to Faith—indeed, what had almost happened to all of them, and he was now quite subdued and withdrawn. There seemed to be nothing for any of them to say.

Faith knew that her uncle had only done what he had thought he must; he had unthinkingly discounted the danger to others and to himself. No doubt he still discounted it, and she could only hope he would not try such a thing again. By now he must surely realize the futility of imposing peace on these men who seemed determined to fight, determined to die, determined to hurl bombs at one another until one side or the other surrendered or was destroyed.

The Americans had no choice but to defend the fort. The conflict was not their fault so much as it was the fault of the British and the Indians. And while she, too, deplored violence and its consequences, she always had differed from her uncle in that she believed in defending oneself, at least. For her, prayer and protest were not enough—though she would still draw the line at offensive measures and especially at the kind of revenge to which Whip Martin had committed himself.

Whip's vengefulness alone would have raised an inpenetrable wall between them; his love for his dead wife was only one more barrier that was impossible to breech.

246

No, she dared not allow herself to hope. She dared not open herself to any more pain than she had already experienced. Her feet were firmly set upon a path along which he could never, would never follow. Nor could she compromise herself by following him along his path.

A wrenching loneliness and despair settled over her, and she wished with all her being that she had never met Whip Martin.

Halfway back to the bombproof, two women settlers stopped them. "Adrienne," one of them said, "can we ask your advice?"

Adrienne graciously smiled and came to a halt. "Of course . . ."

But Uncle Abel interrupted before the women could even state their problem. "Ladies, please excuse me . . . Faith, Madame Langlois, come along when you can, but I must go quickly to Nancy. A minister's first duty, you know—to comfort the afflicted."

He started off in the peculiar rocking gait that served as his fast walk, and Faith let him go. She was afraid that she might meet Whip at the bombproofs, in which direction he had been heading after he vaulted off the roof of the magazine and left without a word. She had no desire to hurry.

Dispiritedly, she stood and listened as the women solicited Adrienne's opinion on how to handle the problem of rapidly diminishing wood for cookfires. Adrienne suggested that the settlers share a common meal over a single fire for the duration of the siege, and after several more minutes of conversation, the women went on their way again, apparently in agreement. No one mentioned the possibility that if the siege proved lengthy, there might not be enough wood to support even a single fire.

They continued walking toward the bombproofs, and Faith finally remembered her manners. "Adrienne, I want to thank you. If it hadn't been for you, my uncle might never have come down from the roof of the magazine."

Adrienne acknowledged that fact with a slight shrug. "It was nothing. Besides, I meant what I said, Faith. I only spoke the truth."

"You mean Nancy is *really* weeping? But I thought—"

"No, *chérie,* I meant about your uncle. He *is* a fine, brave man, and he does not seem to have a selfish bone in his entire body."

Adrienne's eyes took on a soft golden cast as she spoke about Uncle Abel. Faith was startled. Few people besides herself and her sisters truly appreciated her uncle's good qualities. More often, his eccentricities were the first things people noticed, along with his sometimes shabby appearance and his overzealousness in matters of religion.

But Adrienne's large brown eyes seemed to see past all that to the core of the man. And if she felt any conflict of emotions—affection and exasperation—such as occasionally plagued Faith, she gave no sign of it.

"My dear, you are fortunate to have his love. He would do anything for you and your sisters. Only a little while I have known him, but not so little that I cannot recognize how rare and precious a man he is."

Rare and precious. Faith had privately thought of her uncle in those terms, but she had never heard anyone of such short acquaintance voice that opinion. It made her wonder: While she had been so engrossed in her own problems, had she missed the blossoming of a relationship between her uncle and Adrienne? And was Adrienne's admiration reciprocated in kind?

The two women parted at Faith's section of the bombproof, and as she entered the trench, such questions were abruptly swept from her mind. Hope and Charity awaited her, dismay and agitation stamped on their pretty faces. Uncle Abel, she noted, was nearby reading Psalms to a patient, puzzled Nancy.

"Look!" Charity shrieked. "Just look what that awful Mr. Martin has done!"

Faith looked. Shadow looked back at her—and growled. The wolf was sprawled in the far corner of the shelter, and he did not look any happier to be there than she was to see him. Then she noticed the black iron links of a chain wound about the creature's neck and fastened to an iron peg in the ground.

Hope provided the explanation. "Mr. Martin said you would understand why Shadow could not go with him—something about it being too dangerous, and he didn't want Shadow in the way. He said he was going to do what you told him to do, and so you shouldn't mind watching Shadow . . . Oh, Faith, that animal hates us! What have you done?"

Faith felt the blood drain from her face. She was momentarily unable to speak, as the challenge she had so recently thrown at Whip came hurtling back to her with all the stunning force of an eighteen-pound cannonball: *"Why don't you just go off somewhere and kill Indians?"*

He had said he would go, and he had gone. No— first he had saved her life again, and *then* he had gone. Oh, why hadn't she had the sense to stop him, to realize what he would do?

Whip Martin had never yet lied to her. Insulted her, mocked her, ravaged her heart, and made fiercely passionate love to her, yes. But lied to her—never.

Oh, Faith, she asked herself bleakly. What indeed have you done?

Chapter Fourteen

The ominous silence combined with the stares of her sisters finally brought Faith to the realization that she could not continue to stand there berating herself, no matter how much she deserved it. Arranging her face in a serene expression that would have rivaled any of Adrienne Langlois's, she started toward Shadow. At her approach, the wolf raised his head and bared his teeth.

"That animal will die if he is left chained. It would be better to let him go," she said.

"But Mr. Martin said—" Charity began.

"I don't care what Mr. Martin said. I kept Shadow once before, and he would neither eat nor drink nor relieve himself until I let him out of the fort. So that's what I'm going to do now. And if his master doesn't like it, he needn't leave him here again."

Hope and Charity scrambled out of her way as Faith marched determinedly to the animal's side. Shadow sprang to his feet. Realizing that she intended to touch him, he snarled low in his throat,

251

and the gray fur along his massive shoulders stood on end.

Faith returned his amber-eyed gaze with one that she hoped was more intimidating than his. Why had Whip decided to chain him? The last time he had merely issued a firm command, *"Stay,"* and Shadow had stayed, even though his whole body betrayed his eagerness to follow his master.

"There now, Shadow. Be a good boy and I will have you free in no time. I won't hurt you," she crooned, kneeling down beside the wolf. "I'll just slip this nasty old chain over your head . . ."

The wolf's muzzle and sharp, gleaming teeth were only inches from her face. Faith could hear the sharp intake of breath from Hope and the little gasp from Charity as she reached around Shadow's neck with shaking fingers. The moment she touched the chain, Shadow snapped at her.

Warningly, his sharp teeth grazed her knuckles, and Faith realized that he could have taken off her entire hand, if he had chosen to do so. Cowering against the clay wall, she eyed the animal suspiciously. Shadow was just like his master—hostile, malevolent, arrogant, and too proud to accept anyone's help or affection.

"Stupid," she whispered under her breath. "You are as stupid as Whip."

Shadow's ears twitched at the sound of his master's name, but his low growl did not cease. He sounded as if he were issuing an ultimatum. Keep your distance or I'll bite.

Slowly, Faith reached for the chain again.

252

"Faith!" Hope's voice rang out. "It really isn't necessary to force an attack."

"It isn't?" Frostily, Faith eyed her sister over Shadow's raised hackles. "I told you he would refuse food and water while he's tied up like this. He won't even take it when he isn't chained. Besides, I thought you didn't want him here."

"I don't." Hope's level green gaze met hers with unblinking animosity. "But what Charity was trying to tell you is that Mr. Martin expects to be back before tomorrow morning. There's really no danger of the beast starving, and even if there were, he's too mean to die before then."

"He isn't mean." Faith leaped to the animal's defense. "He—he's just scared. He doesn't trust people."

And the same could be said about Whip, she thought with surprise. Was that why he growled when he should be tender and retreated into mockery when he should reach out to others and be kind?

Hope shrugged her slim shoulders. "The point is, you are risking an attack for nothing. Now that he's here—much as I dislike it why not just leave him until Mr. Martin returns?"

"Oh, no!" Charity squealed. "I refuse to share living quarters with a wolf! You have to get him out of here, Faith. I protested to Mr. Martin, but he simply ignored me."

"No, he didn't, sister dear." Hope's tone dripped sarcasm. "He told you to sit down and stop sniveling. Then he as much as suggested that we

253

owed him this favor—and he said he wouldn't have asked us to keep Shadow if it hadn't been an emergency."

An emergency. Faith jumped to her feet. Perhaps Whip had not gone to kill Indians after all. But he *had* gone to do something dangerous. Just stepping outside the fort was perilous. Her palms suddenly felt clammy, and she had to take a deep breath before she spoke.

"Mr. Martin is right," she said quietly. "We do owe him. Please try to show a little maturity, Charity. None of us likes living this way—in a hole, with a half-wild beast for company. But we can't always have things the way we would like them, and it's time you learned that."

Charity opened her mouth, then closed it again. Her blue eyes flashed rebellion, but she forbore to say anything further. Faith did not regret being so hard on the girl. It *was* time that Charity grew up. She could not continue to be a child in a woman's body—and that was what her selfishness was, a sort of childishness.

"If you have nothing else to do," Faith added, "why not pick the weevils out of the flour? I saw several the last time I opened the sack."

"Pick *weevils?*" Charity looked horrified.

"Oh, come on . . . I'll help you," Hope interjected. "God knows there isn't much else to do while the British are blasting away at us."

And there wasn't, Faith discovered to her own chagrin. The rest of the day passed with agonizing slowness. The only bright spot came when Captain

Daniel Cushing, a kindly young man with an engaging crooked smile, stopped by after the sparse and hasty evening meal shared by all the settlers.

The young officer could not stay long, he said, but he thought that Charity and her sisters would enjoy knowing how the defense of the fort was going.

"Only two killed and four wounded today," he declared proudly, clasping a mug of precious coffee brewed over the dying embers of the settlers' campfire. "And we took two hundred and forty shot and shells from the British batteries."

"How do you know that?" Hope asked bluntly. "Did you count them?"

"Indeed we did, Miss Hope. General Harrison has offered a gill of whisky for every musketball brought to the magazine or to the Grand Battery so that we can shoot it back from our own cannon."

"But, *monsieur* . . ." Adrienne raised her delicate eyebrows questioningly. "Do we have so little ammunition that we must resort to scavenging from the enemy?"

Seated on a sawed-off tree stump, Captain Cushing took a quick swallow of coffee, then leaned back against the wall of the trench. "Well, Madame Langlois, there's no point in pretending that we're better off than we are. Surely, you know how difficult it is to get supply boats down the Auglaize and the Maumee, past the Indians, while the British have only to snap their fingers and supplies pour in from Malden and Fort Detroit . . . It's a shame, but while the British control Lake Erie, that's the way it is."

255

"Back home, who would ever believe it?" Charity asked mournfully. "Who in Philadelphia or Erie could possibly understand what it is like out here in the wilderness under siege?"

Captain Cushing fixed a comforting glance on her. "Who indeed? That's why I'm keeping a journal, so that someday my kids and grandkids will know what it was like. Every day I write down what's happened—briefly, of course. I like to think that someone somewhere will enjoy reading it."

"A journal," Charity exclaimed. "What a grand idea! I guess you could complain all you wanted to your journal, and no one would ever scold you for it."

Faith suppressed a smile. She was about to suggest that Charity begin writing one when Adrienne Langlois did it for her. "I even have some parchment you may use," the Frenchwoman offered. "Wait a moment, and I will get it for you."

Adrienne got up to rummage through her things while the conversation turned to the subject of the wounded and how they were being cared for—inadequately, to be certain—in a makeshift hospital fashioned from canvas. Surgeon Smythe was doing the best he could, but by his own admission he lacked experience in treating wounds caused by flying chunks of metal and grapeshot.

Faith glanced at Nancy who was sitting quietly nearby. Would her friend blame Surgeon Smythe for not knowing how to save Jeffrey? But no, Nancy stirred and leaned forward. "Don't you say nothin' bad about Surgeon Smythe, Cap'n Cushing. He's a

256

right good man, he is."

Captain Cushing turned red. "He is indeed. I only meant—well, he wishes he could do better for our poor wounded."

Hope surprised Faith by saying, "Captain Cushing, would it be possible for a woman to help in the infirmary? I feel so useless and in the way. Besides, it doesn't seem fair that men should be the only ones to perform important and dangerous tasks while we women sit around doing so little."

In the corner, Uncle Abel stirred. "Why, Hope, you could come with me when I go there—and read Psalms," he suggested. He had been dozing, but at the prospect of training one of his nieces to do that in which even Faith had never shown any interest, his countenance brightened.

Hope shook her head. "I had rather do something practical, Uncle—something to keep my hands busy."

And your mind, too, Faith thought. Yes, that was exactly what her sister needed—some meaningful task to distract her from whatever was bothering her.

Captain Cushing grinned. "You sure would brighten up the place, Miss Hope. Some of the camp followers help out there, so I don't know why you couldn't too. We need all the nursing assistance we can get."

Envious of the attention being paid to her sister, Charity pouted prettily. "And what can I do, Captain? The sight of blood turns my stomach—but maybe there's some other task I could perform?"

Captain Cushing's eyes twinkled. "Why, I don't know, Miss Charity. You could stand on top of the traverse and call the British shots, I guess." And then, when he saw Charity look thoughtful, as if she were actually considering the matter, he blurted worriedly. "Now, I was just joking, of course. Why, we already have a fella who does that—a member of the militia."

Suspecting that her youngest sister might find such a dangerous activity appealing, Faith said: "Yes, Adrienne, Uncle Abel, and I saw him. It's a wonder he hasn't been killed by now."

Just then, Adrienne returned with a square blue packet of silk tied with a matching silk ribbon. It was an unusually rich object to see in the wilderness, and Faith's attention, as well as that of everyone else, was drawn to it. Adrienne handed the packet to Charity with a slight nod.

"There is some fine old parchment inside, *chérie,* and you are welcome to use as much as you like."

Charity pounced on the packet with a greedy squeal. "Oh, thank you, Adrienne!" She tore open the silk, reached inside, and withdrew a sheet of creamy paper. "Oooohhh! I will write very small, Adrienne, I promise you. This paper is too fine to waste. And I will first think very carefully about what I want to say so my words will not be wasted either."

Charity's childish pleasure in the gift made everyone smile, even Nancy who, Faith noticed, was having a difficult time maintaining a consistently pleasant interested expression. Occasionally, a spasm of sorrow would cross her friend's face or her eyes would water, and Faith would silently share the sharp pangs of grief over Jeffrey's death.

"That parchment came all the way from France, *chérie*," Adrienne said proudly. "It belonged to my family . . . but I have kept it safe long enough without finding a good use for it, so you might as well enjoy it."

"Oh, I *will!*" Charity bubbled, stroking the sheet almost reverently.

Impulsively, Faith gestured to the Frenchwoman to sit down. "Adrienne, tell us about your family—about where you came from and how you happened to come here to America. You said you would tell me one day."

"Oh, that is such a long story, *chérie* . . ."

But Nancy said, "Go on an' tell us, Adrienne. I'd like t' hear it myself. All I know is that your folks was royalty or somethin' like that."

"Royalty!" Charity exclaimed. "But that's so exciting—so intriguing! Oh, you must tell us now—please do!"

Even Hope and Uncle Abel looked interested, so there was no way for Adrienne to escape the task. The sounds of sporadic musketfire notwithstanding, she began her tale, and Faith herself soon lost interest in everything else—the gathering twilight, the presence of Shadow sprawled near her feet, the crowded conditions in the trench, and the rapt way everyone was watching and listening to Adrienne.

Adrienne Langlois's family had been members of the French aristocracy. Following the Revolution, they had all become fugitives from the guillotine. Adrienne had fled to America in the hope of joining

259

her widowed sister who, along with an infant daughter, had emigated several years earlier.

But a bout with smallpox had nearly killed Adrienne while en route to the new land. And when she finally regained her health and journeyed to Philadelphia, where her sister had married a tailor, she arrived in the midst of the yellow fever epidemic of 1793 and could not discover her sister's whereabouts.

Eventually, she met and married a French trader, Antoine Langlois, and journeyed west to Frenchtown. Antoine died soon after in a confrontation with hostile Indians, but Adrienne remained at the settlement to tutor the children there, as well as any passing friendly Indians who showed an interest in learning French or English.

She recited all of this in a carefully restrained manner, as if to gloss over the deeply emotional moments: Adrienne had seen one older brother and her father executed in the courtyard of her family's château; she herself had been hunted like some animal and had only just managed to escape with the help of a peasant family; she had been unable to find her sister after coming so far and enduring so much; and after finally finding happiness with her husband, Antoine, she had lost him to the savages.

"A long sad tale, n' est-ce pas?" Adrienne asked when she had finished. "But I was content for a few years—until the massacre at Frenchtown. I had my teaching and my work among the Indians, who are not all bad, despite what some say."

Uncle Abel sat bolt upright. "My dear lady, you are absolutely correct. Why, you are the only one I have met since our arrival here who has had the vision to see that!"

Startled, Faith noticed how her uncle's eyes glowed in the wavering light of the rush lamp. Nancy had lit it and hung it from a peg sometime during Adrienne's story, and the yellow light bathed his face in a radiance that made him look ten years younger.

"As God is my witness, Madame Langlois, you are an uncommon woman," he bellowed, and Faith was not surprised to see the serene Frenchwoman blush becomingly. Remembering their exchange earlier in the day, she smiled to herself; a relationship was certainly blossoming.

"A member of the aristocracy," Charity breathed, her blue eyes dreamy. "Oh, how I wish I could travel and see all the things that you have seen . . ."

Adrienne's laugh sounded like a small tinkling bell. "They were not all good things, I assure you, *ma petite*. And I promised myself when I got to Frenchtown that I would never again travel so far . . . I would make the wilderness my home, and that, I think, I have done, Indians and all."

Charity turned her eager young face to Adrienne. "But don't you wonder what happened to your family in France—to those who were left behind?"

Adrienne looked down at her lap. When she lifted her face again, her brown eyes glistened. She was on the verge of tears. "No, I never wanted to know. I brought that parchment with me so that I could write to them when it was safe. But somehow, I never did. I was always afraid of finding out that I was the only one who had escaped."

There were several moments of silence as every-

261

one digested this, and then Charity said, "I could never feel that way . . . Why, if there were any chance at all of finding out about *our* family—our mother and father and what happened to them— why, I would be writing letters, traveling about the countryside, doing whatever I could think of. It's terrible to know nothing about your heritage . . . When Hope and I were little, that's all we ever talked about—the mystery of who we are . . . Don't you ever wake up at night thinking about your relatives and missing them?"

Adrienne looked puzzled. "Of course I do, *chérie*. But what is it—*who* is it—that *you* are wondering about? At least you have your dear uncle, and he can surely tell you . . ."

"But Uncle Abel never wants to *talk* about—"

"Do not upset Madame Langlois with your foolish notions," Uncle Abel said gruffly, almost angrily. "Can you not see that she finds it painful to relive old memories? Sometimes it is best to leave the past behind. Let's hear no more about it. I would not have such a dear lady disturbed any further this evening."

The protectiveness in his tone made Adrienne blush again. Hope and Charity exchanged a look of surprise, as if wondering what was going on. Uncle Abel never reprimanded Charity; he left that task to Faith. And Adrienne—after all that she had been through, her blushes must have seemed startling and unusual, as they did to Faith—except that she had already guessed the reason for them.

Faith only wished she could guess the reason for her uncle's continued refusal to discuss the manner in which he had first become the guardian of her and her sisters.

Then Faith noticed that Charity's lower lip was trembling with chagrin at Uncle Abel's unaccustomed public reprimand. The pretty blond girl darted a sideways glance at Captain Cushing, but in a rare act of compassion, Hope rescued her sister from the awkward moment. "Well, this has all been very interesting, but I am exhausted. Now that the bombs have ceased falling, I should like to get some sleep."

Everyone listened for a moment and realized that the evening had indeed grown silent—and dark. Night had fallen and brought a merciful reprieve from the constant bombardment.

Captain Cushing stood and awkwardly made his apologies for having stayed so long and so late. Nancy smiled briefly at one and all and went quietly to her own section of the shelter. Then Adrienne rose and gently placed her hand on Uncle Abel's arm.

"*Monsieur* Cormorand, do not mind so much what others say about you and your desire to teach the savages. I applaud what you did today. To abolish violence sometimes requires drastic measures. In France, had there been more brave men like you who were unafraid to protest what they knew was wrong, there might have been fewer deaths, fewer innocent victims. You were very brave to do what you did . . ."

"And you, Madame Langlois. God has tested you in fire, but it has only made you more compassionate, given you greater vision."

The two stared at each other, and Faith came

close to laughing outright at the looks of amazement on the faces of both her sisters. Never in all their years of growing up together had they seen their uncle display the slightest personal interest in a woman. And of course they found it unthinkable that a cultured, refined, almost pretty woman like Adrienne Langlois could be interested in their uncle.

Yet the interest on both Adrienne's and Uncle Abel's faces was now plain for all to see. The petite Frenchwoman and the tall, stooped minister in his black frock coat might have been alone in the crowded area. They stood staring at each other, alternately blushing and smiling, apparently unaware of or uncaring that anyone might notice the currents of awareness and emotion passing between them.

It was a long time before everyone settled down for the night on the narrow, uncomfortable pallets. Faith lay down on a piece of canvas scarcely a foot away from Shadow, and sometime during the night, she awoke in a spasm of fear as a low growl sounded in her ear.

Somehow she had rolled over and was now back to back with the wolf—or back to front with him. She lay perfectly still next to his furry warmth and felt the rumble in his chest as he protested such threatening familiarity.

The chain clinked briefly, but it must have been stretched out as far as it could go, for the wolf's warmth did not retreat. Faith held her breath, expecting at any moment to feel the animal's sharp fangs sink into her back. Any sudden movement on her part might startle him into violence.

264

But as she lay there, planning a slow, inching departure, she felt something wet and cold touch the back of her neck. She fought the urge to twitch, to make any movement whatsoever. The wolf nuzzled and sniffed her hair, her neck, and her shoulder. He even poked his inquisitive nose beneath her chin. She feigned sleep and welcomed the timid exploration as a sign that Shadow was perhaps not so aloof and self-sufficient as he pretended to be.

He sniffed her thoroughly, then gave a long, low expulsion of breath—almost like a sigh. His body shifted, and she could feel him settling comfortably against her back.

Oh, Lord, she thought. I hope he doesn't have fleas or ticks.

The creature did smell however—a fur smell that was not altogether unpleasant. It reminded her of the furs on Whip Martin's sleeping platform. Had some of those pelts been wolf or fox? She recalled the incredible warmth and softness of that luxurious bed and chided herself for scorning a living animal when she had been more than willing to accept the comfort of dead ones.

Shadow's breathing soon became even and slow, and Faith began to relax. She was still rolled up in a cocoon of blankets, for—though the weather had been pleasantly warm—the bombproof trench had seemed cold and alien. Drowsiness began to overtake her, and the last thought she had was of Shadow's master. Where was Whip sleeping tonight? Was he safe? And did he know how much she missed him, how much she regretted her angry outburst?

Please be safe, she thought groggily. I won't even mind that you asked me to marry you only out of a sense of duty, or that you will never really love me—or at least never *admit* that you love me—if you just come back safely . . . safely. You must be safe . . .

At last she fell deeply asleep again, but this time she dreamed strange dreams in which, like Adrienne Langlois, she was pursued by angry people intent on doing her harm. She called out for her long dead mother, who could not hear her, and she knew a terrible uncertainty and confusion. Who *were* her people? Where had she come from and what had happened to her family?

Kindly and amiable, Uncle Abel's face floated above her, but when she asked him these important questions, he merely smiled and floated away, reluctant to answer her, as usual.

"Uncle Abel!" she cried. "What is it that you aren't telling us? What are you so afraid of?"

Frightened now, she ran *from* strangers *to* other strangers; nowhere in the crowd of bodies jostling her on every side did she see a single familiar face.

I am rootless, she thought in panic. I belong to no one, and no one claims me. Whip—oh, Whip, you *must* come back!

Whip sat in the hollow of an enormous sycamore and regretted having left Shadow behind. He could find no comfortable position in the huge cavity of the tree. Safety, yes, but no comfort. Shadow at least would have given him warmth and a soft furry body to lean against.

The wolf often served that function. As a small pup, he had slept beside Moon Daughter, often curled in her arms, and Whip had found it necessary to ease the wolf off the platform when he wanted his wife to himself. Now Shadow slept beneath the platform, except when he was lonely or when they were off in the woods together. Then the big wolf would curl up beside Whip and act as a pillow and blanket all in one.

But this time Whip had not wanted to expose Shadow to needless danger and so had left him behind. It was one thing to take Shadow along when he intended to strike once or twice and then return to camp, but it was quite another when he intended to strike over and over.

Whip shifted his cramped body and reflected that he might as well have brought Shadow; thus far this foray had been a complete waste of time.

Not that the woods didn't offer opportunities aplenty. The savages were everywhere— behind every tree, hiding in every clump of brush or stand of young willows beside the river. But the lust to kill them, to boldly sneak up behind them and sink his hatchet into their skulls or squeeze the living breath from them, seemed to have disappeared.

On three separate occasions, he had spotted a likely quarry—a lone warrior whose attention was focused on the fort in front of him rather than on the woods behind. But at the last moment, after carefully sneaking up on the man, Whip had felt powerless to launch his attack.

And yet, the boiling rage that drove him to these acts of violence still simmered in his guts, still twisted and ate at his insides until he felt that he *must* do something—anything—to overcome it. Now he would welcome the darkness that usually overcame him at such times; it had always blotted out his feelings and made killing a detached exercise, something he could do without a single twinge of conscience or feeling of remorse.

What had changed him? he wondered. Why did the darkness refuse to come? Before, he had been unable to stay it; now he could not summon it.

He felt oddly bereft and confused. Supporting his elbows on his drawn-up knees, he leaned his aching head on his hands and abandoned himself to self-pity, remorse, guilt, and all the other ugly feelings that he normally held at bay and refused to acknowledge.

Inside the cavity of this great dying tree—with its musty odor, its sly, scurrying creatures, its dampness and decay—he knew that he himself was similarly wounded. Something—lightning, perhaps—had split this giant of the forest, and now its very heart was slowly corroding under the combined force of rain, wind, ice, snow, and burrowing critters.

The sap still rose to nourish a few scattered branches—Whip had seen that when he had first found the tree at twilight—but the irrevocable process of death had begun. Another season or two, and spring would no longer cause new heart-shaped green leaves to erupt from those few scattered branches. The tree would stand, naked and beseeching, for yet another few seasons; and then one day, perhaps during another storm, it would come crashing down, dragging with it some of its fellows,

268

to lie full length on the forest floor.

Its destruction would be almost complete then, and the armies of ants and wood borers would move in to hasten the process. The other trees of the forest would close ranks around the fallen member, would shield and shadow and hide it. Ages would pass, and the only proof that it had ever been there would be the grove of sturdy young sycamores sprung from its tiny tufted seeds so many long years ago.

But what will I leave? Whip asked himself.

The seed of his loins had never had a chance to begin growing in Moon Daughter, and when she was murdered, he became like this giant tree, rent by a bolt of lightning and mortally wounded, with no chance of ever recovering.

But you *have* sown your seed in another, a little voice responded inside him. And the presence of Faith Cormorand was suddenly in the tree with him. He saw her before him as clearly as if she stood there in all the delicacy and beauty of her soft white flesh, glistening hair, and enormous violet eyes.

He yearned for her as he had never yearned for anyone—not even Moon Daughter, whom he had known in the fullness of his young manhood before he discovered hurt, need, and crushing loneliness.

But could he accept the solace Faith offered him? Like the tree, was he not already dying, incapable of prolonged growth, change, vigor? And would she ever believe that he truly loved her for herself, and not as a pale remembrance of the love he had lost?

When he had seen her atop the magazine, only a heartbeat away from death, something inside him had snapped. He had gone nearly mad with panic and fear—had not stopped to calculate the odds against being able to save her . . . and when she had tried to throw her arms around him and thank him, again he had almost come undone. His first impulse had been to strangle her for exposing herself to such danger, and his second impulse had been to flee, to run as far away from her as he could get . . .

He did not understand himself. He did not understand Faith or her uncle or her sisters. So often they all behaved foolishly, yet so often he saw a kind of logic and caring in even their most absurd actions. He was both drawn to them and repulsed by them . . . Especially, he was drawn to Faith.

He did not know how he could live without her— or with her, and he pondered his dilemma until the first light of day crept into the sheltered hollow of the sycamore. Then he stretched his tight, aching muscles and climbed out to discover a dreary gray world. It was raining softly and steadily. In the distance, from the direction of the fort and the British batteries across the river, cannons and muskets were already spewing venom. Their booming sounded like low rumbles of thunder.

Exhaustion made him close his eyes for a moment and sigh deeply. And when he opened them again, a man stood in front of him—a naked, painted, grinning man. He saw the upraised arm, the sharp edge of the tomahawk waiting to descend with murderous intent, the flare of the man's nostrils as he calculated the precise moment when he would strike.

And all his years of training—those endless hours of his boyhood when he had lived, hunted, fought, wrestled, and pitted his strength and cunning against Tecumseh and his brother, Tenskwatawa—flashed before him. He braced himself to deflect the blow and seize the advantage from his opponent.

Is this how it will end? he wondered. And then the moment of wondering passed, and the moment of fighting for his life was upon him.

Chapter Fifteen

It was May 2, the morning of the second day of the siege, and despite the rain, the aim of the British was improving. This information came from Jacob Brent, a gangly redhead who had met Charity at the well and, like a friendly pup, had followed her back to the trench.

Hope and Uncle Abel had already gone to the infirmary, and Faith was fighting a losing battle against the rivulets of water streaming into the shelter and turning the earthen floor into a muddy quagmire.

"I heard they was gonna restrict the settlers to their quarters until the siege is over," Jacob said. "Them redcoats is gittin' lots better. They nearly landed one atop the meat house this mornin', an' one of the blockhouses has been bad hit. I jus' hope they don't discover the whereabouts of the magazine."

Jacob had to stoop beneath the low canvas ceiling. He reminded Faith of a giant hunched bird she had once seen on the wharf in Philadelphia, only

273

this bird had a sprinkling of bright red freckles across his homely beak.

"Well, they better *not* order us to stay inside these trenches!" Charity exclaimed. "Just look at this mess. Where are we going to sleep? How are we going to eat? And look at my dress, will you? The rain has completely ruined it."

Jacob Brent looked and grinned, revealing a set of healthy teeth that would have done credit to a horse, Faith thought.

"Why, Miss Charity, I think you are the prettiest little gal I ever seed, mud or no mud, but if the general says you gotta stay in here, you better stay 'cause I sure wouldn't want nothin' bad t' happen t' you."

Jacob looked so earnest that Charity broke into a dazzling smile. The change of expression, from stormy to sunny, completely distracted Jacob from the devastation of her mud-splattered rose silk dress, bedraggled blond curls, and bare muddy feet. This morning, all three girls had abandoned their shoes, for there was no way to keep them clean and dry, or to stop their skirts from dragging in the mud.

"My goodness, Mr. Brent . . ." Charity tucked a damp curl behind one delicately fashioned ear and gazed up at the young woodsman with an expression Faith immediately recognized as her flirting look. "I certainly do appreciate your concern over my welfare. Not everyone around here cares so much. Indeed, I have been trying to persuade my sister to take in one of her dresses for me, since this is the only one I have in all the world, but she has yet to do so. And now, after my trip to the well, I am soaking wet

274

and sure to catch my death of cold."

Why, you spoiled little minx, Faith thought. She stopped what she was doing—rearranging their belongings to find the driest places—and pulled out the homespun dress she had been planning to alter for Charity as soon as she could find the time.

"Here." She threw the dress at her sister. "Take it in yourself if you are so wet and cold."

Charity caught the dress before it dropped into a puddle at her feet. Her blue eyes widened indignantly. "Well! You didn't have to throw it, Faith. Honestly!" She turned to Jacob Brent for sympathy. "Some people are so cross and churlish. You'd think, since we're all in this together, that we could at least try to be cheerful and uncomplaining."

Faith bit down so hard that she almost broke a tooth. The canvas ceiling and side walls—hung the previous night for privacy—suddenly became so confining that she could scarcely breathe. She had to get away somewhere, rain or no rain, or she would start shouting—and probably shock poor frecklyfaced Jacob Brent into apoplexy and Charity into tears.

"I'm going out," she mumbled. "Look after Shadow and Nancy, too, if she needs anything."

She draped a heavy shawl over her head and shoulders to ward off the rain drumming gently but steadily on the canvas.

Charity clutched the homespun dress to her bosom in exaggerated horror. "You're not leaving me alone with that wolf, are you? When is Mr. Martin coming to take him out of here?"

Shadow lifted his head from his muddy paws and

275

gave them a mournful, miserable look.

"I don't know, and I don't care. If the beast gives you any trouble, you will have to depend on Mr. Brent or Captain Cushing or some other unsuspecting male to rescue you."

Faith climbed out of the trench without a single backward glance and strode quickly away.

The rain felt cool and refreshing, a soothing balm to the hot anger coursing through her. Faith settled the shawl on her shoulders and allowed the gentle wetness to bathe her upturned face. She did not know why she was so upset; Charity was just being Charity—but she was not herself at all.

Where was the solid, responsible older sister who looked after everyone and expected nothing in return? Had she disappeared forever? Faith had no idea, and niggling doubts assailed her. This change of personality might not be temporary. Indeed, the way she felt now, it might go on until the Angel Gabriel blew his horn on the last day.

Aimlessly, not knowing where she was going but loath to return to the shelter, she stopped and watched the soldiers at the gates and the picket fence.

The entire back wall of the fort was lined with soldiers wearing black shako hats, which ordinarily looked jaunty and impressive, but today appeared oddly pitiful. The rain ran off the brims and spilled unnoticed down the sides of the soldiers' intent young faces. But at least they could see to fire their muskets, Faith thought.

Round after round of ammunition splattered the surrounding woods. On command from a nearby officer, the row of soldiers embarked on a procedure that consisted—as nearly as she could tell through the screen of smoke and rain—of thirteen steps to load, prime, cock, and fire.

Half the muskets misfired, the powder failing to ignite, and some fired after a short pause—as had Uncle Abel's when she accidentally shot Whip that night in the forest. The few militiamen interspersed among the soldiers seemed to be having more luck with their Kentucky long rifles. She remembered hearing that one could aim better with the rifles but could not load them quite so fast nor affix bayonets to the ends of them.

She wondered if the men were making any hits. While the British shots and shells being lobbed across the river rarely achieved the wide-scale devastation intended, the relentless attack on the fort from the woods had already caused much wounding and loss of life within the enclosure.

From all sides, the fort was under siege and—suddenly acutely aware of this—Faith experienced a moment of gut-clenching panic. Whip was out there somewhere, beyond the pall of gray-violet smoke. He had said he would be back before morning, but he hadn't yet returned.

She stood in the pelting rain and refused to believe what her instincts told her: Something had happened to him. He would never leave Shadow chained for so long. He would not say that he would return by a particular time, and then not return. His mission had been urgent and, no doubt, fraught with danger. Had his phenomenal luck run out at last?

She closed her eyes and uttered a silent prayer:

Dear God, don't let him be hurt. Don't let him be lying out there somewhere in the rain, suffering and dying all alone.

Such a wave of emotion swept over her that she swayed on her feet. Her knees felt wobbly, and her face felt hot. The rain ceased to cool and comfort her. I'm going to faint, she thought. I'm going to collapse right here in the mud.

"Faith . . . Faith!" Strong hands suddenly gripped her shoulders. She opened her eyes, but the face in front of her swam in a rainy mist. She saw a flash of green and a slant of familiar brows. The hands supporting her were familiar, too—strong, brown, and able to hold up the world.

No, it isn't him. I'm dreaming this, I want it so much that I think he has really come.

"Whip . . . I—I . . ."

Her feet slid out from under her, and a blackness reached up from the earth to swallow her into a dark hole. She felt as if she were falling into a bombproof that had no bottom. She could not resist the sinking sensation, and later, much later, she awoke to someone chafing her hands and muttering under his breath, "Come on, Faith . . . Come on, wake up."

Without opening her eyes, Faith tried to guess where she might be. There were no voices save Whip's. She knew she was inside some sort of structure or shelter, because the rain was drumming on the roof overhead. It sounded as if it was raining harder, but she was not wet. Nor was there even a whiff of the clammy spring breeze or acrid gun-smoke.

Instead, the air seemed blissfully dry, almost

278

stuffy, and she realized that she was lying on something dry and lumpy. The faintly musty odor tantalizing her nostrils smelled like—like old sacking or canvas. Flour bags. She was lying on flour bags, probably inside a store house. Some warm, damp thing—her shawl—had been flung across her, and then quite suddenly the shawl was removed.

Whip's fingers clutched the neckline of her dress. He grasped the fabric as if he meant to rip it down the front, and for a single, startled moment she considered allowing him to do so. But then her limbs found a life of their own. Opening her eyes, she grasped his hands and held them away from her breast. "What—what are you doing?"

A watery gray light bathed the inside of the storehouse, and she had no difficulty seeing the green eyes boring into hers. "Giving you some air," he drawled. "I tried everything else, getting you to a dry place, covering you, warming you—and it didn't work. I thought I would try the opposite, cooling you down."

Trying to make light of the situation, she muttered, "I suppose next you would have thrown me out into the rain."

She made to get up, but he held her down, leaning over her and pressing his hip against her side. "I might have, had it been necessary. But that's where you were when I found you. What came over you? Why were you standing there in a downpour with your eyes closed? Why weren't you in the trenches where you belong?"

His staccato questions irritated her. How could she explain that she had suddenly become so fearful for him and had been struck with such an awful foreboding that she had fainted? It made no sense to her; obviously, it would make none to him.

"Are you feeling better now?" he asked more gently. With one finger, he traced the line of her cheek. "Your color is returning."

"Yes," she admitted. And it did feel good to lie in someplace warm, dry, and dimly shadowed. The storehouse had no windows, and the door was closed against the rain, but light still seeped in through chinks in the logs and under the dripping eaves.

Wanting to assure herself that Whip was truly there, alive and vital beneath her fingertips, she reached for him with outstretched hands. Whip tensed when she touched his buckskin shirtfront, but did not draw away, and she could no longer conceal her anxiety over him. "Oh, Whip, I was so worried about you. I was so scared . . ."

"Hush . . . hush. I am not hurt." He gathered her into his arms so that she could cling to him and feel his body all along the length of hers.

They lay silently for several moments, arms entwined around each other; then Faith began to cry. Huge, hot tears rolled down her cheeks and into her hair, and he must have felt a similar outpouring of emotion, because suddenly he hugged her to him fiercely.

"Oh, Faith, Faith . . ."

To hear him whisper her name in such a ragged, desperate voice against her ear made Faith weep even harder. She buried her face in the hollow between his neck and shoulder and sobbed as if her heart were breaking. Her emotions felt rubbed and scraped raw, and only the balm of his whispered love could heal her.

"Why are you crying?" he demanded in a bewildered tone, the implication being, I'm here, holding you; what more do you want?

Oh, arrogant, insufferable male! Say . . . I love you, Faith. Prove to me that I mean as much to you—more to you—than Moon Daughter did.

He was silent a moment, clinging to her, and then, miraculously, she heard him say it in a shaking, awe-filled voice: "Oh, God, I love you, Faith . . . God in heaven, I love you . . ."

Then he began kissing away her tears, tilting her back on the flour sacks and leaning over her. Kisses rained down on her mouth, neck, forehead, and hair—wonderful, bruising kisses that could not have been meant for anyone but a live, willing, flesh-and-blood woman.

He paused only long enough to draw off his buckskin shirt and fling it aside. She relished the sight of his supple inviting muscles and the glow of passion in his brilliant green eyes.

Softly, she moaned her need for him. "Whip, I want you . . . Oh, I want you so much."

She began to remove her own clothing, and desire flared between them like a lightning bolt. It split the very air around them with a splendid, awesome fire. She set aside her dress in a daze, hardly aware that she did so. Impatiently, ravenously, his hands and his mouth sought her naked flesh.

The rain drummed harder, thunder and cannon boomed in the distance, but Faith heard these things as if in a dream. Reality was Whip Martin—his lean, hard body moving over hers, his tongue tracing circles of fire around her erect nipples.

His lips trailed flames from her breasts to the hollow of her throat. "Woman, I am going to make love to you as you have never even dreamed of being loved. I am going to love you everywhere . . . here . . ."

He kissed her lips and parted them with his tongue; she willingly granted him entry and gloried in his sweet plundering of her mouth.

"And then I will love you here . . ." He nuzzled her breasts, and with exquisite care, made love to them—touching, teasing, kissing, and sucking them into glowing, swelling mounds that threatened to burst with desire and gladness.

Then he moved lower still, to the juncture of her thighs, and his seeking mouth found a spot so sensitive that she gasped in fevered anguish. "Not there . . ."

He raised passion-glazed eyes to caress her with a long smoldering glance. "Most of all there . . . Trust me, Faith. Open yourself to me. I want you, need you."

Before the onslaught of his desire, the last barriers of her modesty fell away. She could hold nothing back from him, would give him anything he wanted or needed.

With deft fingers, lips, and tongue, he ravished her most secret intimate parts. Writhing in total abandon, she whispered a plea from the very depths of her being: "Whip, I want . . . I want . . ."

In desperation, she quickly changed position and

began to make love to him as he had been loving her. "Oh, God, Faith! Wait . . . stop," he moaned.

He rolled her over and mounted her, thrusting into her aching, quivering flesh, claiming her, plundering her, making her his own.

Again she sensed the wildness and violence in him. Only this time she responded with an answering wildness unknown to her before this moment. She felt herself flying apart, being torn asunder, shattering and breaking. Her fulfillment was the sweetest thing she had ever known.

He reached his peak with a muttered cry, and she became abruptly weak and drained, and vastly relieved. This time, he had called *her* name, not Moon Daughter's.

After a moment, she shifted her body to cradle him in her arms and discovered that he had fallen into a deep exhausted sleep. Tenderly, she cradled him against her breasts and allowed herself to doze, the drumming of the rain providing a security she might not otherwise have felt.

Sometime later, his roving hands and mouth awoke her to the building of another delicious surrender—and more sleeping and waking and lovemaking followed, until she lost track of where she was and what was happening and did not even know—or care—whether it was day or night.

"Whip . . ." Gently, Faith disentangled herself from Whip's body so that his rough, stubbly jaw no longer pressed against the tender flesh of her breast. "Whip, I don't hear the cannon anymore."

283

She roused herself enough to really listen and discovered that not only had the firing stopped but the rain had lessened to a lazy patter. The inside of the storehouse had grown dark, and she wondered if night had fallen—yet it did not seem possible that she and Whip had spent the entire day alternately sleeping and making love.

Whip tightened his hold around her waist and returned his jaw to her breast. "Don't be afraid. No one will come."

She smiled to herself. It was a little late to worry about someone coming. Only once had she even thought about it—and then Whip's kisses had driven the idea right out of her head. His kisses could make her forget anything. Indeed, if someone opened the door right this moment—a redcoat or a savage—to say that the fort had fallen and they were now prisoners of the enemy, she believed that she would simply smile and say, "All right. Just close the door and lock us in. I will be happy to stay here forever."

Such was her sense of wholeness and completeness. Nothing, *nothing* could destroy it—not now, not when she knew with certainty that Whip loved her.

Drowsily, she played with a lock of his hair and allowed her thoughts to rove freely, playfully. "Whip, why is the governor of Ohio called Return Jonathan Meigs?"

"What?" Whip murmured, still half asleep.

"The governor. You asked me once if I knew why, and I said I didn't know or wish to know . . . but I just now thought of it and wondered why."

Grunting, Whip raised himself up on one elbow

and peered at her in the semidarkness. *"Now* you want to know? Right now?"

She laughed. It was such a wondrous thing to be able to laugh with him, at him, at herself, and to feel that she could ask him anything she wanted, silly or not. She could say or do anything, and somehow she knew he would not mind—not really, as he had before.

"I just wondered, that's all . . . I don't know what made me think of it."

She saw the glint of his teeth and knew he was grinning. Her heart fluttered joyfully; they had so much to discover about each other, so much to learn. She wanted to spend the rest of her life getting to know this man, learning what made him laugh, what made him happy, or sad. She wanted to be able to read his expressions the way Uncle Abel read his psalmbook.

"Tell me," she whispered. "Tell me about Return Jonathan Meigs. I want to know about the man for whom they named this fort."

He told her, and it was such a simple, touching tale that tears sprang to her eyes. The mother of Return Jonathan Meigs had been a Quaker, but his father, Jonathan Meigs, had not been. The pretty Quaker girl had resisted Jonathan's attentions at first, sending him away each time he came seeking her favor. At last, Jonathan swore that he would never again return to face her endless objections.

He walked away from her, across the meadow to the fence he had to climb to court her in secret. But as Jonathan reached the fence, he turned for one last look at the girl he was losing. Their eyes met, and she beckoned him with her hand. "Return, Jonathan," she called, and so that he might always hear that sweet reprieve echoing across the meadow, they named their firstborn son Return Jonathan Meigs.

"Oh, what a wonderful story," Faith cried. "I can't tell you how much I like it!"

"You just did," Whip responded dryly. "And somehow I knew you would."

They lay still, caressing and holding each other, locked in their own tiny magical world, until at last Faith ventured another question: "Where did you go, Whip? You didn't really set out to kill Indians, did you?"

He stirred at her side, pulling slightly away from her. "The Indians are trying to kill us, you know."

"But that's different. With you, it's somehow—so personal."

"'Killing is always personal. If you think it isn't, you are only fooling yourself. Whether it's a cannonball taking off someone's head or a war club sunk in someone's back or shoulder, there's nothing grand or noble about it."

Whip rolled over and began tugging on his buckskins. His back was to her now, and she could not see his face. Gruffly, he continued, "I don't intend to stop killing Indians, Faith. You can't ask that of me. The first time I let down my guard, I'll be dead."

She reached for her dress, her hands atremble. "You know that is not what I mean."

He paused, glanced back at her over his shoulder, then turned and put his warm, strong hand on top of her suddenly cold one. "I know what you mean, but I can't make any promises, Faith. You will have to accept who I am and what I am." A frown spread across his dark features. "Maybe I'm not the right man for you, after all. I do what I do because I have to. I can't explain it, and I won't beg anyone's forgiveness. Let's just say, I have my reasons."

"Would she—would Moon Daughter have wanted you to spend your whole life seeking revenge for her death?"

Whip removed his hand from hers. "I don't know, and she isn't here to ask."

They finished dressing in silence, but before Whip opened the door, he took her in his arms once more. "Faith . . ." He tilted her chin and entwined his hands in her long, tangled hair. "I don't want to lose you—not now. I never thought . . ." His voice broke, and he could not go on.

But she knew what he was trying to say. He had thought he could never love again, never again feel alive and happy.

"I never thought I could feel this way either," she murmured.

But were feelings enough? What about shared values, shared hopes and dreams? What would their lives be like if Whip continued to put revenge ahead of everything else? Would he—every time he grew angry—run off into the woods to kill Indians?

She clung to the fringe of his shirt. "Whip, did you . . . kill someone today?"

"Yes," he answered. "And I might kill someone tomorrow and the next day and the next. I am not like your Uncle Abel, Faith. I am not a man of peace and prayer."

287

"I *know* that, but did you—?"

"Enjoy it? Yes . . . I won and he lost. I beat him at his own game. I am still alive, and he is dead."

Slowly, she relaxed her grip. "Oh, Whip . . ."

His eyes held hers for several moments, and finally he whispered, "Decide whether you can accept me the way I am, Faith, and let me know. Even if I were willing to try to change, I don't think I could."

"You don't even want to try?" she murmured incredulously.

Frowning unhappily, he stared at her, the glint of his eyes just discernible in the darkness. At last he said, "It's too late, Faith. I'm sorry . . . but I'm afraid it's too damn late."

Chapter Sixteen

"Where were you all day yesterday and half the night?" Hope asked accusingly.

She paused in the act of gathering up a wet blanket and gave Faith a resentful stare. "No, don't tell me; I can guess. You were somewhere with Mr. Martin, weren't you?"

"Shhhhh . . ." Faith nodded to Nancy's and Adriennc's sections of the shelter. Charity and Uncle Abel had gone to buy salt pork from the quartermaster, but she had not seen Nancy or Adrienne depart.

"They guessed that you were with him, too," Hope snapped. "And they think it's wonderful—but I don't. How *could* you sleep with a man like that—or with any man, for that matter? Don't you have any pride, any self-respect?"

Faith sat down on a barrel and wordlessly studied the auburn-haired girl in front of her. She and Whip had made no secret of returning in the dark and the rain to their closely situated living quarters. Everyone had been asleep, or discreetly pretending to be asleep, on pallets and bedrolls piled atop canvas-wrapped bundles to keep them out of the mud.

Only Uncle Abel had roused himself to ask, "Faith, dear, are you all right? Has anything happened?"

And when she had assured him that all was well, Uncle Abel had lain back down again, evidently so accustomed to her self-sufficiency that he thought no more about it. But green-eyed Hope, who saw to the heart of everything while she kept her own heart closely guarded, was ready to believe the very worst.

"Yes," Faith admitted. "I was with Whip Martin, but my self-respect is quite intact, thank you."

Hope grimaced as if she had been struck. She gave the wet blanket a nasty shake. "I don't see how it could be."

Ignoring her sister's hostility, Faith observed, "There's no use trying to dry that blanket until it stops raining."

It was indeed still raining—and the cannons and muskets were still booming, and Faith felt as if the gray depression of the morning had entered her very soul. With an effort, she forced her thoughts to her sister. Now was as good a time as any to deal with Hope's problem—the one that had soured her normally cheerful nature and made her seem old and cynical beyond her years.

"Why do you find the idea so distasteful—my spending time with an unattached male? I'm a woman, too, you know—not just your sister."

Oh, that didn't come out quite right, Faith thought. She certainly had not meant to imply that she found the duties of her station burdensome. But aren't they sometimes? a little voice asked.

Hope folded the blanket, placed it on the foot of a pallet, and seized another—this one also slightly damp. "I just don't understand what you see in him. Oh, he's handsome enough, yes, in a dark, stern kind of way—but he really isn't your sort, Faith. Not at all. I wouldn' trust him as far as I could throw him. He will only disappoint you in the end. Like most men, he isn't truly interested in what a woman could give him; all he cares about is war, scouting, whatever!"

The blanket suddenly fell from Hope's fingers, and she put her face in her hands. Her shoulders shook, and deep sobs issued forth—shocking Faith, who suddenly realized that Hope's problem was another *man,* some man like Whip who was caught up in this conflict and could not escape it. Maybe it was even Whip himself!

Faith leaped to her feet and hurried to Hope's side. She wrapped her arms about her sister's heaving shoulders. "What is it, Hope? Can't you tell me what's bothering you?"

"It's nothing!" Hope insisted. "I just don't want you to make the same mistake I did—falling in love with some stupid man who hasn't the sense to—to come in out of the rain!"

"*Who* doesn't have enough sense to come in out of the rain?"

"A-Alex . . . C-Cummings." Hope choked on the name.

So relieved that her sister hadn't said Whip Martin, Faith could not at first place the name.

"Alex Cummings?"

"The—the sea captain who brought us here."

"Oh, *that* Alex Cummings." Faith did recall now the name of the *Sea Sprite*'s captain. "But he didn't—why, he didn't take advantage of you, did he?"

Her protective instincts leaped to the forefront. Why, she would jump in the lake and swim after the man to bring him to account if he had dared lay a finger on her sister!

"No!" Hope sobbed. "He never touched me. He never so much as *looked* at me in that way—the way Mr. Martin looks at you. All he ever did was shout at me and scold me and tell me he hoped he never saw me or Charity again."

"Oh, Hope, dear . . ." Faith hugged her sister, encouraging her to vent her sorrow by sobbing on a sympathetic shoulder. "You should have told me at once why you were so unhappy."

"How could I?" Hope wept. "I was going to at first, but then I saw how you were all cow-eyed over Mr. Martin, and I was jealous because he was coweyed over you, too, and I couldn't say anything."

"You saw all that?" Faith had not realized that her and Whip's attraction for each other had been so apparent, but then she recalled the way Adrienne and Uncle Abel had been looking at each other lately. Perhaps those two had not yet admitted to themselves either what everyone else already knew.

"Of course, I saw it. So did Adrienne, Nancy, Charity, and Uncle Abel."

Astounded now, Faith gasped. "Uncle Abel saw it, too?"

"Yes, and he thinks Whip Martin is just the man for you—someone strong who can keep you in line when you get too bossy. He said it's high time you started thinking of your own needs and not just his or ours, or else you might wind up a bitter old maid, a spinster . . ."

"A bitter old maid!" Stunned by these revelations, Faith leaned back to view Hope's tear-stained face. "Is that what *all* of you think of me—that I'm just a bitter old maid?"

"Well, no . . ." Hope hesitated, then plunged onward. "But you were certainly headed in that direction before you met Mr. Martin . . . Oh, Faith, will *any* man ever look at me the way he looks at you?"

Tears sprang anew to Hope's eyes, and Faith could only pat her sister's back and shoulders, comforting her as best she could. Once again she must put her own feelings aside in order to comfort someone else—another sacrifice, she thought ruefully, the likes of which had apparently gone unappreciated in the past.

"Of course, some man will notice you someday. You have only to be patient, my dear little Hope."

"But I don't want any man but Alex Cummings," Hope murmured fervently.

Faith did not know what to say to that; in this, she and Hope were alike. Neither could flit from one infatuation to another as Charity so obviously could.

"Someone else will come along," she soothed, sounding unconvincing even to her own ears. "Why, you hardly got to know him that little time you were on board his ship."

"And you?" The accusing tone was back in Hope's tear-laden voice. "Did it take very long for you to know how you felt about Mr. Martin?"

"No," Faith conceded. She wrapped her arms more tightly about her sister. "No, I guess it didn't."

Suddenly, the truth became glaringly clear to Faith: If she could not have Whip, she would not want anyone else either. No other man could command her total surrender with so little as an inviting glance from his compelling green eyes. And now that Whip had awakened her sleeping passions, no other man could bring her to shuddering sweet rapture.

But how could she share her bed and her life with a man committed to violence and revenge? It would go against everything she believed in, everything she had been taught. *Love thine enemies*—yes! That was the right way to live, the ideal to strive for, come what may.

It wasn't always possible to do good unto those who hated you; it wasn't always easy to see the way—but she could not turn from the path she had been walking since Uncle Abel had opened his door to her and showed her what love and unselfishness were all about.

"But why are *you* crying, Faith?" Hope asked in a shocked voice, and Faith realized that indeed tears *were* running down her cheeks.

"I'll never see Alex Cummings again," her sister continued. "But you will probably see Mr. Martin tonight, when he comes back."

"I'm crying, Hope, because I don't think either of

294

us will ever have what we want."

Hope stepped back, brushed away her tears, and looked at her questioningly. But Faith could not explain just then. Her misery was too great. Like the gray, mournful heavens above, all she could do was weep.

"Whip, could I see you a minute?" Peter Navarre stooped down and peered into Whip's shelter. His clear gray-blue eyes squinted, but there wasn't much to see—only Shadow sprawled at Whip's feet, Whip's belongings lined up neatly, and the narrow shelf of furs and blankets that now took the place of his sleeping platform.

The bombproof trench was nowhere near as comfortable as his tepee had been, but Whip had done his best to make his new quarters dry and efficient. He could not understand why the settlers, soldiers, and militiamen spent so much time complaining. Anything was better than the hollow tree or the fallen log or the damp, hard ground where he had often been forced to spend so many of his nights.

"Sure, Pete," he responded. "Climb down, but watch your step. The ground's slippery, and it's getting dark."

It *was* getting dark, he noticed, and the deserted campsites alongside his looked particularly dark and forbidding. Everyone had gathered at a bombproof area farther down the traverse to learn the latest news—news that Whip had already heard.

The third day of the siege had ended—and not

without considerable damage. Today four men had been killed and seven wounded, a number of horses had been lost, and the enemy had mounted a battery on the same side of the river as the fort. The battery was on the left, with artillery stuck in the edge of a small ravine, but thus far the British handling of the howitzer had not been particularly adroit.

They had done better the day before; having discovered the location of the magazine, the redcoats across the river had succeeded in battering the magazine's roof. The Americans had made some repairs, but even General Harrison, cautiously optimistic as always, feared that irreparable damage would be done if the British moved their guns any closer.

Whip had been sitting in the growing darkness thinking about yesterday's damage and today's developments when Peter Navarre interrupted him. He had been remembering what he and Faith were doing at the very moment when the British were hammering away at the magazine's rooftop. And with a quickening of his heartbeat, he thought of it even as he watched Peter agilely climb down into the trench and extend a hand in friendly greeting.

The man had an uncanny knack for appearing when Whip least expected him—and least desired to see him.

"Evenin', Whip . . . You've done right well settin' up your quarters. You ought to give me lessons. Mine is a damn-sight sorrier lookin' than yours."

"Shawnee lessons die hard," Whip muttered. "I like things neat and in place."

He shook hands with Peter but did not ask him to

296

sit down. He had not encouraged visitors in the tepee and had not planned for any in the trenches. If he wanted company, he could always go next door to Nancy's and Adrienne's—but he didn't want any just now. He had too much to think about: Faith Cormorand's lovely silken flesh and her determination to change him into some kind of peace-loving dandy.

Why couldn't she understand that out here in the wilderness one had to dispense justice—seek revenge, she called it—oneself, or there wouldn't be any justice at all? Unless they were wiped out first, the damn savages would wipe out everyone. Hadn't he learned that bitter lesson at a cost he had scarcely been able to bear paying? What would it take for her to learn it? More stupid senseless deaths—perhaps even his own?

While he was asking himself these questions, he noticed that Peter Navarre showed little hesitation in making himself right at home. The leathery-faced scout promptly sat down where Whip had been sitting, then leaned back and looked about as if he contemplated buying the place.

"What do you want, Pete?" Whip recalled that Peter always wanted something when he came visiting.

"Don't want nothin'. I've just been thinkin'—studyin' on our problem here."

Whip waited. Peter's "studyin'" likely meant he had hit on something—something involving Whip himself.

"We're three days into this siege," Peter began. "And despite Harrison's gatherin' up of every unexploded British ball and shell, we're runnin' mighty low on ammunition. Half of our men are sick, and the other half are exhausted from standin' duty night an' day in place of those who are sick. We've got food and water to last us, but firewood is gittin' scarce—and you can bet the British would be right happy if we ventured outside the fort to cut some more. From the vantage point of their new battery, they could cut us down right smartly."

"I know all that, so what's your point?" Whip sat down beside Peter and dropped his hand on Shadow's head. Having been ignored lately and still smarting from the ignominy of those long hours on the chain, the wolf at first refused to take notice—but then, with a sound almost like a sigh of forgiveness, he nuzzled Whip's fingers.

"My point is this." Peter was watching him closely. "I think we need to do something more drastic than sittin' here like a bunch of holed-up rabbits."

Whip tugged playfully at Shadow's muzzle, encouraging his rough swiping tongue. "You have a plan, I take it."

"Not yet, but I figured you an' me together might come up with somethin'. After all, there ain't nobody knows the savages or these parts around here like you an' me."

Shadow grabbed Whip's hand between his powerful jaws and held it, but Whip did not continue the play. Instead, he allowed his hand to go limp. "Pete, it isn't our job to come up with something—it's General Harrison's. He's a capable enough soldier, and he's gone up against Tecumseh before and won.

Why not just keep out of it and let him do his job?"

Peter shot him a sideways glance. "Hunh . . . that don't sound like you, Whip. Are you goin' soft all of a sudden? I would have thought you'd be itchin' t' see what kind of mischief we might cause Proctor an' Tecumseh."

Whip considered this. Ordinarily he would have welcomed an opportunity to do what Peter was suggesting—seize the offensive. But while he could never be the peacemaker Faith so obviously wanted, suddenly he did not want to be in the forefront of planning mischief and mayhem either.

Damn women, he thought. Their unreasonable demands and opinions could change a man almost without his noticing.

"I'm not going soft. You more than anyone should know I have reason not to. It's just that I think we can withstand this siege in fairly good shape if we don't get nervous and do something stupid. Harrison has done a remarkable job on this fortification. We're damn near impregnable. All we have to do is keep the magazine from being blown up—and hold out until Proctor gives up or help arrives, whichever comes first."

Peter shook his head. "Well, I never did think I would see the day when Whip Martin would counsel patience—not an old fire-eatin' forest fighter like you."

"Like me?" Whip glanced at Peter surreptitiously, wondering what he meant. Even Peter did not know of his silent forays in search of backwoods justice. At least, Whip didn't *think* he knew of them.

"Oh, come on now, friend. This is ole Pete you

are talkin' to. I've found the bodies of dead Injuns scattered along your trail . . . You go out an' you come in. An' you never say where you've been. Now, most men brag about bringin' down a savage, if they're cunning enough an' fast enough to get away with their scalps still tight on their heads. But you don't brag—an' most people don't know. Except your old friend, Pete Navarre."

Whip stood up. The toe of his moccasin caught the tip of Shadow's paw, and the wolf hurriedly moved out of his way. "You know why I do what I do, Pete. But don't think, because you know, that you've got the right to nose into my business."

Peter's clear-eyed gaze impaled him. "I didn't come here t' nose around, Whip. I come t' ask your help. If you don't want t' give it, for whatever reason, just say so, and I'll be gone."

Whip could not think of a valid reason. Indeed, his instinct that Faith would not approve was reason enough for him to go ahead. But something still held him back. He could not put his finger on exactly what it was. He knew only that he was suddenly almighty weary of risking his neck every other day, and not knowing, when he stole out of the fort and into the woods, whether or not he would ever return. Before, he had not cared. Now, he realized with a jolt of surprise, he cared very much indeed.

Was Faith Cormorand the reason he had become so cautious and protective of his own life? When had that happened? A little hope is bad for a man, he mused. It makes him rearrange all his priorities.

He looked at Peter Navarre. The scout was watching him with a glint of compassion and understanding in his crinkly gray-blue eyes, as if he had guessed what was bothering him.

"No, Pete," he said firmly. "I'm not in the mood for hatching daring plans tonight . . . but if you and the general come up with something good, something that will decide this conflict once and for all, let me know. I doubt I could say no to that."

Peter smiled a wry, knowing grin. "Fair enough, Whip. Fair enough. And if you don't mind my saying so, that little Miss Cormorand would be mighty proud of you."

Damn you, Pete, Whip thought admiringly. Is there anything you don't know about?

Tightly gripping his large handmade cross, Abel stood in front of the powder magazine. It was the fourth day of the siege and still rainy—damp, cold, and gray. But he noticed that, somehow, despite the weather and the improving aim of the British, the magazine had been reinforced. Occasionally, a cannonball whistled overhead and thumped into the roof of the structure. Mud and dirt splattered everywhere, but the extra layers of earth, animal hides, and beams held steady.

The only other indication of a hit came from the yelping of the Indians outside the fort. Lately, whenever they perceived that a cannonball or shell had struck something, the painted creatures had taken to making the most hideous approving noises. Didn't they know, he wondered, that the Americans would only retrieve the wasted ammunition and throw it back across the river—or perhaps into the woods at *them?*

Abel had not visited the magazine since that first morning of the siege when his protest had failed to bring an end to this madness and instead had almost gotten Faith killed. Guilt and chagrin had kept him away; but at the moment, no one knew where he was or what he was planning.

He had tried to assuage his sense of outrage at the continued bombing by ministering to the wounded and praying over the new graves of the dead. But a lot of good that was doing. Each day, the numbers of wounded and dying rose. And now the men were coming down with mumps, measles, and fever from living in the wet muddy trenches and from getting little sleep and no fresh food.

How much longer could the siege go on? And why would no one except Faith and Adrienne Langlois listen to him when he tried to tell them that fighting and killing would not solve anything?

He thought of the little Frenchwoman's warm brown eyes and her small, erect, aristocratic figure, and his insides did a queer sort of hop, skip, and jump. Surely, Adrienne embodied every virtue known to the human species—courage, patience, gentleness, and a quiet, awesome strength.

She made him feel young and vigorous, stirred him in ways he had thought were beyond him. At his age, fifty-one, he had thought himself too old for such foolishness and, in fact, had never missed it. His ministry had always provided enough joy and excitement to satisfy his modest needs—and he had his three nieces for companionship.

Oh, once in a while, he experienced a pang of

wrenching loneliness, but it was never anything serious. Always an older-looking man, slightly stooped and paunchy, with pewter-colored hair even in his thirties, he had never attracted women. Not like Benjamin Franklin, his lookalike, whom everyone said was a favorite among the ladies.

His religious fervor had always intimidated or frightened women. Certainly he had never expected to discover himself so totally attuned to one—or so thoroughly captivated—as he now discovered himself to be with Adrienne Langlois.

Oh, Lord, he wondered, was he really worthy of her? He could not yet bring himself to make any sort of declaration, but his dreams—oh, Lord! In his dreams he and Adrienne would marry and go to Frenchtown. Adrienne would teach English and French to the Indians, as she had been doing, and he would teach them religion. Together, sharing and caring, they would face the challenges of growing old, and in the process they would convert the heathen and found a new civilization—one in which red men and white could live peaceably side by side without this endless hostility.

Surely, this was why the Lord had kept him single all these years and had brought him so far from home.

But first, this siege must end and peace efforts must be mounted—the sooner the better. He simply could not bear for any more young men to die. Where would Hope and Charity find husbands if all the young men were killed off one by one?

More and more, it looked as if Faith was going to be taken care of—if Abel was any judge of human emotions. And he thought he was. His dear, sweet Faith had found a strong man who needed her in some inexplicable way—not yet understood, he conceded, but clearly recognized. Whip Martin—a tough, unyielding, hard, angry man—would not be too tough for his Faith. His eldest niece was as tough as iron nails herself. In time, she would bring the man around; then Abel need only worry about the two younger girls.

Sighing, Abel contemplated the magazine. Now that the structure was so well fortified, what harm would it do to erect a cross on top of it? Indeed, despite what anyone else might think, he felt certain that the sacred symbol would serve as a deterrent rather than an invitation to bomb the magazine. The British obviously already knew where it was located; a cross should make them ashamed to keep battering away at it.

This time he would simply climb the magazine, erect the cross, and climb back down again before anyone could become upset or alert Faith. There were only two risks: He might be thrown in the guardhouse for doing it, or he might get hit. Then, too, everyone would think him mad. But not Adrienne, his heart told him. She would understand. Grand crises demanded grand gestures, and he was not as afraid now as he had been the first time. Death was utterly capricious—but if the Lord intended for him to marry, to perform grand deeds, to touch the hard hearts of men, then he need have no fear of death.

He need fear only his own weakness.

"You ain't thinkin' of climbin' up on that roof

again, are you, old man?"

It was, Abel saw, the cocky little militiaman with the uncanny knack for correctly calling the British shots.

"I am," Abel stoutly replied. But he cast a furtive glance around for an officer in charge of the magazine and was half disappointed when he did not see him. "I notice that you are still atop the Grand Traverse taking risks yourself."

"I gotta reason t' be up here courtin' death. But you—you're jus' plain addlebrained."

"My good man, I, too, have an *excellent* reason for my actions," Abel asserted. "And as for death, we know not the minute nor the hour."

"The minute nor the hour of *what?*"

"When we shall be called to meet our Maker, of course. It's plain to me, sir, that you could use some instruction from the Good Book."

"Hmmmph!" the militiaman snorted.

"I shall pray for you," Uncle Abel said without rancor.

The exchange having stiffened his wavering resolve, he walked to the base of the magazine and began the arduous climb.

Chapter Seventeen

"*Chérie,* why didn't you tell us sooner? When did the pains begin?" Adrienne leaned over Nancy and gently placed the palm of her hand on her friend's distended belly.

Nancy gasped, closed her eyes, and gripped the edge of the barrel on which she was sitting. Faith saw that her friend's knuckles were white and a rim of white encircled her mouth. Perspiration glistened on her upper lip. The pain was so bad she was gritting her teeth.

Commiserating, Faith gritted her own teeth. She knew that childbirth was painful, but she had never expected anything as bad as this. Or anything as sudden. Only a few moments before, Nancy had been talking and smiling her sad brave smile. The three of them—Nancy, Adrienne, and herself—had been discussing the appalling weather and its effect on life in the bombproofs, where conditions were rapidly becoming intolerable.

But Nancy had said, "Oh, this ain't so bad . . .

really, it ain't. Our first winter in the wilderness was worse. It snowed before Tom finished puttin' up the cabin. We woke up one mornin' t' find ourselves covered from head t' foot in snow."

Then, without any warning, Nancy had gotten a strange look on her face, as if she were listening to something that Faith and Adrienne could not hear. She staggered to the barrel and sat down clutching her abdomen.

"What is it?" Faith had cried. "Nancy, what's wrong?"

Adrienne had responded, "The child is coming."

Now Nancy's grip on the edge of the barrel relaxed. She breathed a heavy sigh and smiled again, a rather wan, embarrassed smile. "It's nothin', I tell you . . . nothin'. The pains started durin' the night. But they ain't too bad yet. Why, I could go on like this all day before the baby comes."

Faith shuddered. She had always wondered what it would be like to bear a child, and now she was certain that she didn't want to find out. She would not want to give birth in a drafty trench where the mud on the floor was now ankle deep—and where there was always the possibility that more mud would splash inside, hitting one in the face, whenever a cannonball landed too close.

"What—shall we do?" Faith could scarcely keep the tremor out of her voice.

"Why, we shall make ready for the birth!" Adrienne responded in a hearty tone. "I only wish you had told us sooner, *chérie,* so we could have begun our preparations at once."

Nancy made as if to get up from the barrel and

help. "Birthin' ain't no cause for fuss an' bother. I had no one but Tom t' help me the first time, an' now I got both of you an' a surgeon, too, if I need one."

Adrienne placed her hands squarely on Nancy's shoulders to restrain her from rising. "You sit right there, Nancy. Faith and I can do whatever's necessary."

Faith and Adrienne exchanged a look of mutual relief over Nancy's head. Surgeon Smythe. He would know what to do. Neither of them had ever delivered a baby before, and they had once discussed how fortunate they were to have Surgeon Smythe available. When the time came, they would help, of course, but Surgeon Smythe would direct them. Well, the time had finally come—but wasn't the baby just a trifle early? Faith wondered.

Nancy had told them only yesterday that she expected the child to arrive no sooner than another week or two at least. By then the siege would surely be over, and Tom might even be on his way to the fort. She had said this with a flare of hope in her warm hazel eyes, and Faith had dearly hoped that it might be so.

"I'll go to the infirmary," she said softly to Adrienne. "Hope and Charity went there this morning."

As usual, Hope had gone to assist in the nursing, an occupation which appeared to be providing a great deal of consolation for her broken heart. Charity had gone because Hope had bullied her into it.

"You can't just sit around flirting while men are dying for a drink of water, Charity," Hope had said.

309

"The infirmary is severely understaffed."

"But I can't stand the sight of blood!" Charity had wailed.

"Then close your eyes, you selfish ninny!"

So the two of them had gone off into the gray morning, and Uncle Abel had left shortly thereafter —no doubt, headed for the same place.

Faith wrapped her damp shawl around her shoulders. "I'll be back soon!" she announced with the same false cheeriness Adrienne had adopted.

"Do hurry, *chérie,*" Adrienne urged. She rolled her expressive brown eyes in Nancy's direction. Nancy wore that same strange listening look. It was almost eerie, Faith thought, and wasting no more time, she clambered out of the shelter.

One could not exactly say it was raining, but the air was so heavy and full of moisture that Faith was soaked and breathless even before the infirmary tent came into view. The tent was a large one, like General Harrison's, but not large enough to accommodate all of the sick and wounded.

Hope had told her that only the newest and worst cases were kept in the tent. Those expected to live and those for whom nothing else could be done were sent back to their own quarters in the muddy bombproofs. The limited number of pallets had to be kept free; new cases were arriving daily.

Faith kept close to the line of bombproof trenches along the safe side of the Grand Traverse. Cannonballs smashing into the barrier warned her that the British had not given up—though they did seem to have become a bit lazier. Or perhaps, like the Americans, they had grown tired of the ceaseless damp weather. No one could be comfortable in weather like this.

Across a short exposed space, the infirmary tent stood in a sheltered area, one side backed up against a storehouse. Faith paused a moment before going up to it. On either side of the main tent, a canvas ceiling stretched from the storehouse to a row of posts. The overhang provided shelter for the overflow of sick and injured soldiers.

But it was a poor shelter indeed, Faith thought. Rain and wind blew in beneath the canvas to batter the patients, most of whom were lying on the muddy ground, with only a blanket or piece of canvas beneath their inert bodies.

She did not see Surgeon Smythe, but just then Hope hurried out of the tent carrying a large copper kettle. Something was sticking out of the kettle, but Faith could not see what it was until she hurried over to her sister. "Hope, I'm so glad I found you! Is Surgeon Smythe inside the . . ."

She stopped, staring in horror. The object sticking out of the kettle was a human foot—a bloody still-twitching foot.

At almost the same moment, she became aware of a man's voice sobbing within the tent. "Oh, my God, my God . . . my God . . ."

"What are you doing in there?" she gasped.

Hope's face was very pale, her eyes like burning emeralds. With a jolt of nausea, Faith noticed that Hope's hands—gripping the kettle so tightly—were stained with fresh glistening blood.

"What do you think we're doing?" her sister rasped hoarsely. "What does it look like?"

311

For one stunned moment, Faith thought she would be sick. She swallowed hard. "Well, I can see what you're doing. What I meant was—what are *you* doing in there?"

Hope moved to step around her. "There's no one else to help. The camp followers refuse to assist at amputations. And the soldiers and militiamen have to man the defenses, those who are still able to do so, that is. So I said that I would do it."

"But Hope!" Faith trailed after her sister as she walked to the edge of a pit. There, looking down, Faith saw another horrible sight: arms and legs piled atop each other, white and washed clean in the rain, but putrefying in various stages. "Oh, my goodness!"

Closing her eyes, she whirled around and fought the convulsive sensation in her throat. Behind her there came a faint thud and a splash as Hope poured the contents of the kettle into the pit.

"You don't have to stand and watch, Faith. I admit it's terrible, but amputation is the only chance these poor boys have. Surgeon Smythe says that once a limb is shattered by a musketball, it's better to cut it off cleanly. Otherwise, infection sets in almost immediately."

Hope came up beside her, set down her kettle, and calmly began wiping her hands on the broad white apron Faith had lent her. The apron and the entire front of her dress were splattered with blood.

"I didn't think I could do it—but I did." Triumph enlivened her pale features. Her eyes glowed with a new self-awareness, a sense of satisfaction. "I just kept thinking to myself: You've got to be strong,

Hope. Think of this poor boy from Kentucky. He's so far away from home—and so scared. He took a musketball early this morning while on duty in blockhouse number four. I told him jokes right up until the time they had to hold him down. At least, I didn't have to do that . . ."

"They didn't give him anything to deaden the pain?" Faith blurted incredulously.

"I don't think so. Even the whiskey is running low." Hope shrugged ever so delicately, then picked up her kettle. "What was it you wanted, Faith—I have to go back now. After this one, there's another. An arm, I think."

And I'll bet you haven't thought of Alex Cummings once all morning, Faith thought, filled to bursting with admiration for her younger sister. Hope Cormorand amazed her. Where had this young woman learned to be so strong?

"I came because Nancy is having her baby. The pains have started, and I thought Surgeon Smythe could come and look after her."

Hope frowned. "I'll mention it to him when I go back into the tent, but as you can see, he's very busy. In addition to the amputations, several of his patients are in shock, and some have raging fevers. This dampness doesn't help any. I'm afraid you and Adrienne might have to deliver the baby yourselves or get one of the other settler women to help you."

Faith saw no way of arguing with someone who had just helped the surgeon cut off a man's foot. Besides, the need for Surgeon Smythe to remain at the infirmary was all too apparent. "Where's Charity—and Uncle Abel?"

313

They could not be in the tent, too, could they?

"I haven't seen Uncle Abel, but Charity's over there. Don't you see her?"

Faith looked where Hope was pointing and did indeed see Charity. The girl was sitting with her back against the storehouse wall, as far away from the main tent as possible. Her shoulders were hunched over, and she appeared to be writing something— not her diary, surely.

"I'll go over and see if she'll come back with me. I don't know how much help she will be, squeamish as she is, but she doesn't look that busy here."

"Oh, I don't know about that, Faith . . ."

But Faith did not wait to hear Hope's defense of the younger girl. Charity Cormorand had a lot of nerve sitting smack in the middle of a crisis and doing nothing useful.

Unnoticed, she advanced on Charity and was taken aback to discover a pale young man lying beside her sister. He looked as if he were dying; his face and lips were grayer than his canvas sheeting, and he was covered over with blankets. Faith could not ascertain his injury, but his breathing sounded weak and shallow.

With a start, she realized that the young man was speaking, and Charity—lips pursed in concentration so as not to miss a single halting word—was copying down on Adrienne's fine parchment each word he spoke.

"What was that again, Ezekiel?" Charity suddenly asked. "Could you repeat it?"

The young man, Ezekiel, grimaced and tried once more. His voice shook, but with a mighty effort he

314

steadied it and continued. He did not even notice Faith. "And don't grieve that I'll be buried so far from home, Mam. Lots of good brave men are buried here. I shall be proud to be one of them . . ."

"Oh, that's very good, Ezekiel." Charity, her blue eyes brilliant with unshed tears, paused long enough in her writing to flash her dazzling smile at the young man. "Your mother will surely feel better knowing that."

"You think so, Charity? You really think so?" Obviously believing that there must be some sort of military protocol for the circumstances in which he now found himself, the young man was trying desperately to be brave and to do the right thing.

Charity leaned over and tenderly patted his gray sunken cheek. "I know so, Ezekiel. Don't you worry. Your mother will be comforted to know you were thinking of her at this moment."

The young man breathed a long-drawn-out sigh. "Don't leave me, will you, Charity? I—I can't see you so good anymore. A darkness is creepin' up on me, an' I'm scared."

"I won't leave, Ezekiel. I'll stay right here as long as you need me . . . Now, let's finish this letter, shall we? And then I'll just sit with you and hold your hand."

A lump as large as a cannonball sprang up in Faith's tight throat. Quietly, trying not to disturb them, she backed away from Charity and the dying soldier. It did indeed look as if she and Adrienne were going to have to deliver Nancy's baby alone. Her two younger sisters—whom she had lately considered feather-headed, foolish, and selfish—

had more important tasks to occupy them.

"Is he coming, *cherie?*" Adrienne's eyes were as worried as Faith had ever seen them.

"No. Surgeon Smythe is tied up in surgery. How's Nancy?"

Faith saw that the pregnant woman was half-sitting, half-lying on Whip's shelf of skins and blankets. The canvas walls were down between all three sections of the trench, and Adrienne had chosen the driest, most comfortable place for her. Nancy's eyes were closed, and Faith wondered if she was sleeping.

"Not good," Adrienne said. "The pains are stronger now, and coming very close together, but occasionally there is a pause between them. Like now. At these times I tell Nancy to try to sleep, so she will be strong for the actual birth."

"What does that mean—a pause between the pains?"

"I don't know, *cherie.* I have never had children, and Nancy does not remember it being that way with Jeffrey."

"What are we going to do, Adrienne? Surgeon Smythe can't come right now; he's in surgery. I couldn't even drag Hope or Charity away. Things are worse at the infirmary than they are here."

"We could take her there," Adrienne suggested. "And Surgeon Smythe could look at her in between his other duties."

Faith thought of the dying soldier, the pit of amputated limbs, and the threat of fevers and other

316

maladies. "The infirmary is no place for a laboring woman. She ought not to see the horrors there, nor should the baby be exposed to the sickness. Besides, there would be no privacy."

Adrienne sighed. "You are right. We must stay here and do the best we can."

A deep moan from Nancy caused both women to jump. They rushed to her side. Another pain had apparently begun. Nancy's eyes flew open. She stiffened and grabbed at the air, then bit down hard to keep from crying out.

Faith seized her hands, while Adrienne put an arm around her shoulders. "There, there . . . breathe deeply now."

Nancy opened her mouth, gasping for air. Her hazel eyes were wild-looking, and her short, blunt nails dug painfully into Faith's wrists. But gradually, the wave of sensation seemed to pass, and Nancy's tortured eyes sought Faith and crinkled at the corners.

"Faith," she breathed. "Thank the Lord, you've come back. Where's Surgeon Smythe? I think I'll need him after all . . . It feels—it feels different from the first time. I don't remember it hurtin' so much . . . or maybe, I'm just gittin' older. Birthin' babies is easier when you're young and supple as a willow tree."

"The surgeon will come in a little while," Faith lied. She did not have the heart to tell her friend the truth. Besides, if Nancy knew how much Surgeon Smythe was needed at the infirmary, she might not want him to come at all.

"That's good," Nancy murmured. "That's real

317

good. He'll be more help t' me than Tom was." The corners of her mouth turned up in a wisp of a smile. "I do miss my Tom, but he was scared t' death of droppin' Jeffrey when he was a newborn. I had t' tell him, 'Jus' think of Jeffrey as a piglet or a wild wee critter. Don't think of him as your son' . . . I hope it's another boy, Faith. If it is, it'll kind of take the sting out of losin' Jeffrey. When I tell Tom about the death of his firstborn, I'll be handin' him his second . . ."

Oh, poor Tom. Poor Nancy, Faith thought despairingly. The cannonball-sized lump in her throat grew even larger.

"Hush now, Nancy, you have to rest . . ."

"Yes, I'll do that now, but you'll wake me, won't you, as soon as Surgeon Smythe comes?"

"Of course."

The minutes dragged by as if they were hours. Faith and Adrienne found the miniature homespun clothes that Nancy had brought for the baby. Knowing that she might not make it back to her home before the birth, Nancy had carefully wrapped a few things in protective buckskin—small blankets and squares of cloth for diapers, several tiny nightshirts, and even a kind of outer garment made of rabbit furs.

They tried and failed to start a fire to heat water; the precious scraps of wood were too green and damp.

"How will we wash the baby?" Faith whispered, so that Nancy would not hear. "Won't the infant take a chill if we use cold water?"

"We'll use bear grease instead," Adrienne in-

318

dicated a small earthenware container. "The Indians swear by it for everything. It is even thought to protect them in battle; they oil themselves all over with it."

"Ugh!" Faith wrinkled her nose at the very thought. "Our poor baby will smell like a savage—or a bear."

Somehow, Nancy's baby had become *their* baby —its welfare as important to them as it must be to Nancy.

Adrienne sharpened a small knife to cut the cord binding the child to its mother, and Faith found a length of narrow twisted rawhide to tie the cord before cutting it. Neither knew exactly what she was doing, but each had heard enough birthing stories to be aware of certain necessary procedures.

"What will we do if—if Nancy bleeds a lot?" Faith was now trying to gather some linen to be used for cleanup. She had to resort to tearing up undergarments and one of the few shirts Uncle Abel had brought with him.

"I have no idea, *chérie*. Surgeon Smythe will surely come if that happens."

No, he won't, Faith thought. Not if he is in the middle of sawing off an arm or leg. She hoped and prayed that this birth would be normal; then maybe Surgeon Smythe would not be needed. It had begun to rain again, and thunder rumbled along the far northeastern horizon—or perhaps it was cannonfire from farther on down the river.

Nancy's agony grew worse as the day progressed. She was still managing not to scream during her contractions, which Adrienne said were the efforts of her womb to expel the child. But she gasped and grunted so that Faith became increasingly alarmed.

She and Adrienne made Nancy lie down flat on her back, and not knowing what else to do to ease her, they massaged her hands, arms, and legs. Nancy was pathetically grateful, but once, her eyes glazed with suffering like those of a wounded animal, she gasped, "Surgeon Smythe—has he come yet?"

Wordlessly, Faith shook her head.

At one point, Nancy cried out sharply, "Tom! Oh, Tom, where are you?"

Faith felt like crawling into a hole and pulling the earth down on top of her. It was because of Hope and Charity that Tom was not there to aid and comfort his wife. And then, abruptly, she remembered that they were already in a hole—and if it kept on raining, might not the whole Grand Traverse eventually collapse and cover them?

Toward midafternoon, Faith heard someone calling her name. She heard it from afar, and then it came closer, as if someone were running to get her. "Faith! Faith!"

Nancy was in the throes of a contraction, and neither Faith nor Adrienne could pause long enough to look outside and see who it was. Then, Faith recognized the voice. "It's Charity!" she exclaimed.

Nancy's grip on her hands relaxed, and Faith turned to see Charity scrambling down the muddy side of the shelter. Ordinarily so fastidious about her clothing, Charity was a shocking mess. Her hair was plastered to her face from the rain, her dress was torn, wet, and muddy, and her eyes were swollen and red from weeping or hysterical excitement or both.

320

"Oh, Faith!" she gasped.

"What is it, my dear? Did Ezekiel die?"

Charity looked momentarily puzzled, her expression seeming to say: Ezekiel? How do you know about him? She gathered her composure and said, "No, not yet . . . and I have to get back to him immediately. It's . . . it's . . . oh, Faith, do you know that man who stood on top of the traverse and was so good at calling the British shots?"

"Yes, what about him?"

"Well he . . . he saw one coming, and he couldn't guess where it was going to land. He started to say, Look out by the meat house—or look out *something* —and he changed his mind and called a different warning . . . and then the shell fell right on top of him and exploded."

"Oh, how awful!"

Faith recalled how the entire fort had been abuzz with praise for the cocky little man's phenomenal ability. It was said that he had called every single shot correctly—and there had been hundreds and hundreds of them. But this one—the one aimed directly at him—must have eluded his precise judgment.

"But that's not all, Faith!" Charity faltered in her effort to tell the rest of the story intelligibly.

"What else?" There could not be anything more—she could not *deal* with anything more.

"Uncle Abel! He was standing on top of the magazine trying to put up a cross, but it kept falling down . . . and . . . and pieces of flying debris from the explosion struck him. The soldiers brought him to the infirmary . . . Oh, Faith. He was covered

321

with *blood!*"

There came a piercing shriek behind her. Nancy, Faith thought. But as she whirled to comfort her friend, she saw that it was not Nancy who had screamed; it was Adrienne.

"Not Abel! Oh, *mon Dieu,* not Abel, too . . . not that kind, good man!"

The Frenchwoman's eyes were wide with horror, and before anyone could stop her, she clambered out of the trench and ran toward the infirmary.

Chapter Eighteen

"Faith, I have to go back now. Ezekiel wept when I left him. The surgeon said he'll be dead before nightfall, and I can't leave him to die alone!"

Stunned by Adrienne's outburst, which had brought home to her the full import of her own dreadful news, Charity sounded on the verge of hysteria—exactly the way Faith felt.

Her little sister blinked, took a deep breath, and went on more calmly. "I only came to tell you about Uncle Abel. I thought you would want to come to the infirmary . . . but you can't leave Nancy, can you?"

They both looked at Nancy, who started to say something and then could not: Another pain had caught her in its savage grip. Faith rushed to her friend's side. "No, I cannot . . . not now."

Faith offered her hands for Nancy to cling to and, for a moment, almost hated Adrienne. The woman should not have run off and left her there alone. Uncle Abel was *her* uncle, not Adrienne's.

Yet Adrienne Langlois was plainly suffering—perhaps even more than Faith and her sisters. The love between a man and a woman was so strong as to be all-encompassing. Grudgingly, Faith admitted that if Whip had been wounded, she would have gone to him at once, regardless of previous commitments. She realized that Adrienne had never even stopped to think about it.

Grimacing with pain, as if she could no longer bear the struggle to bring her child into such a harsh world, Nancy cried out. Charity's eyes widened in stunned pity. "I—I didn't know having a baby hurt so much."

"I don't think it's supposed to." Faith turned her attention to Nancy's twisted face and straining body. She wished she could lean on Nancy's huge taut belly and push the baby right out of her.

As the pain once again subsided, like a beast withdrawing a short distance to savor its victim's agony, Faith urged her sister to go back to the infirmary. "And if Hope can come to tell me how Uncle Abel is, I would appreciate it. I know Surgeon Smythe will do his best."

"Surgeon Smythe admits that he doesn't always know what he's doing," Charity said bitterly. "He can't save Ezekiel—or Adam or Henry. Kentucky will lose three brave sons before this day is finished."

He couldn't save Jeffrey either, Faith thought. She grew angry, but more at Charity for bringing up the subject than at poor overwhelmed Surgeon Smythe. "He does the best he can. That's all we can ask of him . . . Go on now, Charity. And send Hope as soon as possible."

"If she can be spared, I'll send her."

Charity departed the shelter, and Nancy sighed and tossed her head restlessly. "I feel real bad about your uncle, Faith. Maybe you should go t' him."

"I'm not leaving you, Nancy. Forget that idea. Hope and Charity are with him—and Adrienne." Faith wiped Nancy's brow with a clean cloth. Nancy's skin had gotten damp and clammy—a bad sign surely.

"But I'm just havin' a baby. Your uncle is . . . is . . ." Her voice trailed off. Faith recognized the beginnings of another assault and squeezed Nancy's groping hands. She wished she knew how to ease her friend's suffering, and Uncle Abel's, too.

Oh, where was it all going to end? How much more could everyone take?

"Faith . . ." Nancy did not release her hands even though the pain had subsided again. "I gotta get up."

"No. You can't, Nancy. What for?"

"I want t' try t' walk t' the infirmary."

"But it's too far. How would you even climb out of the trench? It's slippery and raining harder now, and . . . and the infirmary is a terrible place. Not fit for a woman in your condition."

"Faith . . ." Nancy's hands gripped hers so hard that Faith was afraid she would break some bones. "My condition ain't good. There's something wrong. I know there is. If Surgeon Smythe could just look at me . . ."

"I'll go get him . . . I'll *make* him come!"

"And have him leave your uncle and the others t' bleed t' death? No," Nancy protested, trying to sit up. "I'll go to the infirmary. It ain't that far."

325

But before she could struggle to a sitting position, another contraction came—this one so strong that she screamed in anguish, then began to sob, "Oh, God . . . oh, God . . ."

Faith was reminded of the young soldier, after his leg had been amputated. "Nancy, stay here . . . Lie down. I will get someone. There must be someone in this fort who can help. Archange Jacques, perhaps. She has had children; she will know what to do."

Archange was a complainer—always bemoaning the loss of goods confiscated by the army—but she would be better than nothing. She had experience, didn't she?

Experience, yes, Faith discovered. But good sense, no. Archange climbed down into the bomb-proof, shaking water from her large plump body like a dog, like Shadow. "Have you examined her?" she demanded. Her black eyes were hawklike and full of accusation. "The army—a bunch of fools and incompetents—t' subject us all t' this."

But they saved your life, Faith retorted silently. Where would you and your family be if the army hadn't built this fort?

Trying to remain calm, she said, "I haven't examined her. I wouldn't know what to look for."

"Well, let's get her skirts up and see what we can see."

Mortified and worried that she hadn't thought of examining Nancy before this, Faith rushed to help Archange pull up Nancy's skirts. No sooner had they gotten them above her knees, when a contraction began. Completely ignoring Nancy's agony, Archange held the laboring woman's knees apart and frowned at what she saw.

"The baby's head is right there—you see it?"

"Y—yes," Faith faltered. She did see something that might be the top of a baby's head, but there was something else ahead of it—a loop that looked like the mysterious cord she and Adrienne had been planning to cut. "What's that bluish thing?"

"The cord, of course. It's likely wrapped around the baby's neck and is chokin' him. I've seen this happen before."

"Choking him! What can we do?"

"Not much," the settler woman said. "We could pull on it an' git this over with. Once the baby's dead, if it won't come out by itself, we can take it out in pieces."

"No!" Nancy's scream drowned out Faith's gasp, and she clamped her knees together. "Get out of here! Faith, make her get out! I don't want her t' touch me. Get her out! Get her out!"

Filled with blinding hot fury, Faith jerked down Nancy's skirt. "Why did you have to say that in front of her? You had better go. She's a very brave woman, but you have frightened her to death."

"She's likely goin' t' die anyway." Archange seemed bent on total honesty regardless of its consequences. "Along with her baby. There ain't much anyone can do. Like I said, I've seen this before."

"I'll tend her myself. Please go now."

"All right, if that's what you want, but you're makin' a big mistake. The surgeon don't have the experience I do. And he'll agree with me, you'll see. When the cord is comin' out first, the baby is in trouble and so's the mother. You got t' kill one t' save the other, and most of the time even that don't work."

"No—no—no . . ." Nancy moaned.

Faith lost all patience. "Get out! Have you no compassion—no common sense? Get out at once!"

"I'm agoin'. It is a shame," she added belatedly. "Her bein' in this spot after jus' losin' her son . . ."

After the woman had left, Faith stroked Nancy's damp tousled hair and tried to calm her. "She doesn't know what she's talking about. We'll save you both, Nancy. We certainly will . . ."

But Nancy shot Faith such a look of doubtful misery that Faith had to bite back a sob. She had to go get the surgeon. This problem had grown too big for her to handle alone. Nancy was moaning and weeping now, tossing her head from side to side. Even if the surgeon had to be torn away from her uncle, Faith must persuade him to come.

If he didn't, Nancy would die. Perhaps, they would all die—Nancy, her baby, *and* Uncle Abel.

Faith had never felt so alone, so helpless. Like a great ugly black vulture, despair settled on her shoulders. She fought to keep from breaking down entirely. Where was the strength of character on which she had always prided herself? Where was her cool efficiency in the face of trouble? She felt totally bereft—overwhelmed.

She heard a splash behind her as someone leaped down into the bombproof. Looking over her shoulder, she saw that it was Shadow, wet and bedraggled, his tail flopping into the mud. Oh, Whip is here, she thought distractedly—and then, her

328

spirits lifted. *Whip!* Whip would know what to do.

"What's going on here?" he demanded in his wonderful take-charge voice.

For once, she actually welcomed his authoritative manner. Like the sun breaking through a layer of storm clouds, hope reappeared. "Oh, Whip . . . Thank God, you've come!"

"We'll take her to the storehouse," Whip said when Faith had told him about Nancy's plight.

Faith did not have to ask which storehouse; there was only one he could possibly mean. But the suggestion caught her by surprise. "Not to the infirmary?"

"If it's as bad as you say it is, the infirmary is the *last* place I'd take her . . . Besides, I don't have much confidence in our surgeon . . . No, we'll go to the storehouse where she will be dry and comfortable. I know a few tricks that might help her."

Faith was overjoyed to have Whip take charge, but she had not expected him to know anything about childbirth. It was moral support she needed—and brawn, so that she could get Nancy safely to the infirmary. Concealing her apprehension, she began to gather things they would need to take with them.

"What sort of tricks?" she inquired timidly.

"Indian tricks." Whip winked at Nancy, who regarded him with a wan relieved smile. She was between contractions—another one of those surprising pauses. "You don't mind if we try them, do you, Nancy? I picked them up from someone who used to work magic with difficult deliveries, broken bones, wounded paws, whatever. She had quite a reputation for never losing a patient."

He had learned them from Moon Daughter, Faith realized. But there wasn't time to give in to jealousy. She had not a single idea of her own; if the devil himself had volunteered his expertise, she would not have been able to refuse it.

They wrapped Nancy in a blanket, and Whip picked her up as if she weighed no more than Jeffrey. With Nancy in his arms, he had to step on top of a barrel in order to climb out of the trench. Anxiously, Faith held her breath. But Whip, strong and surefooted, easily managed the awkward feat.

Then they were hurrying through the rain. Halfway to the storehouse, Nancy groaned and stiffened.

"Stop! She's having a contraction," Faith begged.

But Whip only walked faster.

By the time Faith stepped into the dimly lit shelter, Whip already had Nancy comfortably settled on a bed of flour sacks, her skirts hiked above her knees.

While Faith fidgeted behind him, wishing she knew what to do to help, Whip looked long and hard. When he finally leaned back, he was scowling. "Well, one thing looks certain. The cord *is* wrapped around the baby's neck."

"Oh, Lord," Nancy moaned. "Then me and my baby are goners for sure."

Whip seized Nancy's hands and almost shook her. "Listen to me, Nance." His voice was harsh and commanding. "We're not going to let you die—or the baby either. I think I can save you both, but it's going to be very difficult. It's going to hurt worse than you can imagine."

330

Nancy clung to him, her eyes pleading. "I kin take it, Whip. You gotta save the baby. I can't have Tom come home to find nothin' left of any of us. For Tom, Whip . . . you gotta save the baby for Tom."

"I'm going to save it for *both* of you," Whip insisted.

He motioned for Faith to bring over the pack of necessities they had brought. "Give me that bear grease, Faith."

During the long, tense interlude that followed, Nancy screamed, Whip sweated, and Faith alternately beseeched the Lord for help and cursed him for inflicting such horrors on women. Whip's face mirrored the suffering he was causing. First, he made Nancy lie with her head down and her buttocks raised—to take the pressure off the cord, he said.

Then, smeared to his elbows with bear grease, he managed to slip his fingers in around the baby's head to gently extricate the slippery appendage wrapped about its neck. This delicate maneuver caused Nancy to groan piteously, and then she began to grunt.

"Don't bear down!" Whip shouted. "I know you want to, but fight it, Nancy . . . try to pant. That way you *can't* bear down."

Nancy panted. Tears and perspiration combined to bathe her entire body in a salt-smearing wetness.

"That's it—easy now . . ." Whip had never sounded so gentle, as if his voice were coated with honey. "Easy . . . easy . . . *there!*"

He looked up triumphantly. "The cord is no longer around the baby's neck."

331

Faith could have wept with relief. But the ordeal wasn't over yet. Now Whip made Nancy squat— Indian fashion, he told her. To Faith, the position looked awkward and uncomfortable; it was most certainly not ladylike. Yet Nancy was engaged in a task that expressed the very nature of her womanhood. Dumb and animal-like in her fear and pain, Nancy obeyed Whip's gentle commands. Not once did she voice a complaint.

"Come on, now, Nancy—that's it. If you were a Shawnee woman, you would be in a special tepee with a post and leather thongs to pull on. The ground beneath you would be hollowed out, and you would have a special blanket on which to catch the baby . . . Here, pull on my wrists as hard as you can."

Now Faith was completely fascinated. The squatting and pulling did seem to ease Nancy's discomfort and to give her the ability to concentrate wholeheartedly on her task. She grunted and pushed, with Whip leaning over her, encouraging and applauding every step of the way.

"You're doing fine, Nancy. You're doing wonderfully! Come on, now, another push. Make it a big one!"

Why do women send men away when they are having babies? Faith wondered. If I were in Nancy's situation, there's no one I would rather have near me than my husband—than Whip, she amended silently. This was a gentle supportive side of him she had never seen before.

His habitual scowl had disappeared, to be replaced by a tenderness, a vulnerability, that she had glimpsed only briefly during his lovemaking—when she had been almost too busy to notice. Now she could study him at leisure when he did not realize she was doing so. How fine and strong and caring he could be, the very essence of masculinity.

Her heart thumped wildly at the thought of how much she loved him. He needs gentleness in return, she realized in surprise. Not censure or rejection. If he knew that she accepted him, wouldn't his rough edges somehow smooth over?

Indeed, at this moment, she could not imagine him shooting, tomahawking, or otherwise harming another person. This was the *real* Whip Martin—this tender, patient human being who refused to allow Nancy to give up.

"I—I can't do it, Whip!" Nancy was sobbing as her efforts failed to produce her offspring.

"Yes, you can," Whip insisted softly. "One more push. Think about this one. Forget the last. Don't think about any future ones. Just this one, Nance. You can do one more. I know you can."

He might have been cajoling a child.

"But I've run out of strength."

"No." Whip gripped Nancy's arms, his eyes hard and bright. "Do it for Tom, Nancy. He must not lose this one, too. Do it for the baby; it deserves to live. Do it for yourself; you *want* this baby."

"Yes, yes . . ." Nancy agreed brokenly. She bent to the task once more, furrowing her brow, and straining with all her might. Faith's muscles tensed; she held her breath. The moment was the longest she had ever known.

The only sound in the storehouse was Nancy's

long, low groan. It seemed to come from her very core. Faith bolted forward just in time to see a round dark head emerging.

"Catch him, Faith—don't let him fall."

Faith wondered briefly how Whip knew the baby was a boy—and then she had no more time to wonder. The baby slipped easily into her waiting hands, its body wet and glistening, its tiny fists clenched, its eyes squeezed tightly shut. A slippery white membrane enclosed the child, which made no sound at all.

"Whip! Is it . . . ?" She could not bear to say the word in front of Nancy.

Whip let go of Nancy's hands and seized the baby himself. He tore open the membrane and wiped the baby's nose and mouth with a none-too-gentle finger. When it still did not respond, he briskly tapped the soles of its feet. The tiny blue body jerked and twitched, and then—oh, lovely sounds—the baby coughed, gasped, and began to howl.

The baby's color changed from blue to an angry red, and Faith's eyes sought Whip's across its squirming body. He was grinning from ear to ear, his eyes alight with triumph. "Here she is—here is your beautiful daughter, Nancy!"

Only then did Faith see that the infant was a girl.

"A daughter . . ." Nancy breathed. She leaned back against the flour sacks and held out her hands. Whip placed the squalling infant in Nancy's outstretched arms. "A daughter," she said again.

Faith could not tell if she was disappointed or delighted—until Nancy raised her eyes. They were shining with a glorious happiness. "Oh, Tom will be so proud. He always wanted a wee little girl, and so did I. Oh, she is so beautiful, isn't she?"

Only through the eyes of love could one regard that red-faced, squawling mite of humanity as beautiful. Faith exchanged looks with Whip; his expression was tender, amused, and satisfied. "She's uglier than a horned toad," he said gruffly. "But I expect she'll improve with time."

"She certainly will, Whip Martin!" Nancy scolded indignantly. "Don't you be sayin' nothin' bad about Faith Foster."

"Oh, Nancy . . ." Faith was deeply touched. "Do you really mean it?"

Nancy nodded. "Ain't nobody I'd rather have for a namesake than you, Faith. You're steady and solid as a mountain."

Uncertain whether she liked the compliment, Faith rolled the name around on her tongue. Faith Foster—it had a nice ring. She got out the grease pot to clean off her namesake, and as she did so, taking the baby from Nancy and rubbing the grease onto the velvety soft skin, the baby fell silent. Its blue eyes stared unseeingly in her direction, and its little pink tongue poked out of its mouth.

Why, she is not only beautiful, she's breathtaking, Faith thought. Tiny fingers wrapped around her index finger and despite the slickness, held on with a strength that surprised and delighted her.

Scarcely able to contain her wonderment, Faith gently wiped away the grease with a clean soft cloth. She diapered and dressed the infant, then wrapped it in a blanket. Looking up, she discovered Whip's eyes on her, watching her every move. "You do that as if

335

you were born to it," he murmured.

Their gazes locked and held. Never had she felt so close to him. Something warm and vibrant strummed between them, and all of Faith's doubts disappeared. Whip had changed; surely he had changed. No man could do as he had just done and remain surfeited with vengeful feelings.

She smiled, and Whip smiled back—the first real smile she had ever had from him. She could have remained there, kneeling and smiling forever, if Nancy had not interrupted.

"Are you two gonna give me back my baby—or are you jus' gonna moon at each other for the rest of the day?"

Blushing, Faith glanced away. Whip laughed. It was a joyous sound that startled little Faith into an angry howl. Hastily, Faith picked up the infant and gave her to her mother. While she had been cleaning up the child, Whip had seen to the other messy details—the delivery and disposal of the afterbirth and the cleaning of Nancy herself.

Finally, everything was in order. "I'll get you some clean clothes in a little while," Faith promised. "And I'll also bring back some food and a lantern."

"No matter," Nancy responded drowsily. "I can just lie here and sleep."

It had gotten dark, Faith noticed, and the rain had at long last stopped. She had no idea how much time had passed but guessed that twilight was falling. Her thoughts jumped to her uncle. The day had passed, and she still did not know how serious his injuries were—or even if he was still alive.

"Go on, Faith," Whip urged. "I'll take care of

Nancy. Someone would have come looking for us if it had been necessary."

Having guessed her concern, he was trying to reassure her. But Faith recalled that Hope and Charity did not know where she was. "Yes, thank you. I will go now."

Her tone sounded oddly formal, and Whip looked at her with concern, then rose and strode to her side. He towered over her, his green eyes searching her face. "If you need me, you know where to find me."

Choking on sudden tears, she could not reply. He leaned over and very gently pressed his lips to her forehead. The simple tender gesture unnerved her; she threw her arms around him and hugged him so fiercely that he almost lost his balance.

"I will always need you," she whispered, and then she ran out of the storehouse.

Chapter Nineteen

Whip watched Faith hurry off to the infirmary, and a part of him went with her. Examining his feelings further, he discovered that an enormous peace filled him, body and soul. He could not remember when he had felt so whole and peaceful—or so tired. His weariness bordered on exhaustion, but having arisen from an honest tension and exertion that had culminated in resounding success, it was a pleasant feeling.

Perhaps he should take up midwifery, he thought with a wry inward grin. He could hang a sign from his tepee: "Babies delivered. No birth too difficult."

Moon Daughter had once tried to explain to him how she felt when one of her patients survived an ailment that usually resulted in death—but he had never understood her exhilaration until now. There was so much he understood now—especially he understood that Faith Cormorand had become indispensable to his happiness.

Happiness. He had not thought to ever be happy

again, and the elusiveness and fragility of the emotion made him wary, almost frightened. The first time he had loved, he had been carelessly confident, believing that he and Moon Daughter would live forever, that their happiness would never end, that he would protect and cherish her always.

He now knew that only the very young and foolish could afford such rash assumptions. Love could be brutally sundered not only by death, but by anger, pettiness, or simply by indifference and neglect. Losing Moon Daughter had opened his eyes to human failings all around him. But Faith Cormorand had reopened them to basic human goodness—kindness, bravery, and self-sacrifice, as well as beauty.

Faith simply would not allow him to stay sequestered behind the wall he had so carefully built. Just by being herself, she made demands on him.

He doubted he would have dared to be so bold in helping Nancy if Faith had not expected it of him—had not depended on him. And by helping Nancy, he felt as if he had earned readmittance to the human race.

The feeling was good. Being in love again was good. No matter that he was still living in mud and danger, he felt as newborn as little Faith Foster. The siege would be over eventually, and then, regardless of what lay ahead, he would forge a new life for himself—and for Faith, if she would have him. Perhaps, they could homestead near the Fosters, or live in Frenchtown, if she preferred.

He trusted his ability to survive anywhere—and to make a good life for the woman he loved. Hadn't he escaped death on so many occasions that he had actually lost count? He was meant to live. He was meant to take Faith in his arms and spend the rest of his days loving and cherishing her. Something dead within him had come to life again. Yes, something—his will to live, perhaps—had been struggling all this while, waiting for him to respond to it, waiting for someone to encourage him to respond to it.

Oh, God, he thought. How good it is to be alive. How good it is to love and be happy again.

He did not know how long he stood there in the doorway of the darkening storehouse, but suddenly, an animal came bounding toward him through the mud. Amused and exasperated, he shook his head. He had expressly ordered Shadow to stay put in the bombproof.

The wolf's lips drew back in a grin. Unerringly, he made his way to his waiting master.

Whip bent down to welcome the wolf's affectionate onslaught. Muddy front paws, a wet nose, and a swiping rough tongue attacked him wholeheartedly. He knew he should scold the beast, but instead, he grinned and ruffled its fur. "Who gave *you* permission to join the party?"

"I did, Whip . . . I had to find you so I told Shadow, 'Go get 'im fer me, boy,' and he did."

Startled, Whip looked up to see Peter Navarre standing a short distance away. The man had drawn near while he was busy trying to keep the wolf from putting paw prints across his buckskins. Slowly, not particularly pleased to see his friend, Whip straightened. With a growing sense of wariness and annoyance, he waited—holding Shadow's front

341

paws as if he meant to dance with him.

Peter got right to the point. "You said to tell you if the general and I came up with somethin' good. Well, Whip, we've come up with somethin' *real* good. An' I know you won't want to pass it up."

Try me, Whip thought. He did not bother to hide his scowling irritation. "Is it dangerous?"

Pete shrugged disparagingly. "You know I wouldn't even ask you if it wasn't. Some little wet-nosed officer could do an easy job; there'd be no need for a man like you."

"Maybe I'm not the man you think I am." Whip let go of Shadow's paws, and the animal plopped heavily to the ground. "Will there be killing?"

"There's always killing, Whip."

"Then I'm not interested."

Peter frowned. "Not even if we're gonna be killin' Injuns?"

"Especially not then." Whip saw that his friend was having difficulty accepting this sudden change of heart, and for a moment, he wavered. Then, thinking of Faith, he blurted, "Tell the general I'm sorry, but he'll have to find someone else."

To emphasize his determination, he withdrew a short distance into the storehouse. "You'll have to excuse me, Peter, but I have things in here to see to."

Pete stepped forward persistently. "What's come over you, Whip? This is your chance—the one you been waitin' for. There ain't nothin' Moon Daughter wanted more than to see peace come to these here parts. An' now, when you can help make that happen, you suddenly back off."

Whip almost smiled. "It won't work, Pete. First,

342

you appeal to my baser instincts; then you appeal to my higher ones. Why won't you just accept my answer? No. It's the only answer I'm going to give."

"All right, then . . ." Pete hesitated, but only for a moment. "I'll just tell the general that you're so besotted with a lady's violet eyes that you've plumb lost your sense of duty. Only one thing I can't help wonderin': What would your little Miss Cormorand think if she knew you were leavin' us all in the lurch?"

"That's enough, Pete!"

Whip hadn't meant for his voice to come out so loud, but suddenly, the baby began to cry, Shadow whined, and Nancy's voice came sleepily, anxiously, "Whip? What is it? Is somethin' the matter?"

Peter looked momentarily startled at the commotion inside the shed. Then his gray-blue eyes hardened scornfully. "Well, don't worry about winnin' the war, Whip, or puttin' an end to this siege. I can see you got your hands full right here."

"What you do is your choice, Pete—and what I do is mine."

It sounded strange to hear his own sarcasm turned back on him, but Whip watched impassively as Peter glared at him, then angrily stalked away. He realized that his friend's accusations bothered him more than he cared to admit. No one had ever dared to suggest that he was refusing to do his duty. Indeed, he had always done his share and more.

Kneeing Shadow out of the way, he turned back into the dimly lit storehouse, only to discover Nancy's troubled eyes on him. "Whip, what did that man want?"

343

"He wanted me to take part in some fool plan . . . something to do with killing Indians."

Quieting the wailing infant by putting her to her breast, Nancy was silent for a moment. "But you don't want t' kill Indians," she said at last.

"No, I don't." Whip busied himself with straightening several flour sacks that scarcely needed straightening.

"Still, if it will end the war . . ." Nancy mused aloud. "You can't say they don't deserve it."

"Yes, they do deserve it—for killing Jeffrey if for nothing else."

Jeffrey. Moon Daughter. The old hatred began to boil in him. He distracted himself by furiously rearranging flour sacks. The sacks were heavy and unwieldy; he could not lift more than two at a time. Grunting under the strain, he transported an entire row of them from one end of the storehouse to the other.

Several untidy rows remained, but he finally realized that there was no purpose to the effort; it did not assuage his anger one bit. The dark beast within him was growling and grumbling again, and he did not know which disturbed him more: the growling and grumbling, or the fact that he had not succeeded in slaying the beast once and for all—as, for a few fleeting moments, he had thought he had.

"Nancy . . ." He stood before the shadowy figure propped on the bed of sacks. "Faith should be here soon. Will you be all right if I leave you alone until she comes?"

"We'll be fine, Whip." Nancy's tone was comfortingly neutral.

344

"Nance . . ." He had never before begged for approval of his actions, but now, for the first time in his life, he found he needed it. "Do you think revenge is ever justified?"

"Well . . . I don't know, Whip. The Bible says, 'An eye for an eye an' a tooth for a tooth,' but it also says, 'Love thine enemy.' An' I ain't smart enough t' figure out how you're supposed to do both."

"But don't you ever want to find and kill the savage who murdered Jeffrey? Or don't women ever feel that way?"

"I've felt that way," Nancy admitted slowly. "But I know I wouldn't hardly be a match for no powerful grinnin' savage. So the question ain't a fair one."

It was not a fair one, Whip saw immediately. Nor was it fair of Faith to condemn a man for doing whatever was necessary to punish his enemies for past sins and to prevent them from committing future ones.

Unlike Nancy or Faith, he *was* a match for the Indians. Indeed, there was no one better. He had the experience, the strength, and the stamina. How could he send others in his place? If he allowed them to go without him—and they didn't come back— their deaths would be on his conscience forever.

"Nancy, I'm going to leave Shadow here. I don't know when I'll be back, but tell Faith not to worry."

"I'll tell her, but you know she'll worry anyway. She might not approve, Whip."

He snorted. Of course, she would not approve, and if he had any sense, he would find her and bind her to him before she could question or disapprove of anything he did.

345

"She'll just have to trust that I know what I'm doing. She'll have to try to understand . . . Stay, Shadow . . . you stay." Whip spoke sternly and pointed to the ground in front of him.

Whining, Shadow dropped to his haunches.

"If I'm not back in a couple of days, tell Faith to let Shadow out of the fort. He may come after me, but by then, it shouldn't matter."

"I'll tell her, Whip."

"Take care, Nance . . ." Whip paused before making his departure. Doubts assailed him. He had the sudden absurd notion that he might never see Nancy or this little storehouse again.

Odd, he thought. The shed had come to mean more to him than his tepee. He had spent some of the most satisfying moments of his life in this little log shelter—that afternoon in the rain with Faith, and delivering Nancy's baby.

Struggling to banish his morbid feelings, he saluted Nancy with a wave of his hand and carelessly brushed Shadow's head. Then, on a strangely tender impulse, he walked quickly to the recumbent woman and bent down to steal a last look at the newest Foster.

The baby had stopped nursing and was now asleep. Gently, he traced the feather-soft curve of her cheek. "Good-bye, little Faith," he whispered, wishing this child were his, wishing he had someone to carry on his name, his vital life force, long after he was dead and gone.

"Good-bye . . ." he repeated softly.

A longing for Faith swept over him. His desire to see her and hold her again attacked him like a sharp physical pain. Hurriedly, he left the store-house and went to collect his weapons before he could change his mind.

Faith sat on a rolled-up piece of canvas on one side of Uncle Abel's pallet, and Adrienne sat on the other. Neither had much to say. Adrienne had already apologized profusely for leaving Faith alone to deal with Nancy. She had been overwrought, she said. All the horrible memories of the Revolution and of her husband's cruel death at the hands of the Indians had come rushing back to her.

She had begged Faith to understand that everyone she had loved had died in a startling and violent manner. It had been too much for her to think of Abel dying the same way. Abel, Adrienne had thought, would be spared because he was a man of peace.

Moved to pity by Adrienne's admission that she suffered fear and anguish as much as any other person, Faith decided not to mention how difficult the birth of little Faith Foster had been. Let Adrienne find out from Nancy if that heroic woman chose to speak of it—which she probably would not.

Sighing audibly, Faith minutely examined her Uncle's stonelike visage. She had studied it a hundred times in the last hour, but he showed no signs of regaining consciousness. In the uncertain light of several smoking torches, Uncle Abel's face was ashen. His lips were as unmoving as those of a dead man, and she had to look hard to see the movement of his sunken chest as he breathed in a faint erratic manner.

It did not seem possible that an apparently superficial wound could cause such trauma. A bloodstained white bandage on her uncle's brow was the only evidence of the injury caused by a piece of flying metal. The wound had bled prodigiously—all out of proportion to the size of the deep gash. But it wasn't the loss of blood that worried Faith so much as her uncle's lack of response to any stimulus.

Nothing could rouse him—not shouting in his ear, not touching his hands, face, or body, not even Surgeon Smythe's relentless jabbing with a needle as he stitched the wound closed as neatly as a woman hemming a dress.

Surgeon Smythe refused to hold out any hope, and Faith feared the very worst. Her uncle's health had never been robust—though he could overcome any ailment or discomfort in pursuit of what he viewed as his mission. Faith remembered the many times her uncle had been ill or laid low by an attack of rheumatism. But always, in some miraculous way, he had found the strength to rouse himself and go on.

She recalled the miles they had traveled and the dangers and discomforts they had endured. Few men of her uncle's age and health would still be alive after such an ordeal, much less eagerly looking forward to future challenges. His courage and determination had kept him going—and that same courage and determination had proven to be his undoing. Somehow, it did not seem fair.

Faith reached for her uncle's large, lifeless hand. It was cool and oddly dry, and she could not remember whether it had always been this way or not. Surely,

Uncle Abel's hand had been warm—like his heart. She stroked his knobby knuckles and stifled a groan of anguish. If he did not awaken, she did not know how she would bear it.

"Our Father, who art in heaven . . ." Adrienne began reciting the Our Father, and looking around, Faith saw that Charity was writing a letter for still another dying soldier. Ezekiel had died a short half-hour ago, and his body had been swiftly removed to make room for someone else. Hope was advancing toward her with two gourds full of some steaming liquid that smelled appetizingly of meat, and reminded Faith that she had not eaten since early morning.

"Here . . ." Hope held out a gourd to her. "This broth came from the soldiers' mess. It's nice and hot. You had better eat, or you will be the next one to require nursing."

"Thank you, Hope. Did you have some broth yourself?" Faith accepted the first gourd, and falling silent, Adrienne nodded wordlessly and took the second.

Hope brushed a glistening auburn strand of hair from her eyes. "Not yet, but I will. I'll see that Charity gets some, too."

Faith gave her sister a brief smile. Things had gotten to quite a state when Hope would voluntarily wait on Charity. "Oh—what about Nancy and Whip?" she suddenly remembered. "I told them I would return with food and a lantern. I should get Nancy a change of clothes and another blanket, too."

"You stay here—Charity can go. Besides writing

letters, there's not much else she can do right now, and she's panting to see the baby anyway. It will do her good to get away from dying soldiers for a few minutes." Hope turned to leave, but Faith called her back.

"Hope . . . I just wanted to say I'm really glad you're my sister. You and Charity both, I'm so proud of you."

Hope looked startled by the compliment; then her green eyes lit with a wry smile. "No need to get maudlin, Faith. I think you just never noticed before that we are as grown up as you."

"No, I guess I didn't—but then, you never actually went out of your way to demonstrate that fact."

"Well, maybe not . . ."

The two sisters grinned at each other, and then Hope hurried away. Faith took a sip of the broth, which had been made surprisingly hearty by the addition of chunks of campfire bread. She noticed that Adrienne still had not tasted hers, but was looking down at Uncle Abel as if, for her, nothing or no one else in the world existed.

"Adrienne, you really must eat. What good will it do if you fall ill from lack of nourishment?"

Adrienne lifted her huge sorrowing eyes, and Faith was taken back by the depths of suffering in them. "Do not bother about me, *chérie*. There will be plenty of time later for eating and drinking."

A twinge of anger accompanied Faith's surprise at the woman's bluntness. "What do you mean by later?"

"We must face the inevitable, *chérie*. I have faced it many times, but somehow, it gets no easier."

"I had not thought that you would be one to give up so quickly. You've been through so much, and you've always seemed so brave."

"Pah! What is bravery but the gracious acceptance of what cannot be avoided? Your dear saintly uncle is probably going to die. And when he does, I think perhaps I shall stand in front of the gate, as Jeffrey did."

"You'll do *what?*" Horrified, Faith leaped to her feet. Half of her steaming broth sloshed onto Uncle Abel's hand, but she was so upset that she paid no heed to the mishap. "What on earth are you talking about? I could not have heard you right."

"*Chérie,* you heard me right. Your uncle will probably not awaken, and I cannot . . . continue . . . if he does not. I have lost too many whom I love—members of my family, my sister, my husband. I am too old to begin again."

"Just how old are you?" Faith snapped. "At what age is one entitled to give up?"

"I am forty-nine years old—almost half a century . . . not as young as you may have thought."

Faith stared at her. What she said was true; Adrienne did not look as old as she claimed. But being older than she looked did not excuse her shocking lapse into despair and self-pity. "I cannot believe you would willingly throw away your life, Adrienne. If you love my uncle, you could never do such a thing. He would rise up from his grave to condemn you."

"I think not," Adrienne said calmly. "Your uncle is very forgiving . . . Here, Faith, you have spilled your soup. Take mine instead, I do not want it."

Adrienne held out her gourd, but Faith was so incensed—was Adrienne trying to starve herself?—that she knocked the gourd away, then gasped as it flew out of Adrienne's hand, dumped its contents in Uncle Abel's face, and thumped him on the forehead. The container then bounced to the ground and landed upside down beside him.

Adrienne jumped to her feet. *"Mon Dieu!* Look what you have done!

Faith could not look away. Broth was running in rivulets down her uncle's cheeks and chin and into his hair. A glob of gooey bread spanned the bridge of his nose, and another lay directly on his bandage.

Incredibly, he stirred, reached up, and wiped the bread from his nose. His eyelids fluttered open. "F— Faith," he croaked, looking up at her. "Whatever are you doing, my dear?"

Chapter Twenty

By the glow of a rushlight, Whip stood looking down at the pile of food, weapons, and ammunition he intended to take on his mission with Pete Navarre. He had too much. Putting several items back, he picked up his long gun and fingered the carved stock. His mind was not really on the mission or on his weapons—but on Faith.

What if she refused to try to understand his reasons for going? What if he was throwing away her love and the future he hoped to share with her?

He had told Pete that he would take part in the mission after all, and Pete had been overjoyed. "You're doin' the right thing, Whip," he said. "Hell, I knowed you wouldn't let us down."

Whip knew his help was genuinely needed, but he did not feel that he was doing the right thing. Certainly Faith would not view it as the right thing. Moreover, he had a bad feeling about the mission itself. Something—call it a woodsman's intuition—told him that the mission, whatever it was, would fail. He still knew none of the details, only that he would be working with men whom he did not know in conditions that were difficult and dangerous.

Pete had told him that much, and General Harrison was waiting at the Grand Marquee to reveal the entire plan. Whip had only to gather his things and go there—yet he had been taking his time and thinking about Faith for over an hour.

Let the general wait, he thought. It had to be pitch dark before he and Pete left the fort, and it would be even better if the enemy thought that everyone in the fort had settled down for the night. One should never be too eager to face death—though Whip had broken that rule hundreds of times.

Sighing, he began to gather his things. But at the sound of someone jumping down into the bomb-proof, he quickly dropped them and turned. In the wild hope that it might be Faith, he grabbed the rushlight from its peg and held it up.

"Oh! Mr. Martin, I didn't know you were here." Charity looked at him with wide blue eyes.

Her eyes and her voice were the only way he recognized her. The rain and mud had taken their toll, and she hardly resembled the pretty, voluptuous girl he had brought through the forest not so long ago. But on second glance, he noticed that her curves were still blatantly apparent inside her rain-dampened dress, and he was filled with an urge to scold her for being so heedless of modesty. Faith would have worn an apron or a shawl to conceal the bold outline of her breasts beneath the wet fabric. Was Charity hoping to inflame every man she met?

The girl needed a tongue-lashing or, at the very

least, some paternal advice, but that was for her uncle to deliver.

Charity stepped closer to him. "I thought you were with Nancy. Faith said I should get Nancy some clean clothes and then take some hot food to you and Nancy. Is that why you are here—to find Nancy's things?"

Whip returned the rushlight to its peg. "You might as well do as your sister told you, Miss Cormorand. I came here for another reason."

"You did?" Charity peered at the pile of things on his sleeping shelf. "Where are you going?"

Her inquisitiveness irritated him. In fact, everything about her irritated him. On their journey to the fort, he had had the urge to strangle her several times. As she had first demonstrated in the little boat alongside the *Sea Sprite*, Charity was stubborn, outspoken, and utterly selfish in going after what she wanted. He would not have been surprised to learn that she had screamed on purpose—*knowing* that he would have to flee the British with her and Hope.

"It's none of your business where I am going," he said curtly.

Charity's eyes widened, then unaccountably filled with tears. "Why are you always so nasty to me, Mr Martin? Why, I think you actually hate me!"

"That isn't far from the truth . . ." Whip reached for his long gun, which he had hurriedly put down when he heard her approach.

To his surprise, Charity moved closer, and now he could see that she was deeply angry and upset. She also looked exhausted—badly in need of sleep. Bruiselike smudges beneath her eyes and a pallor about her mouth revealed the strain she must be under, and for a moment, Whip almost felt sorry for her—until he remembered the strain they had all been under. Then he felt only contempt for her youth and apparent weakness.

"I never did anything to *you!*" she accused. "It wasn't *my* fault that we had to leave the *Sea Sprite* without Tom and your precious supplies and ammunition. If you weren't such a beast—such a . . . a . . ."

Abruptly, Whip remembered Charity telling Faith how he had grabbed her and frightened her—the silly little minx. She really did believe he had somehow compromised her virtue. What conceit! Especially when she was the one who spent every waking moment teasing and flirting with any man who looked at her.

Instead of picking up his long gun, he placed one hand on the wall of the trench and leaned over her. Her eyes were bright with self-pitying tears calculated to melt his heart, but he wanted nothing so much as to turn her over his knee and wallop the foolishness out of her.

"A what, Miss Cormorand? Just what exactly do you think I am—a rogue? A rapist?"

"You—you're no gentleman!" Charity cried. "I don't know what my sister sees in you, and I wish you would leave her—and all of us—alone!"

Whip could feel himself growing angrier by the minute. He knew he should take his things and leave immediately. Nothing good could possibly come from trading heated words with Charity. Yet the chit had been begging for a setdown for some time, and he was so tired and so worried that he didn't know if he could resist the urge to give her one.

"The one thing I do not intend to do, Miss Cormorand, is to leave your sister alone. What she and I are to each other has nothing to do with you . . . What's the matter? Does it bother you to encounter a man who has no interest whatsoever in *you?*"

He heard himself saying the words and felt somewhat ashamed. She was only a child, really—a foolish, troublemaking child. But he never could understand why everyone indulged her. Someday she would go too far—thrusting out her full, heaving bosom, pouting her pink lips—and some young stallion would take what she was flaunting right beneath his nose.

Charity Cormorand was headed for trouble far worse than she was equipped to handle—unless someone stopped her first.

Blue eyes wide and disbelieving, rounded bosom indeed heaving, Charity stared at him. "I wouldn't *want* you to be interested in me, and as for Faith, my sister could certainly do better for herself than *you,* Mr. Martin. Why, hundreds of men in this fort might find her attractive if she would only give them half a chance . . ."

"If they were not so busy looking at *you*—right, Miss Cormorand? You've made it your business to advertise your wares on every possible occasion, and don't tell me you don't know what you're doing, because you and I both know better, don't we?"

"A-Advertise my wares?" Charity's mouth dropped open. "Wh-What do you mean?"

Could she really not know? Could the chit really be that stupid? Idly, Whip reached out and traced the air in front of her bodice. "Look at yourself . . . Haven't you seen the soldiers looking at you—in that damp dress, which outlines even your nipples?"

"M—my nipples!" Charity instantly crossed her arms over her chest. But the virginal gesture could not hide the guilty blush creeping up her cheeks. So she *did* know what she was doing; she only pretended to be innocent of deliberate enticement.

A spurt of anger made Whip's temples pound. This was the sister of the woman he loved, and he had a moment's image of Faith weeping broken-heartedly when Charity's dubious virtue was finally lost—or forcibly taken.

"You little slut," he hissed. "Don't you dare come crying to Faith when some young man loses control and goes too far with you. Don't you dare pretend it was all his fault."

"Oooooh!" Tears trembled on Charity's long golden eyelashes. "I hate you! You're a *terrible* man to say such awful things!"

Suddenly, she lashed out with one hand and struck Whip full across the face. The attack was so unexpected that at first he did not react, and then rage bubbled up from within, destroying the last vestiges of his restraint.

"Do you doubt what I'm telling you? You don't think a man can force you?" Whip seized Charity's shoulders. "Just what will you do, little Miss Charity, when some young man who is twice as strong as you are grabs you like this?"

Without thinking of the consequences of his

action, wanting only to teach Charity a lesson, he pulled her nose to nose with him, as if he meant to kiss her. Her blue eyes went wild with fear, and she began to struggle, making him even angrier. "You won't be able to fight off a man once he decides to take you—you silly little goose."

To emphasize the point, he pressed his mouth down on hers. Despite Charity's panicked flailings, he held his mouth on hers for several seconds, noting as he did so the startling contrast between kissing Charity and kissing Faith.

There was no eroticism in Charity's kiss, no arousal or stir of pleasure. Indeed, he felt nothing but disgust and scorn. Kissing Charity was like kissing a bratty child, not a full-grown sensual woman. Whoever finally *did* relieve her of her virtue was going to be almighty disappointed.

At last, he thrust her away from him, then had to hang on to her lest she go sailing backwards into the mud. Regaining her footing, Charity wiped his kiss from her mouth; she was sniveling and crying now.

"I'll never forgive you for this!" she blubbered like a six-year-old. "And if you ever touch me again, I— I'll tell Faith or Uncle Abel!"

"Tell anyone you want," Whip said, feeling more relaxed and calmer now, though still ashamed that he had so allowed her to provoke him. "Just be sure to tell them that you brought this on yourself."

"I'll go tell Faith right now!"

"Go ahead," he urged, suspecting that she was bluffing.

"It won't be necessary for her to tell me anything," a voice said. "I saw and heard it all."

A figure stepped out of the darkness, and Whip's heart missed a full five beats. He had not heard anyone jump down into the trench. Faith's smoky eyes—a burning dark violet, almost black with pain and anger—sought his.

"I came to find Charity . . . to tell her that Uncle Abel has regained consciousness. But I found Charity seducing you, you *allowing* her to seduce you . . . *enjoying* it, actually . . ."

The corners of Faith's mouth quivered. "How *could* you, Whip?" she whispered.

"Faith, you don't understand," he began, moving toward her. "You did not hear everything."

"And you, Charity—my own sister!" Faith turned to the sniveling blond girl. "I always worried about your flirtations, but never really thought they were anything but harmless. Certainly, I never expected you to try to take away *my* man when you have so many of your own to choose from!"

Charity tossed back her tangled blond curls. Tears and dirt streaked her flushed cheeks. To Whip and undoubtedly to Faith, she looked like a fallen woman, only this time she *hadn't* been flirting and teasing. It was only her damp dress and her infuriating naiveté that had so upset him.

"Faith," Charity sobbed unconvincingly. "It's not what you think! Really, it's not. You mustn't jump to—"

"Don't tell me what I should or shouldn't do! I know what I saw . . . You and Whip . . ." Again Faith looked at him with her enormous violet eyes. They were filled with bitter accusation, stabbing him to the heart.

"Now, look, Faith, you can't believe that I—that we—"

"I *saw* you!"

Her words hung in the air between them like the throbbing presence of something darkly evil and supernatural. He wanted to reach out to her, to take her in his arms and make the hurt go away forever.

"Listen to me, Faith . . . *listen* to me." Boldly, he went to her, but when he would have touched her, she slapped his hand away.

"I don't need to listen!"

"Charity did not seduce me, and I was not trying to seduce her!" he finally shouted across the yawning void between them. "I was trying to teach her a lesson, to show her what can happen if she continues to flirt and tease men."

Faith did not blink; he was not sure she had even heard him. She seemed dazed, completely unnerved by what she had seen. "You were supposed to be with Nancy . . . Why did you leave Nancy and the baby?"

Oh, God, he thought. From the way she was looking at him, he knew he would never be able to explain his mission with Peter. Now an even bigger wedge would be driven between them.

"Faith . . ." He seized her hands before she could jerk them away from him.

"Whip! Whip, are you in there?"

Both Faith and Charity jumped. Whip closed his eyes a moment; the last thing he needed right now was Pete Navarre, who had probably come looking for him to hurry him along.

"Whip! Damn it, man, the general's gettin' plumb irritated. We're supposed t' light out of here in five—" Pete Navarre closed his mouth when he saw Whip's face. Pete was halfway down into the bomb-proof, stepping onto a barrel, and as he took in the tense scene before him, he shook his head.

"Uh-Oh . . . Sorry, ole friend. I'll just wait outside till you're through here . . . but don't take long. Five minutes is all we got. Ladies . . ." He tipped his coonskin cap. "Sorry t' interrupt, but this here is mighty important business."

Then, leaving Whip to explain, he clambered out of the trench.

Faith's eyes scanned the pile of weapons and provisions. "There's no need for you to tell me why you came back here . . . I can see why."

Her tone sent icy fingers down his spine. "This isn't what you're thinking either, Faith. My business with Peter isn't a mission of revenge for what happened to Moon Daughter. It's—"

"Don't lie to me anymore, Whip!"

In the little silence that followed, as Whip tried to think of the right words to restore Faith's trust, Charity ceased daubing her eyes and asked, "Who's Moon Daughter?"

"I'll leave you two alone now so you can tell her," Faith said stonily. "Don't wait to explain until she hears you cry out your dead lover's name in a moment of unbridled passion. That really wouldn't be fair, Whip."

He had not expected her to be so cruel. Nothing she could have said would have wounded him more than bringing up Moon Daughter again. "When I come back, we'll talk, Faith. Maybe by then you'll be willing to let me explain everything."

She looked him square in the eye and did not even flinch. "I don't care if you never come back. Indeed, it would be better in every way if you didn't."

Whip was stunned. Death would be easier than this—being torn apart word by word, sentence by sentence, breath by breath. She was killing him by inches, in the Indian manner, causing slow suffering that would continue until he ceased drawing breath. Not even Moon Daughter's death had hurt so badly.

There was nothing else he could say; he picked up his gear and left.

Faith managed to hold herself erect until Whip was gone. Then, shaking from head to foot, she made her way to a barrel and sat down. She leaned forward and put her face in her hands. But she did not weep. Her pain was too new, too fresh, to be assuaged by tears. Nothing could ever assuage it— or her hatred.

For the first time in her life, she actually hated. Whip, Charity—she hated them both. Visions of violence filled her mind. A seething redness scorched and clawed at her insides. She wrestled with it for several moments, but it grew larger and larger, filling her to the point of explosion. She knew what she had seen—that kiss could never be explained away.

She jumped to her feet, almost knocking over Charity, who was standing wide-eyed right beside her.

"Faith," Charity said, reaching out to her in a wordless gesture of comfort.

Faith shoved her sister against the muddy wall. Had there been a knife in her hand, she might have plunged it into Charity's overripe bosom. Very likely that bosom was what had attracted Whip.

"Don't you ever touch me . . . Don't you ever speak to me again, Charity! I am no longer your sister, do you hear? You're a tramp and a harlot, and I don't want to have anything to do with you ever again!"

Charity's hand flew to her mouth. Heedless of the mud in her hair and on her shoulders and elbows, the girl fastened a teary-eyed stare on Faith. "You can't say that, Faith—we're *sisters.*"

"How do you know that?" Faith railed at her. "Maybe we aren't really! I could never be related to you—we're nothing alike! I believe in loyalty and love and kindness, in sticking by my family. You don't believe in any of those things! All you care about is yourself and your next conquest."

Charity pushed herself away from the slimy wall. "That's not true, Faith! I really do love you and Hope and Uncle Abel . . . Oh, I know I'm silly and foolish sometimes, but there isn't *any*thing I wouldn't do for you."

"Well, this time you've done entirely too much, Charity." Now the tears began to come, and Faith wheeled away from her sister. "Please, just go away and leave me alone . . ."

"Faith? Faith, I—I'm sorry. If Mr. Martin hadn't been trying to—to get me to mend my ways, this would never have happened . . . That *was* what he was doing, you know. He called me a slut . . . and you just called me a tramp and a harlot. Do you

364

think that's really what I am, Faith? Do you think I might have inherited a . . . a weakness that makes me act the way I do around men?"

Through the fog of her pain, Faith heard the terror in Charity's young voice. She remembered a dream—a nightmare in which she had kept begging Uncle Abel to tell her who she was. She had feared that there was something he didn't want her to know, some secret he was reluctant to divulge. All these years, had Charity feared the same thing?

Old habits made her turn her back to her sister, though she still could not bear the sight of her. "No, Charity . . . I don't think you behave the way you do around men because of something in your—in our past. You just don't think before you act. You never consider how your actions might hurt you or others. You—you just flaunt yourself. And this time, you flaunted yourself once too often."

Charity's hands fluttered over her breasts. "I—I should have worn a shawl or—or changed my dress after I got damp. Mr. Martin said he could see my n-nipples."

Faith looked down at her sister's bosom; the very thought of Whip thinking about Charity's body was enough to make her feel like retching. "He *could* see your nipples."

"H—he said I advertise my wares on every possible occasion."

"You *do*."

"He as much as said he hates me, Faith . . ." A single glistening drop threatened to fall from the tip of Charity's nose. She sniffed. "He said I shouldn't come crying to you when some man loses control and goes too far with me . . . and that I should never pretend that it was all the man's fault."

"You *shouldn't*."

"And then he asked what I would do if a strong young man grabbed me and tried to take advantage of me . . . and to show me that I couldn't defend myself, he kissed me."

Faith seized and dug her nails into her sister's shoulders and looked deeply into her tear-reddened eyes. "Is that really what happened, Charity? Are you telling me the truth?"

"I swear to you, Faith . . . I *hate* Mr. Martin! Didn't you *hear* those awful things he said to me? I would never want him to kiss me. Besides, h-he kisses like a mean old goat."

A goat. The last thing Whip kissed like was a goat. And now that she thought about it, Faith realized that she had been so stunned to see Whip kissing her sister that she really hadn't heard a word they said. Maybe Charity *was* telling the truth. Maybe Whip had only been trying to scare the girl. Before this, he had never shown anything but irritation and contempt toward Charity.

Faith moved away from her sister. Whip's sleeping platform drew her eye. Well, maybe he hadn't fallen under the influence of Charity's charms; but he *had* gone off to kill Indians again—and just when she had been so certain that he had changed!

She bowed her head; the joy of Uncle Abel's recovery and little Faith's birth seemed like a fleeting distant memory. Was she never to have a moment's respite between crises? Was her world never going to right itself after being tumbled and tossed and turned upside down since the day she had met Whip Martin?

Behind her, she could hear Charity blowing her nose. "Faith, I promise you I'll change. I'll try my very hardest."

Faith did not turn around. She didn't want her sister to see the doubt in her eyes. People *never* change. She had learned that lesson tonight—in a very painful way. And she wasn't likely to forget it.

"Honestly, Faith, I mean it. Tonight I learned a whole lot. I honestly never realized how—how provocative I sometimes am . . . I guess I *do* ogle and tease men. This isn't the first time I've been told I'm a tease," she admitted in a whisper. "In fact . . ."

"In fact, what?"

"What Mr. Martin was afraid would happen to me almost *did* happen the other day with Jacob Brent."

At that, Faith turned around. "Charity, do you love Jacob Brent or Captain Cushing or any of the other men who trail around behind you?"

Charity shook her head. Shame and self-knowledge darkened her eyes. "No, I . . . I just enjoy being the center of attention."

"Oh, Charity . . ."

The girl's tears threatened to spill over again. "Do you still love me, Faith? Will you still be my sister and m-my friend?"

Faith wasn't yet ready to forgive her sister. She could not block out the image of Charity in Whip's arms. "I—I'll have to think about it, Charity," she answered grudgingly.

But then as Charity's shoulders slumped and she started to turn away, Faith reached out to her. Sobbing now, the girl fairly threw herself into Faith's arms. Faith tried to offer words of forgiveness and reassurance, but they still would not come. It would be a long time before the hurt was gone and she could truly forgive Charity—indeed, she didn't know if she could ever forget the pain of this last hour.

Her desire for revenge was still shockingly strong, and suddenly, Faith understood the bitterness Whip had been wrestling with—was *still* wrestling with—as a result of Moon Daughter's murder.

How odd that the man who had taken her to the heights of passion and joy should also have dragged her down to the depths of despair and misery. Love and hate—he had taught her both.

She hugged her sister, but she did so out of habit rather than affection. Until love returned to her heart, she could only go through the motions.

Chapter Twenty-One

He should not have allowed himself to be talked into this fool plan. Whip knew that now—and it wasn't just because of what had happened between him and Faith. In the east, the sky was growing lighter, but they had not yet arrived at the British magazine, and from the looks of things, would not arrive there until long after dawn.

Colonel William Dudley was an ass, Whip thought, and the men in his detachment—most of them members of General Green Clay's regiment of Kentucky Volunteers—were sadly inexperienced.

Eight hundred men who had joined the army in a spurt of anger and patriotism could not be expected to move swiftly and silently through the wilderness like seasoned veterans. Having left their boats several miles upstream, the three columns of exhausted recruits were advancing along the bank of the river with the speed of turtles.

And to think these whey-faced boys had been sent to rescue Fort Meigs. Heavyhearted, Whip trudged along at the end of the column to which he had been assigned—or, more accurately, ordered. As if the fact that Faith now hated him weren't depressing and discouraging enough, he felt powerless to change the course of current events.

Faith just might get her wish; he, along with hundreds of others, was surely marching into a trap from which there could be no escape.

But it hurt too much to think about Faith; so instead he thought about General Harrison. The general was going to be extremely disappointed.

Upon hearing that the Kentucky recruits had arrived eight miles upriver and were preparing to descend the Maumee to the fort, the general had sent Whip and several others to reconnoiter with General Clay. They had suggested that Clay send a detachment of soldiers to the British batteries under cover of night. There, after catching the enemy by surprise at dawn, they were to storm the batteries, spike the guns, destroy the British magazines, then flee across the river to the safety of the fort.

Since the British would be unable to repair their guns, the siege would be brought to a sudden halt.

It was a brilliant maneuver, Whip believed, the sort of daring offensive that just might succeed because of its implausibility. He had thought so when he first heard the plan; neither the British nor the Indians expected an outright assault. Willie Oliver, the young man who had brought news of General Clay's arrival, had assured Harrison that none of the enemy had as yet discovered their presence.

So Peter Navarre had accompanied Whip, a young captain, and two others to the rendezvous with Clay. But after the plan had been accepted by the Kentucky general, Pete had slipped back to the fort to tell Harrison, and Whip had started downriver with Colonel Dudley.

Shortly thereafter, however, the fleshy, arrogant commanding officer had shown his true nature. Ignoring Whip's warning that stealth and darkness were essential to the success of the maneuver, Dudley had assumed the lead of the three columns and marched them slowly but noisily toward his goal. He had even refused to accept Whip's services as a guide over the difficult terrain—terrain on which he himself had never before set foot.

"Just point me in the right direction, boy," he had wheezed enthusiastically. "I'll find those bastards. We'll show 'em a little Kentucky spirit, and they'll take to their heels in pure terror."

Whip knew it was more likely to be the other way around. He had heard it said that Colonel Dudley had never seen an Indian or heard a hostile gun. Thus, the man did not realize that no Shawnee, certainly not Tecumseh, would be intimidated by a bunch of greenhorns, however bold and daring. Instead, the Indians would gleefully don their war paint and plot how best to confuse or lure their enemies into a bloody ambush.

But when Whip had tried to explain these important facts of life on the frontier, the colonel had responded, "Bull feathers and poppycock! Just get outa my way, son, and I'll learn you a thing or two about Kentuckians."

Now, as dawn washed the eastern sky in pale, watery streaks of gray and lavender, Whip noticed that the terrain had not yet given way to the crisscross of brush-choked ravines that would signal the approach to the British batteries. The main battery itself was situated on a small plain, with a wood in the rear and thick bushes on three sides; only in front had the growth been cleared away.

Not only would they fail to surprise the British at dawn, but they would be lucky to reach the main battery by eight o'clock. Whip cast continued anxious glances into the surrounding woods. It was quiet—too quiet. Not a single bird call or rustle of startled forest creature marred the expectant silence.

Pete Navarre would have understood the significance of that; the presence of soldiers or Indians had scattered the wildlife some hours or even moments before.

Whip heartily wished his friend had remained with Dudley's regiment; but Pete was probably safely back at the fort by now and watching from across the river for Dudley to launch his attack. The fort's big eighteen-pounders were probably already primed and aimed to cover their retreat.

Whip stepped up his pace, hoping that by doing so he might hurry along everyone else in the line. But the pompous Colonel Dudley seemed bent on advancing at his own deadly slow pace—and damn the consequences. Whip succeeded only in breathing down the back of the man in front of him.

The man growled over his shoulders, "Git off my heels, boy. If you're in sech a hurry, go on up t' the front of the line an' tell the colonel to move his ass."

"I think I'll do just that," Whip retorted. Knowing it was already too late and probably futile to try and divert disaster, he nonetheless stepped out of line and loped ahead to find Dudley.

For his own life, he didn't give a hoot; but for the lives of all these damned innocents being marched like lambs to slaughter, he could not help but feel pity.

"Where did he say he was going?" After spending the remainder of the night beside her rapidly recovering uncle, Faith stood in the storehouse and looked down at Nancy, the only person who might be able to give her a clue as to where Whip had gone—and why.

Not that she doubted her own conclusions, but she simply had to find out for certain. Setting aside the incident with Charity, she still believed that Whip had betrayed her hope and trust in him—but might she somehow be mistaken?

With every fiber of her being, she hoped she was wrong. It would be the last straw if he really had gone to kill Indians. How much was she supposed to forgive? How much could she overlook just because she loved him?

"Well, he didn't say exactly where he was goin'." Seemingly unaware of the importance of her answer, Nancy continued changing the soiled cloth on little Faith's tiny dimpled bottom. "But I think it had somethin' t' do with winnin' the war or stoppin' the siege—or maybe jus' killin' Injuns."

"Killing Indians," Faith repeated, her heart plummeting into her toes.

Nancy glanced up in surprise. "Why, what's the trouble, Faith? Did I say somethin' wrong?"

Reeling from the impact of her dashed hopes, Faith blurted, "I can't believe he would calmly announce that he was going off to kill people, and then just go ahead and do it, brazen as you please."

"Oh, it wasn't like that, Faith . . ."

But Faith did not stay to hear how it had actually been. Overwhelmed with misery, she stalked from the shed. She had to be alone for a while; her disappointment was too shattering to share with another.

Just as she had suspected, Whip Martin had not changed. How could she have been so stupid as to hope he had?

She would never understand him, never trust him. He lacked reason and common sense, not to mention normal human compassion. How could he be so tender and gentle one moment—then turn into a vengeful murderer the next? Eventually, she could have gotten over the shock of seeing him kiss Charity, especially if he had indeed done so to teach her a lesson. But how she could get over—again and again—the shock of his deliberately going off to murder other human beings?

As she blindly stalked alongside the Grand Traverse, something cold and wet brushed her hand. Startled, she looked down to see Shadow trotting along beside her. She stopped walking and put her hands on her hips. "You mangy, bothersome wolf!

374

Where did you come from—and why are you following me? Why aren't you out with your master on his killing spree?"

As if embarrassed by her undignified outburst, Shadow sat down in the mud and glanced away. His amber eyes were more mournful than usual, and Faith realized that Whip must have left him behind with Nancy. But why the wolf had suddenly chosen to follow her about like a huge overgrown gray puppy, she could not guess. Except for that one night when he had snuggled close to her in the bombproof, Shadow had always maintained his threatening aloofness.

"Well, there's no use trying to be friendly now. I meant what I said last night! I don't ever want to see your master—or you—again! Neither one of you is capable of affection or friendship or . . ."

The curious glance of a passing soldier caused Faith to begin walking again. The wolf complacently followed—goading her to continue her tirade, only this time in a lower voice. "You and Whip make people care about you, worry about you, love you, and for what? So you can break their hearts. Well, I'll tell you something, you stupid wolf—when two beings, human or otherwise, feel affection for each other, they aren't the same as they were before. They become new and different, bigger and better . . ."

She let her voice trail off, trying to find the right words to explain the difficult concept. "What they become, together, is much finer and more important than what they were separately. Of course, in order for this change to occur, each has to sacrifice something—and some people just aren't capable of

375

changing one little tiny bit. They are too wrapped up in themselves and their own problems—like you and your master. You are both too selfish and stubborn to make the changes that love requires . . ."

So engrossed was she in what she was saying that Faith almost walked past the bombproof trench. Only the fact that Shadow had paused in front of Whip's shelter drew her attention to her whereabouts. Absentmindedly, she climbed down into her own muddy hole, then sighed in exasperation. Everything was a sodden mess—and as usual Charity had been responsible.

During the early hours before dawn, the infirmary had grown quite chilly. Knowing that at least this time Charity would not encounter Whip, Faith had again sent her back to the bombproofs to gather every available blanket. Charity had brought back blankets, jerky, two of Whip's warmest furs, and several clean garments for Uncle Abel. And in her usual careless manner, she had torn the bombproofs apart searching for these items.

Despite Charity's new eagerness to please, Faith now wished that she had sent Hope instead. No matter how late the hour or how tired Hope was, she would never have turned the three places into such a disaster. Baskets and bundles stood open, bedding had been rearranged—some had even fallen into the mud—and clothing was strewn about.

How could she let Nancy, little Faith, and Uncle Abel come back to *this?* With a vengeance that helped to ease her frustration, Faith plunged into the task of cleaning, straightening, and rearranging. At least, she decided, there was one good thing about living in a fort in the middle of a siege; you always had something to distract you from your personal problems.

Avoiding Whip's shelter, saving it until last, she worked tirelessly for several moments and simultaneously considered her bleak future. Regardless of the pain it would cause her, she knew she had to forsake Whip. She must thrust him from her thoughts and from her heart. She must somehow dredge up the strength of mind and character, which had always been her saving grace and her solace, and think of duty first.

As last night had painfully demonstrated, her sisters and her uncle still needed her desperately. And when this war was over, there would be plenty of tasks to fill her empty days. Uncle Abel's dream could still come to pass, and this time, instead of secretly resisting it and wishing she could strike out on her own, she would embrace it as wholeheartedly as he did.

But as she finally began to arrange Whip's belongings—his skins, his clothing, his baskets and bundles, which Charity had tossed right and left— she found it difficult to remain outraged. Everything reminded her of the puzzling complexity of the man.

Opening baskets and fringed buckskin bags so as to separate foodstuffs from other items, she found surprises. One basket held Indian ornaments: a necklace of claws from a large animal; a wide belt made of four strands of perfectly matched white shells; an intricately embroidered headband; and a small embroidered pouch, the significance of which

377

she could not ascertain. The pouch contained several multicolored pebbles, three broken dusty feathers, the tooth of some unknown creature, and a handful of assorted bones.

Why had Whip—who professed to hate and despise the savages—kept these mementos of his life among the Shawnee?

It came to her that the vivid white scars on his chest might be claw marks rather than battle wounds, and that the necklace of long curved claws might have come from the guilty animal. In believing that the scars were the result of violent clashes with other men, had she misjudged him—or was she once again indulging in futile hope?

Exploring further, she found a bundle of carefully wrapped books, bound in leather with gilt-edged pages. The volumes were literary classics, save one— a Bible. She was amazed. Whip scorned and mocked religion, yet apparently he did not do so out of ignorance. The book's well-thumbed appearance gave clear-cut evidence of continual perusal, and she recalled his easy use of biblical quotations.

Abandoning all restraint, she began searching through Whip's belongings with a shameless curiosity. She did not know exactly what she was looking for—but when she came to a small ornamental basket, she paused, sat down on the skin-heaped shelf, and considered it thoughtfully.

Thus far, all of Whip's things had been boldly masculine—even the books. But this basket was feminine and graceful, as if it had been designed for a woman's use. Its colors were delicate, its design subtle, and its shape less utilitarian than decorative.

If I owned this basket, Faith thought, I would put something special inside it—not everyday things but once-in-a-while things, festive things.

Realizing that she would be greatly disappointed if the basket contained nothing but salt pork or jerky, Faith removed the lid. Astonishment swept through her. Inside the basket, Whip had placed the neatly folded remnants of Jeffrey's shirt.

So he had not thrown the shirt away after all but had tucked it away in this obviously special container.

Almost reverently, she removed the memento. Then her eye caught something white, and her fingers brushed a velvety softness. Suddenly, she regretted her impulse to search through Whip's things. What if she found something she would rather not know about? What if she found some intimate personal thing of Moon Daughter's?

But it was unthinkable to stop now. Gingerly, she lifted the next item in the basket. The pale white doeskin seemed to glow with a life of its own in the shadowy gray light. Unfolding the object with trembling fingers, Faith saw that it was a dress—a lovely festive dress, intricately beaded and embroidered—that could only have belonged to Whip's Indian wife.

She studied it for several awestricken moments. The dress was the most beautiful, finely crafted garment she had ever seen. She wondered how she herself would look in it, with her hair twisted into braids and spilling down over her shoulders.

But Moon Daughter had been a brown-eyed savage, and perhaps the dress would not become a white girl. Toying with the fringe on it, Faith was oddly touched to know that Whip had saved the keepsake; it demonstrated once again his amazing sensitivity. On the other hand, it also spoke of his deep abiding love for a dead woman.

For all that she had just spent an hour telling herself that she must stop seeing Whip, she could not suppress her jealousy and longing. Unreasonable though it was, she wished he had never loved anyone before her—never lain with another woman, never mourned another woman's death.

Tearfully, she wondered why life could not be simple and uncomplicated. Why had she fallen in love with a man like Whip? In a spurt of objectivity, she realized that he was everything she both loved and hated in a man—courageous, loyal, sensitive, strong—and savage, violent, arrogant, and vengeful.

Vengefulness was his worst sin—but wasn't she herself vengeful? Hadn't she lashed out to hurt him and been glad of the pain she had inflicted? What right had she to judge him?

An oft-quoted scriptural passage resounded in her ears: "He that is without sin among you, let him first cast a stone . . ."

Her reasons for rejecting Whip were no more than weak excuses, she now realized. Uncle Abel could get along without her, especially now that he had Adrienne. And her sisters did not need her either. They were old enough to make—and live with— their own mistakes.

The truth was that if she wanted Whip Martin she could have him. She did not really believe that he cared for Charity. And, oh, God, she wanted Whip more than she had ever wanted anything or anyone in her life!

Losing him—or more accurately, not taking him—would be worse than losing her mother, that dim, shadowy figure she had lost so very long ago.

But I won't weep or despair, she thought. If I have to give him up, somehow I will go on. I have always been strong. I despise weakness. I will never abandon my principles.

Unfortunately, the choice was already out of her hands. Whip Martin might never return. He might be dead at this very moment.

The story of Return Jonathan Meigs leaped unbidden into her head, and her trickling tears began to flow in earnest. Unlike the governor's mother, she had sent her beloved away with a death curse, without telling him how much she loved him—and how much she wanted him to return.

Return, Whip, return, she prayed, wishing with all her heart that she could take back every nasty thing she had said and thought.

Unexpectedly, Shadow nosed her hand. Suspecting that the wolf was really nosing Moon Daughter's dress, Faith nonetheless knelt on the muddy ground and flung her arms around the startled animal.

As she buried her face in the wolf's soft fur, Shadow stood utterly still, as if frozen. Then a low growl began in his throat.

"Oh, stop pretending you don't need anybody!" Faith choked through her tears. She reached up and grabbed the white doeskin dress, impulsively pulling it down and draping it around her neck and shoulders. "Go ahead and bite me, if you must . . . but you've got to learn to trust again sometime. I may be all you have left."

Gradually, the wolf's warning rumble ceased. Timidly, he nosed the dress. Sensing that it was now or never, Faith stroked his neck, scratched behind his ears, and hugged him to her. She murmured endearments—words meant not only for him but for his master as well. His nose pressed close to the doeskin, Shadow suffered this for a moment. Then he heaved a sigh, licked her cheek, and gently laid his massive head on her shoulder.

Faith's moment of triumph was poignant and fleeting.

"Shadow, oh, Shadow," she cried. "If Whip doesn't come back, whatever am I going to do?"

Chapter Twenty-Two

Whip examined the pale gray sky and estimated the time to be nine o'clock. They had arrived at the main British battery an hour later than he had predicted—and now, while he and the captain struggled to spike the guns of the enemy, Dudley and his men were laughing and talking and exploring the small plain as if they had just won a mighty battle instead of a minor skirmish.

Fools and asses all, Whip seethed, his contempt for them overridden only by his anxiety.

Something was very wrong. The redcoats had struck their colors and abandoned their posts too easily, and the attacking savages had fallen back with little more than a smattering of musketfire.

Dudley thought they had all been frightened off by his great Kentucky yell. "Twill send them scatterin' with their tails between their legs," he had officiously predicted.

Whip knew better. He only hoped he would have time to put the British guns out of commission

383

before disaster struck. More than two-thirds of the artillery pieces remained to be spiked, and he had not even touched the magazines. No sooner had he finished spiking a howitzer when musketfire sounded at the fringe of the woods surrounding the abandoned battery.

The militiamen hurried to return the fire, and the young captain, Peter Dudley—no relation to the foolhardy William—came rushing over. His earnest young face was deathly pale as he inquired worriedly of Whip, "You don't think Colonel Dudley's going to pursue the savages into the woods, do you, sir?"

Poor young Dudley, Whip thought. No doubt he had seen what happened to cocky, overeager soldiers.

With the captain trailing behind him, Whip loped toward one of the big twenty-four-pounders that had likely been responsible for some of the heaviest shelling of the fort. "If he does, he's a dead man, Captain. Do you want to make a break for the fort or stay here and suffer the consequences?"

The young captain looked stricken. "We can't leave yet, sir! General Harrison is expecting us to spike the guns. That's the reason we took the risk of coming here."

Whip glanced toward the colonel. Red-faced with anger and surprise, he was barking orders at his men to get back into fighting formation. A few were doing so, but most were too excited by the pop-pop-pop of musketfire to pay any attention to their commanding officer. "Then I think we had better move faster, Captain. My guess is we haven't much time."

More musketfire punctuated his comment, and

the Kentucky volunteers abandoned all semblance of military order and obedience. "Them's redskins out there, boys!" someone called out. "Are we gonna let 'em get away with blastin' Kentucky's finest?"

In answer, another Kentucky yell went up, accompanied by cries of "Hell, no!" and "Damned if I will!"

In the face of his regiment's mounting enthusiasm, Colonel Dudley grinned and hollered, "Well, what're we waitin' for, boys? Let's have after 'em! Them stinkin' yellow-bellies don't have the guts t' come out from behind the trees and fight us fair an' square!"

Appalled by the man's utter ignorance, Whip dropped the spike he had been about to ram down the barrel of the big cannon and sprinted toward the colonel. "Colonel—no! That's what the savages want you to do—chase after them into the woods. It's a trick so they can ambush . . ."

His warning was drowned out by more cheers and yells as the drum sounded the call to attack. Pandemonium broke loose.

"Dudley!" Whip skidded to a stop in front of the colonel, but there was so much noise and confusion and he was so angry that he could scarcely make himself heard.

As men in fringed hunting shirts and ragtag uniforms raced past him toward the trees, Whip finally found the words to confront the puffy-eyed, puffy-cheeked colonel with the full import of what he had just done. "You idiot! You are sending those men to their deaths! The savages will shoot them down like a flock of pigeons. Sound a retreat, for God's sake. Sound a retreat! It's your only chance."

The colonel flushed a brilliant scarlet. "I most certainly will not do any such thing! And when General Harrison hears of your insubordination, he will string you up by your thumbs, boy."

"He won't hear of it—because none of us will live to tell about it. Sound the retreat, you jackass."

Captain Dudley, who had been running close on Whip's heels, offered his white-faced nodding agreement. "Please Colonel, Mr. Martin knows what he's talking about. I've seen this kind of ambush before."

"Gentlemen." The colonel drew himself upright, his jowls quivering with affront. "Such cowardice is downright disgraceful. An' I fully intend—"

Musketballs began to whiz past them, and Whip realized that it was already too late to sound the retreat. Having lured the bulk of the regiment away from an easily defensible location where they might have made a successful stand, the savages were rapidly closing in on those who remained near the magazine.

Just then a soldier ran toward them and breathlessly interrupted the colonel's faltering tirade. "Colonel Dudley, sir! A column of British soldiers is attacking us from the rear!"

Whip could not help wincing. Their position was now beyond defense. While the colonel had been swaggering about the battery, congratulating himself on his easy conquest, the British had been stealing around behind them to block off their only escape route.

"Dudley, you can still save some of your regiment

if you order them to return to Fort Meigs at once. There might still be boats at the river crossing. If the savages have sunk the canoes, you can swim across the river."

"Damn it, Martin! I'm not retreating! We're from Kentucky, after all—the finest volunteer regiment in the United States Army."

A man's dying yelp interrupted him, and musket-balls rained down like hail. Knowing they hadn't another moment to spare, Whip whirled to face the young captain, "What do you say, Pete? Are you ready to return to the fort?"

Captain Peter Dudley took one last longing look at the remaining artillery. "It's too late to finish spiking them, isn't it?"

"You're damn right it is."

But before either of them could take a step, a terrible bloodthirsty yell erupted from the perimeter of the forest. Colonel Dudley's jaw dropped. Splendidly executed, the fearful Shawnee yell was enough to strike fear into even the sturdiest of hearts. Considering the colonel's pride in his Kentucky yell, Whip wondered what Dudley was thinking now—knowing that in a matter of moments they would surely be either killed or captured.

He couldn't resist a last verbal jab: "Well, Colonel, what do you think of the Shawnee war cry? Magnificent, isn't it?"

He removed his long gun from its shoulder sling. Would he ever be able to convince Faith to forgive him for once again killing Indians? Or, after today, would it no longer matter? He had an awful premonition that her forgiveness, if she offered it, would come too late: This time he would not make it through alive.

"You were the one who came to fetch Whip last night—against my wishes," Faith accused the buckskinned stranger with the clear gray-blue eyes and the grimly set mouth. "What do you want now?"

Night had fallen, a terrible dark night after a terrible dark day, and Faith was anxious and frightened. She did not want to speak with this stranger who had called her out of the bombproof and insisted that she walk with him a short distance, out of hearing of the others.

She held up her rushlight in its small iron holder, and the play of soft light revealed that the man was watching her with a sympathetic expression. But instead of being reassured, she felt all the more apprehensive. If this man had returned, why hadn't Whip?

"Please tell me who you are, sir, and why you want to see me. We are now far enough away from the others to preserve your privacy."

"I'm Pete Navarre, Miss Cormorand, a friend of Whip Martin's."

It was on her tongue to protest: She had already made the acquaintance of all of Whip's friends. But as this morning's search through his belongings had proven, there was much about Whip she still didn't know, including his present whereabouts. Had Mr. Navarre come to see her about that?

"Do you know where he is?" she asked bluntly.

"Well, miss, I suppose you've already heard what happened to Colonel Dudley and his regiment."

Faith lifted her chin, steadying herself for the worst she could possibly hear. "Who does *not* know, Mr. Navarre? Of the nine hundred seventy-one men who participated in today's mission, only one hundred and seventy have safely reached the fort. The rest are still . . . out there."

Peter Navarre's eyes held hers. "The rest are likely dead by now—or taken prisoner, which amounts to the same thing."

"You don't know that for a fact, sir, though the reports have been very disturbing." Abruptly, Faith fell silent, as she thought of the awful stories that had been circulating like wildfire throughout the fort. There had been accounts of men being forced to run a gauntlet of howling savages, of other men being herded together in a group and shot, and of still others being stripped, tortured, and slain in the most inhuman manner possible.

Even now, it was being said, the fires of the savages were burning bright across the river, and the wind was carrying the echoes of the captives' screams.

"No, miss, I don't know for a fact what has happened or is happening to those other eight hundred men. But Whip hasn't made it back yet, and he would have been here by now if he was still alive."

Faith stared at Peter Navarre. She herself had thought that very same thing; but something within her refused to accept that Whip was dead. Somehow, she believed, she would *know* if he was dead. She would feel it in her very bones.

"P-perhaps he wasn't with Dudley's regiment. Perhaps he had some other mission."

"No, Miss Cormorand." Sadly, the man shook his head. "He was with 'em. I know he was, because he and I and two others went out together t' meet General Clay. I'm the only one who's made it back. That's why I came to see you, to bring you the news myself. I no longer have any doubts about what happened to Whip."

"No!" Faith cried, nearly dropping the rushlight. "I don't believe he is dead." She gripped the iron holder with both hands, but even then the light wavered and shook.

"I'm sorry . . . I had hoped t' bring you a measure of comfort, an' I've only succeeded in bringin' you pain." Pete Navarre reached out and steadied her cold, trembling hands with his own strong, warm ones. "I'm sorry, Miss Cormorand," he repeated. "Whip Martin was a fine brave man—there wasn't any finer. I wanted you t' know that. Because of you, he didn't want to undertake this mission. At first, he refused, but I bullied him into it. I shamed him into going . . . That wasn't a mission of personal revenge; he was merely tryin' to end this war once and for all."

In the midst of her suffering, Faith latched on to the one shred of comfort. "H-he didn't want to go? Because of me?"

"He didn't want to do any more killin', though God knows he had reason enough t' hate the savages for what they did t' his Indian wife."

Faith drew a deep breath. Fear and grief were still with her, but those crushing emotions did not weigh so heavily now. If Whip was dead, at least he had

390

died for a noble reason, not a base one. But she did not—she *could* not—believe he was dead.

"Thank you for coming and telling me, Mr. Navarre. You have eased my soul tremendously."

Pete Navarre withdrew his hands and cocked his head. "Of course, there's always a slim chance that Whip was taken prisoner and is still alive. But I don't think you can count on it, Miss Cormorand. I once made my home at Frenchtown, and I know first-hand what the savages are capable of doing to prisoners. Proctor didn't stop 'em then, and I see no reason why he would stop 'em now. If anything, he might think that we can be intimidated into surrendering if he lets the Injuns run wild."

"He doesn't know us very well, then, does he?" Faith recalled General Harrison's reply to Proctor only that afternoon. Bearing a white flag, a Major Chambers had arrived at the fort with demands for an unconditional surrender. Harrison had replied, "Tell General Proctor that if he takes the fort, it will be under circumstances that will do him far more honor than a thousand surrenders."

"I don't expect he does know us, Miss Cormorand." Peter Navarre smiled at her; then just as quickly, his smile disappeared. "I wish there was somethin' I could do. But they say that all prisoners have been taken downriver to the remains of the old British Fort Miami. Only God or an Injun could sneak in there, an' once inside, only God could find Whip an' git him out alive."

"I expect you're right, Mr. Navarre." Despairingly, Faith wondered if God really existed, and if He did, whether He would consider stepping in to save one of his creatures—a man whose noble and selfless acts must surely outweigh his sins.

Then she thought of Moon Daughter and her white doeskin dress, and last, almost inevitably, she thought of Shadow. A plan began to assume shape in her mind. Indistinct and hazy at first, it floated like a cloud just above the grasp of her imagination. God and the white doeskin and Shadow: There had to be some connection between them, and suddenly she knew what it was.

"Will you be all right if I leave you now, Miss Cormorand?" Peter Navarre inquired kindly. "I'll see you back to the trenches first, if you like."

"No, that won't be necessary, thank you. I can find my way back myself."

And I can certainly find my way downriver.

Aware that he was watching her closely, she lowered her head, as if wrestling with her sorrow, then turned and walked quickly away from him. Little did he know that she felt no sorrow whatsoever. Instead, she was swept with a wild, unreasoning hope. Whip was alive. She *knew* he was alive. And she knew exactly how to find him. All she needed was a little help from God—and from Shadow.

Whip tried to moisten his dry lips, but he had no moisture left in his body, except his blood. And even that was draining away, drop by drop, from the cuts and welts that covered every inch of his shivering flesh.

The savages had not been gentle with him when he ran the gauntlet at the entrance to Fort Miami. He was lucky to still be alive—or rather, he was unlucky. The lucky ones, like Colonel Dudley, had died on the field of battle. Dudley had been shot, then scalped, and then his heart had been cut out. But the wretched captives had been herded to the old British fort to face even worse sufferings.

Spreadeagled and staked to the ground, Whip could see a scene that was even more terrible and shocking than his worst imaginings of hell. Glowing, smoking campfires cast an eerie pall of light and shadow over the painted creatures darting to and fro among the captives, some of whom were shrieking or moaning or simply praying, as they contemplated—or experienced—the worst tortures the savages could devise.

No one yet had touched Whip, but he knew his hour was coming. Two of the Indians, dressed in American uniforms stripped from the dead or dying, frequently came to look down at him and to argue. They didn't know he understood their language, and so they jabbered freely. From his actions on the battlefield, they had concluded he was a great warrior—as skilled and courageous as any Indian.

According to custom, his death must therefore be an occasion. His tortures must be the most agonizing. His courage must be tested to the utmost. And when he was finally hovering near death, his still-living heart must be torn from his chest and divided among many warriors. In this way, his bravery would be passed on to his conquerors.

Whip knew that he should pray, but he did not know how to frame words to a deity who already knew him and his guilt better than he himself knew it. Praying now seemed a blasphemy, a weakness. He would not beg to be spared. Nor could he beg forgiveness. Everything he had done, he had done for a reason.

The reason was wrong—he realized that now— and justice demanded that he pay for his acts. The old saying was true: Vengeance begets vengeance. With his bare hands, he had murdered others, and now he himself would be murdered.

In an oddly curious way, he was finally at peace. He could even look up at the ramparts and dispassionately observe the British soldiers who were allowing this scene of horror and violence to occur. One day, the soldiers would pay, as surely as he was now paying. They would get what they deserved; for it was as evil to permit violence as it was to perpetrate it.

At this moment, as his death drew nearer, Whip had but two regrets: He deeply regretted that Faith would suffer when she learned what had happened to him, and he also regretted the loss of the years of loving that could have been theirs. He wished he could tell her that he had repented—that she had been right, after all. He wished he could hold her with all of his body's passion and his soul's surrender.

If he could only see her one more time, he would die content.

A man bent over him. It was one of the savages who had been watching him and biding his time. The man's face was painted red. His dark blue military uniform hung open to reveal other items he had stolen from the dead—someone's solid gold pocket watch, a small silver cross, a woman's gold locket. These treasures hung suspended from a leather thong and dangled in Whip's face.

Then he saw the knife in the savage's hand. Its handle was a carved horn, its blade a glowing red. The savage grinned, revealing a missing front tooth. He waved the blade above Whip's chest, and Whip could feel heat radiating from the metal. Slowly, watching his face, the savage pressed the red-hot knife flat against Whip's chest.

The pain was agonizing, worse than anything Whip could imagine. His heart leaped. His body shuddered and tried to shrink away. He had to clench his jaws together to keep from screaming.

Grinning from ear to ear, the Indian drew back. He said something. It sounded like "Good. This one good. We make his death honorable."

Then the man left him.

Whip closed his eyes and lay perfectly still, but his muscles, his sinews, his nerve endings continued to jump. Defying his control, his entire body twitched and jumped.

The Indian is wrong, he thought. His death would not be honorable. The next time, or the time after that, he would begin to jabber like an idiot. He would lose control over all his muscles and die with the stench of his own vomit and excrement in his nostrils.

Even now the scent of his burned flesh so turned his stomach that he could scarcely keep from convulsing.

Don't think about it, he told himself. By dawn, you will be dead. You will feel nothing. The savages almost always kill their victims before dawn. Think about something else. Think about Faith. Think about Moon Daughter and Shadow and Jeffrey. Think about all those whom you have ever loved.

He thought. He concentrated. He reached for their images in the darkest and most unreachable corners of his mind. They would not come. The pain had driven them away . . . and then, just as he was about to despair, he heard a whimpering. Something was nosing his face, his neck, and shoulders.

He opened his eyes. Shadow's muzzle loomed above him. Past the wolf's massive shoulders, he saw an incredible vision. No, not a vision, a miracle.

Through the smoke and fire, out of the night-swirling mist came a woman—a woman dressed in gleaming white doeskin. Head held high, shoulders thrown back, long black braids spilling down over her breasts, she moved like an Indian princess. Alone and unafraid, she walked into the midst of the savages.

Not a single Indian made a move to stop her. Instead, they muttered and stared. They fell back away from her, and several made a sign to protect themselves from evil spirits.

It was as if she had come from another world, another place, and the heathens—superstitious and afraid—waited in awestruck silence to see what would happen next.

Perhaps they cannot really see her, Whip thought. Only I can see her. Perhaps they only sense her presence.

The woman drew closer and finally stopped and stood looking down at him. Whip saw that she was

396

dazed. Shock and distress filled her huge violet eyes, and her lips were trembling. The truth smote him. This was no spirit come to claim him for the afterworld; this was his own dear Faith. And how she had come to be here, dressed in Moon Daughter's wedding dress and looking like an angel descended into hell, he dared not even guess.

He raised his head and again tried to moisten his lips. "You should not have come," he tried to say, but the only sound he could manage was a cry so hoarse and unrecognizable that even Shadow started and jumped back.

Faith dropped to her knees at his feet. "Whip . . . oh, my dearest Whip . . ."

And then the savages were crowding around them, jostling and shouting and reaching for her, their hands like demon claws. Shadow leaped for one brave's throat, and the man fell heavily on top of Whip. His bones crunched in protest. He could no longer see what was happening to Faith, but the prayers he had not been able to say for himself now flowed freely for his beloved.

Spare her, O God, spare her. She doesn't deserve to die.

Chapter Twenty-Three

Faith felt the clawing hands of the savages, saw their painted, leering faces, and knew that her most terrifying fears were being realized.

Having expected to be seized sooner, she was not surprised. It might have been her Indian garb that had held the savages at bay, or it might have been Shadow, trotting along silently at her side, single-minded in his determination to get to his master, or it might have been a combination of both.

In their eyes, she had seen fear and puzzlement. They had watched her, but they had not attacked—until they realized she was a woman like any other, prostrate with grief over what they had done to her lover.

It was useless to struggle against them. She had already convinced herself that it would be better to die pleading for Whip's life than to live without him.

But she had never really expected to find such horrors as she had encountered on entering the carelessly guarded gates of Fort Miami. It was as if she had walked into a living nightmare, the lair of hundreds upon hundreds of devils.

Now, as she was jostled and shoved, grabbed by one savage and pushed by another, she lost her footing and fell to the ground. She realized that she would never find General Proctor, or if she did, it would make no difference. A man who would condone the torture and killing of helpless captives was a man without honor; a woman's tears and admonishments could not persuade him to end his evildoing. She knew herself to be more naive, more foolish, than Uncle Abel. Yet something—some irresistible force—had driven her to come here.

From the moment she had first conceived the idea of sneaking downriver to plead for Whip's life, she had felt a sense of overwhelming inevitability, as if her fate had been wrested from her hand. Dreamlike, she had spoken and acted—and it had been so easy.

She had gone back into the bombproof, murmured smiling lies, taken Moon Daughter's dress, and hidden it beneath her shawl. Then she had gone to one of the back gates, murmured more smiling lies, and slipped out of the fort with Shadow while the guard's attention was fastened elsewhere.

Even finding a small bateau had been easy—one had been waiting for her in the shallows near the fort. Coaxing the wolf to go aboard for the river crossing had likewise been effortless; Shadow had been frantic to get to the other side.

Yes, it had been as easy as child's play. The fires at Fort Miami had provided a beacon for her to follow. And now, looking up into the fierce black eyes of her

400

captors, she wondered if death would be easy, too. She was afraid—yet she was not afraid.

Something—someone—greater than herself, greater than all of them, was watching. Of that she had no doubt.

One of her captors seized her hair and dragged her to her feet—then off her feet, for he was as tall as Whip. He held her with her toes dangling several inches from the ground, and her scalp seemed to scream in agony. She looked into his gleaming eyes, only a few inches from her own, and saw no mercy whatsoever, not even a faint suggestion of humanity.

"Put her down, you bastard!" someone rasped, and Faith realized that the hoarse, strained voice belonged to Whip.

From the corner of her eye, she saw the flash of a tomahawk, flat side down, descending in the direction of Whip's head. She heard Shadow snarling and growling above the din of excited, unintelligible voices. There came the sounds of a fierce scuffle—and then a sharp whimper, a cry of pain, and Shadow's snarls could be heard no more.

No. Not Shadow, too.

Her heart twisted sharply, and then the savage was shouting into her face. She could not understand a word he was saying and answered nothing in return. He let go of her hair and she plummeted downward. Other hands seized her. They tore at the embroidery on the soft white doeskin. They tugged at the fringe. Someone snatched the lovely headband, which had also belonged to Moon Daughter.

The Indians seemed incensed by her clothing, but they also seemed confused. On close examination, they could not have failed to realize that she was a white woman. And now apparently they wanted to know from whom she had stolen the garment. It was so beautifully made, so obviously ceremonial. Had they thought she was some sort of honored person, even a deity, and then been angered to discover she was not?

One of them began to shake her violently. Then he drew back his hand and struck her across the face with a stunning force that sent her sprawling. Stars twinkled before her eyes.

There were more shouts. Against her ear, pressed close to the spinning earth, Faith heard staccato thuds—like the sound of hoofbeats drawing closer. Again, someone dragged her to her feet.

Indians on either side of her scattered and quieted, their attention drawn to this second interruption. A man on horseback galloped toward them through the curling, wavering smoke. Deftly, he guided his mount around the staked-out Americans, and the savages began to leap up and down, shouting like children. They waved the symbols of their victory— articles of American clothing, weapons, severed hands and feet and scalps attached to poles—and it became increasingly obvious to Faith that this man was a leader or hero to them.

Even the British soldiers high on the ramparts saluted him as he rode past, his horse picking its way slowly now, as the rider looked carefully about, seeming to note every detail of butchery and horror.

A thrill of hope shot through Faith. Here at last was someone in authority—a savage by his swarthy skin, shoulder-length black hair, and Indian dress.

But also a man who seemed displeased by what he saw.

Dragging Faith along with them, the Indians converged on the rider. Over and over, they shouted a single word, a name. It sounded like Tecumseh! Tecumseh! Tecumseh!

The rider reined his mount to a halt as the Indians pressed closer and fell silent, waiting for him to speak. He was not a large man, but his bearing was noble and dignified. Faith saw that his face was finely proportioned, that his nose was inclined to be aquiline, and—most important—that his eyes held none of that ferocious triumph common to the other savages. Instead, they reflected barely controlled anger.

Tecumseh—by now, she had guessed it must truely be he—looked hard into the faces of his followers. Not a single Indian moved. The fort had grown breathlessly silent, save for the moaning of the captives and the crackling of the fires. Tecumseh began to speak, stopped, and leaped down from his horse. The Indians fell back. He seized one man by the throat, his other hand snaking to his waist and withdrawing his tomahawk.

Shouting his fury, he brandished the weapon over the savage's head. The man stared up at it. Like a child caught displeasing his father, he looked scared and guilty. Tecumseh threw him back into the arms of his fellows and stalked around the circle of bystanders, stopping at one or the other and brandishing the tomahawk. Faith saw tears shining in his eyes.

At last, he stood still and cried out in a loud

agonized voice. Heads swiveled and looked up at the rampart. Faith looked also. A man in the scarlet and gold uniform of a British general stood impassively looking down at them.

"Proctor!" Tecumseh roared in English. "Why have you allowed this massacre?"

The man on the rampart stood half in shadow, and Faith could not see his face clearly. But his voice carried easily to her ears. "Sir," Proctor said, "your aborigines cannot be commanded."

Contempt and fury contorted Tecumseh's fine features. He was momentarily silent. "Begone!" he finally shouted. "You are unfit to command! Go and put on petticoats."

General Proctor did not move, and Tecumseh bowed his head, his inner turmoil plainly apparent. "Oh, what will become of my aborigines?" he asked in a broken voice.

Faith stepped forward. No one was holding her now. Silently, on either side of her, the Indians began to fade into the shadows. They did not look at one another, nor did they look at her. They walked with the soft, uneasy tread of men who were ashamed.

Tecumseh stood bowed and stricken. Tears ran unchecked down his cheeks. Never before had Faith seen a man weep so openly, and her heart went out to him. She forgot that he was an Indian, that his people were responsible for the ghastly treatment of the American prisoners. This man, she knew, had never meant for it to happen.

"Tecumseh . . ." she said.

Tecumseh looked at her. Surprise flared in his

eyes; then they narrowed in disbelief. He studied her a long moment before he finally spoke. "Woman, how come you to be here, dressed in Shawnee clothing? Do I know you? Or is it only the dress that stirs my memory?

"I am a stranger who came to plead for a man's life," she answered simply. "In order to gain entrance here I attired myself as an Indian."

Tecumseh was still studying the white doeskin dress. He shook his head as if to clear it. "The girl—the woman—who wore that garment is dead. And long have I regretted the circumstances under which she died. When I first saw you, I thought you were she—come from the spirit world to plead for the Americans, or to avenge them."

"Moon Daughter would not have come here seeking revenge."

"Moon Daughter—so you know her name." Tecumseh frowned, his eyes full of suspicion. "Who is this man for whom you came to plead?"

Faith stepped aside to reveal Whip still staked to the ground behind her. "His name is Whip Martin," she managed in a trembling voice. "And if he still lives, I would ask you to spare him—to allow him to go free."

Tecumseh stalked to the prostrate figure stretched out on the uneven ground. Whip's head had lolled to one side. An enormous purplish lump was swelling on his temple, and his eyes were closed.

Faith hurried to his side and knelt down. She bent over him. "Whip . . . can you hear me?"

Tecumseh knelt down across from her. His dark eyes grew darker still as he looked down at the deep welts and bloody scratches, the enormous lump on Whip's forehead, and the charred flesh above his heart. There was not an inch of Whip's naked body that did not bear some darkening bruise or other injury. Foolishly, Faith longed to cover him, to hide his humiliation. Seeing him lying so weak and vulnerable, even his genitals exposed, was more than she could bear. Her breath caught on a sob.

Tecumseh placed his fingertips beneath Whip's nose. "The breath of life is still in him."

"But he will die soon if he receives no treatment. That burn will become infected."

Tecumseh's eyes probed her face. "And what of the other prisoners? Have you no concern for them?"

Now was the moment, Faith realized, the opportunity she had come here seeking. Ignoring the sounds of suffering all around her, she said, "This man is different. He has suffered worse than all the others. He has suffered longer. Your followers killed his wife, whom he loved more than life itself. You owe him this—a life for a life."

Tecumseh grunted. "Once I knew this man well . . . I loved him as a brother. He is not one to allow his need for vengeance to go unsatisfied. He has doubtless taken many lives in return for that of his lost Moon Daughter."

"Still . . ." Faith persisted. "This violence must end somewhere, sometime. Someone—some lone courageous man—must be willing to take the first step, to forgive, to show mercy, to give back what another has forfeited."

A smile hovered about Tecumseh's thin lips. "You

406

think, then, that I am that man . . ."

"You *could* be," Faith pleaded, hoping and praying that her intuition about Tecumseh was correct. This Indian was *not* a savage—not in the sense of the word as she understood it. What had he called his people—aborigines? An aborigine he might be, but he was also a man of compassion, a man of wisdom and education. His emotions ran deep, and she believed that he was no stranger to honor.

He is like no other whom I have ever met, she thought. And I wish I knew him better. I would feel honored to know him better.

"My path is set," Tecumseh said. A shadow of sadness crept across his face. "I am like a star shooting across the heavens. I am like a panther passing by. My power is great, but quickly spent . . . Much as I regret it, it will not be I who brings this madness to its final rightful conclusion."

Faith thought at first that he was refusing her request for mercy, but Tecumseh abruptly stood and motioned to a passing Indian. He said something in the Indian language, and the man nodded, eyes downcast, and hurried away to do his chief's bidding.

She hardly dared allow herself to hope. Silhouetted against the flickering crimson light of the fires and looking down at her, Tecumseh smiled. "Woman, your courage has swayed me. I have sent for a litter. My men will escort you and Whip Martin upriver to your people—but only if you agree to one condition."

"Anything," Faith whispered.

"Do not tell him it was I who gave him back his life. Either he would feel indebted or he would not believe you. In any case, he would be confused and discomfited."

"But—"

"Promise me, woman. It will be better this way. I want no tales of Tecumseh's moment of weakness to travel on the wind to encourage my enemies."

Though she still could not understand why it would hurt if Whip alone knew, Faith swallowed her arguments. "I—I promise."

"The litter is here. Go quickly now, before anyone tries to stop you."

Faith jumped to her feet. "Yes . . . yes, we are going."

Two tall Indians placed a litter on the ground nearby. One of them bent to cut Whip's bonds with a long, sharp knife. "I—I want to thank you," she said.

But to her surprise, Tecumseh had turned and was striding quickly away. Curling wisps of smoke and fog swirled about his figure and soon swallowed him from her sight.

Whip floated in a dream—or rather he lurched through one. He dreamed he was being carried while lying flat on his back. He opened his eyes and blinked to clear his vision, but the night was black and foggy. He could see no stars. Neither could he see the wavering red light that had lately engulfed him. Had he somehow been delivered from hell?

No, I am dead, he thought. And I am being taken away to the spirit world.

Faith—where was she? He had seen the savages seize her. He had seen her fall. And he had seen her swung aloft and dangled by her hair—her beautiful long blue-black hair. Now, in an agony of fear for her, he cried out her name, but no sound reached his ears. Death had robbed him of the ability to speak. Would that it had also robbed him of the ability to feel.

Pain and grief lanced every muscle, every joint, every tissue. The constant lurching, the jolting, set his teeth to rattling. Defeated by his weakness, he again closed his eyes and clenched his jaws.

He felt himself being lowered and heard a scraping sound. Then came the sound of water lapping against a boat. He floated, he dreamed. Then he was being jolted once more. The jolting went on and on. Voices sounded near him. Light shone in his face. He refused to open his eyes to it. He was afraid.

Something cold and hard touched his lips. Water splashed down his chin. "Open your mouth, Whip— please! You need water."

Dear God, he would know that voice anywhere!

He opened his mouth and drank the cool sweet water. It tasted fresh from the well. Could there be wells in heaven?

"He's drinking it! Oh, Nancy, Adrienne! Look— he's drinking the water!"

Other voices babbled—Nancy's, Adrienne's, Faith's sisters, their uncle's. The voices ran together and poured over him like a soothing, healing balm.

He strained to hear and understand only one: "It's all right, Whip. You are safe now . . . You will get well."

Hot tears spilled from beneath his eyelids and slid down his face.

A soft finger wiped them away. "Sleep now, my darling, sleep. Don't worry, I won't leave you—ever."

Chapter Twenty-Four

The morning of May 18, 1813, dawned cool, dry, and breezy. Though it had stormed and blown the night before, the day promised to be sunny. Quietly, Faith crept from the tent she was once again sharing with the still-sleeping Hope and Charity. Inhaling the sweet smells of spring, she adjusted her armful of clean clothing and hurried to one of the less used entrances of the fort.

The guard did not want to open the gate for her, but she pleaded with him, reminding him that the British had withdrawn. The redcoats had lost the support of the Indians. Whether because of the influence of Tecumseh or because the blood lust of the savages had finally been satisfied, Faith did not know. Indeed, no one knew—but neither an Indian nor a British soldier had been seen about the premises for the past nine days.

She smiled at the guard encouragingly; this was her wedding day, she told him, and she deserved a special favor.

"Promise me you won't stray far, miss . . . and if you hear or see anything out of the ordinary, you must return to the fort straightaway."

Faith promised, and the soldier opened the gate for her. As she hurried through it, she assured herself that there really was no danger. And if Whip found out about her leaving the fort and grew angry, she would remind him that during the past week, the soldiers themselves had been coming and going all the time.

The remainder of General Clay's volunteers and those who had escaped injury and illness during the siege had located and buried the American dead, scoured the entire countryside for any stray Indians, and spent hours out on the river, fishing for white bass. Using a hook and line baited with a red rag, Captain Daniel Cushing had caught sixty-two one-pounders only yesterday, and the day before, he had helped to set out a garden some distance from the fort.

I don't care if Whip does lose his temper, Faith told herself. On our wedding day I am going to be clean—really clean. I am going to wade into the river and wash my hair if it's the last thing I ever do.

Slipping into the fringe of wood surrounding the fort, she made her way carefully down the steep riverbank to the fast-running water. There she set down her clean clothes and her precious sliver of soap, and eyed the racing stream with dismay.

The river was much higher and more turbulent than it had been on that day in April when she and the other women had come down to do laundry. The ceaseless rains, including last night's storm, had pushed it far over its normal volume, and bits of debris—tree branches, dead leaves, barrel staves, and a section of a bateau—were being tossed and turned and swept downstream at a speed that alarmed her.

Unhappily, she recalled the difficulties of paddling a canoe upriver against the current on the night when the two Indians had brought her and Whip back to the fort. The Indians had done the paddling, and she had done the praying.

She sighed. On this day of all days, she had no wish to be foolhardy. She had endured enough scolding regarding her attempt to rescue Whip. Completely ignoring the fact that she had succeeded, he himself had roundly castigated her as soon as he had been able. Now that he was once again strong enough to take matters in hand, he might do something drastic if she dared to bathe in the rough swollen river.

Sitting down on a large rock just out of reach of the river's grasp, she wondered how Adrienne intended to make herself presentable for Uncle Abel—or for that matter, how her uncle would make himself presentable for Adrienne. They would all have to wash in buckets, as usual. At least, she thought with wry amusement, she would no longer have to goad her uncle into bathing and shaving. Since Adrienne had agreed to marry him in a double ceremony with Faith and Whip, Uncle Abel had become the most fastidious person imaginable.

"He's like a rooster preening his feathers before a

hen!" Charity had remarked in amazement.

And it was true. Uncle Abel had changed. He looked years younger. He stood straighter, taller. When he spoke, he even sounded more sensible, less fanatical and other-worldly. He still had his dreams and plans for evangelizing the Indians, but now he seemed more inclined to go about them in a reasonable manner.

And as for Adrienne, gone was the Frenchwoman's air of controlled sadness. These days, her eyes gleamed and sparkled. Her tinkling laughter sounded often. Best of all, during the difficult days of Whip's recovery, Adrienne had joyfully assumed much of the responsibility for Hope and Charity.

Looking out across the rushing glistening river, Faith thought about her two younger sisters and wondered what the future held in store for them.

Hope seemed to have found inner peace in the competent performance of her nursing duties, which she continued to perform daily, though now it was measles and mumps rather than gunshot wounds that brought the soldiers to the infirmary. The auburn-haired beauty occasionally spoke of returning to Erie to work in a real infirmary or hospital, and Faith believed that this was a good sign that she had gotten over her infatuation with the sea captain, Alex Cummings.

Faith did not like to think about Hope leaving Ohio, but at least, in Erie, her sister would not be so far away as to make occasional visits impossible. In time, some man would win her affections—a doctor, perhaps. And who could tell? Perhaps she and her

414

husband could be persuaded to make their home on the frontier where medical skills were desperately needed.

Abel and Adrienne would eventually settle at Frenchtown, and she and Whip planned to homestead not far from the Fosters—a prospect that excited and pleased Faith. She could only hope that Charity would, in future years, end up somewhere in the vicinity, too. Of course, with Charity, it was difficult to predict what might happen tomorrow, let alone several years hence.

Faith smiled to herself, thinking how the girl fancied herself an "angel of mercy" now, imagining that she was even more accomplished than Hope. But while Hope performed the true nursing tasks, the bloody and unpleasant ones, Charity stuck to her own methods of healing—flitting from one wounded or ill soldier to another, writing letters, endlessly chattering and giggling—in short, still enticing half the soldiers in the fort to fall in love with her. At least now, she was more careful of her dress and manner, and she did not flirt quite so brazenly as she had before.

Without Adrienne to keep a tight rein on her headstrong youngest sister, Faith did not know what she would have done. "Just keep the silly chit away from me," Whip had grumbled more than once from his sickbed.

Amazingly, Charity had been delighted with the prospect of falling even more under Adrienne's influence, for she admired everything French and particularly admired anything or anyone connected to royalty or the upper classes.

My little sister will probably stow away aboard a ship to France one day. Once there, she'll try to pass herself off as a countess, Faith mused. Several times she had heard Charity say longingly, "Oh, how I wish I were *someone* . . . or at the very least, *descended* from someone . . ."

Fortunately, since their lineage was presumably humble, Charity could not indulge her penchant for snobbery, but Faith often thought how very wonderful it would be if she and her sisters could somehow, someday discover just exactly who they were and where they had come from. She could not forget how Charity had worried that some dark evil thing from their past had somehow tainted her.

Assailed with an unexpected sadness, Faith traced a pattern on the rock with her fingernail. Today was the most important day of her life, and if her mother were still alive, she would probably be fussing about her like a mother hen with a favored chick. What might it have been like—to have known a mother's love all these years?

Determined not to wallow in self-pity and sentimentality, Faith abruptly stood up. If she was going to bathe from a bucket, she had better return to her tent immediately, else she would stand in line a long time at the well, wedding day or not. Once Hope and Charity were out of bed, the bucket would be in great demand.

She picked up her soap and her clothes and was just beginning the arduous climb back up the riverbank when she heard a whimper. Her throat constricted. The Indians were known to send signals to one another by mimicking the sounds of birds and animals. The sound came again, a long, low whine conveying some creature's distress.

Perhaps, Faith speculated, it really was an animal, one who was hurt or wounded. There was only one way to find out. Cautiously, she peered in the direction of the sound. Something leaped and splashed in the water. The sound seemed to be coming from the river—only a short distance upstream.

Trees leaned far out from the shore, blocking her view. Faith again set down her belongings and clambered over and under several of them, catching and tearing her skirt in the process. An amazing sight rewarded her efforts. There, struggling to free itself from a half-submerged fallen tree limb, was a wet, bedraggled creature—a wolf, by its size and the shape of its long muzzle and flattened ears. Caught and held fast by the snagged chain around its neck, the wolf was frantically trying to swim to shore.

Faith stared. Blood rushed to her temples, and her heart thumped wildly. The wolf turned its amber eyes on her and whimpered again. It could not be, she thought—but it was. Shadow had returned from the dead.

Her head sticking through the opening of the tent, Charity tossed her disheveled golden curls and shot Whip an indignant glance from beneath her golden lashes. "Honestly! There you go again getting mad

417

at me. I didn't do anything!"

"You must know where your sister has gone, Charity. Or don't you pay attention to anyone who is not wearing breeches? I thought you had re-formed—or so Faith told me."

Drawing the flap of the tent even closer around her face—Whip had already guessed that she had only just risen from her pallet—Charity let her pink lips turn down in a pout. Again, Whip was reminded of how different the girl was from her eldest sister; Faith had never pouted in her entire life.

Pity the poor man who marries Charity, he thought, and then he remembered that she was going to be his sister-in-law very shortly. Instead of furthering the lingering friction between them, he ought to be thinking of ways to eliminate it.

"Sorry about that last . . . Will you at least tell her, when you see her, that I have been looking for her?"

A look of surprise suffused Charity's delicate features. She grinned radiantly. "Why, Mr. Martin! This is the first time I have ever heard you apologize to anyone!"

Whip cocked an eyebrow at her, but Charity looked genuinely astonished—and also quite charm-ing with her tousled golden curls and engaging smile. Given time, he realized, she just might mature into something less exasperating.

"You *will* tell her, then?"

"Oh, of course! But I don't think you are supposed to see her today until the wedding."

"The wedding, dear Charity, is not until noon,

and there is something important I wish to discuss with her."

Charity's blue eyes danced a question. "It can't wait until *after* the wedding? You should have plenty of time to talk then—the rest of your lives, I should think."

She is pushing me too far again, Whip thought, trying to restrain his annoyance. *"Talking* to Faith after the wedding is not what I had in mind, dear sister-in-law-to-be. I mean to do other things. Shall I name a few?"

"You'd better not!" Primly, Charity withdrew part way into the shelter of the tent.

At her shocked expression, Whip chuckled. "I was thinking of eating, drinking, and making merry— not claiming my husbandly rights, though I will certainly do that later."

"Mr. *Martin!"* Charity blushed to the roots of her hair.

"Ah, Charity . . ." He sighed. "Are you really such an innocent? I hope so, because if you are not, I will have to challenge your suitors, one by one, to meet me in mortal combat."

"M-meet you in mortal combat? B-but that wouldn't be fair!" Charity's lower lip quivered tremulously.

"For heaven's sake, Charity!" From somewhere inside the tent, Hope intervened. "Can't you see that Mr. Martin is only teasing you? Promise him that you will give his message to Faith, and then come in here and get washed and dressed. It will be noon before you know it."

419

"I promise you that I will tell her!" Charity sniffed. She ducked back into the tent and, as if he were a two-headed monster, jerked the flap back into place.

Grinning and shaking his head, Whip walked away. For the first time, it occurred to him that by marrying Faith he was also marrying her family. That unnerving prospect made him groan. Never again would he be alone in the world. Not only would he have Faith but he would also have these others to depend on and worry about. There would also be much visiting back and forth—only not *too* much, he hoped. For a time at least, he wanted Faith strictly to himself.

A little girl, towheaded and solemn-eyed, peeped at him from the entrance of the nearby tent. Knowing her to be a timid new arrival—one of a small group of settlers determined to conquer the land regardless of the Indians and the British—Whip winked at her. Smiling shyly, she winked back, and he was reminded that eventually his marriage would also bring children. If he and Faith were fortunate, they would soon have the opportunity to shape and mold the spirits of fresh new human beings, like clay from the riverbank, with their own two hands.

At the prospect of this, however, he felt not the least intimidation. His hands—his entire being— itched to get started. He was bursting with plans for his new life. And it was about these plans that he wanted to talk to Faith. Waiting until noon would be impossible when waiting another moment was clearly unbearable.

Stiffly, he began to walk faster. His body protested with tiny shooting pains and dull throbbing aches that reminded him of his recent ordeal. He ignored them. He would go first to Nancy and Adrienne, and if Faith was not with them, he would then find Uncle Abel. Someone must know where she was.

On sudden impluse, he veered toward the back gate.

Would Faith have dared to leave the fort? Not after his severe warnings, surely, but then, when had she ever heeded a warning or obeyed an order from him? Faith Cormorand—soon to be Faith Martin—was her own independent person, and just because they were soon to be wed did not mean he could expect maidenly compliance. Fortunately for both of them, he wasn't marrying her for her docility; he was marrying her for—completeness. Without his stubborn Faith, he was only half a being.

Heeding his intuition, he broke into a loping run. Yes, that was probably exactly what she had done— left the fort, though for what reason God alone knew. But it was to him, not to God, that she had better be prepared to make her explanations.

"Shadow, dear Shadow," Faith crooned. "Wait until Whip sees you! You will be my wedding present to him—the finest gift I could ever give him."

She leaned back against the rock and surveyed her handiwork. She had rubbed the wolf clean and dry with the linen toweling she had brought to the riverbank to wrap around her own wet hair. The wolf looked back at her, his amber eyes adoring, as if he knew she had saved his life.

Crouched on his stomach, paws outstretched in front of him, his gray fur now dry and fluffy, he looked like his old fierce self. It was only when he walked that one noticed how he favored his left front foot, and it was only when she ran her hands over him that she felt the long, ugly scars—still pink and tender—hidden by his concealing gray coat.

"If only you could talk, Shadow. What I wouldn't give to hear how you got here—how you ever survived."

Dipping his muzzle, Shadow licked her hand, and Faith remembered her last sight of him—a bloody heap of fur, unmoving, quite obviously dead. Indeed, she had been so certain he was dead that she had avoided looking at him. Only several days later, when Whip questioned her about the wolf, did she begin to doubt her perceptions.

She had not even taken time to mourn the creature without whose help she would never have arrived at Fort Miami or found Whip inside that awful place. But as with all of Whip's questions about that night, she had been evasive, then defensive, finally snapping, "I don't want to talk about it!"

And Whip, realizing how terrible that night must have been for her, had taken her in his arms and pulled her down to him where he lay on his pallet. "Someday," he had whispered, "we will speak of it again. Such things must not lie hidden or they will return to haunt and torment you when you least expect it."

Little did he know that she intended to remain forever silent, as Tecumseh had requested. Only in confidence to General Harrison had she spoken anything near the truth: "Tecumseh arrived and did not approve of the treatment being accorded the American prisoners. Shortly thereafter, he ordered me to depart—and allowed me to take Whip along with me."

Now, as Shadow nosed her hand, pleading for her attention, Faith put aside the past and concentrated on the present. Her visit to the riverbank had not been in vain—indeed, it had been providential. The same sure hand that had guided her steps to Fort Miami had gently nudged her here in time to save the timber wolf as he swam across the river. Already exhausted when she had freed him and dragged him to shore, Shadow would have drowned in not too many more minutes.

She rose to her feet, and slipping her fingers inside the loop of chain still fastened around the animal's neck, gently maneuvered the iron necklace over Shadow's ears. It slipped easily down his muzzle, and when he felt himself come loose, Shadow shook his head appreciatively. "My gift to you, Shadow, is that you will never again be bound and held fast for any reason. I promise you this. You may stay or follow, as you desire."

"Faith! In God's name where are you?"

At the thundering summons, Faith jumped and looked up. The voice had come from the top of the brush-screened riverbank, and there could be no mistaking the anger of the caller.

"Here, Whip! I'm down here!"

Crashing and sliding, Whip descended the bank, arriving on his backside with little dignity. "By God, woman! Have you no care at all for your safety—or for my sanity?"

Startled by the sudden commotion, Shadow had slunk halfway into a thicket behind her. Not yet having noticed him, Whip stood and brushed mud and debris from his buckskins.

"I am not in any danger," Faith insisted. "Or at least I wasn't until you alerted everyone within five miles to my whereabouts."

Whip's head snapped up. He lunged toward her, and at the same moment, Shadow sprang from the thicket and landed in front of her—growling a warning. Brought up short, Whip stared, his green eyes darkening with astonishment.

"I don't believe it," he whispered hoarsely. "Shadow, you old faker!"

The ragged relief in his voice brought tears to Faith's eyes. "He swam the river, Whip, trying to get to you, but his chain caught on a submerged branch. Luckily, I found him before his strength gave out."

Whip dropped to one knee, and Faith could see that he was struggling to keep control of his emotions. His eyes devoured the creature from head to foot.

Half crying herself, she continued: "He must have been close to death not to have made it back sooner. He, like you, was marked by the Indians. There are scars on his neck and shoulders, and he limps."

"But he made it . . . he made it, Faith." Whip glanced up at her, his eyes shining. "God damn, he made it!"

"Yes, my love, I know . . ."

Whip reached out one hand to her and the other to Shadow. His outstretched hand, palm downward, had always been the signal for the wolf to leap on him joyously. But this time Shadow sniffed it suspiciously and refused to budge from his place in front of Faith. Uncertain as to how Whip would react to this sudden reversal of his pet's loyalties, Faith suppressed a grin, then frowned as Whip's mouth hardened at the corners.

"Why, you traitor!" Whip growled. "What's gotten into you?"

"Perhaps," she suggested gently, "Shadow needs some demonstration that you mean to do me no harm. I *did* save his life, you know, and from the way you were shouting at me, he may think he needs to return the favor."

His expression inscrutable, Whip got to his feet. "And just how would I demonstrate that, pray tell?"

"Oh, I can think of something," Faith replied. Moving slowly and invitingly, with a deliberate swing of her hips, she nudged Shadow to one side and walked confidently into Whip's arms.

Some time later, with great reluctance, Faith rose from the bed of violets Whip had found for them to lie on. She brushed away leaves and crushed flower

425

petals; they were on her skirt, in her hair, and, she suspected, in her undergarments. Not only that, but her clothing was damp and covered with grass stains.

With her fingers, she began to rake the evidence of their lovemaking out of her long tresses, and Whip caught her hand. "Leave the violets in your hair . . . They match you. When your eyes are smoky with passion, they are exactly the same shade."

Faith blushed. "Everyone will know what we were doing. Why, we might even have made ourselves late for our own wedding."

Whip pressed her open palm to his lips, his eyes glowing with happiness. "I see no reason to be ashamed."

He kissed her palm, and a ripple of desire ran through her body. She blushed an even deeper pink. Would her hunger for him never be appeased? Abandoning herself to his scorching green-eyed gaze, she studied the way the sunlight filtering through the trees drew lacy patterns on his face and hair. "What time do you suppose it is?" she murmured dreamily. "We really must go back now."

He glanced skyward. "Ten or eleven . . . not more than that."

"Ten or eleven!" The spell was broken. Even Shadow looked startled. "Oh, Whip, I have not even bathed or washed my hair!"

Whip refused to let go of her hand. Instead, he pulled her closer. "You smell wonderful to me— sweet, like spring flowers, warm and womanly, like the earth."

"Ooooh! You don't understand! This is the only wedding I shall ever have, and I want it to be perfect."

"To hell with the wedding! Our life together afterward will be perfect." He lowered his mouth to hers and kissed away all her protests. He kissed her until she was breathless and swaying on her feet.

"Oh, it *will* be perfect . . ." She sighed throatily against his chest.

His muscles tensed beneath his fingertips. "I almost forgot. Besides being sick with worry when I couldn't find you, I had another reason for following you."

She drew back slightly to see his face. "Is something wrong?"

"No, something is very right." He grinned. "At least, I think it will be after we have discussed it."

She waited for his explanation, and as he gave it, she noticed that his eyes sparkled with rare excitement and his manner exuded enthusiasm. These were reasons enough for her to smile and nod her assent, though in truth, she thought the idea was splendid—the perfect job for a man of Whip's many talents.

"Well, what do you think?" he asked, looking as eager as a young boy who desperately desired approval.

"I think General Harrison does you a great honor," she said. "But more important, he does himself a great service by appointing you as his civilian liaison with the settlers. There isn't another man in the fort who is more knowledgeable or trustworthy."

"I can think of one—Pete Navarre, who has promised to help me . . . Don't agree too quickly, Faith," Whip warned. "I want you to think about it first. The settlers will be arriving in swarms before the war with the British is over. And until a civilian government can be reorganized, the military will be in charge. I don't expect everyone will see eye to eye, and I may need to spend a great deal of time here at the fort or traveling back and forth between distant homesteads."

"I'll come with you!" Faith responded enthusiastically.

"Only if there's no danger." Whip's arm crooked around her neck and he nuzzled her violet-strewn hair. "Ah, Faith . . . it's going to be exciting to see Ohio grow and become civilized. One day, I expect, instead of the wilderness we now see, our children and our children's children will see peaceful, productive farms stretched out across the entire state."

This was a side of Whip's complex personality that Faith had not yet discovered—that of visionary. Pressing closer to him, loving him even more, if that was possible, she whispered, "As long as we are together, I don't care what the future holds. For me, it will be a happy one."

"And for me, also." He tilted her chin and looked long into her eyes. His brilliant green gaze reflected her own exquisite joy. Tenderly, his lips met hers, forging a promise of the future, and then he whispered mockingly, "And now that you have ravished me, Miss Cormorand—and healed me, converted me, and turned me inside out and upside down—don't you think that it's time you made an honest man of me?"

"Yes," she agreed demurely. "I'll marry you this very day, this very hour."

"You had better," he growled and, taking her hand, led her back through the sunlit, flower-blooming forest to Fort Meigs and their wedding.

Chapter Twenty-Five

"What God hath joined together, let no man put asunder," the newly arrived army chaplain intoned, and Abel, who had been silently mouthing the words along with him, turned to Adrienne.

His new wife beamed up at him, her brown eyes warm and caressing, her smile gentle and wonderful. Suddenly shy before her, he did not know what to say or what to do, though he had presided over more weddings than he could remember.

"You may kiss me, Reverend Monsieur Cormorand," she whispered so that no one else could hear.

Grateful for her presence of mind when his own had deserted him, he bent and awkwardly brushed his lips across hers. It was not the first time they had kissed, and praise God, it would not be the last. With practice, his humble efforts should improve.

A cheer went up around him from the gathered

soldiers, militiamen, settlers, and camp followers who had come to wish them well. From the corner of his eye, Abel saw that Faith was still locked in her husband's passionate embrace, and he felt embarrassed at his own timidity about performing such private acts in public.

Adrienne wound her arm through his and smiled. "Ah, my heart, I am most impatient to be alone with you. I, too, dislike exhibiting my deepest feelings in front of others."

Abel gruffly patted her hand. His love for this woman who understood him so well sometimes rendered him inarticulate—Abel, who had always had words for every occasion, from birth to death!

He noticed that his bride was wearing a dress of plain gray homespun, her only ornament a collar of fine old lace. She looked as regal as a queen—and as lovely in her own manner as Faith did in hers. And he had never seen Faith look lovelier.

His eldest niece now broke away from her husband and hurried toward him. "Uncle Abel, congratulations!"

She threw her arms around his neck and kissed and hugged him, then drew back smiling, her cheeks flushed, her eyes glowing. The dress she wore was familiar—it was her Sunday best, a dress the color of violets, the color of her eyes. And Abel was almost certain that the tiny blossoms entwined in her hair were the actual flowers themselves—violets, which he had always loved because they reminded him of her.

He also liked her hair the way she wore it today—unbound, flowing down her back in a silky mass.

The style was much more flattering than her usual one, in which she had always looked somewhat severe.

"Congratulations to you, too, my dear sweet Faith . . ." And then Whip was shaking his hand, and Faith had gone on to hug and kiss Adrienne.

So much hugging and kissing—and right out here on the parade ground, too, watched by everyone in the fort.

"Your niece will know happiness—I swear it," Whip Martin said to him, and Abel nodded, certain of that fact now, despite his past reservations about the man who had just married his niece.

Then Hope and Charity were hugging and kissing him, and his spectacles were knocked from his nose. He succeeded in catching them before they fell to the ground and were crunched underfoot, but now all the faces of his well-wishers seemed to blur together; he endured many handshakes and back-slappings before he could find a free moment to anchor his glasses back in place.

With his spectacles once again firmly seated, he saw General Harrison coming toward him. When the general gestured for quiet, Abel slipped an arm around Adrienne and drew her closer. He never wanted her to be far away from him, for in her nearness he found strength, courage, and a deep abiding joy.

She surprised him by leaning slightly against him, letting him know that she felt as he did and would never suffer him to stray very far from her. General Harrison made a congratulatory speech, but lost in a daze of happiness, Abel paid scant attention.

433

Then the general withdrew a parchment scroll from inside his gold-braided jacket, and Adrienne exclaimed for his ears alone, "Oh, Abel, I hope for Nancy's sake that this is good news."

Realizing that he did not know what she was talking about, Abel listened carefully as General Harrison unrolled the parchment and read: "From Captain Alex Cummings to General William Henry Harrison. Belated greetings from the *Sea Sprite*. I trust that this missive shall find you in reasonable good health and spirits. We ourselves are only a little the worse for wear as a result of our efforts of the past few weeks, which we have spent harrying, eluding, and spying upon the British fleet at Malden. Now that British activity in the area has diminished, I wish to assure you that we are still alive, including the gentleman who was stranded aboard my ship during our unsuccessful attempt to land supplies.

"That man, Tom Foster by name, has requested that I enclose felicitous greetings to his wife Nancy, with whom he looks forward to being reunited within the week. Several days from now, the *Sea Sprite* will once more be in the area—our exact time and location to be made known to you on the night before the rendezvous—and we will once again attempt a landing of supplies.

"I also enclose my personal greetings and felicitous thanks to Whip Martin, who I sincerely hope gained the safety of the fort in company with his two charges, Hope and Charity Cormorand.

"Please extend my abject apologies to the above-mentioned young ladies. We did not meet under the

434

best of circumstances, and I may have said certain things which upon reflection, I now regret. I trust they will understand and forgive my temper. Miss Hope Cormorand, especially, does not deserve the scornful abuse I heaped upon her lovely auburn head, and if I ever have the opportunity, I should like to beg her pardon in person."

Surprised that his second eldest niece had been singled out for special mention by the captain of the *Sea Sprite*, Abel glanced toward Hope and was amazed to see her downcast eyes and furiously blushing cheeks. Then she raised her glance, and he became even more amazed. Her eyes glowed with an emerald radiance the meaning of which was only too clear—Hope was in love with Captain Alex Cummings!

"Oh, dear, oh, my, oh, my . . ." Abel muttered under his breath.

Adrienne squeezed his arm and whispered, "What is wrong, *mon trésor?*"

"Hope!" he blurted. "Why, look at my niece!"

Adrienne looked at the girl's shining eyes and glowing face and then smiled sweetly up at him. "I see a young woman in love, and what could be wrong with that?"

"But—but this Alex Cummings! I don't even know the man!"

Adrienne stood on tiptoe and murmured in his ear. "Do not be afraid, *mon cher.* What is meant to be will be. The future will take care of itself."

Abel started to refute that answer, then stopped. Adrienne was right. The future would take care of

435

itself—and those who remained open to love would find it. The years might pass, tragedies might occur, a hundred circumstances might intervene. One could even grow old, infirm, rheumatic—some would even say addlebrained. Then, quite unexpectedly, a miracle could happen. One could suddenly look into the eyes of another and find what one had been looking for all one's life.

Nodding his head, brushing a sudden wetness from his eyes, he reached around Adrienne's slim waist and unashamedly hugged her to him. And then Nancy Foster was suddenly there, weeping and hugging him and Adrienne with one arm, while with the other she held little Faith tightly against her bosom. "Oh, I'm jus' so glad t' hear Tom is still alive!"

"It is truly exciting news, *ma chère*. And to think he may be here within the week! It was wonderful of General Harrison to save this grand surprise for today. I could wish for no happier wedding present!"

Nancy's eyes were streaming tears of happiness. "Of course, you know I can't read a word—but I'm gonna ask the general if I can have the piece of parchment from Captain Cummings that says the *Sea Sprite* is safe an' my Tom is comin' home t' me! . . . Oh, look at me," she wailed. "An' I don't even have a square of homespun to wipe my eyes!"

Abel searched his pockets and found nothing to offer her. But just then, Faith came to hug Nancy and little Faith, and on seeing her friend's predicament, laughingly withdrew something white from her sleeve. "Nancy, stop crying, or we shall *all* be

crying soon! Here. . . . Dry your eyes on this."
She held out the square of white silk, and Abel saw
that it was her mother's fine embroidered handkerchief.

Nancy plucked the handkerchief from Faith's
hand, but instead of using it, held it up for all to
see. "Why, Faith, I don't want to soil something so
grand as this. Why, it's pure silk an' it's got gold
embroidery on it."

The handkerchief fluttered taut in the breeze, and
Abel, seeing the delicate initials, M de H, and the
flowerlike emblem, the fleur-de-lis, remembered
that long-ago day when Faith had exclaimed
indignantly, "That's Maman's!" He was not surprised that his niece had chosen to carry the
memento on the occasion of her wedding.

Beside him, Adrienne gasped: *"Mon Dieu! . . .
But it cannot be!"*

Startled, Abel looked down at her. His wife's face
had gone as pale as her lace collar. She was staring at
the handkerchief—and everyone else was staring at
her. Charity crowded closer to Faith, and Hope
started toward Adrienne, but only Faith had the
presence of mind to ask, "What is it, Adrienne? Are
you ill? You look as if you might faint."

Before Abel could stop her, Adrienne detached
herself from his arm and reached out with a
trembling hand to take the handkerchief from
Nancy. A stream of French burst from her lips,
propelling Abel forward. "What is it, dearest?" he
begged. "You must tell us what is wrong."

Adrienne took the square of silk, looked down

437

at it for several long moments, then raised tear-filled eyes to his own. "Abel, I would know this handkerchief anywhere. 'Twas I who embroidered this fleur-de-lis and these initials, M de H."

"Why, what are you saying, dearest?" There was a mystery here, but Abel could not untangle it. He glanced helplessly toward Faith.

Her face, too, had turned pale, and Whip moved closer to steady her. Hope and Charity looked as puzzled and confused as he felt.

Faith was the first to speak. "That handkerchief belonged to our mother, but she died when we were very small. We—my sisters and I—never even knew her name."

Faith's normally calm voice had a slight catch in it. She paused a moment, then blurted, "Whose initials are those, Adrienne?"

Unhesitatingly, Adrienne answered: "These are the initials of my sister, Marie de Hougoumont. On the occasion of her marriage into the de Hougoumont family, I embroidered this handkerchief for her. She carried it on her wedding day . . . Oh, Abel!"

Adrienne turned to him, her eyes full of questions as well as tears. "You must tell me what is going on here! How can you be the girls' uncle when it is now obvious that I am their aunt?"

"You are their aunt? Your sister was their mother? But . . . but I thought . . . I was afraid . . ." Abel hesitated. He could never admit what he had suspected and feared all these years—and why he had told Adrienne that he and the girls were blood-related. Three orphans, supposedly sisters, yet

438

looking nothing alike ... What would *any*one suspect?

In the darkness of the tepee, Faith lay entwined in Whip's arms, the soft furs of his bed shelf caressing her naked thighs. It was a time of peace and repletion, when their passion had spent itself and she could happily recall the astounding events of her wedding day. First, Shadow had returned. Then had come the double wedding. And finally there had been the amazing revelation of her kinship to Adrienne.

It had been a day to rival all days, a night to rival all nights.

"What are you thinking?" Whip murmured sleepily against her hair.

She rubbed her cheek against the muscles of his bare upper arm. "I am thinking of how shocked poor Uncle Abel looked when Adrienne asked him to explain how it was possible that she was our aunt and he was our uncle."

Whip's laughter rumbled from deep in his chest. "He was not too quick to answer, was he?"

"How could he answer? When they first met, he lied to her, and now, today, he was as surprised as anyone."

"It's an incredible tale," Whip conceded. "And no wonder Adrienne was amazed when she first saw you. She must have been completely stunned."

"Oh, she was! She said that my mother, Marie de Hougoumont"—Faith rolled the name lovingly around on her tongue—"had my same exact coloring, that she looked as I do now when last Adrienne saw her so many long years ago."

"But Adrienne said nothing to you because she believed that Abel really was your uncle, and also because she knew nothing about her sister giving birth to Hope and Charity, whose father was obviously different from yours."

"Yes," Faith mused aloud. "Hope and Charity's father had to be someone my mother met and married here, after she fled the Revolution in France and heard that my father had been guillotined. I dimly remember a laughing red-haired man, a tailor who used to let me watch him measure and sew, but he either went away or died long before my mother did . . . I remember her weeping, sobbing: 'Now I have lost *two* husbands—two whom I loved' . . . I did not know what she meant and had forgotten about it—until now."

"Your poor mother was unlucky," Whip murmured, nuzzling her hair. "And it's a pity about your father, too."

"It *is* a pity," she agreed. "But then so many died in those days, from so many causes. Adrienne herself barely got out of France alive . . . You know, Whip, I might have discovered sooner that Adrienne was my aunt if I had not allowed Uncle Abel's fib to slide by unchallenged."

Whip's fingers idly brushed across her breast, then returned to it and began to gently stroke along its curve. "Why *didn't* you challenge it and tell her the truth? Abel admitted today that he wasn't really your uncle—and that was no secret to you, was it?"

"No, but I think we—Hope and Charity and I—

440

always pretended and finally came to believe that he was our true uncle. At some point, he probably began to believe it himself. We never spoke about it; we just accepted it. I was only five when we went to live with him, and I remember how he kept saying over and over, 'I am your Uncle now. You must call me Uncle Abel.' Hope and Charity don't remember that."

"But why did he lie to Adrienne? He took the three of you in because he found you shivering on his doorstep. What is so shameful about that?"

"Whip, I think he was trying to protect us. After all, we don't look anything alike. He must have thought that our mother was a—a prostitute!"

"Undoubtedly," Whip said dryly. "If he even knows what a prostitute is." His fingers began to tease her nipple, providing a tingly distraction from their conversation. "But Marie de Hougoumont turned out to be a member of the French aristocracy. A wealthy, cultured woman . . . Do you regret your lost heritage?"

"Not I," Faith sighed, as a luscious languor crept over her. "And not Hope, either. Charity is the one who now wants to go back to France and look for our mother's family, if there are any members left."

"But her father—and Hope's—was an American, while you are an aristocrat on *both* sides."

"I am an American through and through, Whip. What happened years ago across the sea holds little interest for me now. I have always longed to know who I was and where I came from. Now that I know—well, I am content."

More than content, I am ecstatic, she thought, as

441

his hand moved to her other breast and began to work its magic there.

"You will not mind living the rough life of a frontier woman? You will not harbor a secret desire for what you might have had—could *still* have, if you had not married me?"

Now Faith saw where Whip had been leading all this time, and she did not like the direction one bit.

"I told you how I felt this morning," she responded tartly. "As long as we are together, I don't care what the future holds."

"But what if there are lands, castles—wealth beyond imagining—awaiting the heir or heiress to the Hougoumont estate? Adrienne said your father was extremely wealthy, as were your grandparents. And it is not inconceivable that the estates confiscated during the Revolution might now be returned to their rightful owners."

Faith had never once thought of that, and she did not want to think of it now. Angrily she pulled his fingers away from her breast. "How do you know about such things as estates and heirs and heiresses?"

Whip traced a fiery trail down her inner arm, but did not return his hand to her breast, as she had hoped and expected he would do. "For a backwoodsman, I am very well read. That is how I know about such things. And I want you to know about them, too. You have choices now that you did not have before. I want you to be sure, to be certain . . . that I am what you want."

Faith scrambled to her knees and turned to face him in the darkness. "You don't believe that I want you?"

442

From beneath the platform, Shadow growled at her disturbed tone of voice.

"You are upsetting Shadow," Whip said.

She saw the glint of her husband's mischievous, mocking grin but refused to be mollified. "I should think—after what we did this morning and what we did scarcely an hour ago—that you would *know* I want you. I want you more than I could ever want wealth or castles or titles or fine clothes or jewels or silk embroidered handkerchiefs—of which I already have the only one I'll ever need—"

"Perhaps," Whip interrupted. "I need further convincing—of a sort both Shadow and I can understand. This ranting and raving is making my head ache."

"I'll give you a headache!" Faith cried.

But in the next moment, as Whip pulled her down on top of him, enfolded her, rolled over on her, and kissed her into mindless oblivion, she forgot about giving him a headache, or indeed giving him anything but herself.

And that she gave with all her soul and all her being, as she would always, every day as long as she drew breath, as long as violets grew in the forest, as long as the sun shone and the rains came and the moon and stars shone at night . . . as long as forever.

Forever she would love Whip Martin, forever and ever.

"Do you know what?" Whip nibbled at her earlobe.

"What?" she sighed, as once again her body throbbed in the sweet aftermath of fulfillment.

"If we keep doing this every morning and every

443

night, we are going to have a very large family."

"Do you promise?"

"I promise."

"I can hardly wait! And now . . . could we please do it again?"

When he did not answer—but only groaned—she laughed softly to herself, rather liking having rendered him speechless.

For once, she thought, I have had the last word.

Afterward from the Author

The siege of Fort Meigs took place in late April and early May of 1813. General Proctor again tried to take the fort in July of 1813, but again failed. Fort Meigs withstood the three-day attack as it had withstood the earlier siege for eight long days.

Today visitors may tour the restored fort, climb the Grand Traverse, and, on certain days, watch costumed soldiers fire its cannon. It is a pleasant place to spend an afternoon with the ghosts of those who lived and died there during the sieges. I am indebted to Larry Nelson, manager of the Fort Meigs State Memorial Park, for sharing with me some of his own painstaking research.

The historical events herein described have necessarily been fictionalized and some details have been changed or eliminated, but the story remains, for the most part, true to history.